Praise for *Stealing the Dragon*

*An Independent Mystery Bookseller Association
Killer Book Of The Month*

"Tough, original, compelling—a perfect thriller debut."
—*Lee Child, NY Times* bestselling author

"Tim Maleeny makes a strong entrance into crime fiction with *Stealing The Dragon*. There is hardly a drought of Asian-themed mysteries, but Maleeny gives readers a fresh and fast take that enthralls."
—*Crimespree Magazine*

"Tim Maleeny captures not only the bright atmosphere of San Francisco but also the darker aspects of its soul, in a manner perhaps previously matched only by Dashiell Hammett."   —*Bookreporter*

"Combines a gumshoe mystery in the tradition of Dashiell Hammett with the exotic action of Trevanian."   —*Mystery Ink*

"Characters and plot twists bring back memories of Ian Fleming's 007 series."   —*Cherokee Sentinel*

"Readers will want to see more of Cape and Sally."
—*Library Journal*

Praise for *Beating The Babushka*

"Maleeny's second Cape Weathers mystery engages the reader without insisting that it be taken too seriously....The snappy writing and a parallel plot of drug-dealing Italian and Chinese mobsters keep the pace lively and will resonate with Elmore Leonard fans."

—Publishers Weekly

"With an obvious understanding of the traditions of crime fiction, [Maleeny] has created a series that tips the hat as it modernizes the plot line. A plot that sizzles from page one and keeps cooking until the twists at the end. I can't wait to hear more from the very talented Maleeny."   *—Crimespree Magazine*

"The vivid characters...enrich the suspenseful plot, providing a perfect reading experience."   *—Fresh Fiction*

"A new San Francisco treat. This series manages to suggest both the quirky characterizations of Elmore Leonard and the take-it-to-the-mat derring-do of Robert Parker."   *—Thrilling Detective*

"The second coming of Travis McGee."   *—Bookgasm*

"...A highly entertaining thriller...Cape and Sally make an engaging pair, and Maleeny does a nice job showing us the cutthroat side of the movie industry. Keep 'em coming."   *—Booklist*

Greasing the Piñata

Books by Tim Maleeny

Stealing the Dragon
Beating the Babushka
Greasing the Piñata

Greasing the Piñata

A Cape Weathers Investigation

Tim Maleeny

Poisoned Pen Press

Poisoned Pen Press
6962 E. First Ave., Ste. 103
Scottsdale, AZ 85251
www.poisonedpenpress.com
info@poisonedpenpress.com

Printed in the United States of America

For Clare Ruth Maleeny and Helen Grace Maleeny
Sisters smart and funny, daughters brave and bold

Acknowledgments

To properly thank everyone who helped me finish this novel would take longer than reading it. That said, I have no doubt you wouldn't be holding this book in your hands without the support of these amazing souls:

My remarkable wife, Kathryn, and our beautiful daughters Clare and Helen. Bob and Jody Maleeny, evangelists and friends. "Purple" Debi Zinn for hanging in there till the end. My agent Jill Grosjean. Michael Barrett for introducing me to bioluminescent squid and other sinister sea creatures.

The extraordinary people who make Poisoned Pen Press a reality. Barbara Peters for giving me a new home built from her passion and generosity. Annette Rogers for smart answers to tough questions. Jessica Tribble for making sure my t's weren't dotted when my eyes were crossed. Nan Beams for keeping us all on track. Rob Rosenwald for making it all possible.

Thanks.

TVM
September 2008

Gli affari sono affari.
Business is business.
(Italian proverb)

El negocio es uno y el parentesco es otro.
Business is one thing, and kinship is another.
(Mexican folk saying)

Chapter One

No one believes they're going to die until it happens, and then it's too late.

If Danny had been watching himself run, he would have screamed *give up*. Surrounded on three sides by men with guns. The pain in his side making it hard to breathe.

Any minute now they'd release the dogs. He could hear them barking in the distance, straining against the leash. Pit bulls, six of them. Beams of light zig-zagged across the grass less than twenty yards away. He was running out of time.

Danny had never been in the Army, never carried a gun, but he played a lot of video games, first-person shooters mostly. His sister always thought he'd outgrow them, but the endorphin release was better than exercise, even better than getting high. Sometimes he gripped the controls so tight his hands would ache, his thumbs flattened like pancakes from trying to make his character run faster or shoot the other guy first.

There's a moment in every game when your world gets turned upside down. You're running along, dodging the obstacles, when suddenly you step on a land mine, a robot hidden in the shadows blasts you to hell, or some guy standing behind you blows your brains out. One second you're invincible, the next you're dead.

No warning, no sound of a bomb whistling down from above. No chance to see your life flash before your eyes. As sudden and irrevocable as a car crash. He'd never given it much thought, but

Danny suspected that's how it would be in real life. You'd never get to see the end coming.

The game would be over. Just like that.

Danny's hands clenched involuntarily as he ran, as if he held the controls to his life and could jam his thumbs to run faster, hit the right combination of buttons to fly away.

He flew sideways before he realized he'd been hit. The pain in his right calf told him where as he landed on his side in a broken heap. He twisted in the mud as the air *snapped*—sharp sounds like breaking twigs—and Danny knew they must be using suppressors. Nobody would hear the shots, least of all him.

He grabbed at his pants and his hand came away wet. Tears sprang to his eyes as he brushed the wound, but it felt like the leg was grazed, not blown apart. There wasn't a slug in him yet.

He wondered if they had night vision goggles. He could see the hotel lights in the distance, but everything close was black-on-black. Clouds obscured the stars, and there was almost no moon. They'd be on top of him before he could even see them.

Danny felt the ground sloping as he scrambled backward. Maybe he could hide behind this low rise until they passed. He tried to ignore the pain in his leg as he slid on his belly, face pressed into the grass.

His right foot suddenly cold and wet. At first he thought it was blood filling his shoe until he realized he'd touched water. Craning his neck he saw the dull sheen of the pond and felt a thrill of hope. Maybe the game wasn't over, after all.

Danny used to be a swimmer. He could hold his breath a really long time, and the dogs might not smell him in the water. All he had to do was lay low, then submerge if they came too close.

He slid backward until the water enveloped his chest. He could feel the bottom under his knees and wondered how deep it was at the center, being careful to keep his arms loose so he didn't make waves. The water was surprisingly cold, given the tropical climate, but Danny could feel the heat from his own blood as it streamed from his leg.

That's when he felt a tugging at his foot. Sudden, sharp, insistent.

The water exploded and Danny felt himself lifted into the air. His first thought was *grenade* until his brain caught up with his nerve endings.

Teeth.

Something was biting his leg, and it was no dog.

Danny's scream was cut off in a riot of bubbles as he was pulled under, the surface of the water only inches out of reach. He sensed movement and twisted violently, his leg almost dislocating. He started to black out.

Lights danced across the surface of the water, criss-crossing and breaking apart. His pursuers had reached the pond.

Danny heard muffled voices arguing as he swallowed water. A burst of light, maybe the report of a gun. Splashing overhead. The sudden displacement of water, like a sailor falling overboard.

Danny wondered if he was still alone but couldn't turn his head. Spots flashed before his eyes. The beams of light drifted away as the voices faded. Danny smiled with the knowledge that they'd never find him now.

And much to his surprise, Danny realized he was dying. He never expected to see it coming, but he did, right before his lungs filled with water and his vision went black.

The game was over. Just like that.

Chapter Two

When he stopped to think about it, Cecil was glad they'd found a dead body.

Anything that made his brother Bud speechless was a welcome distraction, even if it looked like something out of a coroner's nightmare.

They were just shy of the tenth green, working their way through the back nine of the *Pete Dye Signature* golf course in Puerto Vallarta. Bud was playing the best game of his life, Cecil the worst. According to the rules of scratch golfers everywhere, this gave Bud permission to spend the entire day ragging on Cecil's swing.

Bud used his lucky seven-iron to reach the green, the ball rolling tantalizingly close to the hole. He had a jaunty gait as he approached the pin. A day like this, he could probably sink that ball wearing a blindfold.

"Must be that spicy food we ate—put a little kick in my swing."

"Must be." Cecil tried to ignore the bastard and get his stance right. A thirty-foot water hazard sat between his ball and the green, uphill from where he was standing. He'd been slicing everything all morning, which put his ball on the opposite side of the hole from Bud. Within taunting distance but far enough away for a chance to regroup. At twenty dollars a stroke, he could not afford to lose his concentration.

"Use your seven-iron, *Cece.*" Bud didn't even try to mask his delight. "You see the way I stroked that last one?"

"Stroke this one," said Cecil, grabbing his crotch. Jesus, the guy sinks a few putts and now he's Arnold-fucking-Palmer. Pretty soon he'll start designing courses, pushing rental cars in his spare time. *What an asshole.*

Cecil squinted across the water and lined up his shot. He twisted like a corkscrew, elbows high. Held it for a second then snapped forward. As his head whipped around, the ball vanished from his line of sight, only to reappear as a white streak hitting the far bank of the pond like a rubber bullet. It held fast to the muddy shore just long enough for Cecil's heart to skip a beat, then rolled backward into the water and disappeared.

Bud fell to the ground laughing. Cecil cranked his arm to hurl his piece-of-shit five-iron after the ball but caught himself. He'd never reach the water and just have to pick it up again, giving Bud one more reason to laugh his ass off.

Cecil looked over at Bud doubled over on the grass and considered practicing his swing on his brother's head. Maybe he'd switch to a seven-iron first, get a bit more lift in his stroke. See how Bud felt about his club selection then.

Screw him. Make up the lost strokes on the green.

Cecil trudged toward the edge of the water, wanting to make sure the ball wasn't just out of sight. Maybe it was stuck at the bottom of the far bank and he could climb down and chip it out of there, avoid the penalty. Like that French guy at the Masters who took off his shoes, ended up looking like an idiot.

But Cecil wasn't French, and hope springs eternal.

He leaned into his stride as the ground rose slightly, revealing hidden contours of the fairway designed to torment golfers. As he got closer, Cecil lost sight of the water completely until he crested a small ridge and found himself looking straight down the embankment.

That's when he saw the body.

There was no question in his mind. Though it bobbed just below the surface and wasn't exactly the right shape, it was definitely a human body. You didn't see fish that big in a water hazard, and fish almost never wore khakis. Cecil stared at it for a minute, not sure what to do next.

Bud couldn't see a thing, just Cecil gawking at the pond. Maybe Cecil was suicidal over his pitiful game, thinking about drowning himself. Bud shouted as he hopped into their golf cart and drove it toward the small footbridge.

"Hey Cecil, you gonna *swim* to the other side?"

Cecil glanced up from the body, noticing for the first time eyes staring back at him from the water.

Yellow eyes, with slits for pupils. Staring without blinking. Two, no—*three* pairs of eyes, all looking right at him.

A family of alligators, looking at Cecil like it was time for dessert.

Cecil unconsciously took a step away from the bank. He looked toward the body, understanding why it was such an odd shape. He forced a deep breath as he shifted his gaze back to the alligators, unwilling to let them out of his sight.

They didn't move. They didn't blink.

Bud was leaning across the passenger side of the cart, trying to see what was taking so damn long. "*I said*, are you gonna swim?"

Cecil answered slowly, without taking his eyes off the water.

"I don't think swimming's such a good idea."

Chapter Three

"*¿Ha encontrado alguien el brazo izquierdo?*"

The uniformed *polizia* scanned the crowd and concluded most of them were guests at the hotel, so he shouted his next question in English.

"Has anyone found the left arm?"

Chief Inspector Oscar Garcia watched the throng of tourists carefully as the question evaporated in the humid air, but no one answered. They were too busy holding their digital cameras and cell phones in the air as they jockeyed for position.

"The folks at home won't believe this."

"I'm gonna post this on my blog."

"I'm emailing this to my brother's phone right now."

Garcia shook his head sadly and looked at the uniformed officer, whose name was Fernando.

"*El mundo se ha vuelto loco.*" The world has gone mad.

Fernando nodded. Taking a deep breath, he tried again.

"How about the right foot?" he asked. "Anybody?"

Nobody answered, not even the alligators.

"Anybody?"

The body had been mauled before it surfaced, that was clear even from a distance. In addition to the missing limbs, the face was all but gone, ragged holes where eyes should have been, sections of the skull exposed. The corpse was so bloated it looked like a manatee. Garcia figured it had been under for several days, the alligators gnawing away one piece at a time. Alligators typically lodged a carcass under a sunken tree branch, taking their time working on the leftovers. The victim would have been the special-of-the-day for another week if something hadn't dislodged him from the bottom.

Garcia sighed. They knew perfectly well what happened to the missing limbs, but they had to ask. It was their first attempt to politely secure a crime scene that had been trampled by *turistas* long before they arrived. But scaring the pampered *gringos* back to their rooms wasn't going to be that easy.

Garcia made eye contact with Juan Molina, head of hotel security, who was standing on the outskirts of the crowd with a nervous expression on his face. The two men had served together as beat cops in Mexico City a lifetime ago, but Molina knew his old colleague hadn't changed. Garcia still had the balls of a bull.

The tourists were oblivious as Garcia threaded his way into the heart of the mob. All eyes were focused on the alligators, the corpse, or the digital whirring of their cameras. Garcia winked at Molina as he reached under his jacket with his right hand and drew his pistol from a weathered shoulder holster. No one seemed to notice as he raised the firearm over his head.

The gun was a Colt Python, an old-school revolver slightly larger than a catcher's mitt and louder than an atomic bomb. Because he was feeling dramatic, Garcia pulled the hammer back until he heard the metallic *click* over the din of the crowd. That simple action reduced the force needed to pull the trigger from a ten-pound yank of his finger to only two pounds of pressure. Garcia held the gun high while jamming his left index finger into his left ear. No point in losing hearing in both.

He took a deep breath, counted to ten, and pulled the trigger.

The man directly in front of Garcia pissed himself, the stain appearing instantly on his linen slacks. The woman on his left started screaming. The couple to his right threw their hands up to surrender, even though they were facing away from the gun and had no idea who was shooting or why. Two young men ducked and raised their hands in what Garcia assumed was a defensive posture taught in a beginner's karate class somewhere in the American suburbs.

For an agonizing moment everyone froze, as if the shock of the blast was accompanied by an alien strobe light that glued them in place. Garcia had seen it before when chasing a fleeing suspect, the sonic boom of his gun turning a felon into a deer caught in the headlights.

Before anyone could regain their wits, Garcia pulled the trigger a second time.

If a single gunshot said *freeze* to the primordial brain, a second shot was a hot poker up the ass. Men and women screamed and ran in whatever direction they happened to be facing. The two men in the karate stances practically leap-frogged over the other guests as they tried to escape. The mob of *turistas* turned into a starting line for the Puerto Vallarta marathon.

Fernando braced himself against the embankment to push anyone running toward the water away from the alligators and back toward the hotel. Juan yelled at the top of his lungs.

"*Señors y Señoras*. Go back to your rooms. It is safe in your room. *Vamanos!*"

In less than ten seconds, Oscar Garcia had managed to secure the crime scene.

He waved lazily at the ambulance idling at the far end of the fairway. The driver flashed his lights in acknowledgment and slowly drove toward them over the uneven ground.

Garcia nodded toward Fernando. "More men coming?"

Fernando shook his head. "There's a game, remember?"

Garcia felt embarrassed at his own forgetfulness, his unhealthy obsession with his job. Mexico was playing Italy in a soccer match today, an event on par with a sighting of the Virgin Mary. No wonder only Americans had rushed to see the body. The Germans, Italians, and French guests of the hotel were in the bar placing bets. To Americans soccer was a game played by little girls in plaid skirts attending private schools that cost more each semester than Garcia made in a year. Soccer was not a serious sport, and it certainly couldn't compare to the thrill of seeing a mutilated corpse.

Garcia sighed and gestured vaguely at the trampled green, the muddy embankment, the water, and the three semi-submerged reptiles.

"Help the ambulance crew."

"Of course, Inspector."

"Take pictures. Measure things. Put body parts in a bag."

Fernando nodded. He wanted to go home and watch the game but had lost the raffle the local cops held during the World Cup to determine duty rosters. "Yes, Inspector."

"I will meet you at the morgue later."

Garcia secured his pistol in the shoulder holster with a small strap, then turned to face Juan, who was wearing an expression that blended admiration and exasperation in equal parts.

"You know how many complaints I'm going to get?" said Juan.

"About the alligators on the golf course?"

"No, they've been here all season. We tried to chase them away but they came back. The guests were warned."

"You think I was wrong to scare your guests to safety."

"You won't get the angry phone calls," said Juan. "I will."

"I could have started arresting them."

Juan made a face. "Get off my resort, Inspector *pendejo*."

Garcia gave him a mock salute. "Not yet, old friend. I have one more stop to make, and I fear it concerns someone staying at your hotel."

"The detective?"

"*Sí*," said Garcia. "I must tell the *gringo* private investigator that his client is dead."

Chapter Four

Cape Weathers already knew about the floating corpse. He wondered if he still had a client but had to smile when Garcia fired into the air and the tourists scattered like cockroaches.

Watching from his balcony through a pair of Nikon binoculars, Cape could tell Garcia angled his shots toward the ocean. A cop would know those bullets had to come down eventually. Unlike private investigators, gravity never gave up.

Maybe one of the shots will take out a jetski.

The thought almost cheered him up.

After spending almost a week in Mexico, Cape was pleased to discover that he wasn't the least bit prejudiced—he held all tourists in equal disdain regardless of their race, religion, or country of origin. There was something about Mexico that brought out the worst in those who came to visit. People sitting quietly on the plane became loud and obnoxious the moment they stepped on Mexican soil. Reasonable men became bumbling Lotharios ogling anything in a skirt, while demure women transformed into tawdry sirens coaxing anyone with a penis to crash upon their shores.

Cape had never seen anything like it, even in Vegas.

The locals took it all in stride, having long since abandoned any effort to fight off the invasion. They put their culture and pride up for sale along with the sombreros and stuffed alligators. Cape had begun to think of Puerto Vallarta as a stripper, totally sanguine about having her ass slapped and her tits squeezed as long as her g-string was full of crumpled bills by the end of the night.

The cops had spread a blanket over the corpse as they waited for the ambulance to work its way down the course, which struck Cape as odd now that the tourists had fled. He focused the binoculars on the duty officer's face and tried to read his lips but it was no use. Cape's Spanish consisted mostly of menu items and swear words, maybe a few animals, numbers, and primary colors half-remembered from high school.

He figured at least an hour before he could visit the morgue, assuming he could wrangle a guest pass.

Time enough to have a drink.

Cape wasn't much of a drinker, but he wanted to be sure about the body, which meant he had time to kill. He tossed the binoculars onto his bed as he stepped through the sliding glass doors, then crossed his room. The bedspread and walls were rust and ochre with accents in black and brown, the same colors as the tile mural in the lobby designed to make tourists feel they had been transported to another time and place, even though they had passed a Hard Rock Café on their way into town.

Catching a glimpse of himself in the mirror, he turned and met his own gaze. A reasonably fit man looked back at him, maybe six feet tall, blue eyes almost gray in the yellow light of the room. Crow's feet around the eyes and smile lines around a mouth that wasn't smiling. Sandy hair in need of a comb, a complexion that suggested sunscreen might have been a good idea three days ago. Cape leaned close to the mirror and pretended he was looking into his client's eyes instead of his own.

"Hi Rebecca, it's me. Yeah, I might have found your brother. Is he OK? Well, not exactly—"

Try again.

"Miss Lowry, I'm afraid I have some bad news…"

Pitiful.

"Your brother is dead."

Cape broke eye contact and turned away from the mirror, disgusted. He wasn't sure who blinked first.

He looked at the phone beside the bed for a long minute but lost that staring contest, too. Stepping into the hallway, he let the door swing shut behind him and headed for the bar. Just one drink, followed by a visit to the morgue.

Then he could deliver the news that would surely get him fired.

Chapter Five

"I'm gonna nail this fucker, you just wait."

Cecil rubbed his bloodshot eyes and squinted at the man across the pool. As he tried to focus, his tongue crept slowly between his sunburned lips like a malignant eel.

"*Explorer!*" He slapped the table. "Four door, automatic."

"OK…ok." Bud twirled the little paper umbrella bobbing in his drink. He pointed toward a woman in a yellow sun hat and black bikini heading for the bar. He leaned close to his brother and whispered.

"Mus*tang*." Bud put a lascivious emphasis on the second half of the word.

Cecil and Bud high-fived as the woman felt their eyes on her. She gave them a look but the brothers stared back, oblivious. Realizing she would remain the sole object of their attention as long as she stood there, she scowled and moved past the poolside bar into the hotel.

"I think she likes you," said Cecil.

"She was looking at you, bro'."

"You're probably right. My turn?"

Bud nodded, secretly pleased he and his brother weren't fighting for a change. This game was probably the only thing that pushed aside their petty squabbles. It put life in perspective, because the game was a natural extension of the business partnership that had made them rich. Car dealers for over twenty years, Bud and Cecil fervently believed that only two things in life were certain. Forget death and taxes—for every person there was a perfect car, and the perfect car was always a Ford.

Bud and Cecil were an auto company's dream team. Too lazy to jump to the competition and too stupid to question the sales propaganda from the national office. Why let issues like product quality interfere with a perfectly good sale—they were true believers. Now they were among the top ten dealers in the country, this trip to Mexico only a small part of a year-end bonus package. Give a customer a firm handshake, a pat on the back, throw in the floormats, and next thing you know you're sitting by a pool with a drink in your hand. Not bad.

No matter who walked by, the brothers knew they could match them to the car of their dreams. "What do you think of this one?" Cecil was shielding his eyes, trying to get a better look at the figure walking toward them.

"Hard to say," said Bud. "Confident stride. Maybe another Explorer?"

"Too obvious," said Cecil dismissively. The guy wore a loose-fitting white shirt, tan pants, and sandals—those fancy kind that wrapped around your ankles. *Might be a fag.*

Cecil was about to go out on a limb, tell Bud this guy was minivan material, maybe a Subaru owner, when he realized the guy wasn't just headed in their general direction. He moved past the bar and kept coming. Without asking, the man grabbed an empty lounge chair and sat down next to them.

"Can I buy you boys a drink?"

Despite the offer, something in the guy's tone dispelled any suspicion that he was cruising for a threesome. In fact, now that the guy's silhouette blocked the sun, Cecil decided the minivan was a bad call. This fella looked like he might shake your hand one minute, then knock you on your ass the next. A friendly face with eyes as hard as the cement around the pool.

Bud, who amassed a higher umbrella count than Cecil, dove right in.

"Who the fuck're you?"

The man nodded, smiled. Cecil felt himself relax instantly. Damn, this fella was good. Cecil briefly wondered if the guy was a fellow car dealer.

"Cape Weathers."

Handshakes all around. After the brothers introduced themselves, Bud frowned and said, "Cape…kind of name is that?"

"One that's easy to spell," said Cape. "Like Bud—that a nickname?"

Bud gave it some thought. "Never thought to ask."

"Well, what's it say on your driver's license?"

"Bud—what else would it say?"

Cape kept his mouth shut.

Cecil asked, "What kind of car you drive?"

"Convertible," said Cape.

Bud leaned forward on his chair. "Mustang?"

"Yeah, as a matter of fact."

"'65?" asked Cecil.

Cape shook his head. "Close—67."

Bud nodded knowingly. "Figured you for a vintage man."

"The guy at the bar inside told me you were car dealers."

"*Ford* dealers," Bud corrected.

"Right." Cape nodded in acknowledgment of the distinction. "How long you guys been down here?"

"Almost two weeks," said Cecil.

"All expenses paid," added Bud with a self-satisfied grin.

"That right?" Cape gestured to the waitress navigating the maze of lounge chairs. When he caught her eye, he held up three fingers. "Mind if I ask you some questions about your golf game?"

"Cecil's got a wicked slice," said Bud.

"I was more interested in your *last* golf game. This morning—when you found the body."

"Oh, *that* golf game," said Bud. "I won."

"Bullshit," snapped Cecil. "I was about to turn it around."

Bud snorted and drained his glass. Cape counted nine little paper umbrellas on the table and wondered if he was wasting

his time. Before he could ask another question, Cecil narrowed
his eyes and said, "Wait a minute—you said the bartender told
you we were car dealers."

"So?"

"You checking up on us?" Cecil blinked and his pupils contracted, then dilated again. "You a cop or something?"

Cape shook his head. "Definitely not a cop."

"Reporter?" asked Bud.

"Used to be—" Cape began, but Cecil cut him off.

"—for CNN?"

"You know Ted Turner?" asked Bud.

"What kind of car does he drive?"

Cape was about to raise his hands in surrender when the
waitress arrived. As soon as her shadow fell across the table,
Bud and Cecil sighed. When Cape gave the waitress his room
number and told her to put the drinks on his tab, the brothers
seemed to forget all about the inquisition. Nor did they notice
that Cape's drink was a slightly different color. Before he'd come
to their table he'd asked the waitress to serve him the virgin
equivalent of whatever they were drinking. He knew a pair of
functional alcoholics when he saw them and what would happen
if he tried to keep up.

After everyone took a sip, Cape tried again.

"So tell me about your golf game."

One hour and six little umbrellas later, the brothers were still
talking and Cape had no idea what they were talking about. As a
demonstration of the effects of alcohol on stream of consciousness, it was an impressive display. The brothers finished each
other's sentences—sometimes they even finished Cape's, even
if they didn't know what he was about to say. By the time the
brothers started to feel the drinks, all Cape had learned was that
Cecil was a poor loser, Bud cheated on his score if you didn't
watch him, and all the good looking women in Puerto Vallarta
had an unnatural aversion to car dealers.

Cape was about to give up and return to his room when Cecil
slurred, "And that's when I saw the bodies."

Cape leaned forward. "The *body*—you said the body was in the water hazard."

"Ain't you listening to my brother?" asked Bud. "He said *bod—eeeze.*"

"As in plural?"

Cecil nodded. "As in more than one."

Cape looked from Bud to Cecil, then back again. "You sure?"

Cecil shrugged. "Guess I only saw one body, now that you mention it. But there was two down there—must've been. Either that or the dead bastard was some kinda mutant."

Cape felt a sinking sensation in his stomach. "Why do you say that?"

Cecil looked at him like he was an idiot.

"The legs," he said.

"What about them?"

"There was three," said Cecil. "When I looked in the water, I saw three legs."

"Three legs, that means two bodies," said Bud. "Do the math."

"Yeah," said Cecil. "Do the math."

Chapter Six

Frank Alessi snorted derisively as the tall man wearing the clerical collar was shown into his office. Frank sat behind his desk and spread his hands across the considerable girth of his stomach, making no move to stand or shake hands.

His guest didn't seem offended. In fact, the pale man with the shock of white hair didn't seem to care one way or the other, his gray eyes bottomless and unreadable. He took a seat and unfurled his legs, placing his feet only inches from Frank's double chin.

"Get your feet off my desk."

The Priest ran his long fingers through his hair, pulling it back from a sharp widow's peak, and tugged at his collar, displacing the white square slightly, but he kept his feet where they were. His smug expression almost sent Frank into a blind rage.

This was Frank's office, his *town*. Nobody else called the shots in San Francisco, not even the big boys in New York. That was the arrangement. Besides, if they really had a problem with how he ran things, they should just have him killed. Have a little respect for tradition. That last thought gave Frank pause, made him reassess the sociopath sitting across from him. He ran through a mental checklist of what he remembered hearing over the years.

The guy wasn't even a real priest—never had been as far as Frank knew—just had a fetish for wearing the getup. Had some history with the Church that sounded more like rumor than truth to Frank, the kind of urban legend designed to scare the superstitious. And though the guy never carried a gun, he'd been doing contract work for the families since before Frank made *capo*. Was older than he looked. Had connections that went right to the top. It was said that if the Priest showed up at your door, that could only mean one thing—somebody high up in the organization was royally pissed.

That was about it, except for one thing Frank wouldn't admit to anyone. This guy gave him the *heebie-jeebies*. He suppressed a chill and glanced reflexively over his shoulder for reassurance.

On Frank's left stood Bruno Carcetti. Weighing in at two hundred and sixty pounds, Bruno had an impressive capacity for violence and a desperate need to belong, which made him a perfect candidate for mob muscle. To the right of the desk stood Alex Torratzo, tall and lean, mean as a snake and twice as fast. Both men were packing and had no compunction about shooting first and asking questions later. Frank smiled inwardly at the knowledge his guest didn't have a weapon. Like any career criminal, he hated a level playing field.

Priest smiled without warmth as his eyes roamed from one bodyguard to the other. "I see you have matching bookends, Frank. Too bad you're not much of a reader." Before his apoplectic host could respond, Priest cut him off with an upraised hand. "Because if you did, you might have read the headlines in the papers. The ones about the Senator's son—the Senator himself—gone missing. Did you miss those when you were in the can?"

Frank worked his mouth as if he had something stuck in his teeth. "Was that a trick question? Because I just suck at those game shows." He made a vague gesture that encompassed Priest from head to toe. "And now that I think of it, you kinda remind me of that guy used to host *The Price Is Right*. White hair, beady eyes."

"I didn't realize you had a sense of humor, Frank."

"But he always had a hottie on each arm, didn't he? And you—well, based on your outfit—my guess is you prefer the company of young boys, am I right?"

Something flashed in the back of Priest's eyes, a flicker of life buried in the deadly gray, but he stretched his smile taut. "You like publicity, don't you Frank?"

Frank shrugged. "Hasn't hurt my business."

"But has it hurt *ours?*" Priest steepled his fingers and rested his chin against them. "You're a respectable businessman, a major political donor. A civic leader. Makes for a nice resumé, Frank."

Frank was getting sick of hearing his own name, Priest saying it every other sentence, trying to get under his skin. *Frank*-this, *Frank*-that. Sounding like his third grade teacher, another psycho in a black-and-white outfit, only she had carried a weapon: a ruler. Frank unconsciously rubbed his knuckles at the memory. No wonder he hated this asshole. "Wanna get to the point?"

"Your lack of discretion makes some people uncomfortable."

"Tell those people to get over it," said Frank. "Those political connections pay your salary."

The pale eyes seemed to glow. "I'm not on your payroll."

"My mistake."

"I couldn't agree more," Priest replied. "Let's hope it's your last."

"That a threat?" Floorboards creaked as Frank shifted in his seat.

"The kid was an addict. Think that's smart?"

Frank held his hands up. "Kids today...*whattya gonna do?*"

"You don't seem to be taking this seriously, Frank."

"I'm taking this situation very seriously. I think you're worried I'm not taking you seriously."

Priest flashed a smile full of malice, lips closed. "Do I look worried?"

"You look like a retard at a comic book convention."

Priest nodded as if Frank's comment deserved some further thought. "And the Senator...you weren't keeping tabs?"

"He retired. Fell off the grid."

"Uh-huh." Priest pursed his lips. "You know, we're all fishers of men, Frank. Some we catch and keep, watch after them, nurture them as they grow. Some we throw back into the water because they're not worth the time and trouble." He paused as if remembering a summer day, feet dangling in the water as fish darted just below the surface. "But some we gut right there on the dock, because we don't want them flopping around, scaring the other fish. We gut them and then cut their heads off—do you get my meaning?"

"Your feet stink." Frank waved a hand toward Priest's shoes but was careful not to make contact. "And I'm tired of dancing—cut to the chase or go fuck a nun."

Priest collapsed his legs to the floor, leaned forward in his chair. "I—*we*—don't give a rat's ass what you do in San Francisco. But this little program of ours demands cooperation."

"Cooperation." Frank expelled the word, clearly disliking its taste.

"It requires *control*," said Priest. "And you, my portly colleague, seem to have lost control."

Frank's bulk shifted ominously and Bruno rolled onto the balls of his feet, thinking his boss was about to launch himself across the desk. He'd seen it before and it wasn't pretty, like a killer whale breaching, leaping into the air to devour a seal. And whenever that happened, it fell to Bruno to clean things up.

Frank breathed heavily through his nose before settling back into his chair. "I'm on it," he said. "I got a guy in Mexico, looking into things."

"The kid might be dead," Priest said.

"You surprised?" said Frank. "Didn't you just tell me he was a junkie?"

"The Senator is AWOL."

"Who the fuck are you," asked Frank. "CNN?"

"The horse is out of the fucking barn, Frank."

"And the dish ran away with the spoon—I said *I'm on it*."

"So am I," said Priest, his voice suddenly quiet, barely a whisper. "That's why I came here—to tell you that until this is settled, you've got a shadow."

"Stay out of my way and we'll get along just fine."

Priest stood and stretched, his fingers locked together, long arms thrust toward the ceiling. A yoga pose. Frank gave him a look that suggested his testosterone level was being measured and found wanting. Priest arched his back and twisted his shoulders one way, then the other, his gaze locked on Frank, his features vaguely effeminate if not for the soulless eyes.

"Are you threatening *me*?" His tone was suddenly warm, playful.

"What if?"

"Well, that's really my job—to threaten people." Priest ran his tongue suggestively across his full lips. "Tell you to stay out of my way, not fuck up again, keep your *goombah* nose where it belongs."

Frank's head twitched as if a seizure had begun. That was the cue Bruno had been waiting for—he took a long, aggressive step around the desk. It wouldn't be the first time he escorted an unwanted guest out of Frank's office by the scruff of his neck.

Most guys backed away when they saw Bruno coming, even the hard cases, so he wasn't prepared when Priest stepped toward him, an almost flirtatious smile on his face. Before Bruno could bring his hands up, Priest glided past, his right hand sweeping toward Bruno's face.

Priest hooked his thumb into the other man's left eye socket as effortlessly as a child popping a soap bubble. There was a wet sucking sound and suddenly Bruno was on his knees, screaming.

"Jesus." Alex froze momentarily, repulsed by the scene before him. The sound of Frank's chair scraping against the floor brought him back to his senses. Alex went for the gun in his waistband but for once moved too slowly. As graceful as a dancer Priest ducked behind him, arching as he grasped the other man's head, a silent partner in a ballet of pain. He pirouetted to face the other way, twisting his arms as he turned. A loud snap as vertebrae separated and Alex slumped across Frank, his lifeless body pinning his erstwhile employer in his chair.

Frank pushed against the desk frantically, desperate to free himself, but Priest was already behind him. Bruno was crawling across the floor toward the door, his left hand scratching pitifully at his ruined eye socket, blood pouring through his fingers. And Alex was dead weight, more effective than handcuffs at keeping Frank prisoner.

"Now then," said Priest, moving to sit on the edge of the desk. Frank's lips twitched spasmodically. Priest reached forward and ran his hand gently across Frank's sweating scalp, a mother soothing an hysterical child. "I think you'd agree that threatening you now would be, well, *redundant.*"

"I don't do business with psychos." It sounded better in Frank's head than when he actually muttered the words. His voice felt hollow, even to his own ears.

Priest noticed the gore on his thumb, jellied plasma from Bruno's ravaged eye. He removed his hand from Frank's head and extended it for a good look. With the air of a man pulling lint from his suit, Priest brought the thumb to his mouth and wrapped his lips around it as Frank watched in disbelief.

Priest sucked noisily, his eyes flashing with delight as Frank started to gag. He removed the thumb with a dramatic *pop*, then smiled with an open mouth, and Frank noticed for the first time how both incisors had been filed to sharp points. Priest curled his tongue against one of the fangs as if cleaning it, then laid his hand gently on the side of Frank's face. "Believe it or not, I'm a patient man." He caressed Frank's cheek lovingly with his thumb, up toward the left eye, down toward the trembling mouth. "So I wanted to give you the opportunity to share anything that you think could be useful. Anything at all."

Frank's eye tracked the movement of the thumb as if watching a tarantula crawl across his skin. His lips moved but no sound emerged.

"Look at me, Frank." The dull eyes looked like holes drilled into Priest's face, the empty orbs of a pirate skull. "Look at these clothes. Isn't there something you want to *confess?*"

Frank felt the pressure of the thumb increase as it swept upward, the bite of the nail, and started to scream.

Chapter Seven

Cape left the Ford dealers poolside with a collection of mini-umbrellas vast enough to protect the entire population of Lilliput from a monsoon. Bud had passed out, and Cecil was on a rant about the importance of quality, service, and reliability to the educated car buyer. Neither noticed when Cape took his leave and moved inside to the lobby bar.

The bar sat on the other side of a glass wall overlooking the pool. You got the same view of scantily clad women as the poolside bar plus air conditioning and some shade. Maybe it was the gnawing in his gut over Cecil's news, or maybe a lack of sunscreen, but Cape was beginning to feel the heat.

He gestured toward the bartender, a young guy with bleached blond hair and a strand of leather around his neck—this year's variation of a pooka shell necklace. Cape figured him for a college student, just old enough to serve drinks in Mexico. Not a bad summer job. Cape was about to order when the bartender's gaze shifted over his shoulder and a familiar voice spoke first.

"*Trés Generaciones—dos.*"

Cape wasn't surprised when Inspector Garcia took the adjacent stool. The bartender disappeared to the right as Cape nodded at his new neighbor.

"I think the kid's an American," he said, jutting his chin toward the returning bartender. "The leather necklace is a dead giveaway."

Garcia arched his eyebrows. "So?"

"Not sure he speaks Spanish. A lot of the college students working at the resort don't."

Garcia nodded. "Trés Generaciones is a tequila. Very expensive. If a bartender does not know that, he should be fired. And *dos*—"

"—means two," said Cape. "Even my Spanish has that covered."

"Exactly," said Garcia. "And if the bartender at a Mexican resort doesn't know *uno, dos, tres*—"

"— he should be fired," said Cape.

"*Exactemente.* It seems we think alike, my friend."

The bartender set two short glasses in front of them. Not shot glasses but heavy tumblers. The liquid inside was paler than most tequila Cape had seen, almost as clear as vodka. Garcia took a slim folder proffered by the bartender, opened it and used the pen inside to sign for the bill.

Cape held up his glass in thanks. He prepared to throw it back when Garcia put a restraining hand on his arm. "No, *amigo*. This is sipping tequila."

"Sipping tequila."

Garcia nodded. Holding up his glass, he slowly, almost reverentially, took a sip. Cape followed his example and whistled through his teeth as he set his glass down. The tequila had vaporized in his mouth, returned to a liquid state, then sluiced down his throat as if it were alive.

Cape blinked away tears. "That's good tequila."

"Indeed." Garcia took another sip.

"Is that why we're sipping it?"

"One must savor it," said Garcia. "Besides, it costs twelve dollars a shot—U.S., not *pesos*."

"Twelve dollars? Maybe I should ask for a straw."

Garcia sighed contentedly and set his glass down, but his expression became grave as he turned on his stool.

"I am sorry about your client."

Cape shrugged. "My client doesn't know yet."

Garcia arched his eyebrows. "But you know about the body?"

"Bod—*eeze*," said Cape, doing his best to sound like Bud. "I saw—heard—the news."

"I saw you talking to the brothers."

Cape took another sip and felt the lava worm squirm toward his stomach. "You don't miss a trick."

Garcia spread his hands. "But it seems I did, my friend. When we spoke about your search, I was under the impression you were looking for your client—"

"I wasn't looking for my client—I mean, looking *for* her. I was looking for someone else; someone she asked me to find. What I should have said was that I was looking *on her behalf.*"

Garcia studied Cape over the rim of his glass but didn't say anything.

"I might have been a little vague," said Cape.

"I think you were." Garcia set his glass down with thud. "Sadly, a common technique among American detectives. I should have seen it coming."

"You've worked with a lot of PI's from the states?"

Garcia shook his head. "I have studied them. Sam Spade let everyone think he was—what is the word—a *shady character*—so he could get the Maltese Falcon from Peter Lorre and the Fat Man."

"Sydney Greenstreet."

"*Sí, el hombre gordo.* And then there is Jessica Fletcher."

Cape took another sip and wracked his memory, coming up empty. Garcia saw his confusion and shook his head in dismay.

"Jessica Fletcher, the great American detective?"

Cape shook his head.

"*Murder She Wrote?*" said Garcia in a tone that suggested he'd lost all respect for his drinking partner. "Surely you know this show."

Cape almost laughed. "You mean the TV show with Angela Lansbury?"

"It ran for over a decade on your television."

"Not on my television."

"It is very popular in Mexico," said Garcia. "I saw it once in English, while visiting your country, and must admit the woman who dubs the dialogue for *Señora* Fletcher on Mexican television has too deep a voice. She sounds more like a man than a snoopy old woman. Still, she is coy like you, always letting people jump to conclusions."

Cape drained the last of his drink. As the liquid heat found its way down his gullet, he felt simultaneously tortured and at peace with the world. Therein lay the mystery of tequila.

"This case," he said. "It's complicated."

"Your client is a woman?" Garcia smiled ruefully. "Of course it is complicated."

"You want an apology?"

"I will settle for an explanation."

Cape looked at his empty glass and nodded. Garcia caught the bartender's eye and held up two fingers.

"So tell me, Señor Weathers. What brings you to Mexico?"

Chapter Eight

Some women just looked like trouble. Rebecca Lowry wasn't one of them, which should have been the first clue.

The woman who walked into Cape's office two weeks ago was excruciatingly attractive in a remarkably wholesome way. An expensive gray suit and skirt, tailored to reveal the faint contours of a distracting figure. Short dark hair, large brown eyes, a long straight nose, and full lips defined a classically beautiful face adorned with little or no makeup. Within the first few minutes of the interview he decided that, if asked, he might consider compromising his professionalism and running away with her. She didn't ask, and he didn't press the point. A good detective knows when to be patient.

She started to explain why she had called but stopped herself in mid-sentence and looked uncertainly across the desk.

"Mind if I ask you a few questions first?"

"Most people do." Cape gestured toward the client chair, which she took, crossing her legs demurely.

"Your references were excellent."

"They wouldn't be references if they weren't."

"How long have you been doing this?"

"About ten years."

"And before that?" she asked. "Were you a cop or something?"

"Reporter," said Cape. "I worked for the *Chronicle* here in San Francisco, the *Times* in New York. A few other papers and magazines you probably didn't read before they went out of business."

"You covered the crime beat?"

"Some. I stuck my nose where it didn't belong—they call that *investigative journalism* when editors get full of themselves. Local mob activity. Construction scams. Political scandals."

"Why'd you quit?"

Cape shrugged. "My editor said I had problems with authority."

"Do you?"

"Depends on who's in charge."

"You didn't get along with your editor—that's why you left?"

"No. I could have gone to another paper, or freelanced." Cape shrugged. "Over the years, I saw some things."

"What kind of things?"

"Things I don't really like to talk about—things that convinced me the pen isn't always mightier than the sword. I got tired of trying to make a difference only to have guns pointed at me."

"And now?"

"Now I get to point one back," he replied. "And every once in a while I even get to make a difference."

Rebecca studied him for a minute, teeth working her lower lip. Cape could tell she'd already made a decision—she was just working herself up to tell him about it. The intensity of her gaze almost made him uncomfortable.

Almost.

"Anything else you want to know?"

"You mentioned political scandals," said Rebecca. "What do you think of politicians?"

"Not much."

A bitter smile vanished from Rebecca's lips almost before it appeared. "That might be a problem."

Cape raised his eyebrows. "For me or you?"

"Lowry is my mother's maiden name," said Rebecca. "My given name was Dobbins—as in Jim Dobbins."

"The California State Senator?"

"Retired."

"That's right," said Cape. "Didn't he resign suddenly, a couple of months ago? The papers said he wanted to spend more time with his family."

The bitter smile returned and held.

"I haven't seen my father in ten years, Mister Weathers."

"Call me Cape. So you two aren't close."

"You have a talent for understatement, Cape."

"You're saying the story was spun."

"Like a top."

"What about the rest of your family?"

"My mother died when I was in college." Rebecca's teeth flashed white before she brought her lips together into a thin line. "And my brother Danny, well, he's the oldest son. To my Dad—*the Senator*—he could do no wrong, until he developed a substance abuse problem, as the papers called it."

Cape noticed she almost choked on the word *Dad* and practically spat *Senator* when she said it. "Why are you here?"

"My brother has disappeared. So has my father. I want you to find them."

"After ten years, what's the rush?"

"I love my brother."

"And you think the two disappearances are related."

Rebecca nodded. "I think my brother got into some kind of trouble. We used to talk on the phone—he'd call whenever he sobered up. But then he stopped calling. When I tried to call him, his phone had been disconnected."

"You try his friends?"

Rebecca shook her head. "I don't know his friends, so I did something that I swore I would never do."

"You called your Dad."

"And now I can't find him, either."

"Any ideas, hunches?"

"I think my Dad might have gone looking for Danny. I think he might've known what kind of trouble he was in."

"That's quite a leap, don't you think?"

Rebecca's eyes hardened for an instant. "*The sins of the father. My brother is harmless—if something's happened to him, it must be my father's fault.*"

Cape started to say something but caught himself. He didn't grow up in her house. "Mind if I ask you some more questions?"

Rebecca shook her head. "Not at all, but I have one more for you."

"Shoot."

"Did you vote in the last election, Cape?"

"Yeah, I did."

"Did you vote for my father?"

"No, I didn't."

"OK."

"OK what?"

"You're hired."

Chapter Nine

"I was right, this is complicated."

Inspector Garcia said it sympathetically but Cape clenched his jaw anyway. He felt like a failure. You get hired to find a missing person, the client typically wants you to find that person alive. He downed the last of his tequila and turned on his bar stool.

"You have a talent for understatement."

Garcia made a *tsk-tsk* sound. "You forgot to sip that last drink, my friend."

Cape glanced at the bar and tried to remember the count, but the bartender kept replacing their empty glasses with tumblers full of the impossibly clear poison. "How many was that?"

Garcia shrugged. "I am off duty."

"And I'm probably fired."

"But you will be paid for your work to date, no?"

Cape nodded.

"But that's not what bothers you, is it?" Garcia put a hand on Cape's shoulder. "In your line of work, reputation is everything."

"You learn that from watching a movie. Or a TV show?" Cape hated the sound of his own voice, the undercurrent of frustration. His nostrils flared as he took a deep breath. "Sorry, just pissed I didn't find him sooner."

"Who?"

"That's the question, isn't it?" said Cape. "We won't really know who turned up until you visit the morgue."

Garcia looked at his watch. "Too soon. But you have your suspicions."

"Now who's being coy?"

Garcia took a sip of his drink. "I admit it, I think your search has ended. Despite what you might read in the tabloids about crime in Mexico, this sort of thing doesn't happen very often in a resort town. Mexico City, of course, but a place like Puerto Vallarta?" Garcia shook his head. "You find a *gringo* body, it's usually an overweight tourist who had a heart attack in his room."

"While screwing the maid?"

"Or the bellboy," said Garcia. "We Mexicans are free thinkers."

"Glad to hear it." Cape finished half his drink in one gulp. He knew the tequila was slowing him down, but it was taking the edge off a growing depression, turning it into anger. He had no time for self-pity, but maybe he could put *pissed* to good use. "It does make me wonder…" He let his voice trail off as he set the glass down.

"Wonder?"

"Why a Chief Inspector would be hanging around a sleepy town like this."

"Surely you know tourism is critical to Mexico's struggling economy."

"Yeah," said Cape. "Think I read that in a guidebook. And surely the local *polizia* can handle the pickpockets and grifters that pass through here."

Garcia took another delicate sip, closing his eyes as the liquid scorched a path across his lips. "What are you implying, *compadré*?"

"Maybe you knew there was a Senator and his kid South of the border."

"You told me yourself, or are you too drunk to remember?"

Cape shook his head. "The tequila's good, but not that good. I think maybe you already knew."

Garcia shrugged. "It is an interesting theory."

"Would you tell me if it was true?"

Garcia frowned, giving the question the consideration it deserved. "But who would tell me?"

"The Senator had a lot of connections," said Cape. "I've barely scratched the surface, but like any politician, he had a gazillion business and consulting deals on the side."

"I see."

"And then there's my client."

"You think your client called *me*?"

Cape shook his head. "Not you directly, but maybe her lawyer tried to work through official channels before she came to me. She has a lot of lawyers."

"Of course she does," said Garcia. "She is American."

"That's the most likely scenario," said Cape. "It's what I would do if I was her lawyer."

"You could ask her, no?"

Cape crossed his arms on the bar and rested his head on them. "I might, since you're not telling me a damn thing."

"That is the tequila talking," said Garcia.

"But you didn't answer my question."

"There have been so many. Who knew Americans were so inquisitive?"

Cape raised his head so he could make eye contact. "If you already knew about the Senator's kid, would you have told me?"

Garcia didn't hesitate. He met Cape's gaze and said, "No."

Cape smiled. It was impossible not to like this man, both candid and oblique at the same time. "Why not?"

"Why did you not tell me who you were looking for when we first met? I think, my friend, the answer to your question is the same as the answer to mine."

Cape nodded. "Because I had no reason to trust you, any more than you should trust me."

"*Exactemente.*"

"I hear there's a lot of corruption in the Mexican police force."

"Indeed?" Garcia laughed with his eyes but his mouth was a thin line daring Cape to step across. "And where did you hear this?"

"I think I saw it in a movie—*Traffic*, the one with Benicio del Toro."

"He is a very good actor."

"Good point," replied Cape. "So maybe it's not true, after all. He was just acting."

"I did not realize you were so suspicious."

"Failure will do that to you."

"A man who is that hard on himself must be very good at his job." Garcia looked at his watch again. "It is almost time."

"You want company?"

"No, it would make some people…*uncomfortable*. Go to your room and I will call you later with the news. You can come to the morgue tonight if you like—I will make the necessary arrangements." He lifted his jacket off a neighboring stool and took one of his cards from the pocket. "Call me if you think of anything of interest."

"Like a dead body floating to the surface of the swimming pool?"

"Yes, that would qualify."

Cape stood to leave, felt his legs readjust to gravity. He extended his hand and felt Garcia's firm grip in his own. "One more question before you go?"

Garcia brushed lint off his slacks. "Of course."

"How can a police inspector afford twelve-dollar shots of tequila?"

"That is simple, *amigo*."

"Oh?"

"I charged them to your room." The laughter in Garcia's eyes returned, and this time his mouth had begun to curl at the edges as he turned and headed for the door.

Chapter Ten

Cape felt weightless.

That was the sensation from the tequila as he walked to the elevator, a tenuous separation from his mundane concerns, but the Muzak on the way to his floor ruined it. By the time he made it to his room, his bladder was protesting his failure to visit the men's room in the lobby, and he couldn't get an instrumental version of *Hotel California* out of his head.

After two unsuccessful attempts at getting his key card to work, he made a beeline for his bathroom, lifting the seat to the toilet with his right foot while he worked his zipper with both hands. He blinked as he straddled the bowl, anticipating release, and let his eyes come into focus. He exhaled slowly and then, suddenly—*stopped*.

He doubled over in discomfort and dropped to his knees, his head only inches from the porcelain, his right hand clutching the adjacent sink as he let his eyes readjust to the new angle.

I'm not that drunk.

For a second he feared he might be hallucinating, but he knew that wasn't the case. The tequila might have slowed his pupils down, but they still worked. He stared into the toilet bowl and frowned at the fish swimming there.

There are fish in my toilet.

He had a fleeting thought this was something the resort did to amuse its guests. Maybe there was a kitten on his bed playing with a ball of yarn, a dog waiting in the living room with slippers in its mouth. All part of the club floor package, continental breakfast and live pets included.

But these were not *koi*, colorful oversized goldfish or exotic salt water species in rainbow colors. These fish were barely visible, less than three inches long and pale, almost translucent. Their bodies were impossibly narrow and their heads flared. Cape thought they looked like tiny arrows shooting back and forth. Whatever these creatures were, they weren't brought to his room by housekeeping. And since he was staying on the top floor, he doubted they had swum from the sewer, up the pipes and into his room.

Pushing aside his need to urinate, Cape crossed his room and grabbed the phone. The front desk answered after three rings, the voice female and friendly.

"There are fish in my toilet."

A long pause, a wait for the punch line. When none came, the pleasant voice said, "I'm so sorry, señor." Another pause. "Would you like me to call maintenance?"

"Does this happen often?"

"Not that I know of, señor." A polite hesitation, and then, "But this is Mexico. Anything can happen."

"Any suggestions?"

"You could flush, señor."

"Gracias." Cape replaced the handset, then lifted it again as he pulled Garcia's card from his pocket. He squinted as he read the instructions printed on the phone for calling a local number. Garcia answered after five rings.

"There are fish in my toilet."

"Is this how you Americans say hello?"

"I'm not kidding," said Cape.

Before Garcia could interrupt, he described the fish. When he had finished, there was nothing but silence on the line. Cape thought Garcia's cell phone had cut out until he heard the other man's breath as he exhaled into the mouthpiece.

"Describe them again," he said, his voice a heavy monotone cutting across the static of the call. Cape did, right down to their flared heads.

"Don't flush," said Garcia. "And under no circumstances use that toilet—for anything—I'll be there in twenty minutes."

The pressure on Cape's bladder reasserted itself at the thought of hopping around for twenty minutes, but he felt too tired to return to the lobby. "What if I have to take a piss?"

"Use the sink," said Garcia. "Or the shower. Believe me, those showers have been pissed in plenty of times. Pretend you're in a fraternity on Spring Break. But whatever you do, amigo, do *not* use that toilet."

"Why not?" asked Cape. "They're just fish."

"Trust me," said Garcia. "You'll thank me later."

Chapter Eleven

Sally whisked the tea into a green froth and contemplated death.

Four cups were arranged carefully in front of her. The first two were for her parents, dead these many years. The third was for Cape, a man she called friend, though never to his face. Serving the tea this way—as if her parents and Cape were there—was the closest Sally ever came to prayer.

Her eyes tracked the circular rhythms of her hand as she let her mind go blank. Her thoughts drifted, as always, to her childhood. Though it had not been a happy time, her formative years were full of rich memories.

Sally was orphaned when she was five. After her parents were murdered she was taken from Tokyo to Hong Kong, where she was enrolled in a school for girls. The school was highly competitive and very exclusive. Many girls never made it to graduation—some were expelled and sent home, others were transferred to smaller schools throughout Hong Kong. Some chose a different path from Sally, but a surprising number were crippled or killed before they were old enough to make that choice. The instructors were very strict.

The school was run by the Triads, the largest criminal syndicate in the world, the power behind China's underground economy since the time of the Ming emperors. As China flirted with capitalism and the communists looked the other way, the power of the Triads surged. Their organization became a dragon with many heads, its claws sunk into every port, every business, and every politician in the middle kingdom. And the heart of the great dragon was Hong Kong.

To protect their interests, the Triads molded their own weapons from the clay of young minds. The process had been perfected over centuries of practice. The girls were kept in close quarters under tremendous pressure, forged into weapons in a furnace of betrayal.

Sally was their star pupil.

She could speak half a dozen languages with no trace of an accent, disguise herself as any nationality, or disappear into the shadows in less time than it takes to blink. She was proficient with weapons that had not been used for centuries—weapons easily concealed that were almost impossible to trace.

The basic principal behind the training was simple—direct young minds down a path before they found their own moral compass. But Sally's parents had given her more than green eyes and lustrous black hair, or a laugh that sounded like a bark. They imprinted their love so deep within her that she never lost her sense of self, even after they were dead and buried. Sally conformed to the school's training regimen but would never submit to anyone's will except her own. So when the Triads decided to betray her, Sally showed them what a good student she had become.

As she stirred the tea, images of passion and pain flashed before her mind's eye.

Standing on a pole with a sword in her hand, men running toward her with sharp spears and cruel smiles...a bow in her hand, the arrow notched and pointing at a bird in flight...a man's body spinning like a leaf, plummeting twenty stories to the street below...her first kiss, the burn of the other girl's lips against her own...her fingers slick with blood, uncertain whose blood it was, knowing there would be more...

Sally left Hong Kong and never looked back, leaving behind a wake of bodies cut directly from the heart of the dragon. The

Triads knew better than to try and follow her to America, so an uneasy truce existed as long as each party left the other alone.

Buddhists believe you are not the same person today that you were yesterday or will be tomorrow. This means you always have a choice, never bound by your past, and a better path can begin with each step you take. Opening her eyes, Sally wanted to believe all this but knew she never would. Like the metal in a Japanese sword—folded hundreds of times to strengthen the blade—her past was at the heart of every cell, trapped in every strand of hair, and flowing within her veins.

And though Death had been her companion for many years, Sally had no regrets.

She stopped stirring and continued the ritual, pouring tea carefully into the other cups before pouring her own. Though she didn't know why, Sally could always sense when Cape needed her help. As she drank her tea, she wondered if he would live long enough to ask for it again.

Chapter Twelve

"It is called a *candirú* fish."

Garcia was on his knees, gesturing at the fish with a penlight.

"They look mean," said Cape.

"They are more feared than the piranha, my friend, and for good reason." Garcia stood but kept his eyes on the bowl. "They don't always kill you, but you wish you were dead."

"Why?" Cape squinted at the near invisible fish as they darted back and forth.

"They are parasites," said Garcia. "Sometimes called the toothpick fish, very common in the Amazon. They are attracted to warmth. If someone is bathing in a river, the *candirú* will swim into any available orifice and lodge itself there."

"What do you mean, *lodge*?"

Garcia pointed toward the nearest fish. "See that spine on its back—the flared head? It might swim up your ass and gets stuck there, until someone can attempt a cure."

"At least there's a cure." Cape sounded nonchalant but had inched backward from the toilet.

Garcia frowned. "A native cure requires two plants used in combination—they are shoved into your ass to kill and then dissolve the fish. But in most cases the victim gets infected, goes into shock and dies. It is very painful, but it could be much worse."

"It gets worse?" Cape retreated another step until his back was against the tiled wall.

Garcia nodded. "As I said, the fish is attracted to warmth, and as you can see, *candirú* are excellent swimmers. So if one swims up your ass, you are lucky—at least you have a fighting chance."

Cape tried to imagine having a spiny fish up his ass and feeling lucky. He gave up almost immediately as Garcia continued his narrative.

"Say you were taking a piss, as you had planned."

"It was more of an urge than a plan," said Cape. "But let's say that I did decide to piss on the fish—so what?"

"The toothpick fish has been known to follow the urine stream right into the tiny opening in a man's penis—you can see how small the fish are. They can actually swim *up* while you are pissing *down*, going upstream into your body as you relieve yourself. That is why fishermen on the river will piss against the gunwale of the boat, never directly into the water. Do you understand what I am saying?"

Cape understood but it took him a moment to comprehend. He tried to visualize the fish swimming *up, up, up* and then flinched involuntarily. Garcia watched him and nodded.

"*Sí*," said Garcia. "You would be writhing on the floor in agony."

Cape was a sufficiently confident guy to admit having a short but substantive list of things he was deathly afraid of—*being eaten by a shark, crashing in an airplane, being turned into a flesh-eating zombie by a failed government experiment*—but standing there in a bathroom in Mexico, watching fish swim around in a toilet, he had found a new one that jumped to the top of the list.

"Can I flush now?" he asked.

"Why not?" Garcia leaned forward and did the honors. Both men watched as the tiny fish spun, slowly at first and then faster and faster, caught in the inescapable cyclone of an industrial toilet. "It would be impossible to trace where the fish came from."

"How come you know so much about these toothpick fish?"

Garcia shrugged. "I am addicted to the Discovery Channel—did you see Shark Week?"

"Of course," said Cape. "But I must have missed the special on *penis predators*."

"I cannot remember the name of the show, but that was not it."

"You said these fish came from the Amazon."

"In theory, yes, but they have been known to swim upriver, into tributaries."

"We're in Mexico, Garcia."

"Where anything can happen."

"That's what the woman at the front desk told me," said Cape. "Is that the slogan for the Mexico Tourism Board?"

Garcia checked the refilled bowl to make sure it was empty, then turned to face Cape. "I am merely saying—"

"—you're saying that someone put the fish in my toilet," said Cape. "To scare me."

"Did it work?"

"Fuck, yes."

"But why try to scare you away if your case is closed?"

"Maybe it's not," said Cape. "What did you find at the morgue?"

The two men moved into the bedroom. Cape sat on the edge of the bed as Garcia took the seat in front of the narrow desk. It might have been the change in lighting, from the bright fluorescents of the bathroom to the indirect lighting of the floor lamps, but Garcia suddenly looked very tired, dark circles appearing under his eyes. Cape wondered briefly if the tequila had slowed him down, too.

"I was not there very long," said Garcia.

"But you saw the bodies."

Garcia looked away before answering. "Two men died, of that I am certain. But the bodies are still being…" He hesitated, searching for the right word. "Reconstructed. There were different parts, not so easy to tell where they belonged."

"How many parts?"

"Enough to convince me that the bodies they belonged to are dead. Male torso, late-to-middle age. Part of an arm, no hand. A section of abdomen, right *here*—" He patted his right side. "And a leg, reasonably intact."

"Right or left?" As soon as Cape heard the second body wasn't complete he felt a pale flicker of optimism but sensed it would be extinguished as soon as Garcia spoke again.

Garcia smiled knowingly. "Right."

"The Senator and his son, Danny, they had matching tattoos." He grabbed his right ankle with his left hand. "Right here."

"A tiger." Garcia said it as a statement, not a question.

Cape ran his fingers through his hair and exhaled slowly. He felt nauseous. "They both went to Princeton. Danny dropped out—was expelled—but got the tattoo his freshman year."

"Hardly DNA evidence," said Garcia. "I will give you a full report—"

"It's them," Cape took a deep breath. "What are the odds, right? You see a lot of matching father and son tattoos come through here?"

Garcia remained silent. After a long moment, Cape let his gaze drift around the room, back toward the bathroom.

"Which raises the question, Garcia, that you raised before."

"Why come after you now?"

"Exactly," said Cape. "Maybe they didn't want any loose ends—kill those two off, then get me out of the way. Problem solved."

"But why take the risk, if surely your investigation has come to an end?"

Cape shifted his gaze toward Garcia and nodded when their eyes met, as if he had just come to a decision. "Maybe they knew I'd try to find out who killed the Senator and his son. That I'd stay in Mexico until I found out the truth."

Garcia furrowed his brow. "Have you spoken to your client?"

"Not yet."

"Then how can you know that will be her decision?"

"It's not her decision," said Cape. "It's mine."

Garcia gestured toward the bathroom. "I think it will be dangerous."

"I'll be careful," said Cape, knowing he would be anything but. "And I'll have someone watching my back—besides you, of course."

"What do you mean?"

Cape smiled. "I'm going to call in reinforcements."

Chapter Thirteen

"That's a new one," said Sally. "Even for me."

"Knew you'd be impressed." The connection was bad, so Cape stuck a finger in his left ear as he pressed the earpiece to his right.

"I've used snakes before, and the Triad leaders always had a thing for scorpions." The energy in Sally's voice came through despite the static on the line. "And spiders, of course—spiders are great, if you can get them to stay put long enough to bite someone. But a fish that attacks your *wiener*? That's fantastic—you have to give them points for originality."

"How'd you like to visit Mexico?"

"Is it nice this time of year?"

"It's exciting," said Cape. "Anything can happen."

"Think I read that in a brochure once—who's paying?"

"Maybe my client, if I still have one," said Cape. "Maybe me. Does it matter?"

"I like to know who I'm working for."

"I'm hiring you to protect my wiener," said Cape. "Good enough?"

"You might be better off without it."

"Is that a yes or a no?"

"It's not the most worthy cause," said Sally, "but not a lost cause, either."

"I'll take that as a *yes*."

"How do you want me to pack?"

It wasn't an idle question. Though it wasn't exactly a code, Cape and Sally shared a common language that solved the problem of sayings things in public or over the phone that might get them arrested. Cape thought about it for a minute and then made a decision.

"Bring the heavy bag."

Chapter Fourteen

The shower felt good, as showers always do. Cape stood directly under the spray, rolling his head back and forth to work out the kinks in his neck. He had checked the drain twice before turning on the water, getting down on his hands and knees to make sure there weren't any fish, spiders, or sea cucumbers waiting in ambush.

A jackhammer was moving across his frontal lobe and exiting through his eye sockets. He wanted to blame the headache on tequila but knew the adrenaline rush from his close encounter with the fish had sobered him. He was stressed, a condition unlikely to get any better until he talked to his client, and that would have to wait until morning.

The last time they'd talked, Cape had asked her why she stopped talking to her father. Her answers were curt but spoke volumes.

"What's the point?" she said. "He's a politician."

"He's your father."

"Is your father alive, Cape?"

"No."

"You're lucky."

Standing under the dull roar of the shower spray, Cape wondered how lucky she would feel after his call.

After Rebecca left his office that day, he'd spent the rest of the afternoon online. Tapping a keyboard wasn't as romantic an image for a private investigator as pounding the pavement, but

Cape needed to know where he was headed. After several hours of searches he knew a lot more about Senator Jim Dobbins but precious little about his son.

Dobbins looked to be a typical politician—actually he looked better than that, but Rebecca's instincts had been good. Cape liked politicians about as much as an intestinal parasite and often couldn't tell the difference. He'd been a reporter for too long, seen too much corruption, and heard far too much rhetoric from men patting you on the back with one hand while their other hand was picking your pocket.

But even Cape had to admit that Dobbins had a talent for getting things done.

After graduating from law school at Stanford, Dobbins worked in the public defender's office before running for city councilman. He won and became a fixture in both city and state politics—working fund-raisers, overseeing voter registration drives, grabbing photo ops with the party elite.

Dobbins made his name with urban renewal. One article credited him with drafting a controversial referendum to transform an older, industrial part of San Francisco into residential lofts and office space. In a city where *gentrification* was an ugly word, critics claimed the program destroyed the historical integrity of the district, while supporters said it revitalized a neighborhood that had become economically extinct.

Cape thought both sides had a point. The neighborhood in question bore no resemblance to the charming, sepia-toned photographs from the turn of the century—its character had been bulldozed away. But before the developers, the neighborhood had become a war zone where rival gangs fought over the local drug trade. Most voters decided to make the character of the neighborhood the last casualty in that war. The bill passed by a two percent margin, money poured in with the concrete and glass, and less than nine months later Jim Dobbins was elected to the state legislature.

Then he turned green. An easy political decision in California. The Governor had made the environment his top priority, from state-sponsored recycling programs in schools to switching to single-ply toilet paper at the capitol building. Voters cheered and politicians up and down the state went from kissing babies to hugging trees.

Dobbins bought a hybrid car, and made the front page of the paper as he drove it to Sacramento to meet with the Governor.

Dobbins put the squeeze on businesses to reduce their carbon footprint. His message was simple and direct: cut waste, recycle, or sponsor environmental programs unless you want to end up in court. He engineered tax breaks for the companies that complied, went after the ones that refused with an almost religious zeal. As a state senator he had the latitude to cover a lot of territory, working with local coffee houses and major corporations. Every new program meant a picture in the paper, Dobbins' arm around the shoulders of a smiling shopkeeper or beleaguered executive.

Then suddenly the press dried up.

As Cape read through the articles chronologically, it looked like Dobbins dropped below the radar almost nine months ago. No more pictures in the paper, rarely quoted in any articles, never on any of the political talk shows. His profile shrank over the next several months until the man himself disappeared only two weeks ago, resigning from the state senate with no more explanation than a brief hand-written note.

The news didn't get much attention because that very same day the Lieutenant Governor admitted to using treasury funds to pay for underage male prostitutes, which came as a shock to both his wife and the Governor. Just another day in California politics, but the scandal overshadowed Dobbins' resignation. He held a cursory news conference and received a few column inches inside the fold of the local papers.

And then he vanished altogether. *Poof.*

Cape tried the usual tricks and databases used for skip-tracing, but the senator had dropped off the grid. Not easy even if you're trying, damn near impossible if you're not.

So Cape turned his attention to the son but nearly came up empty. Danny wasn't a public figure, so a Google search didn't yield the volume of pages tagged with his father's name. Cape found one article that listed the contents of the weekly police blotter from several months ago. Danny got picked up for possession.

No follow-up stories, no other arrests that Cape could find. He made a mental note to conduct a more thorough background check later. For a senator's son, Danny should have had a slightly higher profile.

But maybe Danny wasn't a phantom, just a guy who made a dumb mistake. If Rebecca's attitude about their father was any indication, Cape couldn't blame Danny for wanting to steer clear of the gossip columns.

It took a few phone calls, one favor, and access to a database of marginal legality to trace Danny to Mexico. Credit cards and cell phones were better than a blood trail. If he'd gone native or switched to cash, Cape would never have gotten that far without help.

The notion of help made him think of Rebecca. He knew she wanted to find her brother and suspected she wanted to see her father again, more than she might admit. But family members rarely told Cape what he needed to know, even when they wanted to help. Relatives saw the person they wanted to see instead of the person as they really were. Blinded by love or hate, or some combination of the two. Too close to the situation.

At the thought of getting close to Rebecca, he took a step out of the shower spray, turned the handle to *cold*, then ducked under the water and gritted his teeth. He stood there a long time, willing his testicles to retreat somewhere inside his body. The last thing he needed was a puerile fantasy about his client. Rebecca was more than a little attractive and desperately needed his help—his very own formula for disaster.

Cape once read that the definition of an addiction was something you knew was unhealthy but which you kept doing anyway. He turned off the water and stood there shivering, forcing himself to remember the last woman he'd tried to save.

It didn't take long, because she'd dumped him the day he'd met Rebecca.

Cape had finished reading up on the Senator and was about to shut down his computer when the email popped up. It was late in San Francisco, even later in New York where the email originated. It lacked punctuation, like all her notes, which gave it a strangely dispassionate tone that delivered the message like a punch to the gut.

cape, it's over...this long distance thing is too hard...you're great...maybe a little overprotective, but don't think you did something wrong...you're really great...it's me...i've met someone here...he's nice...he's a dentist...you'd like him...sorry...you're great...take good care

Cape tried to call but her cell phone was off. He tried again to no avail, resisted the urge to hurl the phone across the room.

What kind of woman dumps a guy over email? Answer: a modern one. She liked confrontation about as much as he liked going to the dentist. The note made Cape feel like a hopeless romantic. It must've taken all of two minutes to write and underscored the difference in their ages. Though less than ten years younger, she came from a completely different generation when it came to communication. If she wanted to reach out and touch someone, she sent a text message. He was an anachronism with an undying passion for complete sentences.

Take good care. Sounded like something a dentist might say, and Cape wondered briefly how long she'd been seeing someone else. Not that it mattered. He read the note again, surprised she didn't remind him to floss.

He'd always hated dentists; now he knew why.

Taking a deep breath, he stepped out of the shower and wrapped a towel around his waist. He paused to give himself a look in the mirror.

"You're hopeless," he said.

The private detective with the broken heart—how original. Too bad I'm not a divorced ex-cop with a tragic past, married to a hooker

with a heart of gold. Maybe I should develop a drinking problem,
become a loner, get a big dog or ornery cat.

The thing that really pissed him off was that he wasn't the least
bit surprised. Cape shook his head in disgust and made a cursory
effort to dry off before pulling open the bathroom door.

The first thing he noticed was music coming from the
bedroom. He wondered if housekeeping had let themselves
in, turned on the radio. Mexico was downright romantic, even
when you were sleeping alone. Maybe things were looking up
and he'd find a chocolate on his pillow.

Before he stepped into the bedroom Cape caught a reflec-
tion of a pair of legs in the mirror over the dresser. Definitely
male legs, crossed at the knee, covered by gray slacks. The idea
of hiding in the bathroom flashed across his mind but Cape let
his own momentum carry him across the threshold, curiosity
driving him forward.

"It's about fucking time."

The man sitting on the bed sounded more pissed than he
looked. His mouth was turned at the corners, more of a double
sneer than a smile. He had olive skin, wavy hair, narrow brown
eyes, and an enormous nose. Jimmy Durante and Barbara
Streisand had nothing on this guy—he was Cyrano de Bergerac
in a suit. "We were thinkin' we'd have to drag your ass right out
of the shower."

"We?" Cape stepped further into the room. Sitting at the
desk beyond the bed was a skinny Latino with slick hair and
a thick mustache. He looked bored, but his right hand rested
comfortably in his jacket pocket.

Cape adjusted his towel and studied his uninvited guests. It
was eighty degrees outside and both of these guys were wearing suits. He ruled out cops right away. Mustache's socks didn't
match, and cops tended to knock. So did hotel security.

Federales?

Cape moved toward the closet. "You boys have me at a dis-
advantage in the wardrobe department." He slowly opened the
sliding door. "Mind if I get dressed?"

"Looking for this?" Cyrano reached behind the pillow and came up with Cape's gun. The pistol painstakingly smuggled into Mexico. The one he had left in the closet, hanging in the shoulder holster—the empty holster he was now clutching in his left hand.

"We're not amateurs, so don't do anything stupid." Cyrano's nasal voice cut through the air as Mustache shifted in his seat and slowly removed his hand from his jacket pocket. From where Cape was standing it looked like Mustache favored a Glock nine-millimeter.

"Did you actually think we wouldn't case the room?" Cyrano stood and took a step toward Cape, closing the gap but keeping his distance.

Cape turned and reached into the closet, felt around for a pair of pants. "You always this defensive?"

"Fuck you," said Cyrano, clearly pissed he was talking to Cape's back. "I mean, what do we look like to you?"

Cape shrugged. "Dentists," he said over his shoulder. "You look like dentists to me."

Chapter Fifteen

The nun walked quickly from baggage claim toward customs, mouthing a silent prayer as she went.

Just over five feet tall, she wore a simple, nondescript habit that gave her an amorphous, asexual appearance. She might have been Dutch or Eastern European with her long blonde hair, high cheekbones, and blue eyes that narrowed when she smiled, which she did often as she navigated politely through the throng. Tourists and airport personnel graciously moved out of her way as she glided through the busy Mexico City airport.

Clearing customs was a unique challenge in every country. After retrieving luggage in a U.S. airport, for example, travelers had to present correct documentation, such as a passport or visa, and then allow a customs official to inspect their bags while asking a series of questions designed to gage the veracity of their story. *Traveling for business or pleasure? Purchase anything while you were away? Have any contraband items in your bag such as plants, drugs, animals?* Depending on how suspicious a traveler looked or acted, the questions might get harder, the search might be more thorough. The lines were long, the signs were confusing, and no one within hearing distance spoke any language besides English. For foreign visitors, the process was an obstacle course combined with a pop quiz.

Security at Mexican airports was predicated on a game show. After claiming their luggage, passengers are asked to form a line in front of a giant traffic light, the same kind that hangs over busy intersections in cities all over the world except this one has only a green and red light, no yellow. The traffic light is mounted on a pole and stands about as tall as a man, with a button mounted directly beneath it. One by one visitors are instructed by a uniformed official to push the button, which causes the light to turn either green or red. If the light is green, you clear customs without another glance. You might be carrying several kilos of cocaine with no one the wiser if you got the green light.

But get the red light and you might get busted. You'll be directed to a stainless steel counter where a customs official might search your bags from top to bottom. On the other hand, he might simply ask some cursory questions not all that different from his counterparts in the U.S., depending on how curious he felt at that time of day. The system was more akin to a casino than a security checkpoint, playing the odds that a random search was just as effective as anything else.

The Mexican government claimed the sequence of green and red lights was random, but frequent travelers knew the sullen-looking customs officials controlled a hidden switch, turning the light red whenever a questionable character came to the head of the line.

The young nun scanned the people from her flight as they took their suitcases over to the customs area. She had checked two matching nylon bags, each with a sticker that read *Women of Mercy, Sisters of Retribution*. The bags were identical except for their weight. Removing both bags from the carousel, she examined the line in front of the nearest traffic light and crossed herself. Then she peeled the sticker and identification tags off the lighter of the two bags and set it back on the carousel, where it would turn and turn until no one claimed it, at which point the nun would be well on her way.

Slinging the heavy bag over her shoulder, the nun queued up behind the other passengers. When she was fourth in line a middle-aged man—a rumpled business traveler—got the red light. She watched as the man stepped over to the counter where a young male customs agent partially unzipped the man's suitcase and glanced inside. Going through the motions. The nun looked across the baggage area at the only other available line and saw an officious looking older woman rummaging through a couple's suitcase. The nun stayed where she was and waited her turn.

Stepping up to the light, she smiled beatifically at the man in uniform directing the line. He was a head taller than she was, with a broad face and large brown eyes. He reminded her of a puppy, eager to please. The customs officer blushed despite himself, gesturing awkwardly at the button below the light. With a shy nod and tentative hand, the nun pushed the button.

The light was green.

"*Seester*, it's OK." The officer gallantly gestured toward the exit. "You can go."

"Bless you." The nun walked through a revolving door into the main terminal, moving effortlessly through the crowd until she stepped into a restroom on her left. Ten minutes later Sally emerged from the ladies room, her black hair tied into a ponytail. The blonde wig was in the trash, the blue contact lenses washed down the drain. The wax prosthetic jammed into her mouth to change the contours of her face had been chewed and spit into the toilet one piece at a time. The habit was turned inside-out and stuffed into the bag on her shoulder. Underneath she wore faded jeans, black high-top Converse, and a white t-shirt emblazoned with the words *Premenstrual and Proud* in red ink.

She looked like just another Asian-American student on break from college, maybe with a little more attitude than most. She walked toward the exit that would lead to the taxi stand, gliding through the crowd like a fish through coral.

An hour later the sun had set and the customs officer with the puppy dog eyes was still on duty, but his attention span was waning. His hand had released the remote in his pocket that controlled the traffic light, and he let the automated random sequence of red and green take their course. When a tall man stepped to the head of the line, the light turned red. The young officer looked more closely at the man and flinched involuntarily at the pale eyes staring back at him—the stranger had let his topcoat fall open to reveal the clerical collar. The officer felt a wave of shame wash over him—like most Mexicans he considered himself a good Catholic and was reminded of the young nun who had passed through earlier. She was a beacon of light compared with this dark apparition before him, but what was the point of sending a priest for inspection?

"*Por favor, Padre.*" The young officer gestured nervously toward the customs table. The priest's mouth twitched, then settled into a smile as he walked over to the counter.

At the counter the priest faced a middle-aged agent whose uniform barely contained his stomach, a sausage about to burst its casing. He was clearly uncomfortable at the prospect of rummaging through the luggage of a man of the cloth and shot a dirty look to his colleague for putting him in this awkward position. He ran his hand quickly through an assortment of clothing when he felt something metallic. Reflexively he pulled his hand out of the bag, dragging the object into the light.

It was a long string of ebony rosary beads with a heavy silver cross affixed to them. The officer awkwardly handed them to the priest, who took the necklace without a word and put it over his head. The cross hung prominently in the center of his chest, over three inches long from top to bottom. Still smiling, he looked down at the nervous officer.

"Do you have anything to declare?" the man asked, anxious for this gaunt figure to be on its way.

"Anything to declare?" Priest's mouth twitched again as he fought a smile, as if he were about to say something amusing, but instead he merely shook his head. "No."

The officer nodded, then dropped his eyes to the bag and pulled the zippers closed. For some reason he couldn't explain even to himself, the officer realized he was suddenly perspiring heavily under his shirt. The feeling left as soon as the priest began to walk away.

As he watched the Priest disappear into the crowd like a wraith, the portly officer crossed himself and mumbled a silent prayer, even though he did not consider himself a religious man.

Chapter Sixteen

"We look like *dentists?*"

"Sorry," said Cape. "Private metaphor."

"*Meta-what?*" Cyrano wrinkled his nose as if the word carried a bad smell. He rose from his perch on the bed and jutted his chin toward Cape.

"Okay, asswipe, time to go. Get dressed."

"But I don't have anything to wear." Cape adjusted the towel around his waist. "You guys are so…formal."

Cyrano dropped his shoulders in a look that said *I-don't-have-time-for-this-shit*. He stood like that a moment, letting Cape know he didn't want to dance. Not pissed, just ready to get to work.

"Save the dry wit for someone wet behind the ears," he said. "I've been doing this a long time."

"Doing what, exactly?"

"I'm just a delivery boy, and you're the package."

Delivery. No way these guys were FBI. *Would feds call me an asswipe?* Cape wondered what the regulations were on that sort of thing. Figured with all the taxes he'd paid over the years, federal agents should have better vocabularies.

Cape shifted his gaze from Cyrano to Mustache, who had moved his chair back from the desk and stood, Glock held loosely along his right leg. The two men followed each other's cues but barely communicated, as if they came from similar yet separate worlds. Cape pegged Mustache as local muscle, but Cyrano's colorful language marked him as a tourist.

"You working freelance?"

Cyrano's mouth twitched slightly. "You want to ask questions, put some fucking clothes on…*now.*" With his left hand he opened his jacket to reveal the revolver on his hip.

Cape made a show of rummaging around the closet. Though he didn't doubt for a second that his uninvited guests would drag him out of the room if they had to, Cape suspected they didn't want a scene. And like most tough guys, they'd rather wrangle a man with his clothes on instead of grabbing a guy in a towel. Cape figured every minute he could stay undressed was one more step toward homophobia encroaching on their macho act. He didn't have a plan beyond stalling, but a sudden knock gave him an opening.

"Housekeeping," a heavily accented female voice penetrated the door. Cape glanced at the door, relieved to see the *Do Not Disturb* sign still inside. He gauged the distance between himself and Cyrano. Already he could hear the scrape of a key card against the lock.

Cyrano looked like he was about to cry out, tell her to come back later, but Cape took a step backward and grabbed the door knob with his right hand. Called out in broken Spanish, "*Abra la puerta, señorita!*"

Mustache brought his arm up just as Cape yanked open the door. The maid, a middle-aged woman with a nest of black hair, screamed when she saw the gun. Cyrano waved at Mustache to lower the gun as the maid thrust her arms into the air and staggered backward, leaving the door clear. Cape knew he wouldn't get a better invitation.

Stripping the towel from around his waist, Cape threw it left-handed. It hooked around the muzzle of the gun and draped around Mustache's forearm. By the time Mustache had shaken it free, Cape was in the hallway. Cyrano caught an unwanted glimpse of Cape's ass as he darted away.

It was much cooler in the hall than in his room, and Cape felt shrinkage occur, but he pressed on.

Halfway to the stairs Cape passed the fire alarm, a rectangular red box mounted to the wall. He stopped, took a step back, and pulled the short handle. At first nothing happened, then a grating, angry siren cranked into high gear as emergency lighting flashed along the ceiling. Cape took the stairs two at a time.

His naked dash across the lobby caught the attention of a waitress and a family of five who had just arrived from Iowa, but Cape made it poolside and grabbed a towel from a startled attendant before he got arrested for indecent exposure. Maybe later he'd wander over to the gift shop and charge a bathing suit to his room, but for now he wanted a front row seat. He sat on a chaise near the pool with an angle on the lobby and watched people stream out of the hotel.

The delivery boys from his room appeared after most of the guests had already exited. Their guns were concealed and there was no screaming maid to call attention to the two conservatively dressed yet mismatched men as they cut through the crowd. They headed toward the parking lot but Cape didn't follow, nor did he try to see what kind of car they were driving.

He knew he would find out soon enough.

Chapter Seventeen

Cape stared at the body lying in front of him and wondered what to do next.

The legs were slightly apart, left leg bent at the knee, arms spread out in a mute gesture of supplication. The corners of the mouth had frozen into the beginnings of a smile, or so it seemed from where Cape was standing. He took a deep breath and stepped closer to the body. After days of frustration, at least some of his investigative skills were coming in handy.

When the eyes fluttered and the lips moved, he knew his instincts had brought him to the right place.

"I think Cape is a lovely name," the woman lying in front of him said in a husky voice. She leaned forward to reveal some rather impressive cleavage, tilting her shoulders to make sure Cape had the proper perspective.

"But it must have been very hard growing up," she added.

"I decided not to," Cape replied. The body was so perfect he suspected bionic enhancements. "Are those your real breasts?" he asked. "Because, you know, they look too natural to be implants."

The woman laughed and leaned back on the towel. "You're not shy, are you?"

"Only when I'm getting undressed."

"Somehow I doubt that." Another adjustment to her shoulders let Cape know the next move was all his—just the challenge he needed after hours of walking aimlessly around the pool and beach. He needed to kill time, and a little company never hurt.

As he began to sit, Cape sensed movement at the corner of his left eye. Before he could react he was knocked backward onto the sand, the wind rushing out of him. Something landed hard on his chest and he blinked away spots, trying to see through watering eyes to the source of the stranglehold on his throat.

The face looking down on him was in silhouette, but Cape instantly recognized the profile and stopped struggling. He knew he was trapped until his captor decided otherwise.

"Did you miss me?" Sally beamed from her perch atop his chest.

Cape moved his head sufficiently to catch a glimpse of the woman he'd been talking to shaking sand from her towel, muttering something about married men. Before he could protest she headed down the beach toward the hotel, an angry but beautiful mirage fading with the heat of the moment.

Cape glowered at Sally, who glanced back at him with a mischievous smile and furrowed brow.

"Did I just mess something up?" She loosened her legs just enough for Cape to draw a breath.

"Are those your real breasts?" he asked. "Because, you know, they look too small to be implants."

Sally barked out a laugh and rolled off Cape. She stood, brushing sand from her legs. She was wearing a black one-piece bathing suit with a sheer diagonal strip across the torso. The muscles of her legs rippled like ocean waves as she moved.

Cape struggled to his feet. "I'm in the middle of an investigation here," he said indignantly. "She might have been a suspect."

"Looked more like a victim to me."

"Ouch." Cape followed her gaze to take one last look at the receding figure of his almost-conquest. And what a figure it was.

"You hired me to protect your equipment," said Sally, gesturing toward Cape's crotch. "Or did you forget?"

"Maybe my equipment needed a tune-up."

"You'd regret it later," said Sally. "You always do. Plus you weren't really interested."

"How do you know?"

Sally shrugged. "She wasn't in trouble."

Cape didn't have an answer for that one. Sally held his eyes for a moment, rubbing it in.

"Besides," she said, "I thought you had a girlfriend."

"*Had,*" replied Cape. "That's exactly the right word."

"She dumped you?"

Cape nodded. "For a dentist."

"Oral hygiene is very important."

"Not that important."

Sally didn't respond and, as usual, her face betrayed nothing. After a long moment, Cape said, "You don't seem surprised."

Another shrug. "You weren't going to New York as often."

"I've been working."

"Or calling as much," said Sally. "That's just a guess."

"She's been working."

Sally nodded. "I think you lost interest."

Cape felt his cheeks get hot. "Let me guess...because she wasn't in trouble?"

"She was when you met her," replied Sally.

"Your point?"

"I see a pattern, that's all."

Cape started to reply but caught himself. Instead he studied his diminutive friend. Jet black hair, emerald eyes that gleamed in the half-light of dusk. A body that seemed to give off a primal energy even when she was standing still. He'd argued with her more times than he could remember, but in hindsight she'd never been wrong.

Cape and Sally preferred verbal sparring to saying hello, a ritual that acknowledged the bond between them without saying out loud what they both took for granted. For two people for whom trust was such a precious and rare commodity, the ability to count on someone was too great a gift to be diminished by words.

"Welcome to Mexico," said Cape. "Anything can happen here."

"I read that in the in-flight magazine," said Sally. "So, you want to come up to my room?"

"Wow, you work fast. And here I thought you didn't like boys."

"I *do* like boys—it's men I have issues with. C'mon, I brought you a present."

Sally pivoted on her right leg and strode purposely toward the hotel entrance. Cape felt like he was being pulled along in her wake as he followed her across the sand and then the cement around the pool. He scanned the bar as they crossed the lobby. Two men in Hawaiian shirts and straw hats sat in a booth at the far corner of the room. He couldn't be sure with the subdued lighting, but Cape thought he saw the tip of a bulbous nose protruding under the brim of the nearest hat.

Cape had not changed rooms nor checked out, but he stuck to public places until Sally arrived. He hung out by the pool, walked on the beach, strolled through the lobby and shopping arcade. Bought a pair of shorts and a t-shirt, charged them to his room. He wanted to be seen, but he didn't want another close encounter until he was ready.

Sally's room faced west, directly across the pool from Cape's. She could see his bedroom window and tell whether the blinds were open or closed; the light on or off.

"Perfect," said Cape, turning away from the window. He looked at the black bag on her bed. "How'd you do with customs?"

"Take a look." Sally unzipped the black duffel, causing it to unroll like a sleeping bag down the length of the bed. Inside a series of pockets had been sewn to secure a variety of metal and wooden objects that had nothing to do with a beach vacation.

The first series of pockets held *shuriken*, throwing stars of various shapes and sizes arranged across the interior of the bag in a deadly constellation. Next was a long pocket holding a pair of *nuchakas*, two columns of wood joined by a short chain. Decades after Bruce Lee used them in *Enter The Dragon* they were still sold through catalogs to kung fu aficionados who usually ended up hitting themselves in the head or breaking a lamp in their mother's living room. But Cape had seen Sally use them and knew they were a serious piece of equipment.

Cape's eyes moved across the portable arsenal. A wooden shaft secured by loops ran the length of the bag; it could be used as a billy club or pulled apart to reveal a six-inch, carbonized steel blade. Nylon rope, a grappling hook, a pair of palm-sized field binoculars. Night vision scope. Sally knew how to pack.

Cape whistled. "You're a dangerous woman."

"Now that's a redundant phrase."

Sally reached into a small zippered compartment and pulled out a black handgun. She held it with two fingers, wrinkling her nose in disgust. "Here's your penis extension." She handed over the pistol as if disposing of a dead rat. "Promise not to lose it. I may not get the green light next time."

"I promise." Cape checked the gun. It was a Heckler & Koch nine millimeter semi-automatic. Composite frame, three-inch barrel. Expensive but reliable. It held 10 rounds, but Cape was hoping he wouldn't need any of them. He handed the gun back to Sally. "Hold it for now."

"So what's the plan?" Sally returned the gun to its pocket and sat down.

"Order room service if you want, while I go back to the pool." Cape opened the drapes. "Maybe in an hour, when you're feeling ready to go sightseeing, turn off the light in your room and come downstairs. I'll be watching your window from outside. Hang around the front entrance, keep a cab waiting."

"Wardrobe?"

"Black."

Sally nodded. "And then?"

Cape smiled. "Then I'll go back to my room and get kidnapped."

Chapter Eighteen

Cape heard the *swoosh* of hangers being pushed aside before he felt the gun barrel against the back of his neck. He had walked right into a trap.

"*Manos para arriba,*" came a voice from the closet. Cape swiveled his eyes without moving his head and confirmed that the gun was held by Mustache, his recent acquaintance with the mismatched socks.

"Where's your friend?" asked Cape. "Or doesn't he want to be seen with you, now that you've come out of the closet?"

"Funny man." Cyrano stepped out of the bathroom. In his right hand was a taser, a squat black device with two silver prongs on the end.

"You're persistent," said Cape.

Cyrano nodded. "Tenacious even."

Cape forced himself not to stare at the taser, though in the back of his mind he registered the absurd truth that he would have been less uncomfortable had Cyrano been holding a gun.

"Thought we were gonna have to wait awhile longer, after seeing you with that Asian *chickadee* on the beach. What happened, she get a headache once you got back to her room? Maybe she got her period. Or you having problems getting the old soldier to salute?"

"She's a lesbian."

"Yeah, right," snorted Cyrano. He held the taser at eye level and pressed the button, letting the tight blue arc of 10,000 volts emphasize his next point. "Now look, jerkoff, there's no maid service for the rest of the night, so there won't be any opportunity to take your clothes off and cry for help. Or do anything else stupid."

"Guess I'll have to do something smart."

Cyrano hit the button again. The taser sounded like pine needles burning. "You won't do shit, understand? We got permission to carry you out to the car, if it comes to that."

Cape eyed the taser. "It won't come to that."

"Good choice." Cyrano lowered the taser as Mustache lowered his gun and used it to sucker-punch Cape in the back. A balloon of pain exploded as the heavy metal of the gun collided with Cape's right kidney, dropping him to his knees. He coughed involuntarily when his hands hit the floor, sending an aftershock of nausea into his gut. Tears streamed down his cheeks as he spat onto the carpet, barely resisting the urge to vomit. He closed his eyes and tried to focus on his breathing.

Cyrano shook his head, a teacher disappointed in a star pupil, and stepped over to block the door. "That's for being such a pain in the ass." Mustache stepped over Cape to reclaim his old spot at the desk.

"You're welcome," said Cape, his voice ragged. He opened his eyes and took a few more tentative breaths before standing. Cyrano watched from the door, a mild expression on his face as if Cape had just dropped his keys and bent to pick them up. None of this was personal for him.

Cape took a deep breath and turned his attention to the closet. He was about to grab a shirt when he had a random thought and stepped past the bed to the nightstand, where he grabbed the remote for the TV.

"The fuck you doing?" demanded Cyrano. He stood up straighter but held his position at the door. As long as Cape wasn't trying to escape, Cyrano wasn't all that concerned.

Cape held up a hand for patience, then thumbed the remote until he'd navigated the on-screen menu to the adult entertainment channel. An instant later, the excruciatingly banal soft-core porn found on every hotel television around the globe shimmered into focus. Cape turned up the volume before walking past Mustache, opening the window, and flinging the remote across the patio into the swimming pool below. He turned toward Mustache and smiled, moving his eyebrows up and down suggestively.

"Hate for you to get bored," said Cape. "Just wanted you to know there's no hard feelings."

Mustache scowled but his eyes darted to the TV, where a woman with impossibly large breasts was moaning as a man dressed like a fireman used a canvas hose to squirt a liquid with the consistency of baby oil onto her from ten feet away.

"For the love of—" Cyrano pushed off the door. He was about to jam his left thumb against the on-off switch built into the base of the television when Mustache raised his gun and pointed it at Cyrano. Without taking his eyes off the fireman and the woman with the silver dollar nipples, he muttered something in Spanish and cocked the gun.

Cyrano held up his hands and retreated to the door. "OK, OK. Jesus." Then to Cape, "What's your problem?"

Cape shrugged. "I like making people uncomfortable."

"It's unprofessional," snapped Cyrano, darting a glance toward Mustache. "I'm trying to do a job here."

"Complain to the union."

"Get fuckin' dressed." Cyrano didn't bother to flash the taser. "Just cause I don't want to carry you to the car doesn't mean I won't."

"You got a bad back?"

"I'm counting to thirty." Cyrano shifted his eyes to Mustache, who had managed to keep his gun up but angle his chair so he had a better view of the television.

Cape returned to the closet and traded his shorts for a pair of slacks, slipped on a pair of loafers. He paused and leaned against the door frame for a minute, as casually as he could. He'd been hit much harder before, but a shot you weren't ready for hurt like hell. He could almost feel the bruise forming as a dull ache radiated from his internal organs across his side.

He grabbed a light jacket, left his wallet but grabbed some cash. Old habit, he felt naked without cash in his pocket. Maybe he'd survive the night and need a cab home. Maybe they'd pass a fast food joint and ask if he wanted anything. Maybe he'd bribe a helicopter pilot to fly him to Neverland.

"Ready when you are."

On the television, a guy dressed as a plumber was struggling to control a leaky faucet that had caused all the dish soap to form bubbles that overflowed the sink, ran across the floor, and enveloped a startled housewife who conveniently was wearing a white shirt with no bra.

While Mustache's eyes were on the screen, Cyrano drew his own gun, but Mustache barely registered it. Either he knew Cyrano would never shoot him or he belonged to an obscure cult that believed the last thing you saw in this life would be the first thing you'd see in the next. They stood there until the bubble scene ended, guns pointed half-heartedly at each other in an obligatory tough guy dance. Even then it took Cyrano a good five minutes to convince his partner they had to leave.

The three men strolled through the lobby like old friends. Cape knew there was no percentage in causing a scene. If they had wanted to do this the hard way, he'd be wrapped in a rug and thrown into a trunk. No matter how many angles he tried to consider, he couldn't find an advantage to that one. Might as well see what's behind the curtain.

The car was a black Escalade, an SUV only slightly smaller than Texas that handled like an oil tanker. Cape sat in the back next to Cyrano, who had the taser in his right hand, his gun holstered. Mustache drove.

The route cut through town, past restaurants interspersed with stores selling authentic Mexican souvenirs made in China. Once the yellow lights and faded neon of the restaurants were behind them, Mustache turned right and headed away from downtown Puerto Vallarta into the hills overlooking the bay.

The climb was steep, and Cape was surprised at how quickly the trappings of tourism slipped away and the natural vegetation took back the land. The trees grew thick, covered in vines that looked like snakes in the half-light from the moon. As they drove deeper into the hills the road turned back on itself, each curve offering a smaller glimpse of the ocean below.

"Isn't this where they filmed *Night Of The Iguana*?"

Cyrano didn't bother to look out the window. "You're asking the wrong guy."

"Richard Burton, directed by John Huston," said Cape. "It's a classic."

"Got any sports in it?"

"Like soccer?" asked Cape. "None."

"I guess soccer's a sport these days," said Cyrano grudgingly, "but I was thinkin' baseball. I only watch baseball movies."

Cape frowned. "I didn't realize there were that many."

"What about that flick with the guy, builds a baseball diamond in a cornfield? You seen that?"

Cape had seen the movie but had no desire to bond. His kidney felt like it had torn loose and was floating around inside his gut.

"Never."

"Never saw it?" Cyrano turned, and for a moment Cape thought he was going to get tasered. "A fucking classic—guy builds a baseball field on his farm 'cause he hears this voice." Cyrano forced his nasal twang down an octave. "*If you build it, they will come.*"

"Then what happens?"

"These great baseball players, they all come to play on the guy's field...only...*they're dead.*" Cyrano shook his head over the sadness of it all.

"The guy who built the field dies?"

"No, the players," said Cyrano impatiently. "They're all dead, but they come back to play anyway."

"So they're zombies," said Cape, hoping to touch a nerve. "There are zombie baseball players in this movie."

"They're not zombies!" sputtered Cyrano. "They're—"

"So it's science fiction." Cape looked out the window, a bored expression on his face.

"It's *baseball*," said Cyrano. "And they're ghosts, OK?" He huffed a minute before adding, "Not fucking zombies."

"Got any unicorns in it?"

"Up yours."

"Mm-hm." Cape closed his eyes and leaned back against the headrest.

Mustache drove like a man who knew the way by heart. Half an hour into the journey the car's tires crunched on a gravel drive. Cape opened his eyes as they stopped at a wrought-iron gate fifteen feet high flanked by two stone columns. The fence ran out of sight on either side, each twenty foot section supported by stone pillars identical to the ones bracing the gate. Two men with submachine guns slung conspicuously over their shoulders stepped forward to glance inside the car.

The house looked like a fortress, two stories high and made entirely of fieldstone. It was set back from the road about thirty yards, the front facing a large circular driveway. The back overlooked the bay and the town far below. Aging willow and oak trees dominated the lawn, their boughs hanging across the fence, the driveway, and the house itself.

Two men stood by the nearest tree, smoking. The one closest to the house restrained two Dobermans as Cape got out of the car. He held them on a single leash, the muscles of his forearm straining. The dogs didn't bark but growled deep in their throats, a subsonic tremor that reverberated deep in Cape's chest. Mustache climbed from behind the wheel and walked over to join them, gesturing for the man nearest the tree to give him a smoke. Cape quickly scanned the rest of the yard but didn't see anyone else before Cyrano jabbed him in the side, making him flinch and stumble toward the front door.

Cape turned to watch the gate close behind them and realized how easy it would be to find this place again. No sharp turns, no unpaved roads or secret entrances. Even with his eyes closed he was able to track the progress of the car.

As he walked stiffly toward the house Cape wondered if he'd made a horrible mistake about his captors. Maybe whomever was waiting inside the house didn't intend for this trip to have a return ticket. Three men had left the hotel with no signs of a struggle. Cyrano wasn't even local, so he could disappear if anyone asked questions about a missing guest. So could Mustache, no doubt.

Cape was ten feet from the door when he felt rather than heard the Dobermans' guttural cry, and despite his efforts to stay cool, his palms began to sweat. The moon grazed the treeline beyond the mansion. Cape imagined the yellow orb as a jaundiced eye tracking his progress as he took a reluctant step forward, away from the gate and any reasonable hope of escape.

Chapter Nineteen

Joe Drabyak hated waiting.

He'd stood on the pier for almost an hour, watching the deck hands scurry around the yacht like carpenter ants. How long did it take for a ship to be ship-shape, he wondered. It was the middle of the night. And where was his fucking host?

He had already attempted to board, but a big Mexican with a billy club and radio strapped to his belt politely explained that no one boarded the yacht without the owner's permission. When Joe asked where the owner might be, the guard pretended not to understand English and began stroking his nightstick like it was a hard-on. Joe retreated a safe distance, lit up a smoke and began waiting.

That was one thing Joe liked about his job in San Francisco, working for Frank Alessi. You could say a lot of nasty things about Frank, and Joe had said one or two himself, but Frank was punctual. He might be a casually abusive sociopath, but he paid well and was always on time, so that made him OK in Joe's book.

He'd smoked half a pack, killed eight mosquitoes and maimed twelve by the time a gray limousine pulled into the lot adjacent to *Marina Vallarta*. The driver practically jumped out of the car before it settled on its shocks and made a beeline for Joe, a thin smile on his face.

"Señor Drabyak, there has been a mistake." The guy said it like Joe was the one at fault.

"No shit," said Joe. "I've been waiting over an hour. Where's your boss?"

The smile went from pleasant to condescending. "On his boat, señor, as promised."

Joe jerked a thumb toward the yacht. "That's his boat—I heard all about it. The wood floors, the plush furniture. Sammy Dunlop told me." He watched the driver's expression change at the mention of the name, so he added, "Yeah, Sammy and I talk. Just 'cause we work different sides of the street doesn't mean we can't share information."

In truth Sammy hadn't shared anything besides the hot air trapped in his lungs. He'd been bragging to Joe, showing off. *Yeah, flew me to Mexico, all expenses paid, took me on his yacht. What, you haven't been? That's too bad, buddy...*

Asshole.

But now it was Joe's turn, and this driver—the hired help—was telling him he got the wrong boat. He pointed at the stern. "What's it say right there, monkey boy? The name of the boat, *The Flying Fish*. Tell me I'm wrong."

The driver nodded, a study in forced politeness. "This is his boat, you are correct of course, but—"

"What?"

"He has another boat."

Joe scanned the marina. "Where?"

"Please come with me, señor." The driver extended his right arm in the direction of the limo. "He is waiting."

Joe stomped to the car and lit another cigarette as he took a seat in the back, secretly hoping the driver would ask him to put it out. He was disappointed by the time they arrived at their destination.

They'd followed the curve of the marina away from the tourist hotels where the piers were crowded with sailboats and yachts to the commercial piers where fishing trawlers crowded the narrow slips, their hulls painted in garish colors. The limo stopped directly behind a forty-footer, the yellow and blue paint scarred with orange streaks of rust that shifted in the harsh lights set on poles along the wharf as the boat bobbed against the current.

"He is already on board, señor."

Joe ground his cigarette out in the door handle before stepping out of the car. He squinted at the stern of the aging vessel and thought for a minute it bore the same name as the pristine yacht berthed less than a mile away. Then he shielded his eyes from the overhead lights and squinted through the night to read the faded letters.

The Frying Fish.

From flying to frying. A minute's drive along the coast but a world away from the eighty-foot yacht and its crew of twenty. The boxy fishing boat with its cranes and nets looked pathetic. Joe was pretty sure he was being insulted.

But he knew there wasn't a damn thing he could do about it.

Chapter Twenty

Cape was glad he wasn't wearing 3-D glasses.

The foyer was a cross between a Spanish manor house and Graceland. The interior was wood, with simple flourishes and elegant molding accenting high ceilings and a broad curving staircase. But clearly Elvis had come back from the dead, fully loaded on painkillers and booze, and went to work on the walls.

The paintings varied from oil on canvas to black velvet—rich, earthy tones juxtaposed to garish greens and blues. Family portraits adjacent to busty women straddling tigers. Small alcoves held busts of people Cape didn't recognize, some finely crafted but others crudely rendered, rough plaster slapped together, making the proportions of the faces seem not quite human.

Cape felt dizzy and found himself thinking of *Citizen Kane*. Following the curve of the staircase, he saw two more guards waiting on the landing.

"Upsy-daisy." Cyrano nudged him along the right wall, standing one step below him as they climbed. "You've kept *Señor* Big waiting long enough."

The muscle at the top of the stairs could have been matching bookends from one of the gift shops in town. The two men had squat bodies with flat, chiseled faces and onyx eyes. In perfect synchronization they pulled open matching oak doors.

At the threshold Cyrano stopped to let Cape enter alone. "If I wanted to give you some advice, I might say don't do anything stupid, but I'll bet you can't help yourself." He started down the stairs before Cape could respond.

As the doors closed behind him, Cape found himself standing on carpet thicker than a Chicago pizza and just as cheesy. Orange shag ran from the door to a massive walnut desk where a lone halogen cast its glow across a high-backed leather chair.

Two men flanked the desk, not quite in silhouette. Their outlines revealed pistols in angled holsters. Cape noticed that the guy on the right wore the gun on his right hip and the man facing the back of the desk on the left was a lefty. That meant their shooting arms would be raised away from their boss, leaving him room to maneuver or be pushed aside by their free hands if anything unpleasant went down suddenly.

Nice to be working with professionals.

Behind the desk was a windowed door leading to a small balcony overlooking the treetops and the water far down the cliff. Given the tight security, Cape wondered if the glass was bulletproof or the angle of the hill made a clear shot impossible. To the left of the desk was a small alcove, completely in shadow from where Cape was standing. Probably a side door for emergency exits in case of fire, Feds or uninvited hitmen. Along the left wall was a bookcase with leather-bound titles older than the Book of Job.

Cape took a step forward and sensed movement to his right. From out of the shadows next to the door emerged another bodyguard, this one close to six feet tall. Long black hair parted in the middle exposed almond eyes and a thin, cruel mouth. His empty hands hung loosely at his sides, but he needed a better tailor. The bulge of his gun was clearly visible through the cheap fabric of his suit. Cape held the man's gaze briefly before turning as his host leaned into the light.

A broad Mexican face with strong features peered into the gloom beyond the desk. Black eyes glittered as they studied Cape with a hint of amusement. After a long minute, the heavy black mustache curled into a smile, revealing small pointy teeth that reminded Cape of a piranha.

Cape scanned the room and frowned.

"Figured you'd have a fish tank for sure," he said. "Exotic species, dangerous. Maybe one or two from the Amazon."

The man behind the desk joined his hands together as if he were about to begin a sermon. "Do you know who I am?"

"What if I said I don't give a shit?"

The man's eyes turned cold, his smile retreating behind the black mustache. After a long moment the smile returned, but the eyes regained none of their warmth.

"I know who *you* are, Mister Weathers."

"Call me Cape."

"I believe we have a mutual interest."

"Double-jointed women?"

Again the smile disappeared, then reappeared, while the rest of the face remained impassive. Like a magician's slight of hand. "You have been looking for someone."

Cape felt his own expression hardening. "All I found was a corpse."

"You were a bit late, perhaps." A small shrug, suggesting the man behind the desk didn't see much distinction between finding a man dead or alive. "But you found this person, and I have found you."

"Never should have joined Facebook."

"My name is Antonio Salinas." The man looked pointedly at Cape as if hoping to draw sustenance from his reaction. "Perhaps you have heard of me."

Cape arched an eyebrow. "You don't look as grainy as those surveillance photos they showed on *60 Minutes*."

"You saw the program," Salinas said approvingly. "And what did you learn?"

"Let's see," said Cape, counting off the fingers of his left hand. "Former arms dealer, drug lord. How am I doing so far?"

Salinas nodded as each finger ticked off a new section of his resumé.

Cape continued. "Related by marriage to the Minister of Defense, who is currently under investigation for questionable campaign contributions during the last election."

Salinas spread his hands in a *what-can-you-do* gesture.

"You were imprisoned twice in your own country, but only on minor charges and never for long. Almost extradited to the U.S., but proceedings were stopped after the sudden disappearance of key witnesses."

Salinas leaned back in his chair. "That was not on television."

"*Wall Street Journal*," said Cape. "Short column a few months ago."

"You have done some homework."

"Tourists research the best diving spots, the local restaurants," said Cape. "I'm not a tourist. I like to know who the local criminals are before I go somewhere."

Salinas nodded. "I run the largest…" He let his voice trail off as he searched for the right word. "…*enterprise* in Mexico."

"Enterprise." Cape managed not to smirk. "You mean cartel."

"Some have used that term. Personally, I find it somewhat pejorative."

"What about Luis Cordon?" asked Cape. "Isn't he a player in these parts?"

Salinas looked like he'd swallowed a jalapeño. "Luis is my competitor." Salinas added something in Spanish too fast and guttural for Cape to catch. "Once, long ago, he worked for me."

"Touchy subject?"

"Cordon has nothing to do with why you are here."

"I was about to ask."

Salinas didn't respond. He took a cigar from a humidor on his desk, opened a drawer and used a silver tool to clip the end before lighting up. He didn't offer one to Cape. Soon the room was filled with thin tendrils of smoke and a cloying smell more sweet than rancid. After a minute of puffing, Salinas sighed contentedly.

"I think you are good at this," he said. "Finding things."

"I'm having a bad week."

"You act the clown, but I was looking for this man, this dead *gringo* of yours, and you did much better—even though he was in my own country." Salinas examined his cigar, rotating it slowly between his fingers. "But you were already here, so you must have been close."

"Close doesn't count," said Cape.

"This is very embarrassing," said Salinas. "I do not like to be embarrassed."

"Next time I promise to give you a head start."

"Like you, I wanted this man alive."

Cape didn't bother to keep the edge from his voice. "So you invited me here to commiserate?" It was tempting to ask Salinas which man he was talking about, the father or the son, but Cape instinctively didn't like giving up information. If Salinas didn't know about the two bodies, Cape wasn't going to be the one to tell him.

"You are not stupid." Salinas' face was etched with disappointment. "I want to know how he ended up in Puerto Vallarta, and how he died."

"He might have drowned. I'm sure you can check with the city coroner—you might even have him on the payroll."

Salinas blew smoke at the ceiling. "You do not believe he drowned, or else you would have gone home...to your client. By the way, who *is* your client, Señor Weathers?"

Cape tilted his head to the right. "Sorry, I'm a little deaf in this ear."

"I could make you tell me." Salinas was sighing smoke as he talked. He seemed almost bored, like a snake with its eyes half-closed, as he jabbed his cigar toward the bodyguard standing behind Cape with a quick, impatient gesture. A sudden rustle of fabric was the only sound in the room.

Without turning, Cape bent forward and windmilled his right arm—back and around—hoping to deflect the blow before it connected. He got lucky and caught the guard under the left armpit. Cape pivoted and grabbed the man's left wrist and twisted hard and fast, as if turning on a water spigot in the dead of winter. The guard yelped as his own momentum carried him across the desk, his legs knocking the halogen lamp and humidor onto the floor.

Salinas shoved his chair back from the desk just in time. Cape straightened, very deliberately holding his hands away from his sides. Before he raised his eyes from the floor he heard the telltale slide and crack of guns coming free of their holsters, safety levers being thumbed into the fire position.

Salinas' face was lit from below by the fallen but still functioning lamp. He looked like a jack-o-lantern as he smiled broadly, with genuine warmth this time. He chuckled softly.

"As I said, Señor Cape, you are good at this."

Salinas snapped his fingers and the bookends holstered their weapons. The guard with the long hair was clearly annoyed at being turned into a human projectile and stared at Cape with unabashed hostility. Cape blew him a kiss.

Long-hair held the edge of the desk and was trying to get his feet under him when Salinas grabbed a fistful of the man's hair with his right hand. The guard's eyes bulged as Salinas slowly moved his left hand—the hand holding the cigar—inexorably closer. Nobody took a breath as Salinas did all the talking.

"My men are good at some things, but not all things." Salinas shifted his left hand, ash falling behind the desk. Cape kept his eyes on Salinas, not giving him the satisfaction of staring at his captive. Every sadist he'd ever known loved an audience.

Salinas didn't blink as he slid the cigar against his man's cheek, barely an inch below the eye. The fallen guard muffled a scream through clenched teeth as Cape gritted his own at the unnerving calm of Salinas' expression. The smell of charred flesh blended seamlessly with the rank odor of his cigar.

"You sure know how to reward loyalty."

"I reward results." Salinas unclenched his right hand and released the guard, who fell gasping behind the desk. "Not incompetence." Then he looked down toward the floor with an almost paternal expression. "But I am willing to give people second chances. And you, detective, you desperately want to have a second chance, don't you? You are as angry about your failure as I am, no?"

Your failure. An obvious jab, almost childish. Still, it had the desired effect. Cape was pissed.

"So here is what we shall do." Salinas smiled as the guards returned to their respective positions. "You will continue to do what you were already doing, only now you have a new client."

"Let me guess," said Cape. "You?"

"*Sí.*"

"And why, exactly, do you think I'll do this?"

Salinas interlaced his fingers. "We have a saying—*plato o plomo*—take the silver or the lead. If you do this, I will pay you."

"And if I don't?"

"The lead."

"You'll force me to chew on a toy made in China?"

"*No.*" Salinas sighed. "I am going to have you shot—with bullets." He gave Cape a deliberate stare. "Bullets made from lead."

"I'll take the silver."

Salinas nodded. "I will pay you ten thousand dollars."

Cape didn't hesitate. "I want fifty."

Salinas laughed. "And why should I give you that much money?"

"Because you're too high-profile—you're on TV. And you don't want to kill me."

The black eyes glittered. "Don't be so sure."

Cape looked skeptical. "You don't know why I'm here. Kill me and you might get another half-hour segment on American television. That won't make your government friends very happy."

Salinas studied Cape like a man trying to pick a lobster from a tank. "Continue."

"I don't think your buddy Luis Cordon has public image problems, do you? I had to really dig to find dirt on him."

Salinas blinked once, almost reptilian, but his face remained placid. He glanced to his right and the guard on that side of the desk bent to grab a stainless steel briefcase that he placed carefully in front of his boss. Salinas spun the combination locks and turned the case around. Cape could see neatly packed rows of American bills.

"Take this case with you. Another case—a bigger one—will be delivered to you once I know *everything*."

Cape came forward and gently pushed the lid closed, then stepped back from the desk. "Keep the case, Salinas."

Salinas worked his jaw. "You are choosing the lead?"

"No way." Cape held up his hands. "But I'm kind of a *first come, first serve* detective. I already have a client, and whatever I have to say, my client hears it first." Cape waited for a reaction. None came. "But if I discover something you can use, I'll come back for the case. The bigger case."

Another crocodile blink, a long pause from Salinas. "And why should I believe you?"

"I like money."

"An honest answer, but can I trust you?"

Cape almost laughed. "You can trust me about as much as I trust you."

Salinas frowned and reopened the case. "I would feel better if you took the money."

"But I might feel worse—I might feel like I owed you something."

"Do you go to the movies, Cape?"

"I only like films about zombie baseball."

Salinas pressed on. "In American movies about criminals, there is often a scene in which the policeman—or the detective—is offered a chance to work with the so-called bad man. And you know what he always says?"

"*Never!*" Cape spoke in an overly dramatic voice. "*You'll have to kill me first.*"

Salinas clapped. "*Plenario!* These scenes make me laugh—"

"Because in reality that would never happen. You don't say no to the bad guy, even if you plan on double-crossing him later. It would be—"

"—insulting."

"I was going to say *unwise*."

"That, too," said Salinas. "Take the money."

"Fine." Cape closed the lid and grabbed the handle of the case with his right hand. It was heavier than he expected.

Salinas studied him for a minute before speaking.

"Do not disappoint me."

"You sound like my mother."

"So bold for a *gringo*. One more thing…"

Cape kept his face open, his mouth shut.

"I am perhaps not as good at finding people as you," said Salinas. "But I am not so bad at it, either."

"The silver or the lead?"

Salinas nodded. "It seems we understand each other."

"Guess those team building exercises really paid off."

Salinas reached across the desk and extended his right hand. "That is my direct number."

Cape took the card, shoved it in his back pocket. "We through?"

"Adios, Señor Cape." Salinas gave a short nod and the bodyguard on the right moved to open the door. "Good hunting."

Cape followed the curve of the stairway to the front door. No one blocked his way or accompanied him. When he reached the driveway he continued past the cars to the large iron gate, which stood open. Cape looked back at the house. He couldn't see anyone in the windows but knew he must be under the watchful eye of security cameras. He looked back toward the open road and sighed.

"Guess I'm walking." He said it to no one in particular, wondering how long it would take to follow the winding road back to town.

Chapter Twenty-one

"Do you like calamari?"

The question seemed idle enough when Joe Drabyak first stepped onto the fishing boat, but now he wasn't so sure. His host had never followed up with the calamari. No snacks or drinks, but thirty minutes out to sea, Joe was glad he hadn't eaten anything deep-fried. His stomach was starting to lurch with every swell as he gripped the low railing near the bow, salt spray stinging his eyes.

He almost lost his grip when the question came again, like a voice inside his head. The man who owned the boat was standing right beside him. He must have come from the cabin but Joe didn't notice until he heard the deep baritone cutting through the wind.

"You never answered my question, *Señor* Drabyak."

Joe was busy trying to breathe through his mouth as he fought the urge to puke, but he managed to yank his eyes from between his feet. He had talked to this man many times over the phone, but this was their first meeting. That was significant. It meant Joe was moving up in the world.

Luis Cordon's profile matched his voice. A rich mane of chestnut hair flared wildly around a distinguished face. High cheekbones, amber eyes that looked almost golden. Seeing him on the street, you might think he was an actor or an opera singer. Maybe a star of a Mexican *telenovela*. But Joe knew he was none of those things.

The golden eyes studied him until Joe managed to respond. "Calamari? Sure, I like it fine. Eat it when I go to bars sometimes."

Cordon smiled, pleased. "Then you will find this interesting."

Joe nodded absently. "When you said we'd be on your boat, I kinda thought—"

"Ah, the yacht. You thought we would take her for a spin."

Joe shrugged but didn't say anything.

"Do not take offense, Joe—you don't mind I call you by your first name?"

"Knock yourself out."

"This boat, it attracts no attention. No surveillance. It is too noisy for listening devices. And we are too far from shore for anyone wearing a wire to be heard. When this boat leaves the harbor, no one follows it."

Joe nodded. "The *federales* are too busy watching the yacht."

"Precisely. I know it has been an uncomfortable journey, but we have arrived."

As if on cue, the throttle was cut and the roar of the diesel engine blew away on the breeze. To Joe it felt as if the boat lurched backward, but he knew that was only an illusion. They had followed the coast for some time before heading into deeper water, and he wondered how far they were from land. He saw flashing lights to starboard and squinted into the wind, trying to gage the distance.

It took Joe a moment to realize the lights were underwater. White, almost fluorescent, flashing less than a hundred meters away. A submarine seemed unlikely.

"Squid." His host seemed to read his mind. "*Calamar* in Spanish. You see the lights, yes?"

"Yeah," said Joe tentatively, wondering if there were divers out there. Guys with spear guns and nets, scooping up squid. Before he could ask, the engines rumbled back to life and the boat seemed to pivot on the crest of a wave, then reverse toward the underwater laser show.

"Come with me, *señor*."

Joe was led to the stern, where two men in yellow slickers and bright orange rubber boots worked a winch. Again the engines dropped to a murmur as they lowered a net over the back of the vessel. In the reflected light from the water below, the workers' skin turned bluish, making them look like animated corpses. Joe suppressed a chill as he looked over the railing.

The sea was boiling.

Blue and white flashes shot across the waves and vanished, illuminating a macabre dance just beneath the surface of the black water. Joe glimpsed a tentacle lashing out to wrap around another twice its length, both as pale as the grave. A bulbous eye in a conical head, its jellied surface alien and trembling. Another electric flash and a beak appeared at the center of a ring of suckers six inches in diameter.

A beak?

Again Cordon seemed to read Joe's thoughts. "It looks more like the mouth of a parrot than a weapon for a squid, eh? And the suckers, those have teeth, too." A deep sigh as the man watched in admiration. "Within that rubbery flesh, to find something so hard, so *sharp*—it is a miracle of nature, don't you agree?"

Joe couldn't tear his eyes from the churning water. "How many are there?"

Cordon shrugged. "Hundreds. Maybe a thousand." A tentacle flashed out of the water, snapped like a whip. It must have been four feet long. "They are big, these squid. As big as a man, some of them."

Joe nodded absently. "What the fuck are they doing?"

"Feeding, of course." Deep laughter echoed over the ship. The two men guiding the net glanced toward them. Something about their expressions made Joe uncomfortable, like they were in on a joke that wouldn't translate into his language.

"But the lights?"

"Ah, that is best part." Cordon pointed to an eerie green light bobbing amidst the flashes of white, its dull glow steady even as it was jostled back and forth. Then he pointed at another ten feet away, a steady beacon amidst the strobing chaos. "You see those lights, the green ones?" They reminded Joe of the plastic glow sticks kids carried on Halloween, or the chemical flares people kept in their cars for emergencies. "The flares were placed into the water before we got here, to attract the plankton that squid like to eat. The squid eat the plankton, and we eat the squid."

But Joe wasn't looking at the little green lights. He was trying to focus on the blue and white strobes, the sudden bursts of energy followed by utter blackness. "But the other lights," he asked, almost worried he was hallucinating. "The glow…"

"These are *Humboldt* squid, and they are…" Cordon hesitated, frowned until he found the word. "*Bioluminescent*. They make their own light when they are aroused, or when they are feeding. Squid are vicious predators, as you can see."

Joe stole a glance toward the men by the net. They were laughing again at some private joke but Joe couldn't hear them. The thrashing of the squid pushed all other sounds past hearing.

Joe took a step away from the railing and immediately regretted it. The sway of the boat was subtle but still there. He tightened his grip, wondering if the railing was wet from the damp air, the ocean spray, or his own sweating palms.

"OK," he said, almost shouting to be hard above the roar of the feeding frenzy. "Here we are. Can we discuss our arrangement now?"

"Our arrangement?"

"Like you said, there's no wires. Can we talk business?" Joe almost said *please*. A thousand tentacles waved, coaxing him overboard, the tiny teeth surrounding each sucker glinting green. A gelatinous eye came into view and froze. Joe would have sworn it was staring right at him, wondering what he'd taste like deep-fried.

"You said so yourself," pressed Joe. "We've got no company out here."

Again the laughter, a deep baritone that made Joe's skin crawl. "But we *do* have company." Cordon clapped his hands.

Two more crewmen emerged from the forward cabin, carry-ing a third man slung between them like a bag of laundry. The man on the left was tall, the man on the right short, so they progressed in a crazy zig-zag pattern that heightened Joe's sense of the boat's lateral motion. The guy in the middle was average height, but his feet dragged as the two men hustled him toward the stern. When the ungainly trio reached the back of the boat, Joe felt his body explode in sweat.

Sammy Dunlop. The name leapt into Joe's head like a child-hood memory.

Sammy, a.k.a. "The Hound" to his friends and enemies, and Joe had been both. They'd come up together in the west coast rackets and were partners for a while before becoming erstwhile competitors, but things had never gotten ugly. The drug trade was lucrative and their territories clearly marked.

At the end of the day, Joe was a middleman and so was Sammy. Any drugs distributed from Mexico to central or north-ern California along the coast, then Joe handled the freight. Anything south of Santa Barbara, it was Sammy's burden.

Now Sammy was someone else's burden, a broken bag of flesh. His mop of blond hair was streaked with blood, his right eye swollen shut, the skin turning purple. His breath was ragged, his nose broken. The two crewman dumped him unceremoni-ously onto the metal deck.

Cordon shook his head sadly. He studied Sammy but spoke to Joe over his shoulder.

"You wanted to talk about our arrangement?"

It took Joe a minute to respond. His eyes were glued to Sammy, his ears to the squid. "Y-yeah. I mean, yes."

"I want to change it."

Joe forced himself to meet the other man's eyes. He didn't want to ask the question but heard his own voice saying, "Change it how?" A knot was expanding in his stomach as the answer dawned on him.

"As I expand my interests beyond narcotics, I need that side of my business handled by men I can trust. How would you and your...*employer*...how would you like to handle distribution up and down the coast?"

Joe didn't like that idea at all, it would bring too much heat. He learned a long time ago that greed got you dead. But he also understood that *no* wasn't in your vocabulary. Instead he tried, "Some people are going to be pretty pissed off."

"I know how it feels to be *pissed off*," said Cordon, mimicking Joe's American accent. "Imagine how I felt, Joe, when I discovered our friend Sammy here had been stealing from me?"

Uh-oh. Sammy, you poor, dumb fuck.

On the deck Sammy writhed, his head lifting just enough for Joe to see the pain in his eyes. Sammy said something but it was snatched away by the wind. Behind them, Joe could hear the squid lashing out in all directions.

"It's true," said Cordon, a pained expression on his face. "I got reports that product was lost in transit. Damaged, the packages broken, the product no good. Sudden trouble with the police, more product had to be dumped to avoid arrest. Thousands of dollars lost."

Joe wanted to say *shit happens*. He had the same problems up North. Everyone did, that's why dope was so expensive. Trashing product along the way became part of the overhead. He was about to make a comment when another thought struck him like a bucket of ice water.

Sammy had been on board the yacht. That meant he'd been seen by whatever law enforcement agencies were watching Cordon's fancy ship. The feds would run Sammy's mug through a database, pull up his name and rap sheet. So if he disappeared, word would spread that the last time anyone saw him alive was in Mexico, visiting Luis Cordon. Nobody could ever prove anything, but everyone would know.

Cordon *wanted* everyone to know.

Joe wanted to speak up, make it clear he understood what was happening, but something in Cordon's expression stopped him. A dull glow to those golden eyes, warning him the story wasn't finished.

"So imagine my surprise, Joe, when new product starts show-ing up from a different source. Finds its way to *my customers.*" Cordon spread his arms, letting Joe know this was bigger than him, out of his hands. "Imagine my disappointment when I get a sample of this product tested. Do you know what my chem-ists told me?"

Joe tore his eyes from Sammy's pulped face. "It was yours."

"*Sí.*" Cordon nodded. "The ruined product, the lost mer-chandise. It wasn't so lost after all. It had been hijacked by your associate, Señor Dunlop."

"My associate." Joe kept his voice neutral.

Cordon put a hand on Joe's shoulder and squeezed. "I spoke too quickly, señor. I should have said former associate." Cordon jutted his chin toward the two crewmen who had dragged Sammy from the cabin. Sammy's eyes were frantic as they grabbed his shoulders. His mouth spasmed around broken teeth but no sound came out.

Joe swallowed hard and tried to look away but Cordon had shifted his hand to the back of Joe's neck. It was a gesture as threatening as a gun pointed at his head.

Sammy flailed his arms as he went over the railing headfirst but he'd forgotten how to fly. He hit the water with a smack, flesh hitting flesh. For a terrible moment he was suspended on the surface, the overlapping bodies of squid holding him aloft, a scene from an H.P. Lovecraft nightmare.

Tentacles wrapped around Sammy's legs, his arms. He opened his mouth and a rubbery arm found the opening, its pointed tip down his throat before he could scream. Then a ring of suckers six inches across wrapped around his neck and pulled him under.

Joe Drabyak watched the water flash blue and white, blue and white—and for an instant red—as the neon horror turned the ocean to foam.

Chapter Twenty-two

Salinas lit another cigar and spoke into the shadows. He didn't seem the least bit surprised when the shadows replied.

"I am not sure I like paying this detective so much money," he said into the darkness.

"He'll never collect."

Salinas shrugged. He had dismissed the men on either side of his desk and felt uneasy. He knew they waited outside the door and would enter, guns drawn, at the slightest signal, but he didn't like talking to phantoms. Without asking permission, he thumbed a switch under his desk that activated lights set into the molding overhead.

Salinas blinked as the figure to his left materialized, but even with the lights up the man looked as if he'd been conjured from the cigar smoke that choked the room.

Priest came around the front of the desk and took a chair, crossing his long legs at the ankles. "Why so nervous, Antonio?"

"I think this *gringo* detective is smart, but not as smart as he thinks he is."

Priest raised his eyebrows but didn't say anything.

"That type of man is always trouble."

"How would you have handled it?" asked Priest, relishing the knowledge that Salinas didn't have any choice in the matter.

"I think maybe we should have killed him after all."

"He is more useful to us alive," said Priest. "And less dangerous."

"Explain again why a man like that is dangerous to men like us?"

"Because a man like that will have *friends.*" Priest handled the word as if it were a scorpion. "People who will look for him if something happens."

"*Ocho ochenta.*" Salinas looked at the crucifix around Priest's neck and suppressed a chill. "I don't like it."

"I don't care."

Salinas studied his unwelcome ally. "Have you ever heard of the *Civatateo?*"

Priest raised his eyebrows. "Do tell."

"Mexican vampires, a legend dating back to the Aztecs." Salinas chewed on his cigar. "But these vampires were servants of God. They would lurk in temples and churches, do horrible things to the unfaithful."

"What are you getting at, Antonio?"

"That is what you remind me of, *amigo*—you are a fucking vampire." Salinas blew a noxious cloud of smoke across the desk. "I am trying to run a business, but you, I think you like the blood. That is why you delay everything, to build *anticipación.* It is almost sexual for you."

"I didn't realize you were the court-appointed psychiatrist." Priest linked his long fingers and cracked his knuckles. "And I'm surprised a pissant private detective could make you so jumpy."

"I do not like things I cannot control."

"We will use him...for now."

"Until our business is concluded."

"Exactly."

"Fine." Salinas shrugged, feigning indifference. "And then?"

"We'll kill him."

"What about his friends?"

"We'll kill them, too," said Priest. "Every godforsaken one of them."

Chapter Twenty-three

Cape got mugged before he was halfway down the hill.

He heard a rustling in the bushes on the side of the road and turned just as a hand wrapped around his mouth from behind, pulling his head backward.

"Did you miss me?" Sally whispered into his ear.

Cape spun around, scowling at his diminutive protector. She was almost invisible, dressed completely in black with a hood pulled tightly around her face.

"Where have you been?"

"Following you for the past half-hour," Sally replied. "I wanted to make sure you weren't followed."

"They know where I'm staying."

"They might have changed their minds and sent a car after you. Give you a ride back to the hotel. You know, a sudden attack of guilt for making you walk."

"Not likely," said Cape. "I think the walk is some sort of lesson. You know—*you might be on the payroll, but you're not one of us.*"

"You're on the payroll?"

Cape held the briefcase high in his right hand.

"You took his money?"

Cape shrugged. "It seemed rude not to."

"You feel conflicted?"

"Why?" said Cape. "Because it's dirty money?"

"There is no dirty money," said Sally. "Only dirty wallets."

"Exactly," said Cape. "Besides, I might have lost my only paying client."

"So where do we stand?"

"Not sure." Cape told her about the conversation with Salinas.

Sally nodded. "I saw the whole thing but could only catch bits and pieces of the conversation. Salinas had his back to the window so I couldn't read his lips."

"You were on the balcony?" Cape should have been surprised but he'd known her too long. "I was worried when the car headed up the hill, you wouldn't be able to keep up."

"That was easy. I grabbed a taxi in front of the hotel and told him I was going to a surprise party for the people in the car ahead of us, then told him I wasn't sure of the address. I had him drop me off a hundred yards past the gate. All I had to do was flash some bills and act helpless."

"You're so convincing at that."

Sally curtsied without breaking stride. They walked in silence for a while.

The road twisted and the lights of the resort became visible, reflecting off the water in undulating streaks of yellow. Cape thought they looked like claw marks.

After another minute he asked, "So how much do you know?"

"Less than you for a change," said Sally. "I did make it to the balcony but it was slower going than I'd expected."

"I heard the dogs."

"Dobermans are a royal pain," said Sally. "Thank goodness for tall trees and dumb dogs."

"Hey, I like dogs. *Dog* is *God* spelled backward."

"God never tried to bite me in the ass."

"You obviously weren't raised Catholic."

Another turn in the road and the lights disappeared, replaced by trees that swallowed the moon.

"So now what?" asked Sally.

"I try to connect the dots."

"How many dots do you have?"

"Dead Senator, dead Senator's dead kid. Client who might be an ex-client, daughter of dead Senator. Mexican drug lord. Out-of-town muscle for said drug lord. Local police inspector. You. Me."

Sally wiggled her outstretched fingers and frowned. "That's eight dots."

"More than enough to make a straight line," said Cape. "But right now it leads to nowhere."

"So where to next?"

Cape patted the side of the briefcase. "Now that we've taken his money, I think Salinas is going to want us close at hand."

"So?"

"So I say we skip town without telling him."

"I just unpacked."

"We're not checking out of our rooms," said Cape. "We're just leaving suddenly."

"Take the money and run?"

"Exactly."

"You think he'll send someone after us?"

"Only one way to find out," said Cape.

Chapter Twenty-four

An hour into the flight Cape was locked in the lavatory. He sensed other passengers waiting but stood transfixed by the small sign posted above the toilet bowl.

Caution! Disposal of any articles other than toilet tissue can cause external leaks which could be hazardous.

"External leaks?" Cape muttered, wondering what sort of article besides toilet paper might send the plane into a flat spin. On the back of the toilet lid was a graphic of a circle with a red slash across it, the circle filled with line drawings of paper clips, dental floss, coins, and what appeared to be a toothbrush, which only served to reinforce Cape's growing suspicion that dentists were to blame for all the troubles in the world.

Cape glanced around the cramped space, searching for bits of plastic, cracks in the mirror, anything with potential for tearing through the fuselage. After a long minute, he took a deep breath and opened the door. A small queue had formed. Cape made eye contact with the first person in line, a heavyset woman wearing a Hawaiian print blouse. He gestured at the sign as she brushed past and shut the door in his face.

He took his seat next to Sally and asked, "Ever notice how turbulence always occurs shortly after they serve you the meal?"

"Never." Sally put down the book she'd been reading, the vertical rows of Chinese characters like tiger stripes across the pages.

"I mean, do you think it's intentional, an effort to shake up your stomach just enough to facilitate digestion of the rubber chicken they serve? Or maybe the pilots eat at the same time and take their hands off the controls, flying the jet like a truck driver eating fries with a Coke stuck between his legs."

"I never eat when I fly."

"You're missing the point."

Sally smiled. "And you're pretty neurotic for a guy who carries a gun."

Cape didn't respond but exhaled loudly, stretching his arms above his head, feeling his fingers bend against the closeness of the overhead compartment.

"You want to fly the plane?"

Cape looked at Sally across the empty seat between them. "What do you think?"

"I think that you can't control everything."

"You seem to manage."

"I only control myself," said Sally. "Everything else…" She let her voice trail off.

Cape looked past Sally and out the window. An ocean of pillows extended all the way to the horizon, an unwelcome reminder of how exhausted he felt.

"Sorry you had to leave your bag of tricks behind." Cape knew the trouble Sally had gone to smuggling their weapons into Mexico.

"We thought things were going to be more exciting."

"I wouldn't call getting hired by a drug lord boring."

"So who are we working for?" Sally raised an eyebrow. "You never told me about your call with our client."

Cape shrugged. "Not much to tell."

"That bad, huh?"

"Shitty."

"How did she take the news about her brother and father?"

"Badly."

"Are we fired?"

"Not yet."

Sally watched while Cape worked the muscles in his jaw. "You want to talk about this later?" she asked. "When we're on solid ground."

"No," said Cape, "I'm just…"

"Pissed?"

"Exactly," said Cape. "Royally pissed."

"You want me to quote a Zen scripture about the healing power of mistakes?"

"God, no."

"Good, at least you're not getting soft."

Cape took a deep breath. "She sounded devastated. She loved her brother, and even if you're estranged from your father, hearing that he floated to the surface of a water hazard probably isn't the epitaph you had in mind."

"And yet we're not fired."

"She doesn't blame me."

"Does she know you blame yourself?"

Cape didn't take the bait. "She wants to find out what happened."

"She wants revenge," said Sally bluntly. Cape didn't challenge the comment. Lots of people talked about revenge, but Sally had spent half a lifetime in pursuit of it.

"I told her I'd find out what happened—didn't make any promises beyond that."

"She might not like what she finds."

Cape said nothing.

"What next?"

"I called Linda and asked for a deep dive into the Senator—I'll meet her when we get back. Then I'm going to Burning Man."

"Burning Man." Sally arched an eyebrow. "Is that a person, place or thing?"

"All of the above. It's a festival in the desert. You really haven't heard of it?"

Sally shook her head. "Why should I?"

"It's been around for almost a decade, attracts thousands of people every year. There was a big feature about it in the *Chronicle* last month."

"I don't read the local papers."

"It's supposed to be a break from civilization. People drive into the Nevada desert, have a big party, and disconnect from the rat race."

"I'm not a rat," said Sally. "I don't race."

"That's why you haven't heard of it."

"Are drugs involved?"

"Of course," said Cape. "It was started by Californians."

"Nudity?"

"It's hot in the desert. Don't need a lot of clothes there."

"Have you been?"

"Never," said Cape. "But I've seen pictures. Imagine a peace rally from the sixties, only with ecstasy instead of acid—better tents, and the Nevada desert instead of Woodstock."

"Somehow I don't imagine you in that picture."

"Me neither, but that's where our client is going."

"Why?"

"She goes every year—says it's like therapy."

"She should study martial arts."

"Besides," added Cape. "I need to see her in order to get some answers."

"But have you thought of any questions?"

"Sure. Why does a Mexican drug lord care about a U.S. Senator?"

"Or his son."

"Exactly."

Sally frowned. "Didn't you ask about her father and brother when she hired you?"

"Maybe this isn't solely about them—maybe it's about her, too."

"What makes you think that?"

"I'm desperate," said Cape.

"And suspicious."

Cape met her gaze, a half-smile on his lips. "How do you know?"

"I know you."

"OK."

"You have a reason for being so paranoid?"

"Sure," said Cape. "She's the only one in that family left alive."

Chapter Twenty-five

Juan Molina used to enjoy being head of hotel security. Compared to being a cop in Mexico City it was like he'd died and gone to heaven. Blue skies instead of pollution, rich women in bikinis instead of back alley whores, and no bureaucracy except for a monthly staff meeting in the general manager's office which got cancelled half the time. For a man whose early retirement plan had been to get shot in the line of duty, this was more like a vacation than a job.

He knew he could never repay the debt of gratitude to the man who got him the job, and every night before he went to bed, he prayed that he would never have to try.

But this past week the job had almost made him miss being a cop. The sore feet, aching shoulders, and the constant river of sweat between his shoulder blades all seemed pleasant by comparison to the inexorable pressure on his balls since those two corpses appeared on the golf course.

Every day he received the same note in his mailbox, written in a simple, nondescript hand.

¿Qué le tienen visto hoy?

What have you seen today? An innocent enough question, taken out of context. But even though the notes were never signed, Juan knew who sent them.

Just as he knew the risk of ignoring the sender.

Juan ran his hands through his hair, feeling the gel stick to his fingers but not caring. He sighed and stared at the telephone a good five minutes before picking up the receiver and dialing. He heard ringing on the other end, and then the sound of someone lifting the receiver. But no voice. No matter how hard he listened, he never heard a voice.

Juan took a deep breath. "The detective left about an hour ago." He waited for a response but none came, which implied a question. "For the airport."

Silence.

"The cab driver dropped him at departures, in the international terminal."

Silence. Only the *click* of the call ending would signal satisfaction.

"I searched his room, and his bags are still here."

Silence.

"That means he didn't check out. I think—I think he's coming back."

Juan couldn't be sure, but he imagined that he heard the whisper of a laugh on the other end of the phone, just before the line went dead.

Chapter Twenty-six

"Thanks for meeting me."

Linda Katz didn't answer right away, but her hair bobbed up and down in greeting. Cape chose a spot on the blanket sufficiently close to seem friendly but far enough away to avoid being blinded by a loose strand or runaway ponytail.

Linda's hair could have been the stunt-double for Rapunzel, impossibly long tresses that seemed to move simultaneously in all directions. Of course it could have been the wind, always intense at Chrissy Field, but Cape had seen Linda indoors on countless occasions and the effect was very much the same.

"You're late." Linda said it calmly. "As usual." She squinted into the glare off the ocean and Cape followed her gaze. A container ship was passing below the Golden Gate Bridge, two sailboats cutting across its wake. Directly below them a woman with a stroller worked her way down to the beach. The hill where they sat was covered in long grass bent backward from the constant breeze off the water. The movement of the waves and the undulating grass combined to create a sense of motion that Cape could feel deep in his gut, as if the blanket they were sitting on was really a sail.

"My flight was delayed landing."

Linda nodded. "SFO or Oakland?"

"SFO." Cape took off his shoes so he could feel the grass. "Nice spot."

Linda made a gesture that encompassed the entire hillside. "No towers."

For as long as Cape had known her, Linda avoided electromagnetic radiation the way Tweetie Bird avoided Sylvester. Dodging between wireless hotspots, detouring around cell towers, generally staying outdoors except when she was at home. No small trick for a reporter working in a major city. She had a computer that she used for short periods of time but didn't own a cell phone. Tracking her down always took two or three tries.

"What do you think of my Senator?" Cape shifted on the blanket.

"Not much."

"You found something?"

"Not yet." Linda frowned. "But I was going through the archives at the paper, especially during the election periods. I even found a few of his speeches. You were right, he was big on urban development at first, but then all his energy shifted toward the environmental movement. Almost overnight."

"A cause close to your heart."

"Dobbins only jumped on board when it became fashionable."

"Didn't he drive a hybrid—I saw a picture."

"Turns out he parked it right next to his Hummer in front of his 6000 square-foot house."

"Must have been quite a heating bill."

Linda nodded. "He was living large."

"That's not a crime, Linda."

"I know." Linda's hair shifted uncertainly. "Call it a hunch."

"Did you vote for him?"

"Yeah, I did, and maybe that's what bothers me. He said all the right things, all the things I wanted to hear, but looking at him with a fresh perspective, some things don't add up. It got me thinking."

"About?"

"Hypocrisy." Linda twisted a wayward strand of hair around her right index finger, then unwrapped it slowly. "This guy was painting himself Johnny Appleseed, but I don't think he ever planted a tree in his life."

"Maybe not, but he was a politician. He's supposed to listen to the voters."

"His speeches about the environment didn't offer any solutions. Just rhetoric. In fact, they were apocalyptic."

"Maybe he wanted to wake people up."

"He played off people's fear to get elected."

"It worked."

"I've lived a certain way my whole life, because I believe in it." Linda looked at the water. "I never tried to be *politically correct*—I just tried to do the right thing."

"And you resent having your cause hijacked for political gain."

"Maybe."

"He's dead, if that makes you feel any better," said Cape. "And I need something I can use."

Linda nodded. "I know—I've got the Sloth looking for connections. Voting records, investments, phone records. There isn't a database on the planet Sloth can't hack."

"A couple of days?"

"One should do it."

"Thanks."

Linda turned to face him, her hair stretching out like a kite behind her. "Want to know why your flight was delayed?"

"They said fog."

Linda's hair contracted in frustration. "They said fog— might've been rain. But you want to know the *real* reason?"

"Did I mention I was a nervous flier?"

"They only have two runways at SFO, and they're too close together, so the pilots have to *land by sight*. That means that if one plane can't see the other plane—"

"—the other plane gets delayed."

"Exactly, which begs a question."

"Why not build another runway?"

Linda's hair practically hugged him. "Want to know why not?"

"I sense you're going to tell me."

"Because so-called *environmentalists* say that another runway would require building a concrete strip into the bay."

"Would it?"

"Yeah," said Linda. "No way around it. And they should start tomorrow."

"Wait one minute," said Cape. "You're the one who wanted to meet away from the cell towers."

"You don't like the view?"

"Don't dodge the question. You don't eat meat."

"True."

"You only take public transportation."

"I prefer to walk."

"You separate your paper from your plastic, your glass from aluminum."

"Don't forget about composting. I'm big on composting."

"You're greener than Kermit the Frog. A friend to all plants and animals. I've never known anyone more concerned about the environment than you."

Linda's hair nodded its assent. "Thank you."

"So help me out with the rant about the airport."

"You know how much jet fuel gets pumped into the atmosphere every hour a plane circles overhead, waiting for an open runway?"

"Lots?"

"More than your car burns in a year. Now multiply that times thousands of flights a day, across the entire air traffic control system, because a delay in San Francisco means a delay for the next flight when it lands in Chicago or New York."

"Never thought of it that way."

"Neither did the nimrods who keep protesting the new runway." Linda sighed. "They say it will displace the fish and ruin windsurfing near the airport—that's the real issue. God forbid we worry about the atmosphere more than windsurfing."

"There's always Half Moon Bay for windsurfers. As for the fish…"

"I bet everyone on the action committee eats sushi," said Linda. "I know their type."

Cape noticed the deep lines around Linda's eyes, the streaks of gray in her hair. She looked older than he remembered, until she suddenly smiled and the lines on her face flattened out.

"I don't think things are ever as simple as the Senator made them out to be." She spoke quietly, as if talking to herself. "He learned the vocabulary of the environment, but he never understood what he was saying."

"Words can be pretty powerful."

"Until they become bankrupt," said Linda. "I used to be a feminist until that word got co-opted by a bunch of strident women with chips on their shoulders. Now I'm just a woman who doesn't take shit from anyone, especially a man."

"Duly noted."

"And I was an environmentalist before anyone knew what the word really meant. In the seventies, when *Newsweek* was warning the world about global *cooling* and the coming ice age."

"I think they changed their position on that one."

"Which is fine," said Linda. "We learn new things, scientists come up with new theories. They might be wrong again, but at least there are some people who do their homework and try to understand the consequences of their actions."

"Feeling old?"

Linda smacked him on the leg. "Feeling sick and tired of being lectured about the environment—*my* environment."

"Glad it's yours and not mine. I couldn't handle the responsibility."

"I voted for that bastard."

"I don't think you have to worry about him getting re-elected." Cape stood and brushed off his pants. He extended his hand. "Help you up?"

Linda shook her head. "I think I'll stay awhile."

Cape bent down and kissed her on the head, feeling her hair intertwine with his own, tugging gently as he pulled away.

Chapter Twenty-seven

"Get out of my hair, Oscar."

Inspector Garcia ignored the man in the white lab coat, who barely glanced up from his computer screen. His was standing, the computer set at eye level, his shoulders hunched as if he spent more time in that position than he did asleep. His head was clean-shaven, his ears small and slightly pointed near the tops.

Garcia popped some gum in his mouth. "You look like an elf, Ramirez."

"Fuck you. This is a sterile environment."

"I took a shower." Garcia looked around the collection of steel countertops littered with scales, test tubes, computers, and a number of machines he didn't recognize. "You called me."

"You're supposed to wait in the lobby." Ramirez pushed his glasses up onto his forehead as he turned away from the computer. "It's the rules."

Garcia blew a bubble and popped it. "You called me."

Ramirez shook his head and walked over to a desk near the door. He selected a manila folder and flipped it open.

"You wanted to know about the floaters?" Ramirez tilted his head forward until his glasses swung down onto his nose.

Garcia waited.

"DNA looks like a match."

"For both?"

Ramirez nodded. "Father and son."

"Have you told anyone else?"

"What do you think happened?"

Garcia ignored him. "Have you told anyone?"

Ramirez looked at Garcia over his glasses. "You said you would get me soccer tickets."

"Yes, I did." Garcia popped another bubble. "How confident are you?"

"I want to run it again, just to be sure. This was the second time."

"Same results?"

Ramirez shook his head. "The first sample was degraded with reptilian DNA. You should have told me about the alligators."

"Then it wouldn't have been a surprise."

Ramirez scowled. "We use a polymerase chain reaction technique, Garcia. Very sensitive."

"You have enough to work with?"

"Sometimes we only have a strand of hair. You gave me a leg, a torso, an arm—I am rich in evidence, poor on time."

"How soon for the final results? I need to make some calls."

"Where are the seats?"

"Goal line—home team."

"Tomorrow," said Ramirez. "You can make your calls tomorrow."

Chapter Twenty-eight

"Drive into the desert and look for smoke."

The woman working the counter at the AAA office smiled at Cape as she gave him directions that seemed as confusing as her wardrobe. Her dress had a shimmering thread woven into it, making her sparkle as she swayed back forth. She wore white gloves that ran up to her elbows. Her graying hair was pinned up, looking like a dilapidated pyramid on the verge of collapse.

"That's it?" Cape tried to sound more appreciative than dumbfounded.

"If you see purple mountains followed by a fruited plain, you're in the Midwest and you've gone too far."

"Got a map?"

The woman shook her head in disapproval as she handed over a map of Nevada. "No maps for the BRC."

"BRC?"

"Black Rock City." She leaned closer and spoke in a conspiratorial whisper. "You've never been, have you?"

Cape shook his head. "My first time."

"I couldn't go this year." She sighed and looked around the empty office, scowling. "Work."

"Bummer."

"You got that right. But you missed most of it—today's the last day."

Cape sighed. "*Work.*"

"Hey, at least you'll get to see the man burn, right?"

"Right." Cape wasn't sure what she was talking about, but he nodded enthusiastically. It was time to leave.

"Just drive into the desert?"

"There's thirty thousand people camped in the middle of the *playa*." The woman spread her arms like Moses. "How can you miss 'em?"

The drive took five hours in a pickup he borrowed from a friend. He had an extra tank of gas, blankets, a sleeping bag, and a cooler filled with water, cold cuts, bananas, and enough pretzels to survive a nuclear winter.

The shadows were getting long by the time Cape turned off the road onto the broken moonscape of the *playa*, a prehistoric lakebed now dry as a bone. Nothing but cracked earth in all directions, white dust covering the windshield like snow as the truck bumped and jostled its way through a desolation so vast that Cape started to wonder if he'd been transported to the Forbidden Zone on *The Planet of the Apes*. He squinted into the harsh light, half expecting to catch a glimpse of Charlton Heston on the horizon.

He began humming the theme from *Lawrence of Arabia* before he saw Black Rock City. It was an apt name for the collection of tents, cars, and RVs clustered at the heart of Black Rock desert, squeezed into an area less than three miles square. Seen from the air the annual gathering formed a giant U, but from Cape's vantage point it looked like an invading army.

Thank God they had a post office.

It was right next to the portable toilets, adjacent to the radio station, and within walking distance of the fire department, first aid clinic, and recycling center. The ramshackle tents and lean-tos that circled the encampment offered more services than most municipalities. And by tomorrow there wouldn't be a trace they had ever existed.

The postman couldn't have been more than a thousand years old. Cape figured it would take that long just to count the wrinkles in his skin, beginning with deep folds below his eyes that creased and turned all the way down his arms, stomach, and legs. His loincloth and sun visor left little to the imagination.

Cape removed his sunglasses so the man could see his eyes. "I'm looking for Hera and the Mud People."

Methuselah nodded. "Nice bunch, them mud people." He stood, his knees popping like firecrackers, and pointed along the arc of tents to his left. "At the end of this row are the Luddites. You see that shack of plywood and silk banners?"

Cape nodded. "Luddites."

The old man shook his head. "Got their name from the 19th century movement against technology—folks that smashed the factory machines to protest the industrial revolution. Bunch of phonies, you ask me."

"How's that?"

"They're rich wankers from Silicon Valley, geeks from the tech capitol of the world."

"Maybe they're being ironic."

"Not likely. They make their millions on stock options, then come out here to get high and hit on college girls from Berkeley."

"How about the mud men?"

"Sure. Turn left at the end of the row, walk into the maze and take your second right. Go all the way to the end—the mud people are out on the rim."

If a three-ring circus had sex with a Renaissance festival and then ingested large quantities of psychotropic drugs during its pregnancy, it might give birth to Burning Man. By the time Cape passed the first dozen encampments he wasn't sure what was real or what he was imagining.

He passed a family of four on stilts, a boy around fifteen and a daughter who looked slightly older, their bodies painted with lurid colors, faces covered with animal masks. A band of women wearing nothing but grass skirts, their nipples painted to look like eyes, navels turned into gaping mouths. Plenty of people in shorts and tank tops, and just as many wandering around naked, their bodies encrusted with dust. As with most nude beaches, the people who walked around stark naked were the ones you most wanted to see fully clothed.

Art was everywhere. Wooden platforms filled spaces between the tents and trailers, some more than twenty feet high. Giant birds and pterodactyls made of wire. A six-armed Shiva with glowing eyes, blue lights running down her animatronic arms. In the distance Cape saw a ferris wheel, and somewhere to his left must have been a trampoline, because a man wearing a horned helmet and wings was soaring into the air at regular intervals.

Cape considered going back to the truck for water. He could taste the dust in the back of his throat as he walked, his shadow stretched before him like a scarecrow twice his size.

When he came to the end of the row, it was clear where he was headed. Nearly a dozen tents clustered around three large mounds of earth that reminded Cape of igloos. Built from the desert floor, each was roughly ten feet in diameter, crude rectangular doors cut into them. As Cape came within ten feet of the closest mound, a man emerged holding a wooden spear and wearing a mask. A brown and gray bodysuit covered everything else except the man's feet, upon which he wore a pair of Teva sandals. The mask was made entirely of mud, a fierce expression carved into its rounded surface.

"Hargabufargas?" The voice was a distorted booming behind the mask.

"Sorry?" Cape contemplated trying another igloo, but he was hesitant to turn his back on the spear.

"Wagafusardus!" The mud face looked pissed, its angry eyebrows deep gashes in the mask, the mouth a jagged line. The spear moved up and down ominously.

Cape spread his hands, open-palmed. "I come in peace."

The mud man spun the spear around in one fluid motion, bringing it over his head with the tip pointing down. Cape was trying to decide whether to lunge sideways or try for a kick to the groin when the warrior thrust the spear into the desert floor between them. His hands now free, he reached up and lifted the heavy mask from his head.

"What do you want?" His voice sounded small without the echo. Black hair tangled with sweat topped a long, narrow face that began with a high forehead and ended in a close-cropped goatee.

"Must get hot in there."

"You must be the detective."

Cape shrugged. "Is Rebecc—I mean Hera—she around?"

The man nodded, sweat running into his eyes. He jabbed a thumb to the right. "Hut number one."

Cape strode to the first hut on the left and ducked inside the door.

"You came!"

Cape blinked against the darkness but couldn't see Rebecca, or anything else. Even with dusk on the horizon, the glare outside had been absolute. He sensed movement and felt Rebecca's arms wrap around him, then release before the blackness turned to spots and then resolved to recognizable shapes within the shadows.

The temperature was the first sensation, the surprising cool. Looking around Cape saw that the walls were actually nylon. They were inside a camping tent covered with mud made from the desert floor. Fiberglass poles placed at regular intervals added support.

Rebecca stood three feet away, wearing a skin-tight bodysuit like the mud warrior outside, only on her it looked a lot better. She seemed to be staring at Cape's shirt.

"Oops."

Cape looked down and saw that his shirt was stained with mud, one streak running down his side onto his shorts. He looked back at Rebecca and noticed corresponding gaps on her suit, revealing bare skin underneath. She shifted her weight and another clump broke off her right thigh, and Cape realized she wasn't wearing a leotard after all. She was completely naked, painted with dust from the playa.

This was going to be a lot harder than he thought.

Cape glanced over his shoulder toward the rectangle of light behind him. "How about we go for a walk?" He didn't wait for an answer, just turned and stepped outside, putting his sunglasses back on. Cape mentally kicked himself. *She's a client—not your ex-girlfriend, and not a damsel in distress.*

They had only spoken of the deaths in Mexico over the telephone, then she'd come out here to run away from it all. True, she invited him out here, but seeing Cape and dealing with reality were two different things, one an uninvited guest. So he shouldn't have been surprised when she started running away from him.

Rebecca brushed past him and strode purposefully across the cracked earth. She headed toward the center of the semi-circle, chunks of clay popping off her thighs and calves.

A client. Cape picked up his pace. *Not a mirage.*

She navigated her way through milling throngs, people in costume all facing in the same direction. Cape lost sight of her, then pushed through into a small clearing between a group dressed like elves and a smaller bunch of robots. And looming over them, stark against the darkening sky, was the Burning Man himself.

A skeletal figure of wood and glass, it stood on a platform that elevated its height to over sixty feet. The head was squared off, tapering toward a flat chin. Arms that seemed too long for the body, exposed ribs covered in neon and fluorescent lights. It looked ominous in the half-light, a warning of the coming apocalypse. Cape heard drums in the near distance, and speakers blared to life all over the camp. People cheered.

Rebecca stopped and turned, all the sadness of the world etched into her face. Cape took her right hand in his and didn't say a word as shadows pooled between their feet like blood. Twilight had come to die in the desert.

A thunderous roar as thirty thousand people cried out as one. Light coursed across the giant's frame, neon lightning. Blue and white flashed outward in all directions, flickering with a manic energy that made the giant appear to move.

Someone at the base of the tower lit a torch and held it against the gasoline-soaked legs of the wooden effigy just as the sun ran for cover.

Flames ran up the sides of the figure with liquid grace. Fluorescent light bulbs exploded from the heat, sending sparks into the night sky, where they disappeared like yesterday's plans.

The burning man was consumed in less time than it takes to think twice. People were cheering, hugging and kissing—*Auld Lang Syne* of the damned. Cape looked at Rebecca and saw her face streaked with tears, their tracks running down her chin, neck, and across her chest. Their eyes met and she pulled him close, sobbing convulsively as her head hit his shoulder.

A woman with orange dreadlocks standing a few feet away took notice and smiled sympathetically, gesturing at the crumbling tower and the dying embers of the burning man.

"Shame it all has to end."

Cape didn't respond, just held on as Rebecca cried away every memory of her brother and father, every regret, missed opportunity, bitter word and forgotten moment. The crowd had dissipated along with the smoke from the fire by the time Rebecca raised her head to look at him.

"Let's talk."

Chapter Twenty-nine

Priest sat in the last pew and bided his time.

About a dozen of the faithful were taking the body of Christ into their mouths, Father Connolly placing the wafers on tongues with fastidious care and exaggerated gestures designed to impress the entire congregation. It reminded Priest of the time when he was fifteen and he bathed the wafers at his local church in LSD. That was a sermon to be remembered.

Connolly blathered on for another ten minutes before cutting loose his flock. Mothers and children, fathers and friends passed Priest on their way to the front door, never realizing there was a wolf in their midst. A handful stayed behind, people waiting their turn for the confessional. Priest remained in the back row while the other parishioners stood or sat a respectful distance away from the twin booths.

It was another thirty minutes before Priest stepped up to the confessional. He stood for a moment outside the priest's side of the booth, then looked around the church, checking to be sure he and Father Connolly were alone before slipping into the parishioner's side.

Priest leaned back against the wall and sighed, head tilted toward the checkered screen. He could discern movement and shadows, but Father Connolly's face was all but invisible.

"I have sinned, Father."

"God forgives you."

"I sincerely doubt it."

Connolly's reply was soft but insistent. "God's mercy is infinite."

"You can't be serious."

"It is a very serious matter." Connolly tried to sound stern but compassionate. "I am merely a vessel for God. Pretend you are speaking to Him, and your sins will be forgiven."

"Just like that?"

Connolly hesitated. "You must be genuinely sorry and resolve to make amends."

"There's always a catch, isn't there?"

Connolly took a deep breath. "You came here for a reason— you must be looking for some kind of absolution."

"Actually, I just wanted an audience." Priest leaned closer to the screen and lowered his voice. "I'm trying out some new material."

"What?" Connolly's voice was sharp.

"Is the Seal of the Confessional something you consider sacred?"

A long moment passed before Connolly replied. Clearly he was weighing his options, but he took the question seriously.

"Yes, it is a priest's most sacred trust. Whatever is said—"

"Good, because you know what happens to a priest that violates that trust?"

"Well, there is censure, even excommunic—"

"No, no, no." Priest's voice echoed around the booth, the sound revealing how claustrophobic the space could feel. "Would you like me to tell you what *will* happen, or would you rather use your imagination?"

Sudden movement on the other side of the screen, followed by the rattle of a door handle. Priest listened to the sound for several seconds before saying anything.

"It's locked from the outside."

The rattling stopped. Priest could sense Connolly shifting on his seat, his breathing more audible now. "What...what do you want?"

"I want you to listen to me, Father. Do you think you can do that? I want you to listen very closely."

Priest didn't wait for an answer to begin his narrative. After a few minutes he saw the shadow of Connolly's head tilt forward as if in prayer, and not long after that he heard the muffled sobs of a brave man losing his faith one word at a time.

Chapter Thirty

"I loved my father."

Back inside the mud-covered tent, Cape was thankful for the subdued lighting. A single candle sputtered on a crate that sat between them. Rebecca obviously didn't feel the need to put anything on, and their outdoor embrace had dislodged more clumps of earth from her body. Cape knew that maintaining eye contact was going to put his unyielding professionalism to the test.

"No, that's not right." Rebecca took a deep breath. "*Worshipped* is more like it. All through school I bragged to my friends what a great man he was, how he was going to change the world. Their fathers might be doctors or lawyers, but mine was a city official."

"So what happened?"

"I got caught smoking pot at the end of my sophomore year."

"You and every other teenager in San Francisco."

"Yeah, but I got my picture in the paper."

Cape shrugged. "Embarrassing—but big deal."

"When your Dad is about to make a move from the city council to the state senate, you'd be amazed what a big deal it is. So I got shipped to boarding school to start a new life."

"With a new name—your mother's maiden name?"

Rebecca nodded. "Lowry—I wasn't good enough to be a *Dobbins* anymore."

"That's a bit harsh."

"My mother insisted they just wanted me to grow up some-where away from politics, out from under Dad's shadow. They had seen too many other politicians' kids get blinded by the glare of publicity. This was my chance to have a normal life."

"OK," said Cape, thinking that it didn't sound OK at all.

"But I didn't want a normal life. I wanted a life with my *fath*—with my family."

"So you didn't have any contact with your parents?"

"Oh no, I saw my Mom every month. She was wonderful. Told me that my father sent his love, but that it was better for me if we didn't see each other."

"Better how?"

"I refused to even talk about him." In the dark of the earthen tent, Rebecca hugged herself. "I know that hurt her deeply, but I never forgave him for sending me away."

Cape waited, watching her expression change in the shifting candlelight.

"One month my Mom didn't show up. A week later I got a call from my brother, telling me she was in the hospital."

"Why?"

"Ovarian cancer," said Rebecca. "She died two months later."

Cape listened to the sound of his own breathing.

"Dad and I didn't speak at the funeral. There was really nothing left to say."

"And your brother?"

Rebecca hesitated. "Danny got away with things."

"Such as?"

"Drinking. Smoking pot. You name it—all the things I wasn't allowed to do."

"That's quite a double-standard."

"He was the first-born son," said Rebecca without rancor. "And I was...I was just a girl. Even the press has different stan-dards for the daughter of a public figure. The boys get to run wild."

"But you stayed in touch."

"It wasn't Danny's fault my Dad played favorites." Rebecca paused. "But I think Danny took advantage, maybe even rebelled on my behalf."

"What do you mean?"

"He was always pushing the limits. I think maybe he got into something illegal."

"Why?"

"Danny never gave me details, but he was always talking about money—he'd say something big was coming down the road—bullshit like that. I never paid any attention. Danny was a big drunk-dialer, calling me after he went drinking with friends."

"But you don't know what he was into, who he worked for, any of it."

Rebecca shook her head. "That's why I wrote to my Dad. I should have just picked up the phone, but I didn't…I wasn't ready for the conversation."

Something that had been gnawing at the back of Cape's skull finally broke through.

"When did you send the letter?"

"The week before-last."

"The week before he disappeared." Saying it aloud, Cape couldn't believe he hadn't focused on it earlier.

"I never heard back from him." Rebecca frowned as the candle sputtered. It was down to the last inch of life. "He had already gone looking for Danny."

"How do you know?"

"I guess I don't." Only Rebecca's left eye remained visible, her body a dark contour against the indigo wall of the tent.

The candle hissed in protest as the flame was extinguished by the pool of wax. Nobody moved to light another.

Cape didn't mind. He was getting used to being in the dark.

Chapter Thirty-one

Joey DeLuca hated lawyers.

Most lawyers, anyway. Not public defenders, they were alright. And the expensive criminal lawyers who defended Joey from time to time, they didn't suck either. The lawyer that helped Joey through his divorce—she was OK, too—at least until he hit on her and the bitch turned on him.

But corporate lawyers were the worst. If you have to be a lawyer, have enough self-respect to work in a courtroom. Get your hands dirty. Don't go to law school for three years just to work in some random company with casual Fridays. A lawyer who wears a fucking polo shirt to work just because it's Friday has got no self-respect.

Joey was big on respect, even though he was only a bag man. Couldn't stand that expression, though—*bag man*. Showed a lack of respect for a very important job. He hated being called a bag man more than anything, even lawyers. If the Feds swooped in, he took the fall. A noble sacrifice for the good of the family. A role like that deserved a title, a little dignity.

Joey liked to think of himself as a courier. *Courier*—like a French diplomat.

A turn-of-the-century gentleman, only without the fag clothes.

Business cards, that's what he needed. Nobody dissed a guy with business cards.

Joey DeLuca

Professional Courier

As he rode the elevator to the 34th floor of the Delta Energy building, Joey made a mental note to order the cards as soon as he got home.

As a twenty-something personal assistant ushered Joey into the corner office, he looked past the huge desk at the view of the bay. You could see the congestion along the Embarcadero and Bay Bridge, rush hour taillights moving like red corpuscles toward the heart of the city. It was a view you could stare at forever and never get bored.

And that's exactly what the lawyer was doing, big leather chair turned away from the desk. His back to the door, totally oblivious to anyone coming up behind him. Unbelievable.

As the assistant left the room she pulled the door shut, making enough noise for the lawyer to swivel around in Joey's direction. His round face was unperturbed, gray hair falling across a pale forehead above gold-rimmed glasses. Watery blue eyes. On one wrist a Rolex, on the other a gold bracelet. A red and white polo shirt, the tensile strength of the fabric tested by a gut that spilled precariously over his belt.

Looking at the man's shirt Joey wrinkled his brow as he realized what day it was. Casual-fucking-Friday here at Delta Energy. He was about to say something when the lawyer called out in greeting.

"Ah, the bag man!"

Joey's jaw clenched. "How you doing," he managed in his best courier voice. A few years ago Joey would turn a nimrod like this into cat food, but not anymore. After eleven guys got nailed in a high-profile RICO operation a few years back, the mantra of the mob was *low profile*. No more Gotti-style nights on the town with two girls on your arm. No more box seats at the Giants games. Stick to the private clubs, the family restaurants. Keep your head down and mouth shut.

And the key to it all was sitting in front of Joey. Corporate lawyers, working for big companies interested in diversifying their portfolios, hedging their risk. Joey's employers provided investment opportunities, and in exchange their own money came back to them with interest, clean as a virgin's snatch.

"Show me yours and I'll show you mine." The lawyer was breathless, like this was some kind of game.

Joey wanted to scream but instead pulled a folded piece of paper from his right jacket pocket.

The lawyer scanned the list greedily. To a casual observer it would be gibberish, a series of letters in the left margin with numbers running across in rows, each spaced at regular intervals. No names, only acronyms, and no dollar signs or decimal points. When he looked up, his face was covered with a bright sheen of sweat.

"Looks like we had a good month."

Joey shrugged. "I guess so."

"My turn." The lawyer proffered a plain brown envelope, his right hand leaving a sweat stain on the paper. These face-to-face meetings didn't seem necessary—they could have arranged a drop or sent an encrypted email—but Joey was beginning to think this was almost sexual for the guy, a cheap thrill he could tell his wife about later. *I got to talk shit to the mob today.*

"Thanks. Mind if I use the men's before I head out?" Joey didn't wait for an answer and the lawyer didn't stop him. The guy was probably going to beat off as soon as Joey left his office.

Joey checked the stalls before washing the lawyer's sweat off his hands. Then he locked himself into the handicap stall and dropped his pants. Taking the envelope from his jacket pocket and a roll of athletic tape from his pants pocket, he carefully bent the envelope under his crotch and secured it. There were some places even the toughest cops wouldn't look during a frisk.

When he was sure he could move without dislodging the tape from his thighs, Joey pulled up his pants and walked calmly to the elevator, pressing the button for the garage.

The garage was half full of cars but no one seemed to be around. The attendant's booth was down one level, out of sight and earshot from where Joey had parked his black BMW. He thumbed the key and heard the soft click of the door locks just before he noticed the shadowy figure standing on the far side of the hood.

"How punctual you are, Joseph."

Joey reflexively started reaching for his piece but stopped when he caught a glimpse of silver in the darkness. Nothing got you killed faster than reaching when the other guy already had his gun drawn. Joey extended both hands from his sides, squaring off to face the voice.

"Who the hell are you?"

The silver flashed again and Joey flinched involuntarily. "I doubt Hell has anything to do with it." The figure moved, coming around the back of the car. Joey saw the white hair first, then a gaunt face with a high forehead. Eyebrows like the old wizard in that Disney movie, the one where Mickey fucks up and makes all the broomsticks flood the castle.

Below the cruel mouth and tapered chin Joey noticed the priest's collar, the silver crucifix reflecting the fluorescent light from the ceiling back into Joey's eyes. By the time he connected the dots and realized it wasn't a gun, it was too late. Priest was standing directly in front of him, looking meaningfully at the left side of Joey's jacket.

"Firearms are *soooo* barbaric." Priest stroked the length of the crucifix absently as he took a step closer. Joey would have to take a step back if he wanted to draw. He wouldn't call himself religious but he went to mass and wasn't in any hurry to gun down a priest.

"The fuck are you?"

Priest smiled. "How rude of me. I work for your employers, Joseph."

"Frank?"

Priest shook his head. "The men who pay Frank pay me."

Joey concentrated on breathing through his mouth. The man in front of him oozed malevolence like an open sore, and Joey could smell his breath. He tried to give Priest a look, the classic hardcase stare, but he couldn't hold it.

"I work for Frank."

"Such loyalty," said Priest, "is to be rewarded. But something has come up, Joseph. Actually, something has floated to the surface, and it could be connected back to your precious boss, Frank."

Joey resisted the urge to cry for help out. He listened intently, hoping for the sound of a passing car.

"So I'm here to make sure nothing ties us to this unsavory business." Priest leaned forward, his mouth opening slightly, just enough for Joey to see the points of his teeth. "I'm sure you can appreciate that, being a *bag man*."

The words sucked him in, and Joey looked at Priest, now standing as close as a lover. He stared directly into those lifeless gray eyes and found he couldn't look away. Joey felt vertigo take hold, his world turning gray, until he glimpsed a flash of silver in the corner of his eye and felt the knife enter his chest.

He looked down and saw the top of the crucifix buried to the hilt just below his ribcage, Priest holding the bottom loosely in his left hand, a silver scabbard for a three-inch blade. Just long enough to penetrate the heart, if you got close enough to the victim.

As Joey's heart seized and his vision blurred, his last thought was how much he hated that expression, *bag man*. It really pissed him off when someone called him that.

Chapter Thirty-two

Cape was barely visible behind his stack of pancakes. It made him feel safe.

Police Inspector Beauregard Jones tossed his newspaper onto an empty chair, then waited until the waitress departed before saying anything.

"You might explode, you finish them off."

"You're one to talk." Cape gestured at an entanglement of bacon the size of a football. It filled one of two plates sitting in front of Beau, the other covered with scrambled eggs.

"Protein. There's a difference. Nobody ever died from eating too much protein."

"Uh-huh." Cape took a forkful of syrup-laden starch and let it work its magic before nodding toward the discarded newspaper. The cover story was about the city council's decision to ban plastic bags from all supermarkets.

"So it's against the law in San Francisco to bag groceries in anything but paper?"

"Your tax dollars at work." Beau selected a strip of bacon and bit it in half. "Like the smoking ban, only for plastic. Supposed to be good for the environment."

"You worried about global warming?"

Beau switched to eggs and scooped a mouthful onto his fork before saying anything. "Found a dead prostitute last week."

Cape drank some water.

"Her pimp beat her to death with a tire iron. Found her in the trunk of his car." Beau reached for his coffee. "She was fourteen."

Cape studied his friend.

Beau shrugged. "Me, I'd love to be worried about global warming."

Cape went back to his pancakes. He had a recycling bin at home, but he didn't really know where it went after it got picked up every week, or what happened to the cans he threw inside. He walked to his office when it was sunny, drove when it rained, but he never gave it much thought.

"Why you ask?"

Cape shook his head and kept chewing. He'd been trying to climb inside the head of the Senator but couldn't find a foothold. Find a man's passions and you could usually find the man.

The Senator didn't seem to care about his family, at least not in the traditional sense, so Cape wondered what he did care about. He claimed to care about the environment, and that helped him get elected. And then re-elected.

Cape thought about Linda, her undercurrent of anger. For a lot of people, turning the city green had become a crusade, not just a personal choice. Sometimes crusades got bloody.

"You stopped eating." Beau seemed to take it personally.

Cape looked up from his plate. "Sorry."

"You look tan."

"Was that a question?"

"Just an observation." Beau dapped the corner of his mouth with a napkin, a surprisingly dainty gesture for a man who weighed almost two hundred and fifty pounds. "Figured you'd be asking the questions, since you invited me to breakfast."

"I've been in Mexico."

"Nice."

"Anything can happen there."

"What did happen there?"

"Long story—you still have friends at the DEA?"

Beau shrugged. "More like *colleagues* than friends, but yeah." He paused to sip his coffee, watching Cape over the rim of the cup. "Why?"

"Ever hear of Antonio Salinas?"

Beau almost spit his coffee across the table. "That man produces half the pot smoked in California, including the legal shit people use for their glaucoma."

"I want to know more about his operation."

"My turn to ask questions." Beau straightened in his chair, eggs and bacon momentarily forgotten. "Why do you want to know about Salinas?"

Cape poured more syrup on his pancakes before answering.

"I'm working for him."

Beau gave a half-lidded stare, a cop look, until Cape finished chewing. Then he sat back and waited until Cape told him about his trip.

"You're on your own on this one."

Cape nodded. "I figured."

"I can't step across the bridge to Oakland without an invitation from another cop, let alone start making calls to Mexico. But you want my advice?"

"Always."

"Tear up your passport and never go back."

"You should see the pool at this hotel."

"Swimming's for pussies," said Beau. "And Salinas is a bad man."

"Where does his product go?"

"Ah, now that's interesting," said Beau. "We're talking marijuana, lots of it. Salinas is old school, with close ties to the mob. That means he gets paid up front and then walks away— moving the drugs is somebody else's problem, but it's also an opportunity."

"Because that somebody gets to mark up the price."

"Big time."

"And you know who that somebody is, don't you?"

Beau shrugged. "Can't prove it, but my money's on Fat Frank."

"You've had a hard-on for Frank Alessi ever since I met you."

"Cops and robbers ain't supposed to get along." Beau stretched, his arms brushing the edge of the lamp hanging over their table. "Frank's the local mob boss, and every beat cop knows it. He's the only one with an organization that could move that much grass. The gangs in the Mission are too small."

"But you can't prove it."

Beau shook his head. "Man's a civic leader. Real estate magnate, friend of the mayor." He paused and gave Cape a sympathetic look. "This helping?"

"Not at all." Cape looked out the window of the restaurant, cars cutting across the view of the abandoned piers on the far side of the street. "What about Freddie Wang?"

"Chinese mostly deal in smack."

"Doesn't he do business with Frank?"

"If you're asking if Freddie's connected, the answer's yes. But connected doesn't necessarily mean involved."

"Got it."

"You're grasping at straws, aren't you?"

"Now you're being optimistic." Cape tried to force a smile but couldn't quite pull it off. "But call me if you think of anything."

"Cool." Beau stood to leave. "But maybe you should think about what I said."

Cape looked at his friend but said nothing.

"You got paid to find some people, and you found them," said Beau. "Not your fault they wound up dead. It's over."

"I don't think so." Cape shook his head. "I think it's just getting started."

Chapter Thirty-three

Sally was dressing to kill.

She stood alone in a small bedroom chamber, the moon visible through a skylight. Through the open door behind her was a large open space with hardwood floors, the walls adorned with racks of arcane weapons. Wooden swords, *yari* spears with double-edged blades, a *masakari* hand axe, a bow alongside a quiver full of arrows.

She arched her back and zipped herself into a long-sleeved dress embroidered with gold thread. In front of her stood a wide dresser with a mirror and lamp, assorted sundries and makeup. Some of the items were familiar to a woman's bedroom, others looked like costume makeup, wigs and face-paint more typical of the theater.

Sally carefully selected two hairpins from an ornate tray, then dipped them one at a time into an old inkwell. The razor tips came out dripping, glinting in the reflected light from the mirror. She waited until each dried, then inserted them carefully into her thick black hair. Finally she took four metal darts the size and shape of collar stays and inserted two in each sleeve before adjusting her cuffs.

Taking one last look in the mirror before bringing her hands together at her breast, Sally wrapped her left hand around her right fist. The *crack* of her knuckles broke the silence as Sally smiled.

Time to paint the town red.

Chapter Thirty-four

"This guy had big feet."

Beau looked from his partner to the legs sticking out of the dumpster. The right shoe was missing, revealing a gold-toe sock, but the left foot still bore a size-twelve black loafer. The rest of the body was out of sight. Beau returned his gaze to Vincent Mango, all five-six of him leaning over the edge of the receptacle with a penlight.

"What are you goin on about?"

Vincent clicked off the pen light and returned it to his jacket pocket. His suit was pearl gray, double-breasted, and immaculate.

"Driver's license says the guy is five-ten."

Beau nodded but didn't say anything. It was too early and the gallon of coffee he'd drunk on the way wasn't working.

"So a twelve is a pretty big shoe," said Vincent. "For a guy his size."

"You're sayin he's got a big cock."

A nearby uniform snickered until Vincent gave him a warning glance. "I'm not saying anything about his cock, I just—"

"Wanna take a look?" Beau raised his eyebrows.

"Fuck you." Vincent extended a hand and the uniform handed him the license, trapped inside a glycine bag. He tossed it to Beau in a spinning arc. "Recognize him?"

Beau held the license at arm's length until his eyes focused. "Joey DeLuca." He whistled, long and low. "Part of Frank Alessi's crew."

Vincent nodded. "Turf war?"

Beau shook his head. "This is nobody's turf." He looked around the parking garage. "Where are we again?"

"Market and First." Vincent shook his head. "You need more coffee."

"I *know* the address...name of the building?"

"Delta Energy."

Beau tossed the license back to the uniform, who caught it one-handed. "I wonder what brings a bag man to an energy company."

"Strange," said Vincent.

Beau nodded and frowned at the legs tangled up with the trash.

"Very strange."

Chapter Thirty-five

Freddie Wang reluctantly agreed to leave the restaurant for a hand job.

Few professional gangsters had survived public scrutiny for so long. Chinatown was unforgiving and San Francisco was a small town. Enemies on both sides of the law had been biding their time for years, waiting for Freddie to slip up.

He almost never left the restaurant that doubled as his office, and he never left Chinatown.

The first bodyguard poked his head out the front door, signaling to the second bodyguard that all was clear inside. The door was almost as old as Freddie, a carved wooden facade adorned with the Chinese characters *Triple Delight*, a popular menu item at a neighboring restaurant and a specialty at the brothel involving three girls at once.

Once inside Freddie was met by a fawning Madame who must've had a good ten years on Freddie. She ushered him down a long hall lined with antiques to a private room filled with furniture dating from the 18th century. Freddie was starting to feel young by comparison until he saw the girl standing next to the massage table.

She couldn't have been more than eighteen, assuming she was even legal. She bowed her head and lowered her eyes, giving Freddie a chance to look her over. She wore a plain white two-piece swimsuit, modest by bikini standards but showing plenty of skin.

The first bodyguard, a heavyset man named Park, stayed inside with Freddie and took a seat by the window, which was open just a crack to allow a gentle breeze into the small room. Park had the foresight to bring a newspaper so he wouldn't have to look at Freddie. The second bodyguard had won the coin toss and returned to the car.

Freddie turned away from the girl and unceremoniously started taking off his clothes, tossing them onto a nearby chair. The chair had taloned feet at the end of its legs and a phoenix motif on its back that took almost two years to carve.

Freddie didn't give a shit. He just wanted a hand job.

Freddie had never been an attractive man, and age had only exacerbated the situation. His left eye was droopy and faint, his right black as onyx and twice as hard. Three hairs sprouted from a prominent mole on his cheek, which some Chinese believed to be good luck.

Freddie must have been the luckiest man in Chinatown, because the removal of his shirt revealed a forest of moles and an explosion of hairs on his back that defied counting. Skin hung off his hunched shoulders in folds as thin as rice paper, a riot of blue veins clearly visible. Freddie smiled inwardly as he sensed the young girl behind him shudder before regaining her composure.

Freddie sighed as the girl's hands touched his back, warm and slick with lotion. He heard Park shift in the seat as he opened his newspaper. Freddie took a deep breath and closed his eyes.

Thud.

Freddie might have dozed off, he couldn't be sure. It happened more often these days, more than he cared to admit. Something jarred him awake, the sound of something falling. Maybe the girl dropped the bottle of lotion. She had stopped rubbing his shoulders. That could only mean one thing. It was time for his happy ending.

Freddie got his arms underneath him, grunting from the effort. He felt the breeze from the window across his back, much cooler than when he first lay down. He called out to Park as he got himself up on one arm and began to turn over.

"Shut that window and go wait in the hall. Time for my happy ending."

Park didn't answer.

Freddie completed his turn and froze, his sunken chest bare, his crotch barely covered by a towel. He couldn't have been more vulnerable.

The girl was gone, and Park was sprawled unconscious on the floor, a livid scratch on his neck. Standing over him was Sally, stretching seductively as she replaced an ornate hair pin.

"Sorry, Freddie, but I don't believe in happy endings."

Chapter Thirty-six

"I brought you a present."

Beau eyed the pastries as he spoke, a mixed assortment of starch, sugar, and chocolate glowing like precious gems under the flourescent lights. Peet's was known for having the best coffee in town, and their pastries were second to none.

Cape gestured at the case. "Go ahead."

"Nah, I got a sour stomach. Up all night looking through garbage."

"You sure?"

"Fuck it." Beau pointed at the glass and smiled at the young woman behind the register. "Two of those, one of those, and…" He looked over his shoulder at Cape, who nodded. "Two of those. And a large black coffee and an iced tea."

They took a table near the window. Foot traffic was light but constant, people moving through the Embarcadero Center on their way back to work, running errands, searching for an ATM.

Cape took a bite of a chocolate croissant. It wasn't a pancake but it had the desired effect. "You said you had a present."

Beau nodded. "A dead body."

"You shouldn't have. Anybody we know?"

"Nobody you know, but he was somebody who worked for somebody you know." Beau tossed an inter-office envelope on the small table and watched as Cape removed a color copy of Joey DeLuca's driver's license, along with another sheet of paper.

"Found him in the garbage—bag man for Frank Alessi. Picked up his dry cleaning, picked up cash from extortion rackets, that sort of thing."

Cape looked at the second sheet, a jumbled list of letters and numbers. "What's this?"

"That's now officially the property of the Feds," said Beau. "Had to give them a copy."

"Which means this might be a smoking gun?"

Beau nodded. "You find a list of numbers like that on a wiseguy, five will get you ten it's some kind of ledger. The hardest part about being a gangster these days is hiding the money. The rest—stealing, threatening people, destroying lives—that part's easy."

"I can keep this."

"Made you a copy. You still work with that computer hacker?"

Cape nodded. "Sloth—and he prefers to be called a programmer."

"Whatever." Beau made a muffin disappear. "He makes sense of that, you can call him the King of Siam. But I got something else."

"Aren't you generous today."

"Frustrated. I got a dead body but shitty forensics. Guy was killed with some kind of knife but no signs of a struggle. The lawyer he visited looks clean but isn't talking, which means he's anything but—I'm not holding my breath on a warrant. Now the Feds want to drive because there might be a money trail. I know Fat Frank is sitting at the end of it, but I don't have permission to rattle his cage."

"I'm always up for a good cage-rattling, but I just want to know what a dead Senator has to do with a Mexican drug lord."

"Can't help you with the Senator, but I found something on his son."

Cape stopped chewing, a supreme act of will.

Beau nodded. "Remember how you told me Danny had a low profile?"

"Just the one arrest."

"The only one that made the papers."

"There were more?"

"Eight arrests, no convinctions. All petty offenses, all tied to narcotics."

Cape shifted in his seat. "Why didn't—"

"—you find anything?" Beau raised his eyebrows. "I should have been able to get the lowdown on Danny with a few keystrokes on my computer, which is how I started. But nothing came up, not even the arrest you read about in the newspaper."

"Does that me—"

Beau held up a hand for patience. "So I dug around, and *low and behold*, Danny got himself into trouble on more than one occasion, but he had a good lawyer. A very expensive lawyer."

"And a Dad who's a State Senator."

"Wanna know who his lawyer was?"

"Sure."

"Bernard Rhonbarr—a corporate lawyer, not a criminal lawyer."

"How come?"

"You have a criminal lawyer, everyone thinks you're a criminal." Beau laid his hands flat on the table. "But the best part is that Bernie Rhonbarr has a day job—he just does some extracurricular legal work on the side."

"For Senator's sons."

"And someone else." Beau looked like the cat that ate the canary. "Frank Alessi."

"You're kidding."

Beau nodded. "And you know where Bernie works?"

Cape glanced at the driver's license of the dead man. "No way."

"Yep…Bernie's the very same lawyer that our dead bag man was visiting."

"That's quite a coincidence."

"But not probable cause," said Beau. "So no warrant, not that I'd expect to find anything in Bernie's office. But you gotta admit, it smells pretty bad."

"Maybe I should call Bernie, try to get an appointment."

"Good luck, he ain't talkin to us."

"Why would a made guy like Frank pay his lawyer to bail out Danny?"

"Leverage."

"Has to be." Cape nodded as he resumed chewing. "Frank wanted leverage on the Senator."

"I'd say he had it."

"Doesn't get me to Mexico, but it might get me to North Beach." Cape brushed crumbs off the table. All the pastries had been decimated. "Maybe I should think about visiting Frank."

"Wonder where you got that idea?"

"Easy," said Cape. "You just gave it to me."

Chapter Thirty-seven

Sloth lived across from Golden Gate Park, with a view of eucalyptus trees and cherry blossoms that he never enjoyed.

He spent all his waking moments surrounded by four plasma screens networked to a server as big as a refrigerator. Plagued with a rare neurological disorder that made physical movement painful and slow, Sloth lived through his computers, and the freedom they provided was more precious than any glimpse of nature, tantalizingly close though it might be.

Linda answered the door when Cape arrived. Over the years Linda had become Sloth's voice-box, an avatar for the things he couldn't do himself and interpreter for the things he saw in cyberspace that no one else could understand.

By way of greeting, Cape handed her the page of letters and numbers Beau had given him.

"Present from the SFPD. Crack the code and win a prize."

"Where did it come from?" Linda scanned the sheet before placing it next to Sloth, whose head tilted fractionally to the side, his eyes straining behind his glasses.

"It was taped to the crotch of a dead man."

Linda's hair shivered at the thought. "Sit down."

Cape took the empty chair next to Sloth, squeezing his friend on the shoulder in greeting. The plasma screens flashed as black words appeared in twenty-point type.

This is quite a case.

Cape nodded. "Tell me about it."

Your Senator was getting squeezed.

"He wasn't *my* Senator. How do you know?"

Linda cut in. "Show him, Sloth."

Sloth's right hand twitched, a movement so subtle it seemed involuntary. Beneath each hand was a pressure-sensitive scratch pad calibrated to his range of motion. The screens filled with colored bars and squares—blue, green, red—in a complex pattern that kept shifting as Sloth's thumb shifted back and forth.

Linda kept her distance from the screens but jabbed a finger at the nearest one. "The horizontal axis is chronological, dating back to the Senator's days in the local assembly. The boxes are his voting record on different bills, resolutions, referendums, and such."

"Got it."

"Now watch this."

Sloth must have moved because the screens morphed, blues and reds fusing into purple, green splitting apart into yellow and blue. Linda's hair jiggled with excitement.

"Sloth created a program to predict the Senator's voting record."

Cape frowned. "Based on what?"

"Party affiliation, educational background and alma mater, state of birth, ethnicity, and about ten other demographics, all cross-referenced against two hundred other politicians in our database."

"Geez."

"Exactly. So this program not only shows how the Senator voted on any given issue, it shows how he *should* have voted based on the model. So the areas in here—" Linda waved her right hand in a broad circle, her index finger pointing toward the purple rectangles. "—are anomalies."

"Times when he crossed party lines."

"Or just broke the mold," said Linda. "By themselves these votes wouldn't mean anything. Could be a personal issue for him, or a change of heart. Politicians break ranks all the time."

"So why should I care?"

Because there's a pattern.

Cape looked at Sloth, who was still blinking at the screen. The corner of his mouth spasmed slightly, the closest he ever came to laughing. Sloth loved patterns as much as Cape loved pancakes.

The screen changed again, rows and rows of colored squares multiplying, folding, and scrolling across the screen. Cape felt himself getting dizzy and had to look away. He turned to Linda.

"In English, please."

"Sloth ran the program for every city councilman, senator and local assembly member we had records for, then looked for patterns. We focused the search on bills or referendums involving big money—taxpayer money—construction projects like renovating the Bay Bridge. Tax breaks for local businesses. Pension plans for city employees."

"And?"

"We found at least eight, maybe ten other politicians moving in sequence with Senator Dobbins. Sometimes with him, sometimes voting against, but always following a distinct pattern. Which got us thinking—"

Cape looked back at the screen. "If you bribe one politician, you only get one vote."

Linda nodded. "And after a while, someone's going to notice the politician in your pocket, because he always votes for your pet projects."

"But if you bribe a dozen politicians, you can play them off against each other from one vote to the next. Al Capone used to do the same thing with juries—he'd intimidate as many jurors as he could, just to get the swing vote."

"So your Senator could seem tough on crime with one vote, then soften on the next one, but as long as another congressman flip-flopped at the same time, the end result would be the same." Linda spread her hands and moved her fingers up and down in a parody of a puppeteer. "Now we need to determine who benefits the most from these votes—find out where the money went."

Cape nodded. "Beau thinks all roads lead back to Frank Alessi." He squinted at the dates running along the bottom of the screen. "But I'd love to know some of the legitimate businesses that benefited from these votes. When the tax increase went through for the Bay Bridge, which construction company was awarded the job? For the tax breaks to local business, get me a list of companies. Can you do that?"

"Way ahead of you," said Linda. "But we're not there yet."

"OK." Cape gestured at the sheet of paper he'd brought. "Maybe that'll help."

"One more thing." Linda gave him a mischievous smile. "We figured you'd want to field test our theory."

Cape felt his pulse quicken. "These other politicians are *local?*"

"But not all current," said Linda. "Some of this data is historical. But there's one local assemblyman—still in office—whose voting patterns move in perfect sync with Dobbins."

"Got a name?"

"And an address."

A house number and street appeared on the screens in huge glowing letters.

"It's in Pacific Heights," said Linda.

Cape took a deep breath. He still had no clue where he was headed, but at least he had an address.

Chapter Thirty-eight

Rebecca sat on the bed as she opened the shoebox.

She closed her eyes, took a deep breath and willed them open again. Tears sprang spontaneously from her eyes before she touched the first picture.

Danny when he was fifteen, football helmet under his arm. Danny again, maybe twenty-one, a concert t-shirt and hair longer than a summer day.

Rebecca gasped.

She and Danny together. She remembered that shirt, her Mom had turned it into a pillow when she got older. She couldn't have been more than six, big cheeks pressed against her older brother's chest.

She held the pictures at arms length, let her tears fall onto the bedspread.

The whole family. Mom, Danny, Rebecca and Dad, bathing suits in the backyard, a sprinkler and a slip-'n-slide in the background.

Who had taken the picture?

A single tear landed right on the photograph, obscuring the smile of the little girl she barely recognized as herself. How old had she been—ten, eleven?

There she was again—aged three, sitting in her father's lap, a book open in front of them, her eyes glued to the book, his locked on her.

Rebecca tried to control her breathing, gave up and sobbed until she was dried out. It took a long time. She walked to the kitchen and poured herself a glass of water, stepped into the living room and sat down on the couch.

She had lived by herself almost her whole life but had never felt so alone. Every hour she spent at her Father's house she wanted to flee. Run away to the desert, a friend's apartment, anywhere but here.

But she could control that feeling—she had before and she would now.

She couldn't confront her past in the desert. Her friends couldn't help her. This was something she had to do by herself.

This room felt more like an office than a living room, the walnut desk dominating the wall facing the bay window. Rebecca stood and walked over to the desk, sat in the red leather chair. Ran her hands over the blotter. Took pens from the coffee mug, put them back. After several minutes of touching, lifting, holding, and procrastinating, she started opening the drawers.

Forty-five minute later she had a stack of bills, old checkbooks, and receipts on one side of the desk. A small pile in the center that included a pocketknife, gold ball, rubber bands, and coins from other countries. She would go through the bills later, maybe after she found the strength to look at the rest of the photographs. She pushed the chair back and leaned forward to open the last drawer, the lower right file drawer.

It was locked.

She scanned the pile of stuff on the desk. Scooting off the chair, she ducked under the desk to check the bottom of the main drawer, but no key was taped there. She thought about going back to the bedroom and checking the end table, but first she pulled on the drawer again. It was a simple latch, turned vertically to slide into the bottom of the drawer directly above it.

Rebecca selected a thin letter opener from the coffee mug and jammed it between the drawers. It stuck when she tried to push it down, so she got on her hands and knees again and slid it straight between the drawers. Holding it steady with her right hand, she brought her left across her body and knocked the letter opener sideways.

The latch gave way and the drawer popped open.

Rebecca didn't know what she was expecting. After all, she didn't really know her father. Maybe a bottle of scotch. Perhaps a gun. Thousands of dollars in unmarked bills. But she found none of those things.

What she did find was something that she never would have predicted, not in a million years.

Sitting at the bottom of the drawer was a padded envelope, and written in the unmistakable scrawl of her father's handwriting—writing she remembered from her childhood—was a single name in red ink.

Rebecca.

Chapter Thirty-nine

Cape knew from the Pacific Heights address that Assemblyman Henry Kelley was living well. It was only when he reached the house that he realized how well.

The two-story home occupied half the block, a rust-colored stone exterior with plenty of windows under a Spanish tiled roof. The property sat at the crest of the street, and from where he parked in the circular driveway, Cape could see a backyard sloping away down the hill. The back of the house must have an unobstructed view of the Bay.

In this town, in this neighborhood, ten million would be the starting bid. Cape tried to remember how much he paid in taxes as he walked across the gravel drive to the front door.

A young Mexican woman in a white blouse and gray skirt answered the door.

"Sí, Señor Weathers—Mister Kelley is expecting you." She turned on her heel and walked across the marble foyer down a short hallway to a large living room.

The first impression was of light—the window facing the door was almost eight feet wide. As Cape surmised, it afforded a view over Marina green onto the endless expanse of the Bay, the Golden Gate Bridge just visible on the left.

The backyard was modest but green with new grass. Three boys, all under ten, were laughing and chasing a small terrier that gripped a ball tightly between its teeth.

The room itself was quite dark, leather and oak. A long couch sat to Cape's right, a duck-hunting decoy on the nearest end table. Facing the couch was a fireplace. Above the mantle a matching pair of shotguns were mounted next to a stuffed pheasant. Presumably the taxidermist intended for the bird to be frozen in flight, but its oblong body and the stunned look in its glass eye reminded Cape of an angry football tired of being thrown.

"Magnificent creatures, wouldn't you agree?" Kelley had come through a side door.

"I understand they're quite tasty." Cape took Kelley's extended hand and shook.

Kelley chuckled—a deep, melodic sound that made you feel warm all over. Cape smiled and reclaimed his hand, which took some effort. He had the impression the handshake would have lasted until the next election if he hadn't allowed the assemblyman to win the man-grip contest.

Kelley was a handsome man, past middle age but striking. His gray-blue eyes were set wide, his white hair groomed into thick, rolling waves. Cape had the sudden urge to ask for his autograph. This guy was a natural.

"Thanks for agreeing to see me on such short notice, Mister Kelley."

"Are you a registered voter?" Kelley had a slight accent, not quite Southern but close. It was a style of speech he noticed in politicians before, whether they were from the south, north, west, or even Brooklyn. Rounded vowels and dropped consonants, just down-home enough for a man of the people yet too vague to be associated with any specific region. Part of the modern political landscape—ambiguity in speech to match a lifestyle of misdirection.

"Yes, I'm registered."

"Well then, you can call me Hank." Kelley gestured to a leather chair in front of the sofa. "Your message said you had news about my colleague, Senator Dobbins. I'm afraid I haven't spoken to him in some time."

"He's dead."

"My God." The pupils in Kelley's eyes contracted, then relaxed. "You get right down to it, don't you?"

"Sorry. I don't have a lot of time."

"What happened?"

"I honestly don't know, but he was found on a golf course in Mexico. I expect…my guess is it'll hit the news sometime in the next few days, if not sooner."

"That's horrible." Kelley looked out the window, tracking his sons as they chased the dog.

"You two were close?"

Kelley refocused on Cape. "We were on the same team—politically."

"But you didn't always vote the same."

"No…no, we didn't." Kelley paused. "Even colleagues don't always see eye-to-eye on every issue."

"When's the last time you talked to him?"

"I don't know." Kelley glanced toward the mantle. "Maybe a week before he retired. We talked about—"

Cape cut him off. "Frank Alessi?"

Kelley blinked. "Excuse me?"

"You think Frank had the Senator's son Danny killed?"

Kelley's mouth opened and closed like a carp but no sound came out.

"Or do you think Danny just got caught up in the whole mess?"

Kelley's eyes darted around the room. Cape stared at him and waited.

"I don't know…" He looked out the window. "I have a family."

Cape nodded. "You took a chance seeing me, I guess that's why. You've been scared shitless since Dobbins disappeared and couldn't resist a chance to find out what happened to the poor bastard."

"You don't…I can't just—"

Cape held up a hand. "You didn't seem surprised when I mentioned Dobbins' son was dead, too. You didn't ask how Dobbins died. Whether Frank meant it as a warning or not, I figure you and everybody else on the payroll connected the dots when Dobbins disappeared."

"*I have a family.*" Kelley's voice was barely a whisper.

"How many on the payroll? Besides you and Dobbins."

Kelley didn't answer. His eyes had drifted out of focus.

Cape looked out the window. The oldest boy had retrieved the ball and was running around in circles, his two brothers tripping over each other and giggling as they chased him, the dog yapping at their heels.

Cape didn't care about Kelley, but there were lines he wasn't prepared to cross. The men he was chasing were harder than he was—they wouldn't hesitate to go after Kelley's family. That thought might help him sleep at night, but Cape suddenly realized that was why he could never beat them. No matter how far he pushed, it wouldn't be far enough. They'd push him off a cliff, along with anyone who got in their way.

He was out of his league and over his head.

Cape took one of his cards from his pocket and laid it on the end table. "If you ever need help, call that number."

Kelley looked at the card like it was a poisonous spider, then shifted his gaze back to the window.

Cape stood to leave. He took one last look at the stuffed pheasant, its glass eye reflecting its amazement that Cape was still alive and it was mounted on the wall instead of him.

Chapter Forty

"That's quite a view you've got, Bernie."

Priest paced languidly in front of the window that ran the length of the office. It was almost midnight. Very little traffic on The Embarcadero, barely a whisper through the glass.

Bernie sat at his desk watching his visitor warily, saying nothing. He noticed the moon was huge tonight, a malevolent eye looking over the Bay Bridge.

Priest stood close enough for his nose to touch the glass. "How high up are we?"

"Twenty-fifth floor."

Priest smiled. "But only twenty-four floors."

"What?"

"There isn't a thirteenth floor, Bernie. Look in the elevator, it skips from twelve to fourteen."

"You sure?"

"It's an old tradition in tall buildings—people are superstitious."

"I never noticed."

"Attention to detail. Wouldn't you say that's important in your line of work?"

"What are you implying?" Bernie swiveled in his chair.

"I think we might have made a mistake." Priest spoke without rancor but Bernie tasted bile.

"*We?*"

"All right." Priest turned from the window and leaned back, his open palms against the glass. "I might have made a mistake, Bernie. How's that?"

"Better." Bernie rested his hands on his gut as he tilted his chair back. "But it doesn't solve my problem."

"*Our* problem."

"OK, our problem. The cops are trying to get a warrant."

"You said they would."

"True." Bernie patted his belly. "The cops I can handle, I guess. That's what you pay me for, right?"

Priest ran a tongue across his teeth. "Among other things."

"But now a private investigator is trying to schedule an appointment."

"So?" Priest glanced out the window, tracking a passing car no bigger than a matchbox. "Just refuse to see him—you're a busy man."

"Genius. Why didn't I think of that?"

"Watch your tone, Bernie."

"Blow me, your holiness. The PI is a fucking problem."

"You know him?"

Bernie shook his head. "I hire PI's all the time—every lawyer does—they do all the shit I'm not supposed to do, unless I want to get kicked off the bar. I guarantee this dick will be picking through my garbage before the week is out, maybe even following me."

"So?"

"So!" Bernie almost came out of the chair. "Taking pictures, invading my privacy."

"You have something to hide?" Priest stepped across the carpeted floor and sat on the desk, his legs brushing against Bernie's.

Bernie rolled his eyes. "Save the Dracula routine for somebody missing his gonads. You know damn well what I have to hide."

Priest nodded. "Perhaps I'm not being clear. That's why I came to see you in person, Bernie, to..." He pursed his lips, clearly not liking the taste of the words that were about to come out. "To...to *apologize* for any inconvenience I might have caused you by dispatching poor Joey in your building. It seemed—"

"—like a good idea at the time?"

"Precisely. Tying up loose ends after the Senator's unfortunate demise."

Bernie exhaled slowly. "You said you had some questions—what do you want to know?"

"Are we exposed?"

"No."

"You're positive."

"Absolutely. I've been doing this a long time. I cover my tracks."

"*Our* tracks."

"Yeah, them too." Bernie spun his chair slightly, to force a few inches of separation from his guest. "Every trail the Feds could follow is a dead-end. They can have all the suspicions they want—they have for years—but they won't find any facts."

"Very good." Priest nodded. "I was worried my rash decision had made us vulnerable somehow."

Bernie looked him up and down. "Mind if I ask you a personal question?"

Priest raised his eyebrows and waited.

"You always wear that getup?"

Priest smiled ruefully.

"My father worked in the local rectory. He would do various chores, repairs, errands—that sort of thing. He was a hard worker and…" Priest paused, a faraway look in his eyes. "And a drunkard."

Bernie slid his chair back another foot.

"At night, he would take my brother and me to the basement. Mother had left years ago—run away—but always the basement, never anywhere else in the house. My brother was older, so he went first. Father would push him to his knees as he undid his belt."

Bernie felt sweat break out across his upper lip. *Dumb ques-tion*, he thought. *Remember not to ask about the wardrobe next time.*

"Father said we had to know sin in order to defeat it." Priest slid off the desk and kneeled in front of Bernie. "Watching my brother was almost worse, knowing my turn was next."

Priest reached forward and took Bernie's left hand in his with a grip that was surprisingly gentle but remarkably cold, as if he'd just come in from outside.

"Afterward, all of us crying and ashamed, he'd beat the sin from our bodies. I had so many concussions I can barely remem-ber a day of grade school."

Bernie breathed through his nose and tried not to blink.

"It was during those times, when I was on the verge of losing consciousness, that I came to know God." Priest's eyes welled with tears, then dried suddenly. Bernie wondered where the tears had gone. "When all seemed lost, I found faith. And I realized that God is vengeance, Bernie."

Bernie didn't say anything.

"Vengeance. *He* doesn't reward the weak, he helps the faithful. And the very next day, He was there to help me."

"How?"

"I came home to find father passed out on the couch. He was a drunk, but he never did that, not during the day. It was providence. My brother was playing with friends, so I was alone with the old man. Providence."

Priest chuckled at some private joke.

"A garden trowel did the job nicely. I was sixteen, an age when most of my friends had no clue what to do with their lives, and suddenly my path was clear. I prayed as if I really believed, and a change came over me. I swore to God that I would become his Sword of Damocles and bring judgment and retribution back to the world."

"You're...you're not a priest." Bernie couldn't help himself. "You must know that."

Priest shook his head. "The seminarians didn't see things the way I did—found me over-zealous, can you imagine?"

Bernie didn't comment.

"And that, Bernie, is what brings me here, at your service."

"Sorry, I must have missed something." Bernie tried to retrieve his hand but Priest sat immobile, kneeling on the floor in some parody of supplication.

"I realized then that *all* men are sinners, Bernie. And since God helps those who help themselves, I sought out other men who had the will, the strength of character to exact judgment here on Earth. Men who made their own laws, like our mutual employers. Might does make right—that is God's law—His *only* law."

Priest sat back, his backside resting on his calves. He looked serene, satisfied with the flawless logic of his life's work.

"Right," said Bernie. "So, um…we done here?"

Priest released Bernie's hand and stood, brushed off his slacks. "I have one small problem."

Only one? Bernie kept the thought to himself. "Shoot."

"That paper you gave the bag man. The one with the list of numbers."

"I told you, it's not a problem. Nobody could decipher it."

Priest pursed his lips. "But what if they could?"

"Who cares?" Bernie rolled closer to the desk. "It doesn't prove a thing without corroborating testimony."

"Legally speaking?"

"It's inadmissible."

"*Ahhh.*" Priest brought his fingertips together. "Someone would have to translate the ledger in court."

"Exactly."

"I see." Priest took his seat on top of the desk and looked out the window. The moon had dropped in the sky, bisected by the suspension cables of the bridge. "I still don't think you're seeing the big picture, Bernie."

"I don't follow you."

Priest's eyes glittered with reflected light. "You could translate the ledger."

Bernie lunged sideways off his chair and reached for the bottom-right desk drawer. Priest kicked him in the side of the head.

"*Fuck.*" Bernie clutched the side of his face. "*Fuck, fuck, fuck.*"

Priest calmly kneeled and opened the drawer. A Kimber .45 automatic lay next to a box of ammunition.

"*Tsk-tsk*...they teach you how to use one of these at Harvard Law?"

Bernie scrabbled backward until his head thumped into the window.

Priest took the gun in his right hand and walked calmly to the window, where he used the butt of the pistol to bang against the glass. A hollow *thunk* reverberated around the office.

"Safety glass."

Priest squatted next to Bernie and stroked his cheek with the barrel of the gun. The *click* of the hammer seemed deafening.

"I abhor guns."

Priest stood and took a step back, raised the pistol over Bernie's prostrate form and pulled the trigger.

The window exploded in a spiderweb of cracks centered around a surprisingly small hole. Priest pulled the trigger again.

And again.

Bernie whimpered as Priest dropped the gun onto the carpet. Before he could react, Bernie felt Priest's fingers in his hair, pulling hard. His right ankle was grabbed and he felt himself being lifted off the floor.

The window lunged at him with impossible speed. He felt the glass break apart as it lacerated his face, the sound like icicles falling. A sudden loss of gravity and then distance, an impossible distance between him and the ground.

Cars moved listlessly below, one in particular looking more and more like it might become a bull's-eye. Bernie twisted in midair and saw stars blinking their warnings, a silent Morse code he wished he had noticed before. The moon was overhead, the bridge its constant companion.

Priest had been right. It really was quite a view.

Chapter Forty-one

"How's the view from up there?"

Cape sat on the floor and watched Sally defy gravity. She was balancing on a black nylon rope six feet above the hardwood floor. Her shoes were split between the second and third toe, providing a narrow channel to guide the rope as she moved. She wore calf-length black tights, a long sleeved black sweatshirt, and a blindfold.

"Funny." Sally reached the midpoint of the rope, arms extended, her head cocked to one side.

Cape told her about his visit with Assemblyman Kelley. When he had finished, Sally bent her knees and brushed the rope with her right hand, then straightened, the motion causing the rope to bounce slightly.

She adjusted the blindfold and continued moving forward. "Freddie Wang says he's not involved."

"Isn't that what you'd expect him to say?"

Sally shook her head. "He wasn't lying."

"How do you know?"

"Let's just say I caught him with his pants down."

"OK, another dead-end."

"Not entirely." Sally sprang straight into the air and twisted, the rope vibrating like a piano wire. She landed in a crouch facing the opposite direction, arms out, the rope snapping into place between her toes.

"Nice," said Cape.

"Freddie says that Frank Alessi has a new supplier."

"Not Salinas?"

Sally shook her head, displacing the blindfold slightly. "Freddie thinks Salinas is still doing business with Frank, but there's someone new."

"Maybe Luis Cordon."

"Freddie didn't know, but he said volume is up, street prices are down."

Cape nodded. "Frank drives demand while he plays one supplier against the other, controls his costs."

"Sounds plausible."

"Only Frank would know."

"Why don't you ask him?"

Cape stood. "Why do you think I'm here?"

"Because you missed me." Sally took a long step and launched herself into space, spinning in a tight somersault before opening her arms and landing noiselessly on the hardwood floor. She stripped off the blindfold as Cape clapped lazily, the sound a hollow echo in the open space.

"Free tonight?"

Sally nodded. "Frank's office in North Beach?"

"Not this time." Cape shook his head. "I think Frank's probably jumpy…someone might get hurt."

"Isn't that the point?"

"You're starting to sound like Beau."

"You have a better idea."

Cape smiled. "I know where Frank eats dinner."

Chapter Forty-two

Inspector Garcia held the soccer tickets at arm's length and clucked his tongue reprovingly.

"You surprise me, Ramirez. You are never late."

"I'm not late," snapped Ramirez. "I said tomorrow."

"You said that yesterday."

Ramirez pointed to the lab's wall clock. "It's a quarter to five. I still have fifteen minutes." He pushed his glasses onto his bald head and rubbed his eyes.

"But you didn't call."

Ramirez blinked. "That's because I knew you would come find me. Like you always do."

Garcia frowned. "My wife says I am not a patient man."

"I thought you were divorced."

"Now you know why."

"Fine." Ramirez gestured to an empty chair adjacent to his desk.

Garcia eyed the chair. "Shouldn't this be a short visit? *Yes, the gringo Senator is dead. So is his son.*"

"Yes, the *gringo* Senator is dead, Oscar—so is his son. There is a positive DNA match for both."

"But?" Garcia studied his colleague's expression. Reluctantly he slid the soccer tickets into his breast pocket and sat down.

"There is a third strand of DNA." Ramirez swiveled in his chair and tapped his computer screen.

"The alligator," said Garcia. "We already spoke of this."

"No, a third person. That's why the first two tests were tainted."

"You're sure."

Ramirez nodded. "Three people died in that lake."

"Who?" Garcia could tell there was more.

"That's what I wanted to know, so I worked with the coroner to separate the various samples we had."

"The arms from the legs—"

"—and the hands from the feet—"

"—and we found someone who happens to be in our database."

"Which means he is a known criminal."

"Or law enforcement." Ramirez hit several keys until a face appeared on the computer screen. A name, dates, and numbers appeared next to a stern man in his thirties with close-cropped hair. "Does the name Gilberto Arronyo ring a bell?"

Garcia's eyes popped. "Arronyo is definitely not law enforcement."

Ramirez squinted at the screen. "The file says he works for—"

"—Luis Cordon." Garcia exhaled loudly.

"So one of the men works for Cordon—but who killed them?"

"That's not really the question, is it?"

Ramirez turned in his seat. "You think it was Salinas?"

"When a man who works for Luis Cordon gets killed, there is rarely another explanation." Garcia shrugged. "But what was our Senator doing with one of Luis Cordon's men in the first place?"

"*That* is not my problem." Ramirez reached forward and snatched the soccer tickets from Garcia's pocket. He turned off the computer and stood, removing his lab coat and draping it across his chair. "Thanks for the tickets."

"You earned them."

"I know." Ramirez looked at the clock. "You coming?"

"You go ahead." Garcia suddenly felt very tired. "I need to make some calls."

Chapter Forty-three

Follow your nose up Columbus Avenue from Fisherman's Wharf and you'll find The Stinking Rose. The exterior is painted a lurid purple and the sign is electric orange—a combination that's hard to miss—but most people smell the famous restaurant long before they see it.

By its own estimation, the restaurant serves over three thousand pounds of garlic each month, which doesn't count the more than two thousand garlic bulbs used to decorate the interior. Along with red wine and dark chocolate, garlic has been widely praised for its health benefits, making the restaurant popular not only with tourists but also foodies and health nuts. The only people who avoid the place are vampires.

Frank had taken a private room in back. The room was normally reserved for parties of six or more, but Frank ate enough for four all by himself and had two bodyguards, so it was close enough.

The waitress brought the second course as Frank mopped the sweat from his brow. He didn't recognize her, figured she must be new. Not much of a looker, big hips and thick braided hair going gray at the roots. A mole on her chin that might have been sexy if only it had been two inches higher. But she was fast, and that's all that mattered. If Frank wanted to see tits and ass he could walk across the street to any of the strip clubs littering both sides of Broadway. Frank wanted to eat.

◇◇◇

Cape smiled at the hostess and blinked away tears as his eyes adjusted to the garlic-infused atmosphere. He scanned the restaurant but didn't see Sally. He headed toward the restrooms, located directly past the private dining area.

He passed red leather booths with velvet drapes overhead, chandeliers and coat racks adorned with bulbs of garlic. A wall mural of San Francisco landmarks populated by cartoon garlic-people, smiling and laughing as they mingled with tourists who would, no doubt, be eating them soon.

◇◇◇

Frank didn't expect any trouble. He'd made his peace with the Chinese, drew neat little lines on the map. There might be some heat from the Feds because of this fiasco with the Senator, but nothing he couldn't handle. They tap his phone again, big fucking deal. Business as usual.

Still, Frank never ate alone. No need to upset the other patrons of the restaurant by having Tommy outside the door looking like a bouncer, but having him inside the door helped Frank's digestion. And with André sitting behind him, Frank had a bodyguard sandwich ready to protect him if anything went down.

He drank some more water and smiled as the waitress brought the main course. *Courses*—plural—Frank had an appetite tonight. He dabbed his napkin across his forehead and scooted his chair closer to the table.

◇◇◇

Cape stood at the sink in the men's room and visualized the room he had just passed. One guy sitting on a chair near the door, looking relaxed but out of place, no table in front of him. Frank with a napkin tucked into his collar, another in his right hand, his florid complexion reflecting the halogens overhead. Another guy behind Frank, presumably a second bodyguard, his face obscured by the waitress' hips as she bent to put a plate the

size of Kansas in front of Frank. Cape noticed two more dishes
on a serving tray behind her.

He ran some water over his hands and splashed it on his face,
nodded to himself in the mirror, opened the door and started
down the hall.

◇◇◇

"Will there be anything else?"

The waitress squeezed the last plate onto the table and
removed the dirty dishes, refilled Frank's glass of water and
poured another glass of wine without spilling a drop. Damn
she was good.

"What's your name sweetheart?" Frank was feeling mag-
nanimous.

The waitress said something he couldn't catch. Sounded
almost Chinese.

"It means *Little Dragon*." She leaned in closer, her voice barely
a whisper. "But you can call me Sally."

Frank started to respond but stopped as he noticed someone in
the doorway, a man about six feet tall, sandy hair, shirt untucked
over jeans. He looked vaguely familiar. Frank half-stood as he
leaned past the waitress to get a better look, just as the man stepped
across the threshold and kicked Tommy in the face.

Cape dropped to his knees, landing on Tommy's solar plexus.
He could taste the bodyguard's breath as the wind rushed out of
him. Cape removed the nine-millimeter from Tommy's shoulder
holster and turned toward Frank. The bodyguard sitting in the
back of the room was already on his feet, his hand reaching
under his coat.

Sally laid her right hand flat on the table and vaulted past
Frank, landing directly in front of André. He sneered and
snapped his left arm out from his body, a football blocking move,
as he grasped the butt of his gun with his right hand.

Sally grabbed his left wrist with both her hands and twisted
inward, toward his body. The effect was dramatic. André's brain
told him to protect the bones in his wrist, which sent a signal

to his legs to leap backward out of harm's way. He levitated off his heels with a distinct lack of grace, airborne long enough for Sally to kick his legs out from under him. He landed in a heap at her feet, his gun clattering across the floor until it spun to a stop directly under Frank's chair.

Frank's eyes darted to the pistol but he wasn't stupid. He looked at the gun in Cape's hand and nodded, then kicked the gun that was under his chair toward the door, which Cape had gently closed behind him.

Cape gestured at Tommy with the gun. The bodyguard scooted backward against the wall, then stood. His chin was red where Cape's shoe had connected but he wasn't bleeding. Cape slid the chair over and Tommy took a seat, looking like he wanted to kill someone. Cape was pretty sure he knew who that someone might be.

The bodyguard behind Frank stood awkwardly, clutching his wrist. Cape smiled when he saw the man's face. It was his old friend from Mexico, the man he thought of as Cyrano. His nose looked the same but his expression had become considerably more sour.

"*Hola, mi amigo*," said Cape.

"Up yours."

"Never did get your name when we were South of the border."

"—his name's André." Frank cut in. "Like André the giant, only more like André the dumbass from the look of things." He glanced at Sally, who took André by the wrist and led him to another chair. She seemed to barely touch him, but André winced with every step and made no move to resist.

Sally stood between the two bodyguards and proceeded to undress. Her wig was the first to go, tossed in a ragged heap on the floor. The mole on her chin was peeled off, then flicked across the room like a squashed bug. The waitress outfit was shed to reveal false hips underneath, padded foam contours attached with velcro.

"Unbelievable." Frank shook his head and turned his attention back to Cape. "You're not here to whack me, so I don't suppose you mind if I finish my fuckin dinner?"

Cape took the chair directly across from Frank and spun it around, straddled it. He placed the gun on the table, out of Frank's reach but well within his own grasp. Then he unbuttoned his shirt to the center of his chest and pulled the two sides apart.

"No wire, Frank."

"Not much chest hair, either."

Cape rebuttoned his shirt. "Does Salinas know you have another supplier?"

Frank coughed, spraying Cape with garlic-infused spittle. For a moment it looked like the Heimlich maneuver might be needed.

"Skip that question for now," said Cape. "Let's talk about the Senator."

Frank drank some water, his face cooling from red to pink. He stared at Cape for a long moment before jabbing a fork into his garlic chicken.

"Why am I talking to you?"

"Oh, sorry." Cape took a card from his pocket. It was the card Salinas had given him in Mexico, the one with the drug lord's private number. Cape slid it across the table far enough for Frank to read. "Want me to ask that first question again?"

"The Senator's dead."

"That hasn't hit the news yet, Frank."

"Word gets around." Frank glanced toward André-Cyrano, who was still massaging his wrist. "Go wait in the car." Frank turned toward Cape. "Unless you got a problem with that?"

Cape made a gun out of his thumb and forefinger and pretended to shoot it at Cyrano, who gave him the middle finger in response. After he was gone, Cape turned his attention back to Frank.

"How long did you own the Senator?"

"You're mighty well informed." Frank took a bite of chicken and spoke with his mouth full. "Too bad you can't prove anything."

"I don't have to—I'm not a cop, or a Fed. I just need some answers for my client, then I go away and you never see me again."

"Somehow I doubt that—you're like a bad penny."

"C'mon, Frank, neither one of us is getting any younger."

Frank dabbed his mouth with the napkin tucked under his chin. "You know that stadium project that made the Senator a local bigshot—guess who built the stadium?"

"Construction is your bread and butter, isn't it?"

At the mention of bread and butter, Frank took another bite. "We underbid the job. Senator Dobbins didn't realize that two major corporate contributors to his election campaign had ties to the—umm, to *us*." Frank smiled at the memory. "So when we won the stadium job, we could make it look like maybe the Senator was playing favorites."

"He either goes on the payroll or you say something to the press. Goodbye political career."

"Hello jail." Frank chuckled. "And no skin off my back, since the press would only have enough to claim *alleged* mob connections."

"The rumors would be enough to ruin him, so you owned his vote."

"Rented, is more like it." Frank shifted his focus to the garlic mashed potatoes.

"How often?"

"We greased him on a regular basis—a few grand a month—but only called in favors once in a while."

"Because you had others on the payroll?"

Frank leaned back, shifting his weight from side to side. "Attracts less attention if you spread the responsibility around. You do your homework, don't you?"

Cape tried to look modest and almost pulled it off.

"I'm not saying I know anything about that." Frank sounded like he was testifying in court. "Just like I'm not saying there is such a thing as organized crime—I'm just a businessman with diversified interests in construction, shipping, real estate."

"How about insurance?"

"You bet." Frank smiled and sucked on his teeth. "Some people buy insurance because they're worried there might be a fire in their store—some dumbass spills lighter fluid or a stock boy gets careless with matches. But if the owner of that store buys insurance—"

"—from you—"

"—then no fire—they're protected. Fire insurance, life insurance. Nowadays they got insurance for everything."

"Legislative insurance?" Cape reached out and spun the gun like a bottle. "Protection in case corporate taxes get raised. Real estate zoning changes, drives up costs. Maybe the right kind of insurance could pay for a team of bi-partisan lawmakers voting on your behalf."

"That's quite an imagination you got there." Frank rested his hands on his belly.

"Was Delta Energy one of the companies that benefited from your voting block?"

"No comment."

"Off the record?"

Frank glanced at the gun resting on the table. "By the time I order dessert, I want you gone."

Cape knew his threat to call Salinas must have an expiration date attached to it. Salinas would find out eventually, so Frank wanted to control the timing. That gave Cape some leverage but not enough, and there were some things Frank would never admit, even under duress.

"Five more minutes, Frank. Then you can have your tiramisu."

"Gonna need a new waitress."

"Why did you hire the son?"

"C'mon."

"Danny do something stupid?"

"Besides working for me?" Frank grinned. "He was a mule, nothing more. And not a very good one. Just an overgrown kid looking for cheap thrills."

"You used him."

"Wouldn't you?"

"What went wrong, Frank?"

"You're the detective. I was hoping you could tell me." Frank shook his head in dismay. "You think I killed him?"

"It was one theory."

"Look, a man like me only wants three things out of life." Frank ticked them off on the fingers of his right hand. "A wife that can cook, a girlfriend who swallows, and a steady stream of non-taxable income."

"Are those in order of priority?"

"If you don't mess with those three, I don't give a fuck what you do. The Senator was my clean-up batter—my ace in the hole. You think I'd throw that away, you're an idiot."

Cape felt like an idiot. He was running out of questions. "Maybe the Senator stopped cooperating. Had a change of heart."

"Nobody bats a thousand. Maybe he did start to feel the heat—if he wasn't dead you could ask him yourself. But I had more than ten years invested in that douchebag."

Cape looked over at Sally standing placidly beside Tommy, who watched her warily but didn't look stupid enough to try anything. Cape returned his gaze to Frank.

"You trust your Mexican associates?"

"About as much as they trust me." Frank pulled the napkin from under his neck, revealing multiple chins. "I'm ready for dessert."

Cape nodded and reclaimed the card with Salinas' number. Then he took the gun off the table and dropped it in his jacket pocket. "Souvenir." He moved toward the door.

Frank called after him. "How's your client?"

"Anonymous."

"Sure," said Frank, smiling without warmth. "Tell her I said hi."

Chapter Forty-four

Cape dropped off Sally in Chinatown before turning down the impossibly steep side of California Street.

He pulled behind a bus claiming to be a *zero emissions vehicle*, twin antenna connecting it to overhead wires running the length of the street. The lights inside the bus flickered on and off every few blocks, illuminating the three passengers with an erratic strobe, making them appear and disappear.

Cape had the top down and was grateful for the night air as he turned onto The Embarcadero. There was something to be said for driving a vintage convertible—the wind off the bay was almost strong enough to flush the smell of garlic from his clothes.

At Townsend Street he parked, grabbed his jacket from the back seat, and walked across the sidewalk to the restaurant he knew so well. Town's End was a favorite breakfast haunt that opened early, but they also served dinner, and the tables were spaced far enough apart to have a private conversation.

Rebecca stood when she saw him and waved. She was alone at a four top near the back. Cape walked past the open counter in front of the grill and said hello to the cooks, including Mary and David, the owners, all dressed in white chefs' uniforms. Cape had never been in the restaurant without seeing at least one of them in the kitchen. He wondered when they slept.

Rebecca hugged him and Cape didn't object. She wore considerably more clothes than in the desert, but Cape was blessed with a good visual imagination.

Nothing had happened between them at Burning Man, though there had been signals even before the candle flickered out. For starters, she had been naked and covered in mud, and he had no objection to getting his hands dirty. But they exchanged nothing but words—no bodily fluids, no moments of intimacy—though Cape sensed that something might have happened if he had taken the initiative. Sitting in the dimly lit restaurant, he wondered why he hadn't.

He could tell himself it was because of professional ethics, but those had more to do with never quitting a case than not sleeping with clients. Another explanation might be the fresh wound from getting dumped by e-mail, but Sally had been right about that relationship—it had been over long before he got the message. Looking across the table, Cape realized his hesitation wasn't from a lack of physical attraction but from a gnawing sense that he still didn't completely trust his client or himself.

Maybe he was pursuing this case out of pride, a refusal to admit failure. And perhaps Sally was right—Rebecca's motivation had less to do with closure than revenge, and Cape was doing nothing more than helping her get blood on her hands.

"Thanks for meeting me." Rebecca's smile was bright enough to cast a shadow on his suspicions. It was one thing to be neurotic, another to be paranoid.

"You said you found something."

"This." Rebecca took a manila envelope from her bag and laid it on the table. "My father left it for me."

Cape reached for the envelope. "What did he say?"

"Not a damn thing." Rebecca's expression was bland, but the bitterness in her voice was palpable. "No note, just a bunch of papers."

Cape undid the clasp and started removing documents, spreading them out on the table. "Maybe he was in a hurry."

"Maybe he didn't know what to say. Men suck at apologizing."

Cape had to admit the latter was more likely, but it prompted a thought that made his skin crawl.

"Rebecca, were you abused as a child?"

Her cheeks flushed but she didn't hesitate. "No...never...why would you ask such a thing?"

"You're positive."

"I think I'd remember."

Cape didn't answer right away. "Never mind...just thought I should ask."

"Why?" Rebecca's expression was less angry than concerned.

"You were the only daughter and got sent away at a young age. Sometimes that happens—the mother steps in and removes temptation. Tries to save the family by breaking it apart."

Rebecca shook her head. "That's not my story. My father sent me away, and it killed my Mom."

"What did?"

"His secrets—I think the stress of living with them ate her alive, one cancer cell at a time."

Cape nodded. "OK."

"It's not OK, but that's the way it is. I can't change it now, but..." Her voice trailed off.

Cape waited, sensing what she would say before she found the words.

"I think the people who killed my brother—my father—I think they might as well have killed my Mom. I think it's all one and the same."

Cape dropped his eyes to the table. The first thing he noticed was a page of letters and numbers reminiscent of the one Beau had given him. He wondered if this was a duplicate and if Sloth had made any progress cracking the code.

Next were stock certificates for a bunch of companies Cape had never heard of before—LandMass Industries, Gaia-Tec Corporation, TerraMax Enterprises, Digest Fuel Corporation— almost a dozen companies, thousands of shares.

Lastly there were three maps, one of the United States, one of Canada, and one of Mexico. Cape felt his pulse quicken when he saw Puerto Vallarta marked with a red dot. Similar dots appeared on all the maps. Places in Canada he had never been, as far north as the Yukon and Northwest Territories. In the U.S. there were dots in the southwest, one in Texas near Austin and one in San Francisco. Cape flipped through the stock certificates and found a company name he had seen before: Delta Energy.

"Wait here." Cape took the page of codes along with the stock certificates over to Mary, who was still working behind the counter. The restaurant took take-out orders by fax, and Cape didn't want to lose any time. After a few minutes he had the pages headed to Sloth for analysis. When he returned to the table, Rebecca gave him a hopeful look.

"What does it mean?"

"It means your father wanted to tell you something." Cape shrugged. "Maybe set the record straight."

"He could've written a note."

"Like you said, maybe he didn't have the words."

"Maybe."

"Maybe he left in a hurry."

"Maybe." Rebecca looked unconvinced.

"Sorry."

"Not all men suck at apologizing." Rebecca reached out and squeezed his hand, then let it go as she forced a smile. "None of this is your fault."

"I know."

"You'll figure it out." She said it as a simple truth, a statement of fact, but it still sounded like a question to Cape.

"Hold on to these—my friend has copies." Cape gathered the papers together and returned them to the envelope. It was late, and the restaurant was almost empty. He stood to leave and Rebecca did the same.

"When will I see you again?"

Cape had been wondering the same thing. "Dinner tomorrow night—tonight I dragged you to a restaurant and we didn't even eat."

"Perfect."

Rebecca had parked a few cars in front of him. Cape got a goodbye hug that might have lasted longer than the one in the restaurant. Rebecca had her arms wrapped around him, her mouth close to his ear.

"I want you to find the people who took my family from me."

Cape nodded as Rebecca started to pull away.

"I want you to find them," she said, "and I want you to kill them."

Her voice was barely a whisper, and Cape thought he'd misheard her. When their eyes met she smiled with warmth that belied her words, and he wondered if he'd imagined it. Before he could ask, Rebecca had slipped into her car and pulled away from the curb.

He watched her drive away as he walked to his car, concluding that the goodbye hug definitely lasted a good four seconds longer, wondering what he should read into that.

Cape started his car and decided he really was a lost cause. He caught the light and made a U-turn onto The Embarcadero, accelerating along the water toward the abandoned piers on the right.

He glanced in his rearview mirror and thought he recognized the late-model Mercedes half a block behind him. An image of a car parked outside The Stinking Rose flashed into his brain, but then the car dropped back and Cape switched his eyes forward.

He picked up speed and caught the next light, then tapped the brakes where the road curved back toward the city.

He tapped the brakes again and felt pedal give way, his foot hitting the floor.

Cape spun the wheel but the car fishtailed and he overcompensated, sending it barreling over the curb. His right leg kicked against the brake pedal, hoping to find some resistance, but the car careened across ten feet of sidewalk into the chain link fence that blocked the wreckage of the pier. The fence flew apart, a stray pole breaking the windshield, as Cape felt his tires skid across the pier and sink into the decaying wood.

He had just enough time to regret wearing his seatbelt as the boards gave way one by one, explosions of splinters and rusted nails that sounded like gunshots. Cape groped for the belt release as his world turned upside down.

He jammed his thumb against the button and felt gravity take him, then his head hit the steering wheel and everything turned black. As black and unforgiving as the water of the bay.

Chapter Forty-five

Sally kept her eyes open as she slipped under water.

The bath was long and deep, almost as wide as a jacuzzi and set into the floor of her loft. Some women took baths to wash away their stress in a miasma of bubbles, but Sally preferred to drown her sorrows by not breathing.

There is a legend in China about a drowning man that sees his future instead of his past. So instead of having his life flash before his eyes, he sees his life as it might have been—if only he had not fallen in the water. If only he had made different choices in life. But like so many Chinese fables, it ends tragically when the man realizes he is dying and will never have the future that the water reveals. There is a moral to the story but no happy ending.

Sally almost drowned when she was barely eight years old. Her school in Hong Kong had a series of interconnected pools that were used to train the girls to swim. Sally's instructor camouflaged one of the tunnels between the pools and she almost lost consciousness before she found an opening.

At that moment, when there was no more air left in her lungs, Sally had seen her parents as if they were still alive. Smiling as if they had never been murdered by the *yakuza*. As if they were still a part of her life. Whenever Sally took a bath she would submerge until she saw spots, sometimes until she had visions. Occasionally she saw her parents, but often she saw only bubbles straining toward the water's surface.

Tonight she lay at the bottom of the tub, her eyes open as she slowly let the air out of her lungs. The water was calm but her hair had come loose, flowing sinuously around her as she stared at the surface of the water. She blinked and focused her energy, slowing her heartbeat as the last bubble escaped her lips.

Sally blinked again as the spots appeared around the edges of her vision. She kept her body still but the water was lapping against the edges of the bath as if a tide was pulling on her. It almost felt as if she had fallen into the sea.

The water grew cold as Sally's hair flowed like seaweed around her face, covering her eyes and turning everything black.

Chapter Forty-six

Luis Cordon stroked the glass of the tank as the jellyfish passed by and wished he could go swimming.

The jellyfish was the size of a dinner plate, but it had plenty of room. The tank had been custom-built into the wall, over ten feet high and twenty wide. Thousands of gallons of seawater trapped behind three inches of glass, big enough to hold a microcosm of the ocean he loved so much. Fish of every conceivable shape and color swam past, bottom feeders and rays, even reef sharks. Some of them deadly, others merely hostile, like the jellyfish.

He almost didn't notice when Enrique came through the door, but his lieutenant coughed to make his presence known. Sneaking up on Luis Cordon was not a big idea.

Cordon gestured at the jellyfish, its tentacles trailing four feet behind the bulbous head.

"What do you think of my newest pet?"

"Very nice." Enrique had a talent for keeping his real opinions to himself, one of the many reasons he had survived this long.

"Do you know these are foreign to Mexico? This is a spotted jellyfish, from Australia."

Enrique stepped closer to the tank, studied the diaphanous membrane of the creature. "How did you transport it?"

"It came to me." Cordon smiled, the beveled glass reflecting genuine affection. "A few years ago these beautiful animals—*Phyllorhiza punctata*—invaded the Gulf of Mexico. Scientists were baffled. They believed the creatures too fragile, too passive to make such a journey. But the spotted jellyfish followed their instincts and came here, where the water is warm."

"And the fish are plentiful?" Enrique always tried to be helpful.

"Exactly." Cordon rubbed his hands together. "In Australian waters things are very competitive, and these jellyfish only grew the size of a man's fist." Cordon clenched his right hand and held it aloft. "But here, in Mexico, they became monsters. Some have grown as big as *hula hoops*."

Enrique tried to look impressed.

"The oceans are changing, amigo." Cordon took a deep breath. "The planet grows warm, the ice melts, currents change. Animals are forced to adapt—and you know which ones thrive, Enrique?"

"No."

"The creatures that bring pain and death." Cordon looked chagrined. "I wish it were not the case, but the climate is not something we can control, though many would disagree with me on that point."

Enrique didn't disagree.

"And as our planet becomes hostile, only the dangerous will survive."

Cordon stroked the glass as the tentacles brushed it from the other side, as if visiting a soul mate in prison.

Enrique clasped his hands behind his back and waited until the moment passed. "They are ready for you outside."

Cordon followed Enrique down a long hallway, the walls made from the kind of rough stone seen in castles more than a century ago. Every few feet another glass tank appeared on either side of the hall, some filled with water, others filled with rocks and sand. Piranha glared from behind tinted glass, their razor teeth too numerous to count. Gila monsters hissed at their reflections as they scampered over pitted rocks. Tarantulas crawled over each other in a tangle of hairy limbs.

Enrique took a deep breath once they were outside, the sun blinding but also healing after the dank feeling inside the mansion. He would never tell his boss, but Enrique was slightly claustrophobic. He opened his eyes wide until they started to water.

Cordon squinted against the glare at his ruined front yard and nodded his approval.

A trench had been dug around the circumference of the property, fifteen feet wide and ten deep. The native soil had been removed, and huge mounds of loose sand lined the edges of the pit, positioned to fill the newly constructed moat.

More than a dozen men worked hurriedly at the bottom of the hole, connecting long pieces of plastic PVC pipe together, the kind used for plumbing projects. Tree-like configurations of the tubing lined the trench where the workers had finished. Even from the front door, standing above the hole, Cordon could see tiny holes drilled along the lengths of pipe.

Every ten feet a giant metal canister sat at the bottom of the pit, leaning against the wall closest to the house, a valve near the base connected to one of the plastic trees. Each tank displayed a warning label with a drawing of an exploding circle, looking almost like a cartoon bomb, the hazard symbol for *contents under pressure*.

"You're sure this will work?"

Enrique nodded. "We tested it on a smaller scale. Three times."

"What happens next?"

"They connect the pipes to the air tanks, we run a switch to the house, and that's it. Then we line the walkway with bricks."

"That is all?" Cordon sounded like a disappointed parent.

"It is what we discussed," Enrique said in a measured tone. "It is a good plan."

"I suppose."

"You have another suggestion?"

"I wish it were water, and not sand." Cordon frowned.

"Not practical."

"I know." Cordon put a hand on Enrique's shoulder and squeezed. "Tell them to keep working, but don't pour the sand yet. I have an idea."

"What?"

"You'll see." Cordon turned and reached for the door. "Come inside when you're done. I have something in one of my tanks that might just be the missing ingredient."

Enrique waited until his boss had left, then he turned his face skyward, staring at the sun until his eyes watered and tears streamed down his cheeks.

Chapter Forty-seven

Rebecca was straddling him, her hair falling across his face as she leaned forward. Her hair was wet and tangled, heavy and cold against his skin.

Cape tried to brush it away but Rebecca snapped her head sharply to the right, her hair whipping across his face. He cried out as she swung her head the other way, a maniacal gleam in her eye, hair slapping hard enough to draw blood. Cape felt it running down his cheek and tasted salt.

The black water surged in a cruel wave and slapped Cape hard enough to wake him. His eyes fluttered as the nightmare of Rebecca dissolved in a spray of sea foam.

He was lifted, then dropped, every surge of current pulling him farther into the bay. He tasted blood and almost blacked again out as he fought the urge to vomit.

Moonlight revealed his car trapped by the wreckage of the pier, trunk pointing skyward. It was growing smaller with every swell of the tide as Cape drifted away from shore.

He couldn't feel his legs, already numb from the cold, until he started kicking. The effort brought spots to his eyes as a sharp pain shot across his forehead and down his neck. His arms felt like lead weights.

He gagged and spit as a wave covered him, then he put his head down and started to swim. Five strokes, ten. Twenty. He raised his head and tried to find his car.

It was even smaller now.

Cape heard blood rushing through his ears, the sound of his own gasping breaths, and knew he wasn't going to make it.

He let the current take him and angled toward the bridge, realizing the direct approach would only take him to the bottom of the bay. He forced his head under and swam.

The car was to his left now, but the retaining wall and the road were closer. With each agonizing stroke, he was moving in the right direction. He could see the steps leading from The Embarcadero to the water's edge.

He could barely feel his arms. The edges of his vision were turning black and narrowing with every stroke. He swallowed more water and kept swimming.

White light exploded behind his eyes as his head slammed into something impossibly hard. Cape blinked away stars and felt his right hand scrape against stone, skin tearing off knuckles.

He had swum headfirst into the steps. The tide sucked at his legs and pulled him back into the water. Cape kicked frantically and used his elbows to climb the first step, then the second. He shoved his chin onto the third step and wrapped his arms around the rough stone like a mother clutching her child.

A rogue wave crashed and pulled him down, banging his head against the lower step. Cape felt a surge of bile deep in his throat as he clutched at the stairway. He felt his legs dangling in the water, tugged by the relentless tide, and he wondered if he could hold on if he lost consciousness.

Then he blacked out.

An hour later two joggers saw him, half in the water and half out. Neither wanted to touch him, so they called the police to say they'd just found a dead body near one of the abandoned piers. Then they ran away just as the tide started to come in.

Chapter Forty-eight

Cape was sinking into the abyss. Bubbles raced for the surface as he plummeted toward the bottom.

But the deeper he sank, the brighter it became, the darkness collapsing into a single black circle at the center of his vision.

"He's awake." Beau's features swam into focus.

Cape squinted against the glare of fluorescent lights. "Your face is a black circle at the bottom of the ocean."

"Even delirious the man's a poet." Beau smiled at the nurse standing at the edge of the bed, a stern-looking woman in her fifties with hair the color of iron. She stepped to the bed and roughly lifted Cape's right eyelid with her thumb and shined a penlight directly at his pupil. Despite his squirming she managed to repeat the procedure with his left eye.

She shot Beau a warning glance.

"I'm going to call the doctor."

Beau nodded. "How long till he stops by, ma'am?"

The *ma'am* softened her a bit. "Probably ten minutes. How much time do you need, young man?"

"Thirty?"

She shook her head. "Fifteen."

"Deal."

After she'd left Cape rotated his head in Beau's direction. The pillow felt like a waffle iron. He tentatively raised his right hand and felt bandages encircling his forehead.

"My car—"

"*Blub…blub…blub…*" Beau pinched his nose. "Was a piece of shit anyway."

"It was vintage."

"You mean old."

Cape tried to sit up but couldn't. He felt faint. "I feel like I'm still drowning."

"Remember what I said about swimming? I take it all back—doctor said you were lucky to be alive."

"What else did he say?"

"Called you an idiot for falling into the bay in the first place. Only drunks and tourists pull that shit."

"What did you say in my defense?"

"Told him you were a tourist from New Jersey who'd had too many Mai Tais."

"I don't drink Mai Tais."

"You're missing the point." Beau moved his chair closer to the bed. "Nobody knows you're here, other than the hospital staff. No one knows you're alive."

"How long have I been here?"

Beau ignored the question. "I take it this wasn't a case of you talking on a cell phone or changing the radio station when you should've been watching the road."

Cape told him about the brakes, the car in the rearview mirror.

Beau frowned. "You sure it was the same car?"

"No." Cape rubbed the back of his neck, which hurt about as much as the rest of him. "Didn't see the driver, either. But my brakes didn't just stop working."

"On that car, don't be so sure—it's not like they made anti-lock brakes or warning lights when that *vintage* automobile was coming off the assembly line."

"What are the odds?"

"I hear you, but fucking with a man's car isn't Frank Alessi's style. He favors the direct approach."

"Bullet to the back of the head?"

"And *then* a swim in the bay—we've found more than one of his rivals washed up on Baker Beach. Still, I won't argue that you managed to piss somebody off."

"You want a list?"

"It might have just gotten longer." Beau reached behind his chair and grabbed several newspapers, which he tossed onto Cape's lap. "The story broke."

The headlines said it all. *State Senator Dies With Son. Senator And Son Murdered In Mexico. Former Senator Eaten Alive And Found Dead.* The story was every newspaper's dream: gory, sensational, and unexplained. Who needed news when you could get circulation?

"The cat's out of the bag," said Cape.

"And it's big and furry." Beau grabbed the top paper and flipped to an inside page where the cover story had been continued. He jabbed his index finger right above the fold where a short paragraph described the family history of the late Senator Dobbins: his deceased wife, his son Danny who died with him, and his daughter, Rebecca. "Your client is on the radar."

"Shit." Cape's head felt like it was about to implode. "Her phone must be ringing off the hook."

"Maybe, but she's not answering."

"Would you?"

"No way, but I called anyway, wanted to let her know what was happening with you. Left a message. She still staying at her Dad's?"

Cape nodded. "As far as I know—I'll go over there." He tried to sit up but only managed to scoot a few inches higher on the pillow.

"Maybe in a day or two."

Cape suddenly had a sick feeling in his gut as he remembered the question Beau hadn't answered. He looked toward the window. No light was coming through the blinds.

"How long have I been here?"

"Almost twenty-four hours. They found you close to midnight." Beau watched him carefully. "You lost a day."

Cape twisted his neck and confirmed there was a phone next to his bed before taking a deep breath and shoving hard against the mattress. He managed to sit up just as the room started to spin. He swung his legs off the side of the bed and closed his eyes, Beau watching him with a look of bemused skepticism.

There was a knock at the door, the perfunctory *tap-tap* of a doctor already on his way in. Cape looked up to see a young doctor with wire-frame glasses and short black hair, flanked by the iron nurse. He gave them a wave and tested his legs on the cold tile floor, then took a tentative step forward.

The room did a somersault. The nurse cried out. Beau started to laugh.

And Cape passed out right before his ass hit the floor.

Chapter Forty-nine

Cape opened his eyes to find Linda's hair looking very concerned. Linda, however, did not seem to share the sentiment.

"Finally."

"Nice to see you, too." Cape managed to sit up without losing consciousness.

Linda's face softened. "The doctor said you were fine. Just rash—"

"Rash?" Cape examined the skin on his arm.

"Abrupt—stubborn—willful. Not a skin irritation."

"Oh."

"How are you feeling?"

"Like a fuck-up."

Linda didn't disagree. Cape grabbed the water glass on the side table and sipped through the straw until it was empty. The iron nurse appeared in the door, as if she sensed imminent dehydration.

"Ah, we're awake."

Cape smiled but her expression made it clear they weren't going to be friends. Several minutes later he had been poked and prodded until he felt like a game hen, but there were no tubes in his arm and no straps on his wrists. The nurse left shaking her head, clearly convinced from her examination that Cape would do something to disappoint her before he left.

Cape returned his attention to Linda. "Beau call you?"

Linda's hair shook. "I called him. You were overdue for a visit after sending us that fax."

Cape held up a hand. "Give me a minute."

Linda watched as he swung his legs over the side and managed to stand, this time without seeing spots. Her hair seemed ready to catch him but he remained upright. He waddled ten feet to the bathroom, less dizzy than he expected. A couple of minutes later he emerged, bladder empty and head almost clear. He sat on the bed facing Linda.

"You saw the news?"

Linda nodded. "Nothing new, just the story about father and son showing up where they didn't belong. A *tragedy under investigation* is what the papers are saying."

"But there's nothing about the Senator's connections to the mob, nothing about Danny working for Frank Alessi."

"Not a word."

"OK, what have you got?"

Linda opened a shoulder bag that had been sitting on her lap. It bulged with papers. She grabbed some that were clipped together and lay them across the bedspread next to Cape.

"This is complicated," she said.

"Everyone keeps telling me that as if I didn't already know."

Some of the papers were articles printed from online news sites. Others were financial reports clipped to the stock certificates Cape had faxed, the names of the companies highlighted in yellow. Three were maps that corresponded to the regions of the map Rebecca had shown him, only these had longitude and latitude designations, along with much greater detail for roads and topography. Cape saw pen marks on certain locations as he did before.

"This *looks* complicated." Cape blew out his cheeks and took a deep breath. "Have you got it all figured out?"

"No way." Linda shook her head vigorously, making her hair look like it was expanding and contracting on its own. Maybe it was.

"Can we start with a simple question?"

"Sure."

"Delta Energy is one of these companies, right?"

"Absolutely."

"So maybe I should start there," said Cape. "Go see that lawyer Beau told me about—the one that bailed out Danny, maybe even pulled some strings to have his record covered up."

"Somebody beat you to it." Linda reached out and pulled a newspaper clipping from the edge of the bed, a short article from the inside of one of the local papers. Cape didn't have to read past the subhead. *Corporate Lawyer Takes A Dive.*

"Shit."

"Police aren't saying whether it was murder or a suicide."

"Does it matter?"

"The article says there was very little evidence at the scene. Beau didn't tell you?"

Cape shook his head. "I think I passed out before he had the chance."

"This isn't as bad as it looks—Sloth found a pattern."

"That coded sheet?"

"There are two." Linda pulled the page in question from her bag and laid it on top of the other papers. "This is the one you got from Beau." She produced an almost identical list of letters and numbers and laid it next to the first. "This is the one from Rebecca."

Cape scanned from left to right and saw that the letter and columns were consistent but the numbers changed.

"What changes?"

"The timeframe," said Linda. "We think these are two months apart. Sloth used the stock certificates as a guide to the letters, then tracked the financials for those companies to see if they corresponded with any of the numbers."

"And?"

"Every stock certificate has a corresponding acronym on this list, if Sloth is right."

Cape had never known him to be wrong. "So these companies are publicly traded?"

Linda shook her head. "Not all of them, but that never stopped Sloth. Having two months made the difference, because he could find numbers in the company financials that moved in the same sequence."

"OK." Cape pressed his hands to his forehead. "But if these are legitimate companies—"

"Some of them. Others we haven't identified—they might be shell companies."

"OK, but if these others are legitimate investments, why would the Senator stuff them into an envelope and write his daughter's name on it? Are they part of his will or something?"

"We don't know." Linda waited until Cape raised his eyes from the papers. "But that's not the point. Sloth took it a step further and reviewed the Senator's voting record. Remember how it moved in patterns around pivotal issues, like—"

"—tax breaks for companies."

"Exactly." Linda's hair bobbed with excitement. "All these companies got some kind of break, allowance, or financial boost from a bill or public initiative that the Senator voted on."

"All of them?"

"It gets better."

"He invested in them?"

Linda smiled approvingly. "You're pretty smart for someone who gets hit on the head for a living. Dobbins was a major investor in all of them—direct conflict of interest. But it gets even better than that."

"You're killing me."

"His wasn't the only prominent investor in these companies."

"Frank Alessi put money in, too?"

"Not just Frank. There were foreign investors—one name in particular you might recognize."

Cape sat up straighter. "Salinas?"

Linda shook her head. "His rival—Luis Cordon."

Cape tried to wrap his head around what he'd just heard.

"It's true," said Linda. "The late Senator's business partner was Luis Cordon."

Chapter Fifty

Luis Cordon put down the phone and nodded to Enrique, who was standing a respectful distance away. The office was the size of a racquetball court, more glass tanks lining the walls, some filling the shelves in between rows of books. Reptiles dominated this room where Cordon spent most of his time conducting business. Enrique found that ironic but kept the thought to himself.

"Everything is in motion." Cordon pressed his hands together and touched them to his full lips. He really was a remarkably attractive man, thought Enrique. He could have been an actor, or a model.

"They will come here?"

"That is the plan, but some things are out of our control."

Enrique couldn't think of any person, place, or thing out of Luis Cordon's control, but he nodded in agreement. "The men are ready."

Cordon looked toward the ceiling, his perfect hair reflecting the overhead lights. "You understand we might have to kill them."

"Isn't that the idea?"

Cordon saw the confusion in Enrique's face and smiled, then sighed as if a great sadness had overcome him. "I don't mean our guests—I mean our men."

Enrique breathed through his nose, not trusting himself to say anything.

"I want this thing buried," said Cordon.

And what about me—am I to be buried, as well? But Enrique kept the thought to himself. He took another breath and then met the gaze of the unnaturally attractive man sitting across the desk, a man who could have been an actor or a model, but instead chose *this*. Enrique wondered, not for the first time, about the choices he might have to face in the end.

"Of course," he said. "I'll see to it myself."

Chapter Fifty-one

"I wish they had pancakes."

Cape scanned the overhead menu of the hospital cafeteria and frowned.

Linda wrinkled her nose. "Looks like they have French toast."

"A poor substitute."

"It's the middle of the night."

"Breakfast is the most important meal of the day."

Linda moved past him to the cereal, where she grabbed a package of trail mix and put it on her tray. Cape pointed at the French toast through the glass and waited patiently while a portly woman wearing a hair net used tongs to separate three slices from the rest of the pile. He grabbed a bottle of iced tea, paid for both of them, and followed Linda to a table where she had papers organized into neat piles.

"Thanks for coming downstairs." Cape cut into his late breakfast.

"You're not supposed to leave your room."

"Actually I'm not supposed to leave the hospital. I was hungry."

"They can bring food to your room, you know."

"I needed some air."

"Is that why you got dressed?"

"The hospital gown was drafty." Cape looked down at his clothes, torn and scarred from his drive off the pier but almost presentable, thanks to the hospital laundry.

"Don't bullshit me." Linda's hair rose up in warning. "You're going to sneak out."

"The thought had occurred to me."

"Then take that off." Linda glanced at his head. Cape had forgotten about the bandage. He undid it slowly, watching Linda for a reaction. Lines multiplied around her eyes as she grimaced. "Your forehead is purple."

"I'll buy a hat in the gift shop."

"Get a pair of sunglasses while you're at it."

Cape took a bite and managed to hide his disappointment— the French toast had probably been in the hospital longer than he had. He and Linda ate in silence for a while. The iced tea kicked in after a few minutes. His head still felt like an over-inflated football, but he was awake.

Cape pushed his plate aside and started thumbing through the stacks of paper. "The Senator invested in companies and then influenced public policy in their favor…"

"Right."

"…and his co-investors included local mobster Frank Alessi…"

"Correct."

"…and Mexican drug lord Luis Cordon."

"Check."

"But not his rival Salinas?" Cape shuffled some papers around, scanning for the name of his erstwhile employer.

"Not as far as we can tell."

Cape leaned back in his chair. "That would explain Salinas' interest in the Senator. Anything that benefited Cordon would presumably hurt him."

"If you say so." Linda's right hand lay atop one of the stacks, her fingers tapping impatiently. Cape finally took notice.

"Am I missing something?"

"Don't you want to know what the companies do?"

"Sure, but I figured it was some kind of money laundering operation. Guys like Frank and Cordon need legitimate companies to cover their tracks."

Linda nodded. "Absolutely, but aren't a lot of those cash businesses? A lot of small operations, like pizza parlors, laundries, restaurants—even retail. A business where it's easy to cook the books."

"Not always. Might even be a hotel—no one really knows how many guests you had, how much money came across the front desk."

"This is different."

"How?"

"It's insidious." Linda's face darkened. "They're messing with my environment."

Cape thought about the names of the companies, with prefixes or suffixes like *Terra, Gaia, Energy.* He considered the Senator's political rise. "All the companies sound vaguely green, or at least energy-related."

"This is a classic case of greenwashing, only on a global scale."

"Is that anything like brainwashing?"

"You've never heard the term—it's in the press all the time."

"I think you and I might read different magazines."

Linda's hair did nothing to hide her disappointment. "OK, think about food labels. A bag of potato chips might have a sticker that says *Zero Trans Fat.*"

"Sure."

"Or a can of mixed nuts might say *Loaded With Antioxidants.* Saltines come in a *Low Sodium* variety now."

"Got it."

"But that bag of potato chips has eight times the amount of sodium you're supposed to eat on a daily basis. The nuts are loaded with fat, not just antioxidants. And the low sodium saltines will give you an ass so wide it'll snap your thong."

"I don't wear a thong."

"Thank goodness, but the point is that if you're on a diet, you shouldn't eat chips. But if you really, really want a bag of chips, don't apologize or pretend you're being healthy—just eat the damn chips and enjoy."

Cape nodded. "And this is related to our problem because…?"

"Because the latest thing in product packaging is to highlight the green components. *Made from 20% recyclable material. Low emissions vehicle.* All the catch phrases designed to alleviate guilt."

"So while you might not be saving the planet by buying this product, you're not killing it, either."

Linda frowned. "That's the idea, but it's *greenwashing.* Because 80% of that product is still crap that goes in a landfill, and if you really want to reduce emissions, walk or ride a bike."

"Not everybody can live like you do, Linda."

"I'm not saying they can. And I'm not saying making a coffee cup out of recycled paper isn't a swell idea. But don't act self-righteous because you drive a hybrid car to Starbuck's. The battery that powers that car is messy to manufacture, and that empty cup is still trash."

Cape knew this was deeply personal for Linda, but he needed to knock her off the soapbox long enough to figure out what the hell she was talking about.

"Can we fast forward to the part where I catch the bad guys?"

"Sorry." Linda took a deep breath. "I don't think you can catch these guys, but maybe you could expose them."

"For what?"

Linda made seven separate stacks of paper between them, then tapped the one in the middle. "Delta Energy is at the heart of it—it's a major energy company."

"Oil company."

"Used to be, but they reinvented themselves around today's politics. They're building wind farms, hydroelectric plants, you name it."

"All legitimate enterprises."

"*These* companies get funding from Delta Energy." Linda smacked the tops of the other piles with both hands. "And Delta gets tax breaks for supporting them."

"And these other companies—what do they do, exactly?"

Linda pointed to the stack on the far left. "This one is an alternative energy venture that builds solar cells from recycled silicon chips after they've been thrown away by computer companies. They don't have a working prototype, but that's the idea." She moved to the next pile. "This one sells carbon offsets—know what those are?"

"I think so." Cape tried to remember an article he'd read recently. "You go away for the weekend, but you feel guilty about filling the atmosphere with your car exhaust, or the jet fuel from the plane trip, so you buy a *carbon offset*, which pays for someone to plant a tree somewhere." Cape looked to Linda for confirmation. "Close?"

"Close enough. It's a very shady business."

"I thought you'd love the idea."

"I do love the idea, but I don't trust it."

"Why not?"

"It's too…*lazy*." Linda's hair looked ready to pounce. "What happened to the three R's?"

"Reading, writing—"

"You are such a clod sometimes." Linda scowled. "*Reduce. Re-use. Recycle.* The three R's of taking care of your personal environment. You want to help the environment, you have to make changes."

"And offsets—"

"—send the wrong signal." Linda looked like she might levitate. "Take your tree example. You drive enough to empty your tank, then pay some company a hundred bucks to plant a tree, because supposedly the tree consumes enough carbon dioxide to offset the effects of your drive."

"There's a catch?"

"Tons of them. The whole industry is unregulated. No standards or system of measurement. And it takes a long time—years—for a tree to consume enough greenhouse gas to make a difference. If the tree ever burns, or dies and then decomposes, it releases much of the carbon back into the atmosphere. So it's very hard to quantify any impact."

"But it's nicer to have trees than not."

"Sure, but it matters *where* you plant the tree. Near the equator, the tree sucks up carbon dioxide and throws off oxygen, which is good. But plant a tree farther north, say in Canada, and it might not have the same effect. The trees up there might absorb sunlight and make that part of the planet warmer than it once was."

"Is that good or bad?"

"That's the hundred million dollar question."

Cape thought of the maps Rebecca showed him with dots marking Canadian territories. "I guess you've looked into these companies."

"You bet." Linda reached into her bag and produced a copy of the map. She brought her index finger down accusingly on northern Canada. "See these two dots? Both represent tree farms run by Delta Energy's carbon offset company."

"Too far north?"

"It gets better." Linda unrolled another document, this one an aerial photograph. It was a satellite photo that looked utterly desolate, a virtual moonscape in the middle of nowhere. "This is the location of one of their tree farms."

"I don't see any trees."

"Glad you're paying attention." She unrolled another satellite photo. This one was almost entirely covered in black smudges, trees running off the edges of the paper. "Here's the other location."

"Looks better."

"It does, doesn't it? Except it's a national preserve where logging is prohibited, and there hasn't been a new tree planted since this company was founded—I checked with the park service."

Cape sat back in his chair. "Both locations are bogus."

"Precisely. It's a scam, people paying for a placebo effect. They tell you that you're a bad person if you drive that car, unless you give them cash to alleviate your guilt. Nobody ever checks to see if a tree was planted, or if planting it ever made a difference—people just want permission to avoid changing their lifestyle."

"How many people?"

Linda smiled without warmth. "This company has sold over a million offsets, and the cheapest one is a hundred bucks. For longer trips they charge up to five hundred. That's a hundred million dollars minimum."

"And the company is non-profit."

"And its investors get tax breaks. Legally and politically, they are protected like you wouldn't believe. And if you say anything against them, well—"

"—then you're not very politically correct."

"A tough position to take in this town." Linda rolled up the photographs and pushed the map in front of Cape. "I hate these people."

Cape didn't argue. Linda had walked the walk since he'd known her, and now that everyone finally seemed afraid for the environment, crooks were lining up to exploit that fear.

"We can give this to the press."

Linda nodded. "But the investors will plead ignorance. And the news will make it harder for legitimate companies doing good work with the environment to raise money. People will feel burned—all these companies have received massive amounts of funding."

"Enough to launder a drug lord's cash."

"And generate plenty on their own. This might be more profitable than marijuana."

"God damn."

Linda shook her head. "I don't think God has anything to do with it."

Chapter Fifty-two

"God helps those who help themselves."

As he talked, Priest curled his tongue around his front teeth like a man searching for a piece of food. "So in the thirteenth century, the Catholic Church started one of the first money laundering operations."

Antonio Salinas studied his guest with a skeptical eye but said nothing. Experience had taught him that sometimes it is best to let a madman rant.

"The idea was beautifully simple." Priest started pacing. "Sinners were supposed to repent in confession, then await God's judgment and forgiveness. But the Church decided people should not only repent, they should pay some sort of retribution here on Earth. So the Church began selling *indulgences*. Merchants, nobles and peasants alike could pay for their sins in cold, hard cash."

"You're joking." Salinas bit the end off a cigar, then lit it. "All of Mexico is Catholic, and I never heard of this."

"It doesn't get brought up in many sermons, but it's true." Priest breathed in the secondhand smoke with relish. "If you sinned you could alleviate your guilt by *doing good works*, but why not erase your sin entirely by paying the Church to do good in your name?"

Salinas waved his cigar in a circle. "What is your point, my friend?"

"This became very popular with the merchant class, who could afford to pay for indulgences. They would bring gold, and the Church would issue a printed slip of paper, the currency of absolution. People didn't have to change their lifestyle to avoid purgatory, and the Church became wealthy beyond measure. Souls were cleansed, the money was clean, and everyone was happy."

Salinas blew smoke rings. The ceiling fan pushed them across the room, where they enveloped Priest's head like a succession of halos.

"This went on for hundreds of years." Priest sighed as if he had been there. "Then that killjoy Martin Luther came along and complained, which caused a great schism among the faithful. By this time the printing press had been invented, so the Church was printing indulgences faster than the Mexican government prints *pesos*—no offense."

"None taken."

"It was a beautiful system, because it was based on a simple truth: people do not want to change. They do not want to repent. You know what they want, Antonio?"

Salinas said nothing.

"They want forgiveness. Absolution. And they are willing to pay for it, again and again. That is the genius of Luis Cordon's plan."

Salinas narrowed his eyes. "Cordon is no fool, but he is not a genius. The *gringo* Senator had the idea, I am sure of it."

"Perhaps. But the environmental movement is the new religion, make no mistake."

"You are being melodramatic, *amigo*."

"Am I? Question global warming and you'll be called a heretic. Drive the wrong car and it might get set ablaze by the faithful. Vote against the greener candidate and you'll be ostracized by your neighbors. The God you and I grew up with is dead to this generation, Antonio—he has been replaced by *Gaia*, the earth goddess. We are surrounded by pagans."

"Pagans with money."

"Yes." Priest nodded. "Willing to pay companies that promise them absolution. Live your life the way you want, and we will plant a tree in your memory. Everything old is new again."

"Too bad Martin Luther is dead." Salinas puffed on his cigar. "But so is the Senator. And the lawyer."

"Yes, the money machine of your rival is being dismantled, but it has many arms and legs. Some right here in Mexico."

"You mean the operation in Monterrey."

"It's very profitable."

"The lawyer is dead. There will be an investigation."

"There will be other lawyers—they tend to multiply. And investigations take time."

"Regulators will come, shut everything down."

"Perhaps." Priest pursed his lips. "But can you afford to wait that long?"

"You have a plan?"

"I have something better." Priest smiled, his teeth glinting with malice. "I have God on my side."

Chapter Fifty-three

"Hell of a day."

Beau sat down heavily next to Cape, the park bench creaking from the strain. His long legs almost touched the water of the duck pond. A small melee of ducks was under way as Cape lobbed pieces of white bread into the water.

Cape took off his baseball cap, removed the sunglasses. "Guess my disguise didn't work."

"Your forehead's purple—practically glows under that hat. How'd you get here, anyway?"

"Took a bus."

"No shit?" Beau turned sideways. "And how was that?"

"Not as bad as I though it would be."

"You know the buses in this town kill people every month. MUNI drivers nailed almost 20 pedestrians already this year."

"Maybe that's part of the city's strategy to get more people riding them."

"Convince them it's safer *inside* the bus?"

Cape shrugged. "Made better time than I thought."

"Linda must be rubbing off on you. Feel better about yourself?"

"I'll feel better when I get my car fixed."

"Ain't gonna happen. I saw it, after they got a crane to lift it away from the pier. Even the little mermaid couldn't drive that car."

Cape laid a fat manila envelope on the bench between them.

"We cracked the code."

Beau opened the clasp and flipped through the pages. "What's the Reader's Digest version?"

Cape laid it out for him. The money funneling through Delta Energy and back through the subsidiaries. The tax breaks, the financials of the alternative energy ventures, and finally the list of investors.

When Cape was finished Beau whistled and reached into the bag of bread. He tossed a few pieces over the heads of the bigger ducks toward the little ones that were getting boxed out.

"My associates in the Federal Building will be much obliged."

"Think they'll get Frank?"

"Not a chance." Beau snapped his arm and sent a piece of bread flying. "Bastard's too slippery. He'll assume the role of naive investor."

"But the law isn't his only problem, is it?"

"You read my mind, brother." Beau smiled wickedly. "If your hacker is right—"

"—he's always right."

"—and Luis Cordon is investing in bogus companies with Frank, that would certainly explain why Cordon's product is showing up in more places—"

"—and why Salinas is losing market share?"

"Bingo."

Cape put his sunglasses back on. "Isn't that a little dangerous, if you're Frank?"

Beau squeezed enough bread together to make a wad the size of a golf ball. "Frank is trying to play both sides. Salinas has old-school mob connections, so Frank can't refuse to distribute his product. But Cordon is the future—he's diversified into semi-legitimate businesses."

"Like Frank."

"Yeah." Beau timed his next throw carefully. A big duck was nipping at the rest of the group, snatching all the bread for himself. Beau raised his arm and waited...waited...and then snapped his wrist. The ball of dough struck the bully right above the bill, knocking it backward into the water. It swam off, quacking in protest, looking over its shoulder to check for any more breaded missiles headed its way.

"Feel better?" Cape took the bag of bread and idly tossed some loose pieces to the remaining ducks, which were suddenly on their best behavior.

"Didn't feel bad," said Beau, "just frustrated. We got nothing on the lawyer, in terms of forensics."

"You've got the connection to Delta Energy."

"Yeah, but all that shit will go federal. I don't have a case to work here."

"They tried to kill me."

"So what?" Beau shrugged. "No offense, but that's *attempted* murder. You gotta be dead if you want me to take an interest."

"I could drown next time."

"Nah, then I'd just have to do the paperwork."

"And the ties to the cartels..."

"Not my jurisdiction."

They sat in silence for a few minutes and watched the ducks. A small island dominated the center of the pond, overgrown with trees twisted by the wind. This part of Golden Gate Park often got overlooked but Cape loved it. The city might have been a thousand miles away.

"You think Salinas killed the Senator and his kid?" Cape tilted his face toward the sun but couldn't feel any warmth.

"Absolutely. Happened in his back yard. The papers said there were three victims, the third identified as having ties to Cordon. So Salinas had the means and the opportunity."

"And the motive?"

"Sure, killing them hamstrings a nice little operation that Cordon set up."

"No." Cape took off his sunglasses. "I mean the motive for paying me off—Salinas had already killed the Senator, so why ask me to dig into it?" He threw the last of the bread in a long overhand arc. He'd been avoiding this question, even though he already knew the answer.

"You got used." Beau said it simply, without any judgment in his tone, but Cape felt bile in his throat anyway. "Salinas might have killed the principals behind Cordon's little environmental scam, but he wanted it torn down. He can't do that, can he? What's he gonna do, call the FBI and leave a tip?"

Cape lowered his voice. "*Hi, it's me—Antonio Salinas, Mexican drug lord and concerned citizen...*"

"*...and I thought you guys might wanna know about some shady investments...*" Beau patted the manila envelope. "Salinas wanted somebody to do the legwork for him."

Cape looked at the envelope and fought the urge to throw it into the pond. If he didn't turn it over, a lot of hardworking people with good intentions would continue to get fleeced. But if he did, Salinas would get what he wanted.

"Fuck me."

Beau put a hand on Cape's shoulder. "Things don't always work out the way you thought they would."

"Tell me about it." Cape watched as the bully duck worked its way back into the throng. The bag was empty. There was nothing Cape could do short of jumping into the pond.

"I'll give you a ride back if you want." Beau grabbed the envelope and stood to leave.

"I'll walk. Dobbins lived next to the park—hopefully Rebecca's still there."

"You talk to her yet?"

"Not since I took a dive off the pier and her name hit the press. Can't get through, so I'm going in person."

"What are you gonna tell her?"

"That it's over," said Cape. "The case is closed."

Chapter Fifty-four

The Senator's house overlooked the western edge of the park, a twenty minute walk from the duck pond. Cape got there in thirty. He was anxious to finish this conversation but wasn't in such a hurry to get it started.

A good long-jumper could clear the front lawn, but by San Francisco standards it was sizable. The grass was freshly cut and the plants groomed. Cape figured a lawn service came every other week. The house itself was mostly wood, white with dark accents around the windows, and a slate roof reminiscent of a gingerbread house. Cape might have called it quaint if he was in the right mood.

He rang the bell and listened to the chimes echoing around the foyer. He knocked and got no response. He considered leaving but knew procrastination would only feed on itself and he'd end up finding some excuse to put things off until tomorrow. Then it occurred to him to check her brother Danny's apartment in the Mission. Even though Rebecca had said she'd be staying here, Cape knew how hard it must be on her. Maybe Danny's place had fewer bad memories.

Cape checked his notebooks to make sure he had the address. He did and turned toward the street before he remembered he didn't have a car. He knew a bus must stop somewhere near the park but didn't have a clue where, and cabs in San Francisco were about as common as Bigfoot sightings.

He decided to take a walk around the house, if only to put off his quest for transportation. The side yard was as manicured as the front, small bushes looking prim and expensive, no bugs in sight. The backyard had some wooden lawn furniture, a sundial and a bird fountain that was dry. Maybe the birds hadn't paid their taxes.

As Cape came around the other side of the house he saw something he hadn't expected. An open window, as tempting to a professional snoop as online pornography is to a teenager with a laptop. He stepped up to the sill and peered inside.

The living room was unoccupied, papers scattered across a coffee table, a desk in the corner. The lights were off but enough came through the window to illuminate the back hall. The house had a stillness about it that said no one was home.

Cape looked toward the front yard and thought about his long walk to the Mission, then decided breaking and entering sounded like more fun. The window was open far enough for him brace his hand on the bottom of the frame. He gently pushed and it rose easily on its tracks.

He walked back to the backyard and grabbed one of the lawn chairs, carried it back to the window. It saved him from having to hoist himself up by his arms. Swinging his right leg over the sill, he managed to slide and then tumble into the living room ass-first without knocking anything over.

Cape stood completely still and listened, but the house was dead silent. No creaks, no water heating kicking in, nothing. He looked at the coffee table.

Photographs were scattered over its surface. Rebecca as a young girl. Her mother and father holding hands. Her brother Danny. Her father at some event, a tight shot of him smiling in a tuxedo, his wife next to him, her hair pinned up. Rebecca again, standing with a group of girls wearing uniforms. Cape couldn't tell what type of team it was—softball, volleyball, lacrosse—but all the girls looked like they could kick his ass.

He stepped over to the desk, where the originals of the stock certificates lay, adjacent to the maps Rebecca had shown him in the restaurant. Cape stopped and listened again.

Silence.

He took a seat in the desk chair and started to reach for the top drawer when a yellow envelope caught his eye. It lay to the right of the maps and had been torn open. Through a clear window in the envelope Cape could see Rebecca's name and this address. It was a telegram.

Cape always felt a slight pang of guilt when he read other people's mail, but years as a reporter and then as a PI had reduced the feeling to a millisecond of doubt followed by a thrill of anticipation. Usually the contents were mundane. In all the years he'd been poking his nose where it didn't belong, he'd never had a case where opening an envelope revealed something totally unexpected.

Until now.

Cape read the telegram twice. By the time he finished, his mouth had gone dry.

Someone had asked Rebecca to meet him in Mexico. Someone claiming to have information about her brother and father. Someone who said he needed her help. Someone who couldn't be reached but would meet her when she came. Someone who said she should hurry.

It was someone Cape knew as well as he knew himself.

He stared at his own name at the bottom of the telegram and felt his blood run cold.

Chapter Fifty-five

Oscar Garcia hated loose ends. As if to illustrate the point, he tugged on a stray thread at the edge of his cuff and watched as the *gringo* bartender poured two more glasses of tequila.

"Whose room are you billing this to?" Juan Molina knew as head of hotel security that too many free drinks would get noticed, and eventually someone in the back office would ask him about it. The women in accounting were a bunch of Nazis. Another headache he didn't need.

"The American detective?" Garcia raised his glass and took a sip.

"He isn't coming back, Oscar."

"Is his credit card still on file?"

"An outrageous suggestion—I am head of hotel security."

"He never checked out—you said so yourself."

"Guests leave all the time without checking at the front desk."

"I think he will be back."

"You told me the investigation was closed."

Garcia nodded. "Señor Dobbins, father and son, are being shipped back to the United States—what is left of them."

Juan raised his glass. "Congratulations. And where do you go next?"

"Are you so glad to see me go?"

Juan didn't answer, which was answer enough.

Garcia smiled. "I am awaiting orders." As he spoke, a woman in a bikini walked through the lobby. It looked as though the bottom of her bathing suit had been exchanged for dental floss without her knowledge. "Until then, I thought I would stay here and enjoy the view."

Juan followed his gaze until the woman reached the safety of the elevators. "For a man on vacation, you don't seem relaxed."

"I'm not wearing a tie."

"But you are wearing a jacket, and it's over eighty degrees outside. Most of our guests are half-naked."

"I don't want to intimidate the other men." Garcia waved to the bartender who poured another shot before Juan could intervene.

"What's bothering you?"

Garcia glanced toward the sliding glass doors fronting the pool. "I have a case file in my hotel room that is as thick as a phone book. It has crime scene reports. Autopsy reports. Photographs. Charts. Names, addresses, dates of birth. There must be hundreds of pages that all say the same thing."

"What?"

"Nothing." Garcia drank the shot in one gulp, then hissed as the tequila vaporized in the back of his throat. "Two men came to Mexico and died. Another man died with them. This we knew when the investigation began. That is all we know now."

"And you think the gringo detective knows more?"

Garcia shrugged. "He was going home to investigate the Senator. Perhaps he found something."

"You haven't spoke to him?"

"No." Garcia sighed. "I tried to call him when we identified the bodies, as a courtesy, but I couldn't reach him."

"You think something happened to him, don't you Oscar? You're the most paranoid cop I've ever known, even when we were in Mexico City together—you want to know what I think?"

"Absolutely." Garcia said it as if he couldn't care less.

"I think he got paid and lost interest once he had money in his pocket. He's an American."

"You could be right."

"Of course I'm right." Juan drank off the last of his shot. "You should listen to me, Oscar. You work all the time, have no life. Look at me—fat and happy." He patted his belly as the woman in the bikini-floss walked past in the other direction. "Now which of us is smarter—the investigator with no answers, or the head of security enjoying all the fringe benefits of a luxury resort."

The mention of *fringe* reminded Garcia of his cuff and the thread he couldn't tear loose. He wished he had a pocketknife.

"You are wise beyond your years." Garcia stood on shaky legs.

"I am older than you, Oscar."

"Regardless, I appreciate your perspective." He gestured thanks to the bartender.

"Where are you going?"

"To pack."

"So you're leaving?"

"I don't know," said Garcia. "I just have a feeling I'm going on a trip."

"Just like you have a feeling the American will return?"

"Yes."

"And why would he come back to Mexico?"

"Because I would."

"Why?"

Garcia didn't answer. He looked at Juan and played with the thread on his sleeve until it rested firmly between his thumb and forefinger. Then he yanked decisively and felt a satisfying snap. He let the loose thread drop to the floor, then he turned and walked away.

Chapter Fifty-six

"We should have seen this coming."

Sally said it softly but the words stung. She wrapped both hands around the cup of tea and drank, her green eyes clear and hard above the rim.

"You trying to make me feel better?" Cape took some crunchy noodles from the dish between them.

Sally called to the waitress, a young Chinese girl in her teens. They spoke rapidly in Cantonese for a minute, the girl looking from Sally to Cape, then smiling and bowing before she went downstairs.

"What was that about?" Cape looked around the dim room. The second floor of the tea house was empty save for the two of them, at Sally's request, but the scars on the floor and the tables crowded along the walls were testaments to its popularity. Cape thought he knew Chinatown but Sally always managed to find someplace he never knew existed.

"I asked her to make something special." Sally studied his face for a moment. "You look better than you did in the hospital, but your forehead is still—"

"—purple. I know. You were in the hospital?"

"You were unconscious. I left before Beau arrived, once I knew you were going to come around."

"How did you know?"

"I checked you out." Sally smiled and Cape had an image of her running her hands along his neck, squeezing his temples. He suspected she could give the doctors a run for their money.

"How did you know Beau was there?"

"I saw him."

"He didn't mention seeing you."

"That's because he didn't." Sally took another sip of her tea. "Doors are over-rated."

The waitress brought a mug that smelled so bad she held it at arm's length. Cape could see her eyes watering behind the steam. After she set it down she bowed once and then disappeared again.

"What is it?" Cape looked at the noxious liquid, a bluish-green concoction with flecks of brown floating on the surface.

"Ancient Chinese secret."

"It smells horrible."

"Then make a face when you drink it," said Sally. "Just drink it."

Cape frowned but didn't say anything.

"Trust me."

He did. Cape grabbed the cup, which was almost too hot to touch, and poured its contents down his throat. He figured the best thing to do was get it over with, so he tried to open his throat like a beer-chugging contest.

He almost fainted. Cape had a sensation of lava hitting his stomach, then an explosion in his head that cleared not only his sinuses but his ears and tear ducts at the same time. His eyes started to water and his nose ran like a faucet.

"It's working." Sally handed him a napkin.

"Thanks." Cape wiped his nose, let the tears run down his cheeks. He took a deep breath and realized the pounding headache that had plagued him since the car accident was gone. Not diminished, utterly gone. He looked around the room and could've sworn his eyesight had improved. He wondered if X-ray vision would develop if he drank another cup.

Sally smiled, laughter in her eyes.

"What's in that drink?"

"You don't want to know." Sally shook her head. "If you did, you'd never swallow it."

Cape took a deep breath and gingerly touched his forehead.

"It's still purple," said Sally.

"But it doesn't feel it."

"You're welcome."

Cape leaned back in his chair. "You were telling me how I should've seen this coming?"

"We—I said *we*. You're not always as suspicious as you should be."

"Salinas got what he wants—it's over. The Senator is dead, the racket he and Cordon set up is bust."

"Look at it from his perspective." Sally set her cup down. "I was raised by men like Salinas."

"And what would they do?"

"When Salinas first discovered what the Senator was up to, what do you think he did?"

Cape remained silent.

"He would threaten the Senator's family." Sally's eyes seemed to harden with memory. "You always threaten first, to see if there is any leverage. And if the target does not respond—"

"—you act on that threat to let them know you're serious."

"Yes."

"But his wife was already dead."

Sally nodded. "So our attention turns to the son."

"And Danny was an easy target. Already in the life, because of Frank. Just an arm's length away from Salinas."

"You said the Senator resigned suddenly."

The buzz from the drink was fading but Cape still felt more lucid than he had in days. "They must have snatched Danny, demanded the Senator come down to claim him. And then they killed them both."

"But we forgot something." Though her face was unlined, Sally suddenly looked incredibly old. The moment passed and

Cape wondered if it had been a trick of the light or an after-effect from the drink. "A threat always has two audiences."

"It does?"

Sally nodded. "The victim and…" She let her voice trail off, then found it again. "The people watching."

"Salinas had an audience."

"A man like that always does. Business associates. Rivals like Cordon. Law enforcement. Even the press. As long as he avoids proof of his guilt, Salinas doesn't mind rumors—in fact he covets them."

"Because every threat carried out sends a message to everyone else. Fuck with me and I'll kill your family."

"Your *whole* family." Sally's mouth was a straight line. "That means the daughter, too."

"The daughter with the different last name." Cape banged his hands against the table and wished it had hurt more. "Who was sent away for her own good when she was young. Who was invisible to Salinas and men like him."

"Until the press found her."

Cape said nothing. Sally sat immobile. Traffic whispered and honked two stories below. Finally Sally broke the silence.

"You want to go after her." She said it as a statement.

Cape met her gaze. "Yes."

"They'll try to kill you, too."

Cape touched his forehead and tried to look nonchalant. "What else is new?"

"She might already be dead."

"I know. You coming?"

"Of course."

Chapter Fifty-seven

Rebecca Lowry was exhausted.

The United flight from SFO to Mexico City was delayed by almost four hours. The gate attendant said it was because of weather, but when several passengers pointed out that it was perfectly sunny in both San Francisco and Mexico City the plane suddenly had a mechanical problem.

Rebecca calmly made her way to the front of the line and pointed at a button the attendant wore on her blouse. *Ask me about our on-time performance!* The woman tersely explained that the crew had been delayed getting to the airport, but her tone of voice made it clear that she suspected the delay was really being caused by Rebecca's inquisitive attitude.

Rebecca had tried to follow the instructions in the telegram to the letter, but she missed her connecting flight in Mexico City. After pacing the airport for three hours she caught a bumpy AeroMexico flight to Monterrey. There she stood in line for twenty minutes waiting for a taxi, her carry-on bag feeling like it was filled with lead.

The taxi navigated busy streets, the architecture a blend of modern-ugly and colonial, the Sierra Madre Mountains visible at every turn. The driver cruised past Fundidora Park and Macro Plaza, movie theaters and discos exploding with neon to spare. It was almost midnight when he pulled into the driveway at the Calinda Plaza hotel.

The lobby was empty save for a balding man in his fifties behind the desk. He had been sitting on a stool but stood and gave Rebecca a huge smile. She almost fainted with gratitude.

"*Señorita* Lowry?"

"How did you know?"

"We have been expecting you—I held your room."

Rebecca remembered they had asked her for her flight information when she made the reservation. She smiled and pulled out her credit card.

"Thank you—*gracias.*" She wished she remembered her high school Spanish, but it had been too many years.

"It is a long trip from the U.S." He pronounced *U.S.* like *oooh, yes.*

"Ooooh, yes," repeated Rebecca lamely. She could barely keep her eyes open. She had tried to rest on the flight but couldn't close her eyes, though the adrenaline rush from receiving the telegram had long since faded. She had too many questions, too many stray thoughts to relax. But now that she was here at the hotel, all she wanted to do was sleep.

The man handed her a key card. "*Ocho cientos doce*—eighth floor. Elevators right over there."

Rebecca rested her head against the side of the elevator as she watched the numbers light up above the door. The eighth floor was quiet save for the humming of the ice machine. Judging from the ambient noise as she walked toward her room, it might have been empty.

She slid the key twice before she got a green light, then stepped into her room to let the door shut behind her. The room was pitch black. A green light glowed on the far side of the room, and she could hear the tortured grinding of an air conditioner. Dropping her bag, she reached along the wall to find the light switch.

Her right hand slid along the stuccoed surface almost two feet until she felt a something smooth. Just as her fingers shifted to push it into the wall, Rebecca felt it move suddenly. Her tired brain sent sparks but no clear signal, telling her the smooth surface wasn't hard like plastic but surrounded by something warm and calloused. Rebecca backed against the door as she realized it must have been a nail, and she just touched a human hand.

The lights came on and Rebecca blinked as she tried to find her voice.

A man standing not more than three feet way had hit the switch. He had a dark complexion and a mild expression on his face. He wore a navy suit and loafers. His overall appearance was non-threatening, but his eyes were hard.

"*Hola, Señorita Lowry.* You have kept us waiting."

Rebecca opened her mouth to scream but no sound came out, and she wondered if maybe the hotel was empty, after all.

Chapter Fifty-eight

"We're going to a pig farm?"

In answer to Cape's question a satellite image appeared on the plasma screen in front of Sloth. He slid his hand awkwardly across the scratch pad and the image zoomed, revealing a cleared area on the outskirts of a city. It was hard to judge the scale, but there appeared to be a series of long buildings arranged near a body of water too symmetrical and square to be anything but man-made.

Linda's hair jutted toward the screen. "This is one of the biggest operations in Cordon's portfolio of companies. It not only received seed money from Delta Energy, which got huge tax breaks for investing in this place, it also got funding from the Mexican government."

"But it's a pig farm."

"A huge source for bio-gas."

"Translate please."

"Pig farts—a terrific energy source, and a really good source of cash."

"You're kidding." Cape turned toward her but stayed out of reach of her hair.

"I'm serious, and this plant might be legitimate, at least as far as the law is concerned."

"I don't have a lot of time, Linda. Our flight leaves in four hours."

"We traced Rebecca's flight to Monterrey, Mexico. Sloth accessed her credit card and she checked into a hotel there a few hours ago. Now guess where the pig farm is?"

"Monterrey?"

"Just outside the city."

The image on the screen changed, replaced by a series of photographs from ground level. Linda talked in staccato burst as new pictures flashed onto the screen.

"This is a farm that raises pigs for the usual reasons pigs are raised—"

" Bacon?"

"—and ham sandwiches, and pork chops. And all the other forms of pork that carnivores like you eat."

"—*delicious*."

"Don't interrupt if you're in a hurry. And that's still the principal activity on the farm, but it's not the most profitable. See that lake?"

Cape nodded.

"It's not lake." Linda wrinkled her nose. "It's a waste lagoon."

"Pig piss."

"Among other things. Now see those long sheds?"

"That where they keep the pigs?"

"Yes. Notice the pipes running from the sides of them, into that series of tanks?"

"Sure. It looks like the pipes all connect and lead to that shed next to the lagoon."

"When pigs fart, which they do constantly, they release methane—just like cows."

"And people."

"And methane not only smells bad, it burns. Which means it can be a source of fuel."

Cape studied the photos. "Isn't burning methane going to release pollution?"

Linda nodded. "It releases carbon dioxide, a greenhouse gas, but methane is considered much worse for the atmosphere, so there's a trade-off. Capturing methane on pig farms gives you a cheap source of energy to make electricity that's slightly better than burning coal or other fossil fuels. For a developing country it can be pretty lucrative."

"I get why it's cheap, but how is it profitable?"

"This operation also gets money from Delta Energy for carbon offsets."

"I thought that was about planting trees."

"An offset can be sold for anything that supposedly reduces greenhouse gases, so funding a methane-burning pig farm qualifies as much as planting a tree. This farm gets a check every month. A big one."

"And since the tree-planting venture was corrupt—"

"—I'm betting there's some creative accounting going on among the pigs."

Cape closed his eyes for a second, tried to get the kaleidoscope of images from the screen off his retinas. He needed a minute to think. When he opened his eyes the plasma screen had turned a dark blue, a calmer color. Sloth must have sensed he was getting overwhelmed.

"OK, say it's another shell company." Cape turned to Linda. "But why this place instead of somewhere else in Mexico?"

Linda took a printout off the desk. It was a newspaper article from the previous year. "Remember how you said the press on the Senator dried up suddenly, about nine months ago?"

Cape looked at the photo next to the article. It showed Dobbins smiling at the camera along with a bunch of well-dressed men. They were standing in front of a low shed with pipes running into it. Mountains were visible on the horizon, trees in the near distance. It looked tropical.

"This is the pig farm that Luis Cordon owns in Monterrey, Mexico." She tapped the faces of the men in the picture. "When Delta Energy got its big tax break, the alternative energy venture got some press. Politicians on both sides of the border hyped their greener-than-thou achievement to woo voters. One of them was Dobbins."

Cape stared at the photo, cursing himself for overlooking the article in his original search. Once he had found the trail to Mexico he'd left the background check behind.

"Salinas must have seen this."

"That's what we think." Linda spread her arms to include Sloth. "Dobbins realized too late his love of the press might have exposed his connection to Cordon. So he lowered his profile, but by then it was too late."

"Salinas took a few months to do some homework, then came about the Senator." Cape ran his hands through his hair. "So this place is significant for Salinas."

"It must generate a fortune for Cordon. If Salinas is going to press his advantage, he'll go after this place. Unless he wants to bring the fight to Matamoros."

"What's there?"

"Cordon lives there—it's a big smuggling port, right near the Texas border."

"But why would Salinas lure Rebecca to Monterrey and not bring her to him?"

"In Puerto Vallarta?" Linda's hair shrugged a little. "I'm just telling you how these places are connected."

Cape thought about what Sally had said about Salinas. About carrying out a threat in such a way that it sent a signal to everyone.

"He wants her to see it burn," said Cape. "It's the crown jewel of Cordon's empire, and she's a stand-in for her Dad—Salinas wants Rebecca there when he destroys the farm."

"As a witness?"

"And part of the message." Cape didn't want to say his next thought out loud but he did. He was starting to understand Salinas and hated the feeling. "She'll never leave there alive."

Before Linda could say anything the plasma screen directly in front of Sloth wiped itself clean. Stark words appeared in bold type.

You'll need these.

A printer hummed to life somewhere behind them. Cape followed the sound to a small alcove where a paper tray caught page after page.

"What are these?"

Schematics of the methane plant. Floor plans. Elevations.

Cape walked over and squeezed Sloth's shoulder, their normal substitute for shaking hands.

"What's the head count on the farm?"

About thirty thousand.

"Thirty thousand men?" Cape knew some drug lords kept standing armies, but he wasn't prepared for this. "I'm fucked."

Thought you meant livestock. Thirty thousand pigs. Don't know how many guards.

"That's better, but I still don't like the odds."

The screen cleared and a name and address appeared next to a photograph of a middle-aged man in a labcoat. The address was local, south of Market Street.

Go see him.

"Sloth, I only have about an hour."

Go see him. Tell him I sent you. He can help.

Linda stepped closer and her hair seemed to nudge Cape toward the door. "Go see him."

"Why?"

"Has Sloth ever been wrong?"

Cape didn't need to answer that. He bent down and kissed Linda on the forehead, her hair tickling his nose. "Thank you."

Linda didn't say anything until he'd reached the door.

"When you come back, I'll buy you breakfast."

"You buy the pancakes," said Cape. "I'll bring home the bacon."

Chapter Fifty-nine

Cape was trying to figure out how to get past the steel door when he started to hear voices.

The door was seven feet high and three wide, with pronounced rivets along the edges and covered hinges. He couldn't really gage the thickness but Cape suspected a rocket launcher couldn't penetrate the door or the brick wall that surrounded it.

What do you want?

The voice reverberated inside his skull.

Who are you?

Cape felt a buzzing in his ears like a mosquito before the words took shape.

Who sent you?

Cape whipped his head around the small courtyard. It was empty.

How did you get this address?

He scanned the walls of the converted loft and saw a red bubble of glass about ten feet up. A security camera. Adjacent to the camera was a small black rectangle with something sticking out of it that looked like a straw. As Cape moved his head, he noticed the straw tracking him. He waved at the camera and explained that Sloth has sent him.

Bolts slid with a loud *chunk, chunk, chunk* and the door swung open. Cape peered inside and took a tentative step forward.

"I apologize for the elaborate precautions, Mr. Weathers, but industrial espionage is a very real threat."

Cape looked up to see the man from the photograph from Sloth's computer walking toward him, his voice the same as the one Cape had heard inside his head. No lab coat today, just a polo shirt and jeans. He had black hair going gray near the temples, an aquiline nose and piercing blue eyes. As he came within ten feet Cape noticed a headset wrapped around his chin, the kind toll-free operators wore in TV commercials.

Cape extended his hand. "You're Dumont Frazer."

The man nodded. "I got an email from Sloth saying I should expect company. I apologize again if I alarmed you."

"That's a pretty neat trick with your voice—mind telling me how you did that?"

"Follow me."

Beyond the short entryway the space opened up to reveal a giant room, thirty foot ceilings and fifty feet in diameter, a converted factory turned into a gigantic laboratory. The first impression was chaos, but Cape began to discern groupings of various apparatus, as if each collection of tables, funnels, trestles, and wires was a separate experiment. It reminded him of the Exploratorium, the children's science museum near the Marina.

Dumont stepped in front of a long table near the center of the room. On it stood a tripod holding a ball-and-socket contraption from which a black straw protruded, identical to the one mounted in the outside wall.

"You're familiar with lasers, Mr. Weathers?"

"Call me Cape."

"Lasers are concentrated beams of light. Industrial lasers can cut through steel, tactical lasers are used for gun sights, laser pointers are used in boardrooms across the country to highlight PowerPoint slides. But they all follow the same basic principals. To build a laser, we direct light in a tight beam, precisely where we want it to go."

"Got it."

"What if you could direct sound the same way?" Dumont gestured at his black straw. "What if you could focus a sound wave like a laser?"

Cape looked at the innocuous device. "That's what I heard outside?"

Dumont nodded. "Through an amplifier, yes. But it was directed at you and you alone. Do you understand what that means?"

"It sounded like you were inside my head."

"I was." Dumont stroked his device. "Or more precisely, my voice was. If someone had been standing next to you, do you know what they would have heard?"

Cape shook his head.

"Nothing." Dumont smiled. "Absolutely nothing."

"Not even spillover, like you get from headphones?"

"Not a sound. No white noise, no echo. Nothing." Dumont beamed like a proud parent. "My voice was aimed at you, just like a laser."

"You could make someone think they were schizophrenic."

"The technology has the potential to be abused." Dumont looked around the vast warehouse of contraptions. "That's why our mutual friend Sloth sent you to me."

"But what is it used for?"

"Right now, very little." Dumont shrugged. "I'm still deciding about engaging in commercial pursuits. Suppose, for example, you were grocery shopping and standing in the soup aisle. When you reached a certain spot on the floor, imagine hearing about a discount on tomato soup or a promotion for a new flavor? Only you could hear it, until you moved further down the aisle. So your fellow shoppers wouldn't be annoyed by an overhead speaker droning on about soup while they were in the produce section."

"It sounds vaguely—"

"Intrusive?"

Cape shrugged. Best not to insult your host, especially if he's capable of penetrating your skull with sound waves.

"That's what I'm worried about." Dumont clapped and rubbed his hands together. "So I'm holding off until I determine the best course of action. But Sloth and I have become acquainted—online of course—he doesn't get out much, does he?"

"Have you met him?"

"Never in person. He must be a remarkable man."

"Smartest guy I ever met." Cape looked around the hall of invention and added, "No offense."

Dumont smiled. "I'm just a humble engineer. Like Caractucus Potts, the eccentric inventor in—"

"—*Chitty Chitty Bang Bang.* Played by Dick Van Dyke."

"You're a man of culture." Dumont nodded approvingly. "Sloth described your problem to me, in very cursory terms, and I may be able to help you."

"What did he say my problem was?"

Dumont looked at the floor. "He was vague, to be honest. You're not in law enforcement, are you?"

"No."

"Military?"

"No." Cape looked at Dumont until their eyes met. "I'm just an ordinary guy in an extraordinary situation who needs a little help. But I have no intention of sharing your secrets."

Dumont held his gaze and then nodded. "Very good." He steered Cape by his elbow over to another table.

Ten spheres sat on octagonal stands. They were somewhere between a golf ball and tennis ball in size. Black plastic divided hemispheres of silver metal. Within the metal quadrants were vents, horizontal slits with tiny grillwork covering them.

"I mentioned that an industrial laser can cut through steel plate."

"I remember."

"Naturally the military is very interested in lasers. They think one day they'll have a Buck Rogers ray-gun to decimate their enemies. But most laser applications are for sighting, measuring precise directions or zeroing-in on a target. To use light as a weapon you need to keep the laser on a target for several seconds, and even then light can be reflected or dispersed. A laser weapon isn't practical—not today."

Dumont picked up one of the black and silver balls. "But what if you could weaponize *sound?*"

"What do you mean, weaponize?" Cape thought of the buzzing that preceded the voice inside his head, a sonic mosquito about to wreak havoc in his brain.

"When you were a teenager, did you ever go to rock concerts?"

"Sure."

"Remember how your ears used to ring for hours afterward? Sometimes until you woke up the next day."

"And you could feel the bass deep in your chest if you stood close enough to the stage."

"Exactly!" Dumont's eyes lit up. "People become sick at concerts when the acoustics are bad or the volume too high. Everyone assumes it's alcohol or drugs, and it usually is, but sometimes it's because of sonic nausea." Dumont said the term as if describing a state of ecstasy.

"Sonic nausea."

"Right here in this little ball." Dumont held it out for Cape. It was heavier than he expected. "See that button?"

There was a red button in the center of the black plastic strip. Cape kept his thumb far away from it.

"Push that button twice and this ball will scream to life." Dumont took the ball gingerly from Cape. "I like to think of these as sonic mines, like the mines that used to stop the U-boats."

Cape saw an image of shrapnel and fire in his head. "Are these explosive, like stun grenades?"

"Not at all." Dumont frowned. "I could demonstrate, but Sloth said you didn't have much time."

"I have a plane to catch in a couple of hours."

"Ah, that won't do. It would take a while to recover."

"From what?"

"Ever have food poisoning?"

"Bad chicken salad." Cape grimaced at the memory. "Puked my guts out on a drive to L.A., thought I was going to die."

"Wracking chills, uncontrollable sweats, violent nausea?" Dumont listed the symptoms with relish.

"All of that. It lasted five hours. I didn't feel better until the next day, and even then I was weak."

"That's how this makes you feel." Dumont placed the sonic sphere back on its stand. "Only instead of five hours, it takes five seconds."

"You're kidding."

"Think about that buzzing inside your head, Cape. Remember those rock concerts. Imagine all the force of a laser—a sonic laser—burning through your skull."

Cape looked at the balls with a new appreciation. "What's the range?"

"Indoors—a normal-sized room—devastating. Total disorientation, absolute loss of equilibrium for any human being with normal hearing."

"What if the room is crowded?"

Dumont rubbed his chin, a near pantomime of the absent-minded professor. "Bodies will absorb sonic waves, so there will be a—" He paused, searching for the right term. "—blast radius. Someone near the back of the room might become disoriented but not debilitated."

"And the people closer in?"

"On their knees within seconds. Better than a taser."

"Outdoors?"

Dumont screwed up his face. "I don't have a lot of field tests. A lot depends on the terrain, but I'd say anything within twenty yards will go down."

"By *anything*, do you mean people and animals?" Cape saw an image of thirty thousand stampeding pigs.

Dumont raised his eyebrows. "Animals have a different range of hearing from humans, so in some cases the effect will be worse. In others not as bad."

"OK. What's the catch?"

"You have to protect yourself."

Dumont walked to the end of the table and opened a leather box. Inside were small Ziploc bags, each with two pieces of beige plastic inside.

"Are those what I think they are?" Cape stepped closer to take a look.

"Ear plugs." Dumont tore open a packet and demonstrated by placing them into his ears. "They have special contours and a noise-canceling motor—like the high-end headphones they sell for iPods. They diminish your hearing, but you can still hear—you won't be deaf."

"So I insert those into my ear canal before I push the button."

"That's the idea. In theory these earbuds will filter out the specific frequencies of the sonic bombs."

"In theory?" Cape realized what the catch was going to be.

"I'm afraid I haven't tested these yet."

"I'll let you know if they work. I might not be able to, if they don't."

"How many do you want?"

"I'll take two."

Chapter Sixty

The United flight to Mexico City was delayed, an event that didn't make the evening news or surprise anyone in the terminal at SFO. The Mexicana flight to Monterrey was only slightly less terrifying than a tax audit.

The topography of Monterrey is similar to Las Vegas, mountainous and hot as hell, so landings are always memorable. The Sierra Madre Mountains conspire to send thermo-climes into the path of any incoming aircraft. The turbulence was so severe that Cape was convinced the plane had struck a flock of birds, then he changed his mind and decided on pterodactyls. Sally slept the whole flight.

Sally had left her black bag in a locker at Mexico City airport when they departed Puerto Vallarta the week before. The bag was still there, and transporting it on a flight within Mexico proved uneventful. Cape had two sonic disruptors, which is how he liked to think of his new toys, hidden inside two hollowed-out tennis balls next to a racket he intended to throw away as soon as he unpacked. He wondered what his fellow passengers had hidden between their socks and underwear.

The rental car was a Ford with a brake pedal just big enough to overlap with the accelerator that required absolute concentration. They made good time, Cape driving and Sally navigating, but it was late by the time they reached the Calinda Plaza hotel. The lobby bar was empty, the restaurant closed.

A stout woman in her forties who looked like she was in her fifties greeted them at the front desk. She had sad eyes at odds with the warmth of her smile. They checked in and then Cape cut to the chase.

"Have you seen this woman?" Cape pushed a photograph of Rebecca across the desk. He had borrowed quite a few pictures from the Senator's house. She was younger by ten years but still the same woman if you looked at the shape of the face and the eyes.

The woman behind the desk shook her head, her eyes older than time.

"She would have checked in last night." Cape nudged the picture a little closer.

"*Lo siento,* I did not work last night. My husband, he was at the desk."

"Is he around?"

"He never came home last night, Señor." Again the heavy shake of her head. "*Pienso que hay otra mujer.*"

"*Gracias.*" Cape turned toward Sally, who had already headed toward the elevators. They went to her room and took turns using the bathroom, then they unpacked. Sally laid her essentials on top of the bed closest to the door, then arranged the items she had carried for Cape on the bed nearest the window.

Cape peeled open his tennis balls and deposited the sonic disruptors next to a nine-millimeter handgun. Ten rounds in the clip, two spare clips. Compact binoculars. A night vision scope. Cape had brought a photographer's vest but hadn't checked to make sure everything fit in the pockets.

Assorted knives, throwing darts and *shuriken* adorned Sally's bed. Near the pillows she laid a *katana* almost three feet long attached to a lanyard. The sword was sharp enough to cut through flesh and bone like paper, and Sally never removed it from its sheath unless she was going to draw blood.

Without ceremony Sally stripped off her travel clothes, a loose pair of gray sweatpants and white sweater, and started changing.

Cape followed her example but was slightly more self-conscious, turning toward the wall as he took off his shirt.

"No peeking."

Sally snorted. "Not sure I could stand the excitement."

Cape turned around to find her almost invisible. Her clothes were matte black, the fabric so tightly woven that it seemed to absorb all the light in the room. Her hair was tied into a ponytail and she had a scarf wrapped tightly around her neck that she could use to cover her face up to her eyes. On her feet she wore black shoes split near the second toe.

Her outfit looked skin-tight, but Cape glanced at the bed and saw all the metal objects except for the sword were gone. He wore a black sweatshirt over jeans, black sneakers, and a black cotton vest with bulging pockets. He patted them one at a time, then again, forming a mental image of which pockets held which gadgets.

"Ready?"

"You know this is probably a trap." Sally looked up at him. She was a foot shorter but her presence filled the room.

Cape nodded. "Probably, but what else can we do?"

"We could go home."

"You mentioned that in San Francisco."

"I can be pedantic sometimes."

"I never noticed." Looking into Sally's jade green eyes had always calmed Cape, even though she was the most lethal person he'd ever met. "I couldn't live with myself if we didn't go have a look."

"You might not have to if you do."

Cape smiled. "Then I guess it's a win-win situation."

"OK." Sally lifted her sword off the bed and slung it across her back. "Let's go herd some pigs."

Chapter Sixty-one

"You lied to me."

The man with the cane hobbled across the great room toward Luis Cordon, who sat on a brown leather couch under a tank filled with piranha.

"Santiago—*amigo*—that is quite the accusation." Luis Cordon looked wounded as his guest approached.

"Stop calling me that."

"We are not friends?" Cordon's handsome features assumed a troubled expression. The fish directly overhead bared their teeth.

"A man like you doesn't have friends." Santiago gestured at the glass wall, leaning heavily on his cane. "Except for your *pets*."

"I see, you are upset."

Santiago pulled a newspaper clipping from his pocket and tossed it onto Cordon's lap. Above the article was a photograph of a row of well-dressed men standing in front of a pig farm in Monterrey. Some were American and several were Mexican. Cordon didn't even glance at it. All week he had been getting phone calls from nervous investors and scared politicians.

"I was in that picture." Santiago shifted his weight and looked as if he wanted to sit down, but the nearest chair would have required that he backtrack, and his anger wouldn't allow that. His forehead was beaded with sweat below his white hair, his eyes jumpy.

"So were many other investors and government officials, but they are not here in my house, complaining." Cordon made an all-inclusive wave of the hand. "I do not recall you hiding your face at the time. You didn't even wear dark glasses."

Santiago leaned forward, exhaling loudly from the effort of keeping his balance, and snatched the article from Cordon's lap. He shifted his cane to his other hand and jabbed his forefinger at the photo. "*That* man is Senator James Dobbins."

"You talk as if neither of us knew him."

"An *American* politician."

"You have a point?" A hint of menace crept into Cordon's tone.

"He's dead now, do you understand that?"

"This is not *your* problem." Cordon rolled his neck, closing his eyes until he was looking up and backward, toward the tank. The sight of the piranha seemed to calm him. "What are you so worried about?"

"People are saying that Antonio Salinas killed the Senator."

"The facts are certainly suggestive."

"Salinas may not like the attention."

"You think Salinas cares about another rumor?" Cordon rested his arm along the back of the couch and studied his guest. "Or did you forget he killed the man's son?"

"*I have forgotten nothing.*" Santiago banged his cane against the floor. "This is your fault, Luis."

Cordon's eyes flashed a warning. "Nothing has changed—you are a rich man, a Mexican citizen, much like your compatriots in that newspaper picture. Above suspicion. Salinas is not your problem, he is mine."

"But the rumors—"

"What about them?"

Santiago took a deep breath through his nose. "They would suggest that Salinas is coming after you."

"He always has." Cordon sounded bored with the conversation. "He always will."

"But what would you do, if you were Salinas?"

"What are you driving at *amigo?*"

"We know he has seen this photograph."

"Of course."

"And by now he has heard the rumors about the Senator."

"Then what is to prevent him from coming after every man in that picture?"

"Nothing."

"He will kill them."

"And torture them." Cordon shrugged. "Salinas is a sadist."

"*Then he will eventually find his way to me!*" Santiago looked as if he were about to faint. "He will work his way through that line of men, one by one."

"I do not think so."

Santiago straightened. "Why not?"

"He will be dead soon."

"How do you know?"

Cordon smiled, and his teeth reminded Santiago of the piranha.

"Because I am going to kill him when he comes here."

"He's coming here?" Santiago grasped the cane with both hands. "Why on Earth would he do that?"

"Because, my friend, he is going to get an invitation."

Cordon stood and turned his back on his guest. The conversation was over.

It was time to feed the fish.

Chapter Sixty-two

The great thing about sneaking up on a pig farm is that no one can smell you coming. The stench hit them before they got out of the car, the methane plant still a mile away. By the time they had climbed the hill overlooking the farm, Cape's eyes were watering and Sally was breathing through her scarf.

"It doesn't smell like they're burning much methane down there."

"We're smelling ammonia, I think." Cape pointed toward a square lake. "I don't know how the operation is supposed to work, but I think that's the waste lagoon. Millions of gallons of pig piss."

"Remind me never to order *Mu Shu* pork again."

The topographical maps Sloth had provided showed the best vantage point was from the East, where a steep hill leading up from the road leveled off onto a small plateau before sloping gently down into the valley that thirty thousand pigs called home.

The moon was as full as a drunk's bladder. The night was clear but a low rumbling rolled up the hill toward them in waves, thunder from an invisible storm.

The enterprise was massive. Five long sheds—semi-circular roofs covering huts that ran horizontally down the center of the valley. At the south end of each shed was a huge tank, the kind Cape associated with oil refineries, pipes running between them. They were all inter-connected.

Adjacent to the last shed was a rectangular one-story building with a smokestack three times its height. The pipes from the tanks all routed into this building, which looked like it was made of cement. Small windows covered with wire mesh were set high in the walls. Only one door was visible.

"That must be the plant where they process the methane."

Sally nodded but didn't say anything. She was using the binoculars to scan the area. The entire compound was illuminated erratically by security lights mounted above the doors of each building.

Next to the plant was the waste lagoon, looking much larger than it had in the photographs. Much bigger than the duck pond in San Francisco. Adjacent to the lagoon was a drainage ditch that ran parallel to the long side of the factory. It looked deep and seemed to run past the far side of the lagoon into the open field, where it disappeared in the darkness. On the far side of the valley was the hulking outline of Cerro de la Silla, the four mountain peaks looking like a saddle without a rider.

"Definitely a trap."

Cape dug in his pocket for the night vision scope. "Why?"

"Nobody down there."

"How far did you get?" Cape pressed the power button as he placed his right cheek against the rubberized eyepiece.

"I'm on the third shed."

Cape closed his left eye and opened his right as wide as he could. A green circle of light appeared, lines slowing becoming sharper as the scope reached full power.

He started from the far end, working the opposite direction from Sally, beginning with the refinery building. Pools of light around the windows and door looked impossibly bright, as if the noon sun had appeared while he was looking through the scope.

Sally muttered under her breath in Cantonese.

"What?"

"Ten o'clock." Sally kept her eyes pressed to the binoculars. "Past the last shed, before you get to the refinery."

Cape focused between the buildings where the pools of light didn't overlap. At first he didn't see anything, just clumps of weeds and moist earth. He started to wonder if he was looking at the two o'clock position instead of ten o'clock—he always got those confused—when he saw something that made him want to learn Chinese just so he could curse.

"Drag marks?"

Sally nodded. "Follow them left toward the drainage ditch."

Two shallow streaks in the mud about a foot apart framed a deeper indentation that followed the same path. They were about the depth and spacing you'd expect if you dragged a dead or unconscious body backward. Cape stopped breathing as he followed the streaks past the door of the refinery toward the drainage ditch a few yards away.

At first he saw nothing, just a river of blackness where the ditch started. Then his eyes adjusted and he moved slowly away from the building. He didn't have to look for long.

"Is that a shoe?"

Sally traded her binoculars for Cape's night vision. "Yes, and it's attached to a foot."

Cape squinted through the binoculars but it was no use. "Can you see anything else?"

Sally nodded. "Another shoe."

"His other foot, presumably."

"Not unless he has two left feet."

Cape resisted the urge to make a dancing remark. "You sure?"

"Here."

Cape took the scope. A left leg jutted up from the ditch, twisted at an unnatural angle, but there was no sign of the right. Several feet further down the ditch, too far to be connected to the same body, another left leg appeared. They'd have to get closer if they wanted to know whose bodies were piled there.

"What do you think?"

"I think we never should have left California." Sally adjusted the sword on her back.

"I think the excitement's over—nothing's moving down there."

"Which side do you want?"

"You check the sheds, I'll take the ditch, we meet at the refinery."

Sally slid down the hill like a figure skater, right leg forward and left bent back, her hands out for balance. She didn't make a sound as she disappeared into the shadows. Cape scrambled after her like a fat kid on a slip-'n-slide.

The rolling thunder was louder on the valley floor, much louder. Cape realized it must be reflecting off the hillside, which meant it was coming from inside the valley. He looked at the sky, the moon surrounded by stars but not a cloud in sight.

It wasn't a storm coming. The thunder was the sound of thirty thousand pigs snoring. Grumbling in their sleep, pushing, grinding against the walls of the sheds and each other to make room for their beds. By the time he reached the drainage ditch the air was vibrating with the bass notes coming from the sheds. Cape could feel the reverberations deep in his chest.

He looked back toward the first shed. He thought he sensed movement near the window closest the door but it barely registered, a shadow blowing on the wind. Cape guessed Sally was inside.

He stuck to the shadows, veering left toward the side of the drainage channel that was furthest from the refinery door. He gauged the distance—it looked like the ditch was about four feet deep.

Cape took one last look around, crouched low, and jumped into the ditch.

Chapter Sixty-three

Sally pressed against the wall as she moved away from the window.

The catwalk was wide enough for two people to walk abreast along the perimeter of the shed, but Sally preferred staying in the shadows. A waist-high railing with evenly spaced supports ran the length of the catwalk, which was a grilled surface of wrought iron. It afforded an unobstructed view of the tenants below.

The first impression was of a single organism, a seething mass of pink and brown that might have oozed out of a 1950s horror film. It took Sally a minute before she could distinguish individual pigs from the undulating sea of flesh.

The animals were enormous, prize pigs one and all, no runts in sight. The smallest would outweigh Sally by fifty pounds, the biggest by two hundred. The collective animal stench tore through her scarf like a razor dipped in shit.

The shed looked bigger inside than she expected, half as long as a soccer field. She scanned the room for other signs of life but it seemed empty. Just her and the pigs.

She moved down the catwalk. At the peak of the roof directly across from her was a giant tube flared at one end and covered with a screen. The open end was aimed at the pigs. The back end connected to a central pipe that ran along the center beam of the shed until it reached another flared tube about ten yards away. Sally counted five such tubes, the last mounted on the far wall of the shed, where it followed the curve of the roof until it disappeared through a hole. Sally visualized it connecting to the massive tank seen from the hill during their surveillance.

The workers must wear some type of filters or masks. Sally stopped every few feet and tried to control her breathing. Her scarf wasn't up to this. She fought a rising sense of vertigo whenever she looked at the pigs through the grill between her feet, even though she never had trouble with heights.

The pigs crashed together in thunderous packs, many snorting in anger or frustration over a lost position. The sound was deafening. A wave of hunger surging toward the catwalk.

A memory crawled out of Sally's subconscious, images buried for many years. Twelve years old, still in school but already hard at work to pay for her tuition. Triad schools were very expensive, and most girls spent their entire lives working off the debt.

She was sent to the estate of a local gangster named Shun, high in the hills overlooking Hong Kong. The house had a spectacular view of Causeway Bay from the front of the house, but in the backyard Shun had erected wooden pens to keep chickens, goats, and pigs. Not because he needed to raise livestock but to remind him of the miserable farm where he grew up. He wanted the life he had left in his backyard, behind him at all times as a reminder of what he stood to lose. Too bad for Shun he never looked out his kitchen window anymore, only through his front windows toward the city beneath his feet.

Shun had taken something that didn't belong to him—the daughter of a banker who sometimes did business with the Triads. She was ten years old when Shun molested her after coaxing her away from friends and into his Mercedes.

The leader of the Triads, a man known only as *Dragonhead*, was very clear about the punishment. Sally's instructors had decided to turn the mission into a training exercise. Her job was to distract Shun until one of the older girls from the school named Dandan could sneak into the compound.

It wasn't a difficult job. Sally arrived in a school uniform and pig tails under a false pretense. Shun wouldn't have opened the door any faster if she'd been delivering a pizza. She was supposed to let him *play* with her until her backup arrived, but when he put his hand on her thigh, Sally decided to demonstrate her initiative.

Dandan entered the house thirty minutes later accompanied by two *forty-nines*—male foot soldiers—and found Sally reading in the living room. Shun was unconscious on the floor with a livid bruise on his cheek.

Sally and Dandan sat on the second floor balcony eating rice cakes and admiring the view while the foot soldiers disemboweled Shun and threw him in with the pigs.

The police never found the body and the rival clan assumed he had skipped town. Pigs had voracious appetites, especially once they tasted blood. Sally remembered feeling sorry for the pigs.

If she closed her eyes, she could still recall the sounds from the backyard.

She was halfway across the catwalk when she turned to look back the way she had come. She was standing at the mid-point between two of the flared intake pipes, so her line of sight was clear. Her eyes found the window where she had entered and moved past the railing, onto the floor and finally to the main door.

Sally froze and cursed herself for not checking the door first. She could have hung upside down over the railing, but it was too late. She hoped Cape hadn't reached the refinery.

She started to run, her feet clanging against the metal grill of the catwalk as the pigs thundered and roared below.

Chapter Sixty-four

Cape crawled through the mud looking for corpses.

He tried to be stealthy and managed to stay low, but he was moving too quickly and making too much noise. If he was right about Salinas then he wouldn't find Rebecca here, not in the ditch with the others. She would be part of a bigger message, a witness to a show that hadn't occurred yet. Cape believed that rationally, but emotionally he was a wreck. His hands were shaking as he scuttled forward on his knees, praying he wouldn't see her face half-buried in the mud.

He practically rammed the first body, banging his head into the poor bastard's knee. Cape fell back against the side of the ditch, tasting bile in his throat. It was a man, middle aged with black hair and olive skin. He wore a guard's uniform.

Cape took a deep breath. He found an LED penlight in his vest and leaned over the body. There were no signs of violence around the face or neck, just some minor scratches that could have been caused post-mortem by getting dragged across the ground, or even cuts from shaving. A billy club, radio and stun gun were still clipped to a utility belt, none of the straps loose. He had been taken by surprise, very quickly.

Cape moved the light across the torso and stopped right below the heart. A stab wound had bled out, the shirt tacky with blood. He switched off the light and crawled further down the ditch. This time he saw the body before he reached it.

Another guard, same uniform and equipment. This one had his throat cut. A professional job, the windpipe severed so he couldn't cry out. The wound was ragged, scraps of flesh trailing into the collar and onto the shirt. Someone who hadn't seen this kind of thing before would swear that a wolf had torn the man's throat out.

Cape squeezed his eyes shut for a minute before putting his head down and crawling forward.

Ten yards.

Twenty.

Nothing.

The compound wasn't that big. Two guards on night duty could probably handle it under normal circumstances. Cape stood until he could see over the edge of the ditch, looked back toward the refinery building. He wondered if Sally had finished searching the sheds.

Hoisting himself over the edge, Cape decided to abandon caution and jog back to the refinery building. If anyone was watching the compound with night vision goggles they would have seen him by now. Maybe not Sally, she was a ghost, but Cape had no illusions about his own lack of grace.

Still, he wasn't completely reckless. Once he reached the door to the plant he braced against the wall and stood perfectly still, listening as hard as he could.

Humming from inside. Lights, maybe a generator. Clanging in the near distance, as constant as a metronome. The door was metal, the walls stone, but neither seemed very thick. Cape pulled the handgun from his belt and flicked off the safety with his right thumb as he grabbed the door handle with his left hand.

He crouched as he spun inside the door but was stunned by the glare from the lights. The entire plant was lit up like a stadium, countless 100-watt bulbs inside wire mesh hanging from the ceiling. Pipes, motors, and pumps grew from the floor and walls, twisting and turning in an industrial maze that seemed to lead toward a series of giants vents mounted on the far wall.

The noise was disorienting, funneled toward the open space in front of the door. There was a generator near the center of the room with a circular motor spinning like clockwork, clanging every time it completed a rotation. Humming came from every direction at once. And directly in front of Cape there was an insistent beeping, a manic high-pitched chirping that sounded like an alarm clock in a cheap hotel. He hadn't heard that sound before he opened the door.

Cape stood slowly as he tried to see what was making the noise.

A three-legged stool sat twenty feet away from the door, set against the wall next to a small desk. On top of the stool was a lumpy bundle of plastic, tape, red putty, and wires, one of which led from the stool to the wall, over the desk and along the door frame, where it was attached to a magnetic trigger that Cape had broken when he opened the door.

On top of the bundle was a red LED screen flashing in time with the beeps. Then the beeping stopped—and so did Cape's heart—until it was replaced by a shrill whine. Cape tried to get his feet to move but they wouldn't, and suddenly the countdown started.

The lights had been nonsense during the beeping, all the LED lights illuminated at once. But now they resolved into numbers.

Someone had a sense of humor. Instead of numbers, letters appeared, and instead of counting down, the timer was counting upward.

Uno   Dos   Tres

Cape tried to remember his high school Spanish and wondered how high he could count before he died.

Chapter Sixty-five

Sally heard the explosion from four buildings away.

She skidded to a stop on the catwalk and gripped the railing. *One second. Two seconds. Three seconds.* When she reached five she heard a second explosion. Closer.

The explosion was igniting the methane in the pipes, working its way through the buildings.

One second. Two seconds. Three—

She felt the next explosion before she heard it.

Sally whipped around to watch the intake vent at the far end of the building, the countdown still going in her head. Six buildings, counting the refinery. Three to go, less than five seconds apart and getting closer.

Sally looked toward the front door and the window where she entered. She would never make it. A dull roar was building in the pipes, the sound of gas expanding, getting hotter and looking for a place to burn.

One second. Two—

The walls shook as if hit by a hurricane. The catwalk jumped. Pigs squealed and trampled over one another trying to find a way out. Two explosions to go, and then the air would turn to fire.

Sally jumped onto the railing.

The pigs were in a frenzy. Butting heads, biting. Sally saw blood mixed with manure and mud on the floor. It was a mosh pit from Hell.

She almost lost her balance when the next explosion hit, the blast wave shoving superheated air through the walls. The roaring in the pipes had become a scream. The lights flickered and went out.

Sally closed her eyes and reversed her footing, so she was facing the catwalk and the wall. The pigs were behind and below her, churning the mud, their backs shifting like waves.

One—two—

Sally spread her arms and tilted her head back as her heels slipped off the railing and she fell backward into space.

Chapter Sixty-six

"Shit."

The sound of his own voice shocked Cape out of his stupor before the timer reached *Cinco*.

He crashed through the door and leapt for the drainage ditch. He landed hard, twisting his ankle, just as the walls of the refinery building turned into shrapnel.

Blue flame erupted into a mushroom cloud that turned yellow and then orange as it expanded into the night sky. The metal door screamed past like a discus thrown by an angry giant. Cape wrapped his arms around his head as flaming bits of metal, stone, and plastic fell like meteors.

He felt something hit his leg, a napalm hailstone, and his pants started to burn. Cape rolled in the mud and tried to scramble backward but it was raining fire all around him. The second explosion took off the roof of the adjacent shed. The walls disintegrated into splinters that flew like darts.

Cape wondered where Sally could be, hoping she was still in the first building. Then the next shed erupted in a fireball and he realized that she wouldn't be safe in any of them.

A shard of two-by-four plunged into the earth only three inches from Cape's ear. Another one narrowly missed his foot. By the time a third penetrated the ground between his legs, he felt like Dracula being hunted by angry villagers. He got his legs under him and pushed backward. Only a dead man could help him now.

He reached the first corpse and pulled the body on top of his own, careful not to leave any extremities exposed. Cape was slightly taller than the guard so he bent his knees and angled his legs.

The next building blew up. Cape held his breath and hoped it was over.

It wasn't. The next shed exploded and Cape saw pigs fly. A two hundred pound sow landed only a few yards away, bursting on impact in a shower of entrails. A three hundred pounder followed, a porcine asteroid big enough to kill the dinosaurs.

A pig's head complete landed with its snout only inches from Cape's nose. A pair of smoldering pig's feet bounced off his sneakers. He heard squealing and the thunder of cloven hooves. The last shed went *ba-boom*, the gas explosion followed immediately by the sound of the building cracking apart like an egg.

Cape counted to three and threw the corpse to the side, scrambled up the side of the ditch and started running toward the building where he'd last seen Sally.

He ran headlong into a stampede and had to dive back into the ditch to avoid being trampled to death. Thousands upon thousands of terrified pigs were running in every direction. Some were horribly maimed but most were surprisingly unhurt. A few were smoking along their backs where their wispy hair had caught fire and burned itself out.

Cape ran along the ditch until it began to fill up with panicked pigs climbing over one another. He put his head down and shoulder forward, assuming a linebacker pose as he tried to redirect the scared animals. He rolled out of the ditch and tried to hold his ground as the herd parted around him, too terrified to be aggressive. He dug his heels into the mud, straining to see into the darkness, desperate to keep moving forward.

In minutes that seemed like hours, but eventually the pigs had fled to all points of the compass, scattering across the broad valley as fast as their stubby legs could carry them. Cape's legs gave out and he collapsed into the mud.

He managed to get his hands under his chest and crawled for several yards before stopping and sitting back on his knees, panting heavily. He felt blood running down his face and snot pouring from his nose. His hands were bleeding, half the nails gone.

He stood up and almost fainted, then stumbled forward. Ten yards. Another ten. Shapes started to emerge in the darkness, his finally eyes adjusting to the moonlight after flame had lit up the sky forever.

A lone figure stood twenty feet in front of him. Sword drawn and covered in blood, her clothes shredded. Her hair matted and torn. Mud and manure smeared across her face and hands.

Cape had never seen her look so beautiful.

Sally smiled and slid her sword into its scabbard.

"Can we go home now?"

Chapter Sixty-seven

Cape looked in the bathroom mirror and wished he hadn't.

He wondered how he managed to drive to the hotel. A gash over his eye explained why he had trouble seeing clearly through the windshield. Splinters stuck out of his nose, cheeks, and ears in all directions and stung whether he smiled or frowned. He looked like a porcupine.

His skin burned, so many nerve endings had been overloaded. He knew he was in shock and should be in a hospital, but he and Sally had agreed that was a bad idea. Showing up at the emergency room smelling like smoked ham the same night a pig farm was destroyed might attract the wrong kind of attention.

It hurt when he moved in a million different ways. It hurt when he breathed. He couldn't smell anything besides over-cooked ribs. His ears were ringing. It was almost like being at a Tony Roma's on a Friday night.

Cape turned on the shower and let it run until steam clouded the mirror. He had seen enough. A sign mounted on the wall asked him to use only as many towels as he needed. Judging from what he'd seen in the mirror, Cape suspected he was going to need them all.

He stifled a scream when the water hit him and grabbed for the handicap bar. There wasn't one. He went down hard, landing on his tail bone. He decided to shower sitting down.

He must have passed out, because when he awoke the water was ice cold. His skin was turning blue so the hot water must have run out a while ago. It occurred to him that he might have a concussion.

He turned off the water and gingerly stood up, grabbed a towel off the rack and patted his face dry. He looked at the towel, which now had red and pink blotches all over it. This was going to take a while.

He needed caffeine. Cape tried to remember what the doctor had told him the last time he got a concussion, but that was the problem with head injuries, you tended to forget things. *Don't go to sleep.* That was it. Caffeine must be the right answer.

He remembered there was a soda machine in the lobby.

Cape made it to the bed where his suitcase lay open. The first aid kit he always carried seemed laughably small given the task, but after twenty minutes he had enough band-aids deployed to look like a mascot at a sticker convention.

He managed to pull on a fresh pair of jeans and a t-shirt from the Orbit Drive-In Theatre, then sat on the bed and pulled on a pair of Converse. Trying to pull on socks might have killed him, so he let the Chuck Taylors protect his bare feet.

Cape took a deep breath and walked over to the desk where he'd left his wallet and hotel key. He felt like he'd been run over by a bulldozer but at least he was clean. Now he needed a drink, anything that wasn't Mexican tap water.

The lobby was empty, the front desk deserted. Not unexpected given the hour.

Less expected was the man sitting alone at the lobby bar. Two shot glasses were placed deliberately in front of him next to a bottle of tequila.

"Ah, you are awake *amigo*. I was hoping you could join me for a drink." Inspector Oscar Garcia smiled and nudged the stool next to him with his foot.

For some reason he wouldn't understand until much later, Cape wasn't terribly surprised to see his old friend.

Chapter Sixty-eight

Sally stripped naked and ran the bath.

She took her clothes and wrapped them in the plastic laundry bag from the closet, then stuffed the bag into the garbage can. She could still smell only blood but knew that was probably because she hadn't yet bathed.

She also knew it could be her own sense-memory. At other times, under different circumstances, the smell of death and copper taste of blood had been a comfort to her. But not now.

Sally padded across the bedroom and opened a side pocket in her suitcase, from which she extracted a bag of dried tea leaves. She shook the bag searching for the ones she wanted among the many-colored leaves. Green, black, rust, red. She found a large leaf almost as big as a maple but gray with dark green veins running out from the stem. She folded it into a ball, popped it into her mouth and chewed slowly. It tasted horrible, bitter and moldy, but it was a natural analgesic that promoted healing.

She wished the tub were bigger and pulled the plug, deciding to take a shower first. It took a long time. When she was finished she looked at herself in the mirror, taking for granted the perfect contours and hardened muscles but making mental notes about every new scar or injury. Sally had been trained as a girl to always make the health of her body her top priority. She was a weapon that had to be honed every day so it was always ready for battle.

When she had cleaned the filth from her body she cleaned the tub, then ran the bath. By bending at the waist she was able to run her legs up the wall and submerge her head underwater.

She closed her eyes and wondered what she would see when she started to drown.

Chapter Sixty-nine

"You tracked me here." Cape sat down heavily on the bar stool. "You've been keeping tabs."

"You leave quite a trail behind you."

Cape looked around for a glass but they were all behind the bar, save for the two shot glasses. He reached across the bar, grabbed the bar gun and found the button for Coke. Then he pressed the button and sprayed it into his mouth. His eyes cleared as sugar jacked up his blood sugar and caffeine dilated his blood vessels. Garcia held his gaze the entire time.

When he was finished, Cape wiped the bar gun on a napkin and replaced it. "Uncouth, I know, even for an American. But the thought of getting a glass is beyond me right now."

Garcia nodded sympathetically. "You have had a rough week."

"I don't know how much you know, but you don't know the half of it."

"You smell like bacon."

"I just had breakfast."

Garcia smiled and poured two glasses of tequila. The liquid was as clear as water. Cape glanced at the bottle.

"What are we drinking tonight?"

"It is almost morning." Garcia twisted the bottle so Cape could clearly read the label. "Don Julio Blanco—one hundred percent pure agave."

"Expensive?"

"Of course." Garcia raised his glass. "When the bar is open."

They clinked glasses and Cape took a sip. His nostrils cleared and for the first time in hours he smelled something other than pig. He blinked as his eyes started to water.

"*Gracias.*" Cape took another sip.

Garcia nodded and set his own glass down. "I wanted to apologize."

Cape shifted on his stool. "For what?"

"I had to inform the media about Danny and his father, the Senator, before I could warn you." Garcia sighed. "And before you could warn your client."

"Not your fault. I saw that you called."

"Twice—you were busy?"

"I went sailing."

"A charming sport."

"In my car."

"You lead an exciting life."

"I didn't a week ago." Cape reached for the bar gun. The caffeine-alcohol-sugar therapy seemed to be working. "My life was nice and boring before I came to Mexico."

"Anything can happen here."

"I believe you now."

"And what brings you to Monterrey?" Garcia refilled Cape's glass.

"I understand there's a lot to see."

"It is true. Mexico's third largest city—shopping, world class museums. The discos. And the mountains, of course. Hiking is very popular. Have you *been* to the mountains yet?"

"A valley," said Cape. "I made it to one of the valleys."

"Monterrey is also a city of industry. Banking. Technology. Agriculture."

"Agriculture." Cape took a slow sip of tequila, breathing in as it burned its way along his esophagus. "Farming."

"*Sí*, there is a very large pig farm just outside the city. Perhaps you saw it on a map."

"I don't think it's on the map anymore."

Garcia chuckled and refilled his own glass. He studied his companion but didn't say anything.

"Oscar, who did you say you work for?"

"I am an inspector with the Mexico State Police."

"That wasn't the question, Oscar."

"I thought I gave you a business card." Garcia raised his glass to the light and admired the clarity of the liquid. "There are other branches of law enforcement, of course. The AFI—*federales*—our version of your FBI."

"Do you work for them?"

"Sometimes."

Cape arched an eyebrow. "Sometimes."

"Did you find what you were looking for, Señor Cape?"

"No." Cape turned on his stool so their knees were almost touching. "Are you going to help me?"

"I already have." Garcia rubbed a hand across his mouth.

"How?"

"I bought you a drink on two occasions."

"Oscar—"

"—and tried to give you some advice. You're not terribly good at taking advice, are you?"

"No."

"Neither am I." Garcia tapped his fingers on the bar. "Perhaps that is why we get along."

"You knew about the farm."

"Of course."

"Then you must know who owns it."

"Luis Cordon—everyone in Mexico knows who owns that property."

"Even the government?"

"Especially the Mexican government."

"But does the government know about the money laundering—the bogus carbon offsets?"

"Offsets?" Garcia frowned. "You mean credits."

Cape shook his head. "Not sure what they're called here." He explained the scam that Linda and Sloth had discovered in as much detail as he could remember. When he was finished Garcia clapped his hands together.

"You have done much homework, my friend. But there is more to Cordon's empire—much more."

"More." Cape felt lightheaded. He reached for the bar gun.

"You have heard of the Kyoto Protocols?"

"Sure." Cape nodded. "Big treaty between countries around the world to try and stop global warming."

"Which the United States voted against."

"Don't blame me—I'm just an American taxpayer—we don't get to vote on anything our government does."

"You are too defensive." Garcia patted Cape's arm. "Most developed countries did sign the treaty, so now they have to limit their greenhouse emissions, unless..." He let his voice trail off.

"Unless?"

"Unless they buy something that lets them keep polluting."

"Carbon credits?"

Garcia filled both their glasses. Cape didn't remember emptying his.

"I think you are feeling better, my inquisitive friend."

"You're saying there's money in carbon credits?"

"Say you have a factory in Germany."

"OK." Cape injected more Coke into his system before reaching for his shot glass. "What kind of factory?"

"It doesn't matter. It could be a chemical factory, an automotive plant. Let us say you own a manufacturing facility for a toy company that makes wind-up animals—little plastic flying pigs."

"I understand they're very popular in Mexico."

"You have already installed the latest filters, the newest technology. All the anti-pollution equipment available. But you can't lower your greenhouse emissions any further without closing the factory, which of course is not an option. What do you do?"

"Buy a carbon credit from somebody else?"

"*Exactamente.* Perhaps you buy them from a pig farm in Mexico which is reducing emissions by turning methane into carbon dioxide. As the farm reduces greenhouse gases, it earns carbon *credits.*"

"So the Mexicans earn credits which they sell to the Germans."

"*Sí*, on the open market."

"For how much?"

"Carbon trading has reached over thirty billion dollars on the European market alone. That is U.S. dollars."

"Billion, with a *b*?"

Garcia nodded. "There have been many articles in the global financial press. *The Financial Times. Forbes. El Financiero.* Serious money is crossing borders."

"But it's all regulated, right?" Cape watched Garcia carefully.

"I wish that were the case." Garcia placed both hands around his shot glass and rolled it between them. "*Verdad*, I really do. And I think it could work one day."

"But?"

"One cannot expect U.N. inspectors to tour every pig farm in Mexico, India, or Mongolia—their oil for food program was *un desastre*, and that was only one country. These exchanges take place between developed and undeveloped countries, farms and factories all over the world."

"So how does it work?" Cape sipped some more tequila.

"Many factories and farms exaggerate their claims, driving up the number of credits they earn. We estimate that twenty percent of credits earned in Mexico are inflated."

Cape almost spit. "That's almost six billion dollars."

"Globally, yes." Garcia held his glass close to his nose and inhaled. "Right now carbon credits are a cross between the free market and the honor system."

"And you think Cordon's operation might not be all that honorable?"

The right side of Garcia's mouth turned up but stopped short of a smile. "All Cordon would have to do is exaggerate the production of methane by a few percentage points to earn more credits, then he could sell them as pure profit on the European market. It is like printing your own shares in a publicly traded company."

"Tempting even if you're not a criminal."

"Indeed." Garcia drained his glass. "Now do you understand why someone might want to kill your Senator?"

"As if hundreds of millions of dollars weren't reason enough—"

"Compared to billions...most men would stop at nothing."

Cape shot the rest of his tequila. "Why didn't you tell me this before?"

"I was hoping you would go home and forget about Mexico."

"Was that what you meant about not being good at taking advice?"

Garcia made no comment. He reached out and tilted the bottle. It was half empty.

"I should have listened to you," said Cape. "I've been a pawn in somebody else's game the entire time."

"And now you know what the game is."

"But the stakes have changed, Oscar. I've lost my client."

"This reminds me of the conversation we had when we first met."

"I'm not being coy this time."

"I know." Garcia exhaled loudly, blowing out his cheeks. "I know about the Senator's daughter."

"So does everybody else. It was in the papers, remember?"

"I am deeply sorry."

"You were just doing your job."

"Perhaps." Garcia rapped his fingers on the bar again. He seemed to be making some sort of decision. "But what is *your* job?"

"What do you mean?"

"You have a client, but who have you been working for?"

Cape started to reply but caught himself. "You mean Salinas—I've been working for Salinas this whole time when I thought I was just taking his money."

"That certainly *seems* to be the case…" Garcia sounded like he didn't believe a word of what he was saying. He looked at Cape to make sure he noticed.

"But tonight he tried to kill me." Cape stared at his empty shot glass.

"Why?"

Cape shrugged. "Tie up loose ends."

Garcia plucked at his sleeve. "He could have killed you when you were in his office. Why now?"

"Why now?" Cape repeated the question, then said it to himself again.

Why now.

Something had been gnawing at the back of his brain since he met Rebecca at the restaurant. A stray thought that got knocked down when his car drove off a pier. A feeling in his gut that got a little heavier after Linda explained Cordon's operation. Something that didn't fit with the facts. Something that broke the pattern if you looked at things from a different angle, turned the whole thing upside down.

Why now.

"Salinas could have killed the Senator nine months ago. He could have killed me last week."

"Now you know what has been troubling me."

"But why, Oscar? Why now?"

Garcia shook his head. "Only one man can answer that question, and it is not Antonio Salinas. Because if you ask him and are wrong, there is very little chance you will live to see the morning."

"If you're suggesting what I think you are, my odds aren't going to be much better."

"They say you haven't really seen Mexico until you visit both of our drug lords."

"Who says that?"

"I just did."

Cape stood and braced himself against the bar. "I need to go see Luis Cordon."

"So it would seem."

"Can you help me?"

"Why not?" Garcia stood and pulled a stray thread off his jacket. "I know where he lives."

Chapter Seventy

"Do you want me to kill you now?"

Sally sat cross-legged on the bed wearing what looked like loose black pajamas, though they might have been her regular clothes. Cape could never tell.

"Was that a rhetorical question?"

"You seem intent on killing yourself." Sally spoke calmly but her eyes were unyielding. "Thought I might save you some time."

"I've lost my client."

"She was taken—there's a difference."

"I have to get her back."

Sally muttered something in Cantonese.

"You don't have to come."

"I know." Sally stood and stepped over to the other bed, where she had arranged her weapons. She began sorting them into various piles.

"I don't see any other way."

"Neither do I." Sally turned to face him. "*A lack of options is the quickest path to defeat.*"

"Art Of War?"

"Common sense." Sally sighed. "You said Cordon lives in a castle?"

"That's what Oscar called it."

"He's coming with us?"

"He'll meet us there. He needs to call some people, make arrangements."

"So we go in alone, just you and me."

"Drug lords don't come to the door when police are ringing the bell."

"Any idea how many men will be inside?"

Cape almost smiled. "Of course not."

"Floor plans?"

"Nope."

"No time to get them, either, I suppose."

Cape shook his head. "*Time is not our friend.*"

Sally raised her eyebrows. "Confucius?"

"The sad truth."

Sally smiled despite herself. "When do we leave?"

"As soon as I make a phone call."

Chapter Seventy-one

Antonio Salinas put down the phone and smiled.

"Who was that?" Priest sat in the shadows on the far side of the room. The blinds were drawn and the only lamp was next to Salinas on the desk.

"Someone I never expected to hear from again."

"The news we've been expecting?"

"No." Salinas shook his head in wonder. "I never expected this."

"I told you to have a little faith." Priest stretched like a cat. "Good news?"

Salinas pressed his fingers together in a mock prayer and brought them to his lips.

"Miraculous."

Chapter Seventy-two

They took turns driving.

Sally slept for the first few hours, curled up in the back seat. When it was his turn, Cape tried to rest but couldn't—his mind was racing, in part because of Sally's driving. He had forgotten she didn't have a license.

"I never needed one. You don't need a car in Hong Kong, and in San Francisco I tend to stay near Chinatown."

Cape nodded. Even compact cars couldn't travel across rooftops and through windows. He took the wheel.

They drove in silence until *Matamoros* started appearing on the signs. Sally counted off the distance whenever they passed a new one, in case Cape had fallen asleep at the wheel. They were still more than an hour from the city when he told her his plan.

Sally didn't say anything for a long time.

"It's hard to believe it could work."

"The only angle I could think of—it's worth a try."

"You're going to blow this whole thing up."

"They tried to do the same to us."

"I'm not saying I don't like the plan." Sally turned in her seat. "But blowing things up can get—"

"—messy?"

Sally nodded. "We won't really know until we get there. You could be wrong."

"So we stick to the plan."

"Planning only leads to failure. A successful warrior relies on preparation, not planning."

"So we stick to the preparation?"

"Just stop."

"Trying to let off some steam. To mentally *prepare*."

Sally scowled. "*The ability to gain victory by changing and adapting is called genius.*"

"Art of War?"

"Very good—extra credit for the Occidental kid in the front seat."

"I'm not as uncultured as you might think—for a *gwai-loh*. Ask me another."

"Just drive."

Chapter Seventy-three

The private jet landed on the small airstrip north of the city and taxied to a stop near the terminal.

"You are staying behind?" Salinas turned to his companion.

Priest shook his head. "I'm going to wait until dark—I think you should, as well."

"You are too superstitious."

Priest tugged at his collar. "Perhaps."

Salinas gestured to the six men standing near the door of the cabin. "*Vamanos.*"

One of the men stood apart from the rest of the group. He had a bulbous nose and a nasally whine to his voice. His name was André but not everyone called him by his real name. He jutted his chin at Priest. "Want me to stay with you?"

"No, thank you." Priest gestured toward Salinas. "Go keep our host company."

A black Escalade was waiting for them. Salinas sat in front next to the driver.

As the men took their seats they each grabbed a suitcase from the floor in front of them. Hard-sided Pelican cases filled with custom padded foam. They set the cases on their laps and opened them to find a Heckler & Koch MP5 submachine gun with a folding stock capable of firing in burst mode—three bullets at a time—or fully automatic at over 600 rounds per minute. Next to the gun were two 50-round clips and a single hand grenade.

"Holy shit," said André. "You don't mess around."

Salinas turned in his seat to smile at his American guest. "I prefer the direct approach."

As they pulled onto the city streets the driver looked over at Salinas.

"Playa del Bagdad?"

Salinas nodded. "*Castillo* Cordon."

Chapter Seventy-four

Cape drove around until they found an American hotel. They didn't have much time and wanted tourist-friendly directions and maps in English. They pulled into the Best Western Plaza Hotel on the corner of 9th and Bravo and checked into a single room, double occupancy. They didn't plan on spending the night.

They hit the gift shop before going to their room, grabbing hats, shorts, shirts and sunglasses. When they returned to the lobby they looked completely different.

Sally was wearing a loose cotton blouse over black pants that flared at the ankles. Her face was shadowed by a wide-brimmed hat tied around her chin. With her darker skin, light freckles, and almond-shaped eyes, she could almost pass for a local.

Cape had gone for an equally innocuous look, a long t-shirt hanging over baggy shorts, Teva sandals. Around his neck were a camera and a pair of sunglasses. He smiled as they passed a full-length mirror next to the elevators.

"You look like a native."

"You look like a tourist."

"Wait a sec." Cape rummaged in his cargo shorts. He sorted through the photos he had taken from Rebecca's collection and handed two to Sally. "You take these, I'll keep the rest."

"You sure this will work? You said Cordon lives on the beach."

"Bagdad Beach, about twenty kilometers east of here." Cape spread his hands. "There's apparently nothing out there, just this monstrous house that Cordon built right on the ocean."

"So if anyone came into town—"

"They'd come here." Cape put his photos back in his pocket. "And I don't want to go the castle until it's dark."

"OK, let's go for a walk."

"You take north and east, I'll go south and west. Meet here in two hours."

Sally tipped her hat. "*Adios.*"

"*Hasta luego.*"

Cape checked the street signs against the map whenever he reached a neighborhood that looked a little different from the one before. He was trying to see the city through someone else's eyes. The ground was relatively flat, the architecture mostly colonial. The streets busy but not terribly crowded. Cape glanced at the tour book as he walked.

Matamoros is located directly across the Rio Grande from Brownsville, Texas, its sister city on the other side of the border. Because of its proximity to the United States it is known as *La Gran Puerta de Mexico*—the Great Door To Mexico—a distinction celebrated by a massive red sculpture, a post-modern arch welcoming visitors from both countries.

In 1826 the city got its name *Villa de Matamoros* in honor of the independence hero Don Mariano Matamoros, but prior to that the town had been called many things. When Capitan Juan José de Hinojosa explored the region in 1706 he was struck by the natural beauty of the wetlands surrounding the area, so he called it *Paraje de los Esteros Hermosos*—Place of the Beautiful Marshes. Almost a hundred years later Franciscan monks came, and while they were also impressed by Mother Nature, it was their job to claim territory in the name of Mother Mary, so they renamed it *Nuestra Señora del Refugio de los Esteros*—Our Lady of the Refuge of the Beautiful Marshes, a compromise worthy of their order.

The locals simply called their city The Refuge—*El Refugio*—or town of refuge, a name that seemed to suit it best. Because of its location near the ocean and directly across the river from the States, it was the perfect border town. A hub for smuggling everything from drugs to guns to human beings. A place to pass through on your way to a better life. Sometimes a place to hide. A gateway to freedom for many, the city of refuge was also an open door for men like Luis Cordon.

There are almost half a million people in Matamoros, and Cape knew the odds against finding one person in a city that size. But he knew something about the person he was looking for, and Cape had a hunch about the type of places to visit.

He had two hours to see if he was right.

Chapter Seventy-five

The house looked like a castle.

It overlooked Bagdad Beach on what until recently had been public property. Following his deal with the Mexican government for building refineries that turned methane into electricity, Luis Cordon found allies on the zoning commission. They discovered a portion of beachfront property unsuitable for public bathing because the soil had been contaminated with hazardous waste. The government could not afford to clean it up, so that section of the beach had to be closed. Cordon graciously agreed to buy the land from the state and clean up the spill. No one ever determined how the ground was contaminated in the first place.

But the castle also looked like a house. It had huge picture windows in the front, welcoming until you noticed the heavy leaded glass, which a security expert would tell you was bulletproof. The walls were rust-colored stone, the color of an adobe house but the shape of a medieval fortress.

The front was only one story high, but the ground sloped sharply beneath the house, the back facing the ocean. It was deceptive rolling up to the driveway, but on foot from the beach side it was clear that the house was huge. The top floor stretched four stories above the churning waves and rocks below.

Salinas had the SUV stop directly in front of the house. This was no time to be subtle. Luis wouldn't be expecting him, not at his home. Never in person.

Luis wouldn't do anything stupid until he knew why his old boss had come to visit. He would expect a conversation, a little respect. Maybe a business proposition.

Salinas would give him none of those things. He had something Luis never expected him to have: inside information. Luis might threaten him physically, but Salinas could threaten him with publicity. He had already made all the necessary arrangements.

He snapped his fingers and his men piled out of the car, guns over their shoulders, grenades concealed in pockets or clipped to their belts. *Gauchos*, thought Salinas. I have a bunch of cowboys working for me. But they were loyal, and in the end that would make the difference.

No guards were visible in front of the house. The outer gate was open, a simple brick walkway leading up the door. On either side of the path the earth was hard-packed sand raked clean. It looked like the ground was being cleared for a landscaping project. Salinas wondered idly what kind of plants would grow in this sandy soil so close to the beach.

He waved his hand in an abrupt gesture and his five men spread out on either side of the brick walkway, three on the right and two on the far left. The American with *una nariz grande* stayed close to Salinas, immediately on his left but practically in his shadow. Typical American, always talking tough until the action started.

Inside the house, Enrique watched the men fan out across the sand. He waited until they had spaced themselves evenly, then he checked the security camera to see where Salinas was standing. With a nervous hand, he held the remote control in his hand, his thumb sliding back and forth across the top button. He waited until Salinas took another step forward, then Enrique pressed the button. He held it down so hard that his thumbnail turned white and only released it when the walls started to shake.

Earthquakes are caused by a sudden and violent disruption of earth. Tectonic plates floating on liquid magma collide, one slips under its neighbor and shakes it up a little. But what topples buildings and kills people isn't the magma or the plates—it's the ground resting on the plates, the soil beneath our feet that supports our weight when we walk, holds our buildings erect, and keeps our world on solid ground.

But ground isn't solid. It's porous. For every million grains of sand on the beach there are ten million air pockets between them. For hardened clay it might be less, but no speck of dirt really touches the one next to it. Like people, the earth needs room to breathe.

Give the ground too much air, though, and something terrible happens. It turns to liquid. Air pockets cause dirt to slip and slide. Pump enough air into sand and it liquefies, the grains flowing over each other like water. A patch of ground solid enough to support the weight of a car can be transformed into a churning wave as ephemeral as the human soul.

Salinas staggered backward on the paving stones as the ground opened its mouth on either side. The bricks bucked and yawed, the ones nearest the edges of the path disappearing into the sand like sinking ships. The earth roared and the men on either side of him were yelling. André had leapt onto the walkway directly behind Salinas and was clutching his shoulder like a drowning man.

The five men sank up to their waists instantly, sand spraying into the air, cross currents pulling the men sideways. Salinas saw one man lurch three feet to the left and then get yanked deeper into the sand, down to his chest. It looked like he'd been taken by a shark.

A muffled explosion and a cry of pure terror. The man on the far right must have worn his grenade on his belt and the pin was torn free by force of the wave. All around him the sand churned red. Salinas watched in horror as the man screamed until his head disappeared beneath the surface.

Salinas tried to run but the walkway was disintegrating. He felt the bricks wobble like rogue surfboards beneath his feet.

Then it stopped.

The earth went silent. Only the sound of grown men whimpering filled the courtyard. Salinas and André crouched together on the bricks. The four men still alive were stuck, held fast as if they were trees.

Once the air stopped pumping through the sand it went from liquid to solid in an instant. The men grunted and yelled, pressed down on the sand with their arms. Two tried to reach one another to get some leverage, but they might as well have been dropped into cement. They seemed to be able to move an inch at a time, but at this rate it would take them hours to dig themselves out.

Salinas had already decided to leave them behind when they started screaming.

The man on the far left was the first, then his companion a few yards away. Salinas saw something dart across the surface of the sand near one man's arm, then disappear. He looked to the right and caught more flashes of brown. Scuttling across the surface with the speed of many legs—insects, maybe some kind of crab. Salinas narrowed his eyes and took a step closer to the center of the walkway.

Scorpions.

Three inches long, barbed tails curling behind segmented bodies built for speed. One of the few creatures on the planet other than a shark whose only purpose in life was to bring death.

More breached the surface. Small and nimble enough to squeeze through the sand in a way that a human body never could. The men were delirious with fear, spit flying from their mouths as they shouted for help. They slapped the ground with maniacal energy but were not nearly fast enough to swat creatures that swam through the sand to sting their arms, legs and genitals.

Salinas watched in horror until the last man stopped twitching and died.

The front door opened.

A man in a haz-mat suit with a silver tank connected to a metal rod by a plastic tube stepped into the yard and took aim at the scorpions. Whatever yellow liquid was in the tank was deadly, far more toxic than the scorpions. It smoked when it hit them. They ran but couldn't escape. The spray made them whither and shrink like dry leaves under a magnifying glass. In less than five minutes the yard was clear.

The man in the suit disappeared and another man stepped into the doorway.

Enrique smiled and held up the remote control. This time his thumb hovered over the second button.

"That walkway has its own channel, a different set of pipes beneath your feet. You saw how quickly your men sank into solid ground. You might have noticed a few stray bricks disappeared as well."

He waited to make sure Salinas was paying close attention.

"What do you think will happen when I press this button?"

Salinas started to respond but André cut him off. The American stepped in close, and Salinas felt the barrel of a handgun press hard against his spine.

"That won't be necessary." André's nasal tones echoed around the open courtyard. "Just tell Cordon we want to come inside."

Chapter Seventy-six

Night brought a change in the weather.

Clouds scudded across the sky and rain slanted sideways by the time Cape and Sally left the hotel. The man behind the front desk reminded them it was hurricane season.

Wind buffeted their rental car as they drove east toward Bagdad Beach. The windshield wipers seemed to get weaker with every mile. Between the rocking and the lashing of the storm it felt like being at sea.

The house stood out like a third nipple in a topless bar. It was the only permanent structure on a bluff overlooking the ocean. From the road it looked like a bunker, low and immovable. They drove past from both directions, then parked half a mile down the road near a footpath that led to the beach.

They were soaked before their feet touched sand. Whitecaps danced all the way to the horizon as waves crashed onto the shore. The waves got bigger as they moved further up the beach.

"This sucks."

Cape leaned into the wind. His hair was plastered against his forehead. Sally's ponytail streamed behind her like a kite.

From this angle it was clearly a castle. The beach narrowed until it disappeared into a rock wall that sloped outward ten degrees and up three stories until it morphed into the foundation of Cordon's fortress. At the base of the cliff was a small tide pool with jagged rocks around the edges. The sand reappeared a short distance beyond the pool, as if Cordon's presence had put a chokehold on the beach.

The castle would cast a long shadow on a sunny day. Cape wondered if anyone ever dared explore the tide pool.

Lights were on in every window, and there were a lot of them. Even from three stories down the glass looked heavy, patterned with lead and set deep into the stone walls. The roof was flat with crenellations, stone diamonds on all sides jutting into the sky like spears.

Cape raised the binoculars but couldn't see a thing. The windows were too high and the rain ran down the lenses faster than he could clean them. Water was dripping into his eyes, down his neck and into his jacket.

"We could come back tomorrow." He had to raise his voice over the wind.

Sally patted her clothes to check that everything was where it belonged. Rain dripped off her nose in a miniature waterfall.

Cape went through his pockets and started dumping things onto the sand. The binoculars were useless, so was the night vision scope. The receipt from the gift shop wasn't going to stop a bullet, either. He adjusted his handgun on his hip and switched his pocketknife to his jeans.

"You know they'll search you." Sally ran both hands over her ponytail and squeezed. A torrent of water spilled onto the sand.

"I'm counting on it. If they find some things to confiscate, maybe they'll overlook some other things."

"In places they're less inclined to search."

"Yeah."

"That reminds me." Sally held out her hand.

"What?"

"Give me your balls."

Cape took a step back. "You're not the first woman to try and take them."

"Yeah, but I might be the first to give them back."

"How about I give you one and I keep one."

"Deal."

Cape unzipped his fly and rummaged around.

Sally rocked back and forth on the balls of her feet. "Having trouble finding it?"

"Shut up." Cape found what he was looking for and pulled. He winced as the duct tape tore hairs off his thigh. He took the sonic disruptor and placed it in Sally's upraised palm. "Careful, you don't know where it's been."

Sally turned it over in her hand. "I push this button?"

"Twice—make sure you push it twice."

Sally tugged on her ears to make sure the filters were still in place. Cape did the same and felt water spill down his wrists.

"Ready to walk back to the car?"

"I'm not coming."

Cape stopped in mid-stride. Sally was looking at the windows. He followed her line of sight up the broken wall of rock.

"We're in the middle of a hurricane."

Sally turned to face him. "I don't like doors—especially front doors."

She had a point. An image of the methane refinery flashed into Cape's brain and he reflexively started counting to himself in Spanish. He held her gaze for a long time, then turned his eyes toward the open ocean. Fifteen-foot swells were crashing onto the beach. The water was gray flecked with white, turning black at the edge of the horizon. The storm was getting worse.

"See you inside."

Sally nodded but didn't smile.

"Not if I see you first."

Chapter Seventy-seven

Cape wiped water from his eyes and knocked on the front door.

The door had a small window cut into it—a little hinged door-within-a-door set at eye level.

The eye that looked out was clearly not happy to see Cape.

"*¿Qué usted desean gringo?*"

Cape didn't catch the meaning but there was no mistaking the tone. He pressed two photographs through the hatch, which slammed immediately. A second later he heard the voice through the door.

"*¡Chingate!*"

Footsteps. Silence. Cape stood in the rain and counted the seconds. The front yard was a cleared patch of ground, recently raked but soggy, puddles interspersed with mounds of sand.

The door opened. The man who greeted Cape had different eyes from the one that had glared at him.

"Señor Weathers, what a nice surprise." The man tilted his head foreword in a mock bow. "I am Enrique—I work for Luis Cordon."

"How's the benefits package?"

"Won't you come in?" Enrique looked past him into the storm as he held the door.

Cape walked into a human wall. He looked up and came shy of the face. Tilted his neck back as far as it would go and landed on a face that even its mother would disown.

The giant's long hair was pulled back in a ponytail, streaked with gray. The face was as craggy as the cliffs outside, the nose lacking cartilage, broad cheeks criss-crossed with hundreds of tiny white scars. Cape wondered how many knife fights you had to lose to get a face like that.

The Incredible Hulk opened his mouth and Cape unconsciously took a step back, bumping into Enrique. The man in front of him had no tongue. A jagged stump flicking back and forth suggested he wasn't born that way. He smiled with malice in his eyes and revealed teeth big enough to be found inside a horse's mouth. On the biggest one, right in the front, a golden skull was embedded in the enamel.

"Meet Julio." The voice in Cape's ear was meant to be soothing—Enrique was the perfect host. "He cannot say *hola* himself, as you can see."

Julio gargled at Cape and pushed him against the wall.

Cape spread his arms out from his sides and let Julio paw him from his ankles to his ears. He grabbed Cape's belt and tugged at his pants but didn't go anywhere near his ball. He didn't touch his balls, either.

When he found the gun Julio gagged and spat, shoving Cape into the wall again. The gun looked like a toy in Julio's hand, which looked big enough to palm a basketball player palming a basketball.

"You were expecting trouble, *señor*?" Enrique's tone was mild.

"I'm in Mexico." Cape shrugged. "Anything can happen here."

"So true."

Julio found the knife and Cape bounced off the wall like a well-behaved guest.

"Any other surprises?"

"I forgot to bring wine."

"We have a cellar." Enrique nodded at Julio, who took up position behind them. "Come this way."

The hallway was a cross between a museum of natural history and an aquarium. Cape peered into the tanks set into the wall as they moved deeper into the castle. Spiders, scorpions, centipedes as long as his hand.

Brightly colored fish swimming contentedly between stalks of pastel coral were the exception.

They came to one tank lit by ultra-violet light that held a single fish. Razor-sharp teeth jutted from a distended jaw, two milky eyes bracketed a fleshy lure dangling in front of its mouth, brightly lit by its own bioluminescence. Scary enough to put in a Disney film for that mandatory moment of blinding terror that had shaped so many childhoods all over the world.

"Señor Cordon is a collector." Enrique almost sounded apologetic.

"That's why I'm here." Cape extended his right hand, trying to feel if the stone was the real thing or a surface applied to a much thinner wall. "He has something that belongs to me."

"The photographs you brought."

"And something else."

The hallway had begun to feel like a tunnel. It branched off at various intersections but they kept moving forward and down. Cape forced himself to take a deep breath.

"You must get claustrophobic working here."

"What makes you say that?" Enrique had stopped walking. His eyes shone brightly.

Cape sensed the change in tone. He patted the walls gently. "These—they can feel a little close."

Enrique breathed deeply through his nose and resumed walking. "We have almost reached the great room."

The room was great indeed. The hallway-tunnel ran into a dogleg and Cape blinked from a sudden explosion of light. Twin chandeliers that might have once adorned a real castle hung from a heavy oak beam running the length of the room, which must have been forty feet long and thirty wide. To the right two huge windows faced the ocean. They were eight feet across and fifteen high, almost as tall as the ceilings. Cape heard the rain whipping against them but could barely see the streaks of water in the bright room. It was utterly black outside.

Directly across from him was a large rug leading to a desk. Dark wood, impossibly wide, with feet elaborately carved into talons. A second door to the room was in the wall behind the desk and to the left. Cape made a mental note and turned to his left.

A leather couch dominated this side of the room, surrounded by smaller chairs and tables. A globe with detailed markings over the bodies of water sat next to a side table piled high with books. Flanking the couch were two suits of armor with visored helmets, one holding a sword and the other a halberd, a spear with a hooked blade that looked like a can opener from the Middle Ages.

Set into the wall was a fish tank filled with piranha. Sitting on the couch was one of the handsomest men Cape had ever seen.

"Luis Cordon."

The man smiled as he stood. "Mister Weathers—"

"—call me Cape."

"*Como usted desea.*" Cordon extended his hand. "I was worried you wouldn't be joining us."

Cape didn't really want to shake but understood the risk in not doing so. Cordon's hand was strong and smooth, his palms drier than Cape's.

"Please, take a chair."

"Maybe later when you're not looking."

"Can Enrique get you anything?"

"How about a towel?" Cape ran a hand over his hair. Water spattered the carpet. "Sorry."

"Anything else? A drink perhaps."

Cape shook his head. "You saw the photographs I brought?"

"You would like me to get them?"

"Both of them."

Cordon patted his pockets. "Let me see, where did I—"

"You can keep the pictures."

Cordon looked up but said nothing, a smile spreading across his handsome features.

"Just get the people in them."

Cordon arched an eyebrow. "Both of them?"

"Yes, both of them."

"Very well." Cordon smiled. "Wait here."

Chapter Seventy-eight

Sally walked alone on the beach but she had plenty of company.

Lightning flashed across the sky. She couldn't hear the thunder over the sound of the wind. Rain stung her face.

The best thing about being a half-Japanese, half-American girl raised by the Chinese Triads was that Sally could embrace or reject the best and worst of her rich cultural history.

The Chinese cherished nobility but made political corruption an art form, oppression by the emperors leading to subjugation by the communists. That was why all their stories about personal loss and sacrifice were so beautifully sad. Everyone dies in the end. Chinese had survived without hope for centuries, which is probably why they still cherished it so much.

Americans were unapologetic cowboys, though fewer would admit it, even to themselves. One person could make a difference. Sally loved their optimism and confidence as much as she hated their absolute certainty they were always right, especially when they were wrong. Americans still wanted to buy the world a Coke, even if they insisted on drinking bottled water.

Sometimes Sally thought the Japanese were all crazy, and she could feel their blood coursing through her veins. From the noble perfection of the samurai to the rape of Nanking, everything Japanese was measured by extremes. They could soar to heights that surpassed the imagination and sink to soulless depths from which there was no return. Perfection was a goal, not an ideal that could never be realized. A samurai that fails blames no one—he disembowels himself to regain his honor. There were no half-measures in Japan.

Sally looked at the windows of the castle as she stepped carefully between the rocks of the tide pool and remembered her lessons from school.

In the 16th century a ninja army scaled the walls of Kyoto castle to overthrow the ruling *Shogun*, an assault considered utterly impossible. The victory led to the unification of Japan. The ninjas used grappling hooks wrapped in cloth, scaling the castle walls silently in the middle of the night. No one then believed it could be done, and even today it was considered more legend than fact.

The Japanese are crazy. Better to blame her heritage than herself.

Sally reached the rock face and felt for a handhold. She thought she saw an opening and thrust her hand into it, then cursed as she jammed her fingers.

The American in her just knew she could do it, though that side of her didn't have the slightest clue how. The Chinese in her said there was no hope, which made her more determined than ever to try.

She asked herself how her old instructor would teach her to scale this wall. She cursed again, already knowing the answer.

Sally took a step back and untied the scarf from around her neck. Carefully she wrapped it around her eyes until she was completely blind. Then she tied it fast behind her head.

She raised her hands to the wall and felt the shape of the rocks.

Sally started to climb.

Chapter Seventy-nine

Cape sat on the couch and dried his hair while Enrique served drinks and Julio cleaned his fingernails with a hunting knife.

Enrique arranged a silver tray on one of the low tables. A bottle sat in the center, surrounded by a perfect circle of shot glasses. The bottle was beautiful—shaped like a conch shell, inlaid with silver and gold thread. Enrique did a quick count with the fingers of his right hand, tapping each with the pad of his thumb as he muttered a name under his breath.

Cape took a wild guess. "Tequila?"

"Very expensive." Enrique adjusted one of the shot glasses. "This bottle cost over a million *pesos*."

Cape did the math and figured he must have gotten the exchange rate backward. "That's over a hundred thousand dollars."

"*Sí.*" Enrique moved a glass a few centimeters to the right, then shifted it back to its original position. "Pure agave, fermented for six years."

Cape was about to ask a question when Rebecca stepped into the room.

She came through the door behind the desk and saw him right away. Cape was on his feet and headed toward her when she ran over and gave him a hug. As she squeezed the life out of him, Rebecca pressed her lips to his ear and whispered fiercely.

"They're going to kill you."

"I know." Cape held her close and inhaled deeply. Jasmine and coconuts. She didn't smell anything like scorched pig. He held her at arm's length and smiled. "You OK?"

"Better now." Rebecca's eyes were bright, almost panicked. "My f—"

"Santiago!"

Cordon was standing in the door, looking back into the hallway. Cape heard a muffled response, then the sound of footsteps. The steps were uneven, each footfall followed by the hard tap of a cane.

"Vamanos, Santiago."

"Godammit, stop calling me that, Luis."

Cape heard the voice and felt his stomach do a somersault. He had listened to audio clips on his computer for days, watched newsreels for hours.

"I told you to stop calling me that."

Senator James Dobbins looked just like his picture. He stepped over the threshold with an expectant look on his face like a man who spent a lifetime making entrances at fundraisers and rallies. His white hair was shorter, his face more tan, but otherwise he might have just stepped out of one of his campaign posters. Cape thought he looked damn good for a dead man.

The Senator was graceful despite his obvious discomfort from the new prosthetic. It took most people several months to get used to an artificial leg, but vanity required hard work, even for a politician.

Dobbins scanned the room, eyes resting on his daughter for a long minute before turning their attention to Cape.

"Aren't you the trouble-maker."

"Pleasure to finally meet you Senator."

"You've fucked everything up by coming here, detective."

"How's the leg?"

"What leg?" Dobbins hobbled over to the nearest chair and sat down, his right arm shaking from the strain of supporting his weight.

"The one they cut off and threw into the water hazard to throw off the investigation."

"Hurts like hell." Dobbins scowled. "Sometimes I'd swear it's still there."

"You're a brave man."

Dobbins ignored the sarcasm. "Not like I had a lot of choice in the matter. The people that I'm hiding from don't stop looking unless they think you're already dead."

"The tattoo give you the idea?"

"Is that why you came to Mexico, to ask me about my leg?"

"I came to find your daughter." Cape looked at Rebecca, who was watching her father with nervous eyes. "You were just a Lucky Strike extra."

Cape felt lightheaded. He knew his chances of escaping the castle decreased exponentially with every new shred of information, but he was past caring. Dobbins was alive, and Cape wanted to know everything no matter what the cost.

"What business is it of yours where Rebecca goes?" Dobbins shifted in the chair and adjusted his grip on the cane. "She's my daughter."

"You lied to get her to come to Mexico. You used my name."

"To protect her."

"From Salinas?"

At the mention of the name, Cordon moved further into the room and stood behind his desk. He watched the exchange between his two guests with mounting interest.

"Of course from Salinas." Dobbins rapped his cane on the floor. "That bastard murdered my son—who else would threaten my little girl?"

My little girl. Cape saw an opening and decided to jump in with both feet.

"Is that why you sent your little girl to boarding school?"

"I wasn't going to let those bastards touch my daughter. I knew eventually they'd forget she even existed—and they did."

"That's why you changed her name."

"Of course."

"Not exactly the witness protection program."

Dobbins narrowed his eyes and his voice dropped several degrees. "Are you trying to goad me, detective?"

Cape shrugged. "You never told her why—ever think what that might do to your little girl?"

"*Don't you dare* lecture me on parenting." Dobbins' face turned red. He surged forward but couldn't get the momentum to stand up. "You know how hard it was to say goodbye to your only daughter—make that kind of sacrifice?"

"Must have felt like cutting off your own arm—or leg."

"Fuck you."

"But apparently not as hard as giving up your political career."

Dobbins got enough steam to stand up. He staggered forward, dragging his cane in his rush to get his hands on Cape. It looked like he might make it until Cordon grabbed Dobbins by the shoulder and shoved him back into his chair.

Cape watched as the Senator's face ran through a range of emotions, finally settling on something that resembled self-loathing before he regained his composure.

"Let's have a drink." Cordon waved at Enrique, who began pouring. He turned to Cape. "How did you know?"

"I didn't at first." Cape steered Rebecca over to the couch, where he sat down next to her. Enrique brought them both drinks. "And even after I figured it out, I didn't really believe it until I saw Dobbins walk through that door."

"*I told you Luis—*"

Cordon silenced Dobbins with a wave of his hand. "The photographs."

"You saw them." Cape glanced at Rebecca. "One showed Rebecca as a teenager, her arms wrapped around her father's waist. Probably taken the summer before she went to boarding school."

Rebecca nodded. "I remember that picture. They told me the week after that I was going away." She looked across the room at her father but he didn't meet her gaze.

"Rebecca looks much younger, but you can still recognize her. But it's a clear shot of Dobbins." Cape looked at Cordon. "The other photo showed Dobbins with Danny and Rebecca. Figured I should cover all the bases."

"You showed them in town, *sí?*"

"I thought word would get back to you—I dropped your name, too. It made people nervous."

"This is my town." Cordon didn't say it with any hint of bragging. It was a fact, a simple statement of ownership.

"And I thought Dobbins might get antsy cooped up in your house. So I asked around."

"Did anyone recognize him?"

Cape nodded. "I got a few *maybe's*, a lot of *no's* from people who didn't even look at the picture. A couple of people told me they thought his name was Santiago—I thought I was striking out until I remembered that Santiago is *James* in Spanish."

"Muy bien." Cordon clapped slowly, the sound echoing off the high ceiling. "But why so suspicious?"

"I was more confused than suspicious." Cape leaned forward on the couch. "I only recently became paranoid."

"Fish in the toilet will do that to a man."

"I have you to thank for that practical joke?" Cape looked over his shoulder at the piranha. Their teeth reminded him of Dobbins' smile and he wondered if piranha ate their young, too, or if only politicians did that.

Cordon glanced at his prized fish. "I was hoping you would go home."

"On a stretcher?" Cape shifted on the couch as he unconsciously laid a protective hand over his crotch.

"The odds of the *candîru* fish actually swimming up your *aparato* are very small."

"Have you seen my *aparato* or are you generalizing?"

Cordon smiled. "Had you been in the water, swimming, that would have been a different story. Besides, if I wanted you dead..." He gestured at the tank set into the wall. "There are so many possibilities."

"Why did you want to scare me off? I'm not that hard to kill."

"Now you are being modest, Señor Cape. I am beginning to think you have nine lives."

"But I'm on number ten. You didn't answer my question."

Dobbins cut in. "*Nobody cares* about a detective who drops a case. The client goes home disappointed, people forget there was ever an investigation. If you had minded your own business—"

Cordon raised his hand, then let if fall to his lap. "But when a detective gets killed working a case…"

Cape nodded. "Maybe the case deserves a second look."

"*Exacto.*"

"You had it all figured out."

Cordon raised his glass. Cape lifted his own and out of the corner of his eyes saw Rebecca do the same. He heard her gasp as she took a sip. He drank and the liquid seemed to evaporate without ever touching his tongue. It didn't burn like most tequila, even the expensive stuff he drank with Garcia. This infused his mouth with something primal. He looked at the glass in his hand, both terribly sad and relieved that he couldn't afford to drink it even if he won the lottery.

Cordon raised his glass again. "I think *you* are the one to have it all figured out."

"I'm still not clear about something." Cape took another sip and had an out-of-body experience. He felt like he had nothing to lose.

Cordon held his glass to the light. "What isn't clear?"

"Why did you kill Danny Dobbins?"

Chapter Eighty

The man at the door pulled the hood tighter around his head and knocked loudly.

A small hatch opened at eye level.

"What do you want?" The guard behind the door sensed he should speak English to the dark figure, though he couldn't say why.

"I want you to invite me in."

The guard started to laugh. "And why would I do that, señor?"

The stranger pulled down the hood. His priest's collar was clearly visible. Lightning flashed, illuminating his teeth as he smiled.

"Because it's the right thing to do."

Chapter Eighty-one

Time stopped.

Rebecca's heart froze.

Enrique looked like a bug staring at a fly swatter. Julio's eyes swiveled like gun turrets, zeroing in on Cordon, awaiting orders.

Dobbins dropped his shot glass, which bounced off the rug and rolled under the desk.

Cordon finished his drink. As he lowered his glass, he revealed a pair of eyes that had lost all their warmth.

"What did he say?" Dobbins rocked forward in his chair.

Cape held Cordon's gaze. Neither one of them answered the question.

"*What did he just say*, Luis?"

Cape kept his eyes on Cordon. The drug lord remained silent.

"Salinas killed my son." Dobbins was clenching and opening his hands, over and over. He looked at Rebecca. "*Salinas* was threatening my daughter."

Cape broke the silence. He turned so he was facing the former Senator.

"Dobbins, if you were going to kill someone, would you do it in your own backyard?"

Dobbins blinked and refocused. He looked at Cape with a confused expression.

Cape tried again. "If Salinas wanted to kill Danny, why dump the body in a water hazard on a golf course? Why not bury it in the jungle? Or feed it to the sharks? They might even drain water hazards once a year, looking for lost clubs or balls. I don't know, it just seems like a piss poor place to hide a body."

"He didn't want to hide it." Dobbins clenched his hands until the knuckles turned white. "He wanted to send a signal."

"I think you've got your drug lords mixed up." Cape stole a glance at Cordon, who was watching him the way he looked at his fish, a rare specimen in his collection that lived or died at his whim. "Salinas wasn't the one sending a signal."

"I don't understand." Dobbins looked like he might get sick.

"Why dump your leg in the same pond?" Cape looked at the empty glass in his hand. "Say that Salinas did kill Danny—once word gets out that you're dead, too, Salinas is going to wonder what's going on. *Because he didn't kill you*, did he?"

Dobbins sat up straighter in his chair. "He would have—if Luis hadn't given me sanctuary. Helped me disappear."

"He brought you here to kill you."

"Luis could've killed me anytime, at home in California."

"And it would have been investigated as a murder of a U.S. politician on American soil. Very high profile—if papers in your office or financial records led back to a Mexican drug lord, what do you think happens? The FBI, DEA, and even the CIA can't let that slide. They have to come down here and kick ass." Cape took a deep breath. "But if some crackpot Senator has a mid-life crisis and disappears to Mexico, then winds up dead under mysterious circumstances—"

"—the press has had a field day. You've seen the papers."

"Newspapers have a short attention span—I used to work for one. They lose interest as soon as the next teen celebrity shaves her head or dumps her boyfriend. But the police investigation, Dobbins, that's the real issue. Cordon has friends in the Mexican government, probably with the *federales*. By the time they sorted out jurisdiction with the States, nobody would even remember your name."

"Then why am I still alive? You didn't find me on that golf course."

"You were bait." Cape laid his hand on top of Rebecca's, which was ice cold. "You were bait for Rebecca and she was bait for me. No loose ends."

"You were right, you are paranoid."

"You left documents behind for Rebecca, and maybe something in a safe deposit box. Either way, Cordon doesn't have to worry about it now. If no one's left to pursue the investigation, go to the press, or testify in court, then all you've left behind is a stack of papers."

"Nonsense."

"We all came here to die." Cape tried to put some sympathy into his voice but discovered that he'd run out. "How did Cordon know where to dump the leg? If he didn't kill Danny, how did he know where the body was going to be found?"

Dobbins was shaking his head back and forth like a metronome. "One of Luis' men was found in that pond, remember—Salinas killed him, too—how do you explain that?"

"You're right." Cape let his voice grow quiet. "A man like Luis Cordon would never kill one of his own men."

Dobbins just shook his head and rocked in his chair, his artificial leg rapping the floor in a dull rhythm. Cape squeezed Rebecca's hand.

"I think you liked the press too much for Cordon's taste, Dobbins. You always liked the press, until about nine months ago. Maybe your old friend Luis talked to you about it—and you blew him off. He probably doesn't like it when his minions talk back. Or didn't you notice the giant without a tongue when you checked into *Castillo* Cordon?"

"I wasn't his fucking minion." Dobbins stopped rocking. "We're business partners."

"Maybe that's not how Cordon sees it."

"Those government deals?" Dobbins wheeled to face Cordon as he answered Cape. "Luis couldn't cut those fat deals without me—where did *he* get off telling me what to do? I was a fucking *Senator*."

"You weren't the only politician on the payroll." Cape waited until Dobbins looked in his direction. "But you're right, you were important. *Really* important."

The flattery seemed to calm Dobbins, almost a visceral reaction for someone used to sparring with the press. Maybe his old political instincts for grace under pressure were kicking in.

"So maybe while he lined up his next Senator, your friend Luis conjured up the boogey man to scare you back into line. A character like Salinas might do the trick. He certainly scared the hell out of me."

Dobbins shifted his gaze from Cape to Cordon as if something he'd suspected all along had finally been proven in a laboratory. The earth was flat, after all.

Cape knew he'd struck a nerve. "Too bad you can't ask Salinas yourself, Senator."

"Oh, but you can."

Cordon's voice boomed off the rafters as he stood. He stepped to the center of the room and shook his lion's mane of perfect hair back and forth, his handsome face etched with disappointment. "I was hoping for *un pequeño teatro*—some magic for my guests. But you have given away my best secrets, Cape."

"I thought I'd save you the trouble of lying through those perfect teeth."

"Now I have only one last trick before the show must come to an end."

The speech sounded rehearsed. Cordon was a theatrical guy, but this bordered on the surreal. Cape looked around and realized Enrique and Julio were no longer in the room. He'd been so focused on breaking Dobbins that he didn't notice them leaving.

He didn't have to wait very long for their return.

Cordon clapped his hands and Julio backed into the room pulling something heavy on a wheeled cart. Enrique pushed from the other side and a third man was hidden behind whatever was resting on the platform. A burgundy cloth draped over a rectangular object taller than a man.

"We all know Houdini, the great *gringo* escape artist." Cordon stepped over to the platform and clapped his hands together. "His most famous trick was the underwater escape. He would be submerged upside-down in a strait jacket and miraculously he would escape. *Increíble!* No other magician ever attempted such a dangerous feat of skill and daring—until now."

Cordon made a gesture and the three men began turning the box in a slow clockwise rotation as he continued his narrative.

"Tonight's trick will be more *peligriso* than anything Houdini attempted. Do you know why?"

Cordon looked at each of his guests in turn but didn't wait for a response.

"Because…in my tank there is a monster. *Sí, senora y cabelleros—un monstruo*. One of the most venomous creatures in the sea, a box jellyfish." Cordon looked over their heads with his golden eyes, as if they were sitting in the front row of a theater only he could see.

"Our magician must not only escape the tank, he must escape the jelly." Cordon clapped in time to his own counting. It sent a chill down Cape's spine.

"*Uno…dos…tres…*"

With an exaggerated flourish Cordon grabbed the red cloth and yanked it free of the tank. Rebecca started screaming. Cape felt bile surge in his throat.

The tank was an exact replica of the famous trick, a metal frame holding heavy glass in a rectangle big enough to suspend a man upside-down underwater, which is exactly what they saw. Antonio Salinas stared blindly at them through a death mask of agony, his inverted features distorted by the pulsing, waving mass of tentacles that had latched onto his face.

Cordon looked at the tank and feigned surprise. "I am terribly sorry, *señora y cabelleros*." He shook his head sadly. "It would appear that our magician was not as talented as the late Houdini."

Cape glanced toward the door in the vain hope that someone who wasn't bat-shit crazy would suddenly appear. No one did. It wasn't a good night for magic acts.

Cordon brought his hands together and smiled.

"But I think we have time for one more trick. May I have a volunteer, or should I pick someone from the audience?"

Cape took a deep breath and raised his hand.

Chapter Eighty-two

Magic tricks work by misdirection. Wave your right hand in the air to get the audience focused in that direction, then palm the little red ball with your left hand while no one's looking.

"Pick me."

Cape waved his right hand like a first-grader as he slipped his left down his pants like a teenager.

"Pick me...*pick me!*"

He thrust his hand past the two balls that were permanently attached and tore the sonic disruptor off his thigh. His hand still in his jeans, Cape found the button and pressed down on it once. He palmed the metal and plastic ball and slid his left hand out of his pants, then dropped his right arm as if he'd suddenly lost interest.

He rested his left thumb on the activation switch and waited for Cordon to make the next move, but it came from a direction nobody expected.

"Don't I get a turn?"

All eyes turned toward Dobbins, but it wasn't his voice that begged the question. Dobbins was on his feet, another man's arm curled tightly around his neck, a knife at his throat.

Priest tightened his grip and dragged Dobbins a few feet closer to the door behind the desk.

Rebecca tried to stand but Cape put his right hand on her thigh and forced her down. He kept his left hand wrapped around the sonic grenade.

Julio drew his hunting knife.

Enrique pulled a slim pistol from under his jacket. The man standing behind Salinas' little tank of horror stepped away from the rolling platform and drew a semi-automatic handgun. It was the first clear view of the man since he'd entered the room, and it was a gun Cape had seen before.

"Cyrano."

André scowled at Cape. Apparently he'd been called that before, maybe when he was growing up. Kids can be so cruel.

"How many paychecks are you collecting," asked Cape, "two or three?"

"More than you, dickhead." André raised his gun slowly as if he couldn't decide whom to shoot.

"Ah, my traitorous friend." Priest ran his gaze over Salinas floating dead in the tank before turning his attention to André. "It would appear that we have—"

"—a Mexican standoff?" A new voice entered the room. "How fitting."

Oscar Garcia stood in the main doorway holding a .45 caliber handgun, which he pointed at Cordon's head.

"Hello Luis."

"*Chingalo!* Who let you into my house?"

"Someone left your door open." Garcia glanced at Priest.

"*Zurramato.*" Cordon shook his head in disgust.

Cape looked from the drug lord to the cop. "You two know each other?"

"We went to high school together." Garcia kept his gun at eye level. "Luis was a *pendejo* even then."

Cordon looked hurt. "We used to get stoned together under the bleachers after soccer practice."

"Luis always knew where to get the best pot."

Because he entered through the main door, Garcia was standing behind Enrique and Julio, with André and the windows on his right. Cordon stood directly in front of him, an easy shot. Cape and Rebecca were directly to his left, maybe twenty feet away. Priest was across the room at the ten o'clock position, near the desk and the other door.

The great room suddenly felt very small.

Enrique tried to pivot counter-clockwise so he could see Garcia without twisting his head. Julio began to turn in the opposite direction. They moved tentatively, unable to see Garcia's eyes and knowing they could be shot at any time.

"Hey…hey…hey." Garcia pulled the hammer back on the forty-five. He kept it pointed at Cordon but the *click* filled the room. Enrique froze in place. Julio shuffled to the left, coming closer to Rebecca and Cape. "Hey!"

"Julio is deaf, Oscar." Cordon sounded bored with his high school reunion.

Julio had turned sufficiently to see Garcia, who jabbed his gun in the air toward Cordon. Julio opened his mouth and made a phlegmy sound that might have been a roar, but he stopped moving. He understood the downside of having his boss shot.

Enrique looked around the room and realized he couldn't get an angle on Garcia. He pointed his gun at Priest. "Who are you?"

Garcia nodded in approval at the question. "Sí, why are you here?"

"I came to collect a debt." Priest shifted his weight. Dobbins started gagging.

"*Daddy!*" Rebecca's voice was a hoarse whisper. Cape held her arm with his right hand. She was getting colder, going into shock.

Garcia waved his free hand at the corpse of Antonio Salinas. "I do not think your employer cares, *padre.*"

"I work for a higher power." Priest sucked on his front teeth. "And all my contracts are binding." He pressed his cheek lovingly against Dobbins' hair. "*Especially* this one."

"Shoot him first," said Cordon. "He's crazy."

"You have no idea." André leveled his gun at Priest and thumbed the hammer into firing position.

"Maybe we should all discuss this over a glass of tequila." Enrique gestured encouragingly at the silver tray, the perfect host to the end. Julio gargled in response. Everyone else ignored him.

Cape looked at the bottle inlaid with gold, half-empty on the silver tray. He thought about Garcia's taste in tequila, their long talks—conversational journeys that had led inexorably here to this castle. Inside his head, Cape could hear Cordon counting in time to his own clapping—*uno...dos...tres*—just as he could visualize the timer at the pig farm in Monterrey.

Oscar Garcia had been there, too.

Cape felt paranoid and wondered if the feeling ever stopped once it started. He increased the pressure of his thumb on the button.

"Oscar, who do you work for?"

Garcia spared him a glance, saw the expression on his face. "Do not think too much, amigo." He kept his gun on target.

"Who do you work for?"

"I don't remember." Garcia pulled the trigger.

A perfectly round hole appeared in the center of Cordon's forehead at the precise moment a red mist of blood and brains sprayed from the back of his head.

It was almost like a magic trick.

The sound wave caught up with the bullet and filled the room with a deafening roar. Cape twitched involuntarily and jammed his thumb against the button just as he shoved Rebecca onto the floor. Out of the corner of his eye he saw Garcia pivot left to line up another shot.

Enrique started firing before he rounded on Garcia. Cape could see the muzzle flashes before he heard the *bang...bang*. The shots ricocheted off the wall as Priest ducked behind Dobbins and dragged him beneath the desk.

In the background Cape heard an urgent whining, a rising pitch building to a shriek of sonic agony. He looked for his disruptor and saw it had rolled to the center of the room, then wondered why no one had noticed. He remembered too late what the inventor had said.

It takes five seconds.

He should have pushed the button sooner. Cape started counting in his head.

Uno...

Cape could feel the sound waves spreading across the room. They felt like butterflies in his stomach.

...dos...

André failed to track Priest behind the desk and made a split-second decision to shoot someone else. Anyone, he didn't care. He just knew he wanted to be the one shooting, not the one getting shot. He looked left and saw a target that made him smile.

...tres...

Cape dropped to the floor, trying to put his body mass between Rebecca and the room. The nearest table was too far away. His only cover was Julio's bulk, but the giant was turning in their direction, his hunting knife already drawn.

...cuatro...

André saw he had a clear shot. The asshole detective was a sitting duck.

...cinco...

André squeezed the trigger just as the window directly behind him exploded and a hurricane roared into the room.

Chapter Eighty-three

Sally somersaulted into the room.

Glass and wood flew behind her like shrapnel, propelled by hundred-mile an hour winds. She stayed tucked in a ball until she had rolled past André. He swung his gun at her back and finished squeezing the trigger.

When the bullet left the barrel of the gun, Sally wasn't there.

The shot hit the floor under the desk and ricocheted upward. Dobbins screamed as it tore through his left ear. Priest dragged him closer to the side door.

Sally had gone into a flat spin, her stomach pressed out as she scissored her legs violently. Her right foot caught André behind his left leg and he went down on his kneecaps. The gun kicked as he involuntarily clenched his hands. Sparks flew from the floor where Sally's head had been an instant before.

André's face bulged and it looked like he was going to be sick. Sally could feel the sound waves deep in her chest but didn't hear the whine over the roar of the hurricane. She spun to a halt two feet away from André and jammed her thumbs into her ears to make sure the filters were still in place.

André was still holding the gun.

Sally shielded her eyes from the rain pouring sideways through the window, and she realized the wind might be interfering with the disruptor. It had to be. She reached for the one hidden in her clothes just as André swallowed hard, his Adam's

Apple jumping. He was still on his knees. He blinked and looked at Sally, then summoned all his strength and pointed the gun directly at her chest.

Cape staggered to his feet. It felt like the whole room was vibrating, disintegrating in an earthquake, but his eyes told him everything remained solid. Rebecca was curled into the fetal position next to the suit of armor, hands tearing at her hair, eyes wide with fear.

Rain lashed his face like a whip and Cape tasted blood. He held his hands in front of his face, trying to see the room through his fingers. The rain was turning to hail, its velocity undiminished. The lights flickered overhead as the wind tried to tear the chandeliers off the ceiling.

Sudden darkness, then a hint of movement and light. The wind seemed to have subsided. Cape lowered his hands and saw Julio standing directly in front of him, knife held low, the tip pointing directly at Cape's stomach.

Julio is deaf.

Cape lunged to the right and knocked the suit of armor between them. Julio swatted it aside with his knife hand as it fell, the halberd clattering onto the floor. With his free hand he punched Cape in the stomach.

Cape felt a rib snap and blacked out, but only for an instant. He landed on the couch and opened his eyes in time to see Julio make an overhand lunge with the hunting knife.

Julio staggered sideways as Rebecca rolled against his legs, her arms wrapping around his left thigh. He reversed the knife and slashed at her hands but swung wide. Rebecca jammed her thumbs beneath his knee cap. Julio snarled as he brought the knife around for another swing.

Cape vaulted off the couch and kicked Julio in the face. The knife sank into the couch, the indentation of Cape's body still visible where the blade had torn through the leather.

Julio kicked free of Rebecca, whose face twisted in agony as the shrill whine that Cape could barely hear tore through her brain like an angry hornet. She crawled a few feet away and collapsed facedown, legs kicking as if she were having a seizure.

Julio set his eyes on Cape and took a giant step forward.

Julio's boss had been murdered right in front of him. It might not be Cape's fault, but Julio wanted to kill someone and Cape was willing to put up a fight. The math was simple.

Julio gave a guttural cry and slashed sideways, catching Cape across his right arm. Blood flew into his eyes as Cape yelled, clutching his torn bicep with his left hand. He fell to the floor, his knees landing on the shaft of the medieval spear.

Sally rolled and kicked André in the stomach just as he squeezed the trigger. The shot was wide but she felt something rip across her cheek below her right eye. She heard a *crack* somewhere behind her, loud enough to cut through the rushing of the wind and the incessant whine that was working its way into her head.

André doubled over, hands on the floor, his right still clutching the gun. Sally thought for sure he was going to throw up but she was wrong. He lurched forward, dragging the gun across the floor and twisting his hand so the barrel pointed at her legs.

Sally grabbed him by his shirt and used his body weight for leverage, launching herself over his shoulder. By the time her ass hit the floor behind him, Sally had her legs wrapped around his neck. André pulled the trigger one last time, aiming at nothing, before Sally twisted her legs like a corkscrew and broke his neck.

Cape heard a *crack* overhead but couldn't risk taking his eyes off Julio, who had flipped the knife and was holding it underhand, stepping in for a slash at the throat. Cape pawed at the ground and wrapped his left hand around the shaft of the halberd, then forced his bad arm against the couch and pushed against it as hard as he could. He lurched sideways as the knife cleaved the air.

Another *crack* and a wet sudden explosion. Cape felt a stabbing pain in his back and thought Julio had found his mark.

That's when he saw the piranha.

Julio fell facedown next to him and tried to crawl away, but there was no escape. He had been standing directly in front of the tank when André's second bullet ruptured the glass. A dozen piranha flipped and flopped across his massive back, panicked as their gills failed, razor-sharp teeth trying to find purchase wherever they could, jaws locking as they died.

Two piranhas had embedded themselves in Julio's neck, and one had found the jugular. Blood streamed onto the floor, a river as endless and unforgiving as the Amazon.

Cape dropped the spear and stood up. He arched his back and used his good arm to feel around until he found the shard of glass from the fish tank. He pulled it from his back and tried not to faint. It had penetrated just below the shoulder blade, not dangerous but painful enough to remind Cape that he was still alive.

The same couldn't be said for Enrique. He lay facedown in a pool of his own blood, the back of his head missing. His gun was on the floor next to his right hand.

Cape picked it up. Then he turned his attention to Garcia, who sat on a chair near the door with his gun resting in his lap.

Chapter Eighty-four

The rain was still pouring through the window but was on a diagonal. Cape found that he could open his eyes wide without worrying about being blinded by water darts.

The subsonic humming had stopped, and his skin no longer felt like ants were crawling all over him. The sound grenade had burned itself out.

He kept Enrique's gun down, held loosely against his left leg. Enrique wouldn't be needing it again, thanks to Garcia.

Cordon lay on his back, his lifeless eyes open in disbelief that someone who had once signed his high school yearbook had just shot him in the head. Only a few feet away the box jellyfish had detached itself from Salinas and was pressing against the glass of the tank, as if trying to get a closer look at its fallen master.

Blood streamed down Cape's right arm where Julio had cut him above the elbow. Cape was right-handed but could pull a trigger with his left. He hoped he wouldn't have to—he took a step closer to Garcia.

Sally stayed close.

Vomit stains streaked Garcia's shirt and blood ran down his left cheek below his ear. His face was sweaty and pale, but he managed a weak smile. He tried to talk but his lips were stuck together. He tried again and they came apart with a pasty *pop*.

"What was that noise?" His voice was ragged. "That insect noise that almost killed us."

Sally reached into the folded cloth she used as a belt and removed the black and silver ball. She held her thumb over the button to show Garcia it could happen again.

Garcia's eyes went wide with fear.

For a split-second Cape thought Garcia must really believe Sally was going to push the button, just to teach him a lesson, until he realized Garcia was looking past her toward the center of the room.

Cape turned in time to see Priest lunge at Sally, holding a dagger shaped like a crucifix that was already covered in blood. Sally spun on her heels as Cape swung his left arm up and pulled the trigger. The gun bucked in his hand and he almost dropped it.

Cape would have sworn it was direct hit, but the bullet didn't slow Priest down at all. It must have gone wide. He heard another shot and realized Garcia must have squeezed one off, but it was another miss. If anything Priest was moving faster.

Cape adjusted his grip and started to pull the trigger, but he was too slow. Priest was too close to Sally for Cape to get a clean shot. The dagger seemed to fly as Priest launched himself off the ground, teeth bared as he raised his arm for the strike.

Sally stepped into the arc of his jump and crouched, thrusting her right arm almost straight up. The heel of her hand hit his solar plexus like a battering ram. Priest crashed in a heap to the floor, his mouth open and gasping for air.

Sally did not hesitate. With her left thumb she pressed a tiny button once, twice.

She dropped to a squatting position and rammed the silver and metal ball she'd been holding into Priest's mouth with enough force to break off his incisors. His eyes bulged as Sally kept pushing, jamming it down the back of his throat.

She grabbed the back of his neck with her left hand and pressed hard against his chin with her right, her thumb digging into the soft spot above his vocal chords.

Tilting his head back, Sally forced Priest to stand and half-walked, half-dragged him over to the open window. A few stray rays of light broke through the clouds. It was almost dawn.

Sally pulled Priest close enough to whisper in his ear.

"*Yat...Yi...Sam...Sei...Mm...*" Sally loved counting in Cantonese. It reminded her of her childhood.

She threw Priest out the open window just as the sonic disruptor came to life.

A shrill and horrible cry filled the room and then vanished, a sonic explosion that disappeared as if it had been dragged back out the window. Damnation at the speed of sound.

No one looked out the window. It was still too dark to see the rocks four stories below.

Cape heard sobbing.

Rebecca had dragged herself across the floor. Her father's head was in her lap. Blood poured sluggishly from a single hole in his chest, a puncture wound through his heart.

Dobbins opened his mouth but only gargling noises emerged. His vocal chords were flooded with blood. His eyes spoke volumes as he gazed at his daughter, communicating what he had never been able to put into words. Tears streamed down his cheeks.

Cape saw more love and regret in those eyes than he had ever felt in his life. He wanted to know which would win out in the end but turned away, not wanting to intrude. Sally was watching him from the window, the wind blowing her hair in a thousand directions. She gave him a half-hearted smile.

Rebecca cried out—no words, just a gasp of anguish. Cape turned to see her cradling her father's head, his eyes open and unblinking. He had stopped crying, and then he had stopped breathing.

Rebecca looked at Cape until her eyes dried. It took a long time, but he didn't move until she nodded once, as if she'd just made a decision.

"I want to go home."

"Señorita Lowry has the right idea. We must be leaving." Garcia was standing next to his chair. He looked shaky, as if he might collapse at any moment. His gun had fallen to the floor and he made no move to pick it up. He checked his watch. "In five minutes."

"Why Oscar?" Cape knew the answer but asked the question anyway. If he hadn't been so exhausted he could have been pissed. "Why the fuck do we have to leave in five minutes?"

"Because it is almost six." Garcia gave him an apologetic look. "And that is when I sent the timers."

"The timers."

"Yes." Garcia gestured toward the door. "The timers for the bombs that will blow up the castle."

Chapter Eighty-five

A fireball brighter than the sun welcomed the dawn to Bagdad Beach.

The charges had been set on the first two floors, shaped against the walls facing the beach. The windows erupted in geysers of flame, the concussive force tearing the sea wall apart like paper. With the foundations destroyed, the castle tumbled over the cliff onto the rocks and sand below, burying the tide pool in smoldering debris.

Garcia had parked close to the castle, and Rebecca drove fast. The effects of the disruptor had faded, and she was the only one with a driver's license and effective use of both arms. Sally sat in back with Cape while Garcia navigated. They were a mile away when the pressure wave chased them down the beach road. The car bounced on its shocks but kept going.

Rebecca gripped the steering wheel until her knuckles turned white but didn't speak. Cape didn't know what to say. They had left her father's corpse behind along with the rest of the bodies. Not giving him a proper burial was the only way to bury his secrets.

After twenty minutes they left the highway and headed into Matamoros. Garcia made a call on his cell phone and said a few words in Spanish, then directed Rebecca to drive into a neighborhood that was little more than a maze of alleys. They stopped in front of a house too dilapidated and spooky for the Addams Family.

"This is a safe house." Garcia opened his door and stepped out of the car.

Cape joined him on the sidewalk as the lone streetlight died in a shower of sparks. "It doesn't look very safe."

"Would you rather go to the *polizia*?"

"I'd rather go home."

"I see, and what would airport security say about that arm? Or the man at the front desk of your *turista* hotel?"

Cape looked at Garcia and wished he trusted him just a little bit more.

Garcia gave Cape a look. "I could have shot you in the back at the castle when you turned to help her." He jutted his chin toward Rebecca through the window of the car. "Why don't you come inside and have a drink."

"I'm not drinking with you anymore—I think it affects my judgment."

"Are you coming inside or not?"

"Who do you work for, Oscar?"

"Have a drink with me and I'll tell you." Garcia summoned a half-smile. "But I think you already know."

Inside, the house was nicer than the hotel Cape and Sally had checked into the day before. It was a hotel of sorts, known only to a select group of guests. No swimming pool or free cable, but there were other amenities, like an infirmary and dispensary. The staff was friendly and paid to be discreet.

It took them three hours to attend to their injuries. Adrenaline had kept them from realizing the worst of them, and by the time they were shown to their rooms they were all wrapped in enough gauze to be stunt doubles for Boris Karloff as The Mummy.

Cape lay on the bed after agreeing to meet Oscar downstairs in an hour. He didn't wake up until nightfall. Not surprisingly, Oscar was waiting in a lounge off the main entrance, the safe house equivalent of a lobby bar.

"Tequila." Cape sat down heavily. "What a surprise."

"1800 Silver." Oscar poured them each a shot. "It's not one hundred thousand dollars a bottle, but not bad for a safe house in a Matamoros ghetto."

Garcia raised his glass. "*Salud.*"

Cape started to sip and then changed his mind. He swallowed the tequila in one shot. It made love to his tongue and then burned like regret.

Garcia waited until Cape's eyes stopped watering.

"I am one of the good guys."

"You almost blew us to kingdom come." Cape poured himself another glass. The aspirin he'd taken were wearing off.

"The castle—I set the timers too early."

"I'm not talking about the castle."

"See why I said that you already knew the answers to your questions?" Garcia winked at Cape over his glass. 'You are perhaps the smartest *gringo* I have ever met."

"That almost sounds like a compliment."

"*De nada.*"

"The pig farm, Oscar. We almost got killed."

"I said I was sorry."

"No, you didn't. You showed up at the hotel and apologized for releasing the Senator's name to the press."

"True, that was the conversation we were having." Garcia smiled. "But that is not what we were talking about."

"Do you ever give a straight answer?"

"I could ask you the same question."

"I made a phone call before we left for Matamoros." Cape turned the bottle to admire the label. "I had someone check on your background, something I should have done earlier."

"You've been under a lot of stress lately."

"And you have a lot of jobs, Oscar. An Inspector for the Mexico City *polizia*. Special agent for the AFI. Another organization I can't remember."

"What were the letters?"

"Never mind—they're all listed as current jobs—how is that possible?"

"I am what you might call a contract employee."

"But the most interesting thing I found was your service record."

"Here it comes." Garcia took a long sip.

"You handled demolitions for the army."

"And I still have all my fingers." Garcia wiggled his right hand.

Cape studied him for a minute, saying nothing.

"I arrived at the hotel too late, after you had already visited the pig farm." Garcia spun his empty glass. "I am deeply sorry."

The two men drank in silence.

"What was your last *official* job?"

Garcia seemed to consider the question for a long time. "I was assigned to a joint U.S.-Mexico task force."

"To go after the cartels?"

Garcia nodded. "But I resigned."

"So you could really go after the cartels."

"*Exactemente.*" Garcia sat up a little straighter. "The cartels own the government in Mexico, just as the gangsters own the politicians in your country."

"They're called lobbyists, not gangsters."

"It is the same thing." Garcia made a vague gesture. "Do you think the U.S. or Mexican government can stop men like Salinas or Luis Cordon?"

"Ever been to the DMV?"

"You see my point." Garcia made a fist with his right hand, as if holding a stick. "Politicians are like *piñatas*. If you want something good to come out of them, you have to beat them up sometimes."

"Never heard that one before."

"It just occurred to me."

"So you work outside the system."

"No, I make the system work." Garcia shook his head. "I work inside the system, but the system doesn't know I'm there."

"The ghost in the machine."

"Perhaps I should have that printed on my next business cards." Garcia ran his hands through his hair and Cape noticed the gray streaks for the first time. He looked the way Cape felt—completely and utterly exhausted.

"You used me, Oscar."

"So did Salinas."

"True."

"And Cordon."

"Also true. Maybe I'm not such a smart *gringo* after all."

"But I think you are." Garcia stood. "I could also claim that you used me."

"I was just doing my job."

"Exactly."

"Who do you work for, Oscar?"

Garcia smiled wistfully as if he'd forgotten himself, then he turned and walked out the door.

Chapter Eighty-six

It was a week before Cape could lift his right arm beyond ninety degrees, and his one attempt at shaving left-handed left him scarred, physically and emotionally. His bandages made showering awkward and even brushing his teeth was challenging, so he decided to spend the week recovering at home. He spent most of his time watching the Discovery Channel.

It took an invitation to breakfast to lure him outside again. Beau even offered to buy.

"You look better than I expected." Beau wore his usual jeans and black t-shirt, size XXXL.

"You look tired." Cape felt full just looking at the table. Beau told him he would order if he arrived early, and he had outdone himself. "And hungry."

"Got you pancakes, just came out. Good thing you were on time for a change."

"Thanks."

"Want some?" Beau shoveled some bacon onto his own plate, then held it across the table.

Cape felt his stomach do a back-flip as the all too familiar smell hit him. He shook his head. "Think I'll stick with the pancakes."

"Watching your cholesterol?"

"Something like that."

"Everything in moderation." Beau scooped the rest of the bacon onto his own plate, where an omelet as big and yellow as the sun waited patiently for his hunger to bring about a total eclipse.

"Any word from the Feds?"

"Those papers you turned over got them all excited. But it's the Feds—it'll take a while. My guess is Delta Energy might go the way of Enron and implode from the scrutiny."

"Any chance of nailing Frank?"

"I wish." Beau frowned. "Other investors got burned. Frank will just call his lawyers, claim he's the victim."

"Respectable businessman duped into a shady investment?"

"Fat Frank is teflon."

"So he walks."

"Until someone pulls the trigger on him."

"He's not worth it."

"No argument." Beau shrugged. "I'm not gonna lose my badge taking that fat bastard down. My new plan is to watch Frank eat himself to death."

Cape surveyed the damage on Beau's plate. "That's quite a statement, coming from you."

"You see an ounce of fat here?" Beau took a deep breath, straining the seams on his t-shirt, his mahogany skin tight as a drum.

Cape had to admit he didn't, just enough muscle to bench press a Buick. "Can't say I'm surprised about Frank."

"You could press charges, say he sabotaged your car."

Cape shook his head. "I think Cyrano—sorry, André—"

"—seized the moment?"

"Yeah." Cape conjured the image of the car in his rearview mirror, tried to put a face into the memory. "I don't know, but you said Frank would've just had me shot—I think that's true. When André got sent outside, I think he acted on impulse."

"He was two-timing Frank—and Frank was two-timing Salinas."

"Frank doesn't have to worry about Salinas anymore."

"You never did tell me what went down in Mexico."

Cape let his eyes drift to the gold badge clipped to Beau's belt. "You really want to know?"

"No." Beau shook his head. "I really don't."

Chapter Eighty-seven

Linda squeezed Cape hard enough to get sap out of a tree. By the time she let go he felt like maple syrup, a thought that made him wish they'd met at a breakfast joint instead of a coffee shop in the Mission district.

Linda ordered for them while Cape got plates, spoons, and napkins. The plates were china and the spoons metal. A hand printed sign on the wall read *Napkins = Trees*. He set everything on a table in the corner before meeting Linda at the counter.

"You like Mexican coffee?" Linda's hair looked as if it didn't care whether Cape liked it or not.

"Not really."

"I ordered two."

"Great."

"They make it with a special recipe here. Instead of Kahlua they use tequila."

Cape smiled. "Perfect."

A young woman with a metal stud in her cheek and hoop in her eyebrow stepped to the counter and handed Linda two carefully wrapped confections. She set the coffees on the countertop.

"I thought you didn't eat sweets—corner table." Cape took a coffee in each hand and followed Linda to the table. "Sugar is a killer."

Linda's hair told him to mind his own business but she was more polite. "*Dia de los muertos.*"

"Excuse me?"

"Day of the Dead—when Mexicans celebrate loved ones they've lost." Linda handed him one of the treats. "Or loved ones we thought we lost."

Cape almost blushed. "Sounds like a loophole in the holiday."

Linda gestured at his plate. "Go ahead."

The paper opened like a flower to reveal a perfectly formed human skull the size of a strawberry. Its mouth was grinning wickedly at Cape, the teeth outlined with inlaid chocolate. The eyes were big and round, tiny flecks of blue and gold making the lines. On the top was a mosaic of brightly colored tiles running from the forehead to the nape of the neck. The body of the skull was pure crystalline sugar. A sugar skull.

"It's beautiful."

Linda unwrapped hers. It had earthier hues, reds and orange and streaks of brown, but it was just as festive. She took a small bite and her hair vibrated from the sugar rush so unfamiliar to her diet.

"What's come over you?" Cape had known Linda for years, and even granola wasn't crunchier.

"I wanted to come someplace that reminded me of Mexico. I keep thinking about your investigation, how you almost died."

"I didn't." Cape took a tentative bite. Sweet didn't accurately describe the sensation.

Linda frowned. "Dobbins and Cordon preyed on people's fears."

"That's what criminals do."

"But they were *my* fears." Linda wrapped her hands around her cup and let its warmth flow into her. "I read an article about ethanol on the bus ride over."

Cape reflected on the differences in their reading habits. He had a stack of comic books on his nightstand. "What did it say?"

"That ethanol from sugar cane might be a clean fuel source, better than gasoline."

"Some good news, right?"

"Maybe for Brazil." The posture of Linda's hair suggested there was a catch. "Unless they cut down the rainforest to grow the sugar cane, which they might be doing. But for those of us living in the States, the news is not so good."

"Why?"

"Because you can't grow sugar cane in the continental United States. You can only grow corn."

"Isn't that what they're doing, burning corn into ethanol?"

"Corn doesn't burn as easily, so it takes more heat. Know what ethanol factories burn to generate the heat?"

Cape shook his head and sipped his coffee. When he was around Linda, he didn't know much about anything. He almost felt like Sam Cooke.

"They burn fossil fuels like coal. So making ethanol from corn can actually produce *more* greenhouse gases than sticking with gasoline. Not to mention the effect of forests getting cleared to plant more crops. Bottom line, the science doesn't support the investment."

"Isn't that kind of counter-productive?"

"Not if the government wants to spin a green fairy tale to justify taxes. We're paying millions in subsidies to plant corn and giving energy companies hundreds in millions in tax breaks to build ethanol factories."

"Even though it doesn't work."

"Sound familiar?" Linda poked a hole in her skull and licked her finger. "Why not fund solar panels or wind farms, something that actually works?"

"Maybe they're not as trendy. Politicians like social currency."

"My environmental movement has become a fashion industry." Linda scowled. "Green is the new black."

Cape sighed. "You can't save the world, Linda."

"That doesn't mean I should stop trying."

"Now you're starting to sound like me."

"No." Linda's hair shook. "You care about people. You don't really give much thought to your surroundings."

Cape didn't argue. Linda lay awake at night worried about global warming. He went to bed thinking it was a cold world out there.

"I'm tired of being judged by posers." She forced a smile. "I'm tired of having my environment turned into a religious movement."

"Why is it always *your* environment?"

"Because that's the way it works." Linda blew on her coffee. "*Waste not, want not.*"

Cape smiled. "My Dad used to say that all the time."

"He grew up during the Depression?"

"Yeah."

Linda turned her skull around so it was facing her. "I needed to let off some steam."

"You just might be a renewable energy source."

"Thanks for listening."

"Thanks for keeping the faith."

Linda smiled.

Cape glanced at the clock above the counter. "Shit."

"What?"

"I'm late for a tea ceremony—it's a standing date."

"You're having tea after you have coffee?"

"Caffeine is my friend."

"Didn't you have breakfast before you came here?"

"I drank iced tea with breakfast."

"I'm glad I'm not your stomach."

"Me, too—I couldn't stand the guilt."

"Don't forget your skull."

Cape wrapped up his hypoglycemic treasure. "Going to grab a taxi—you want a ride?"

"I'll walk. Say hi to Sally."

"You bet."

"How is she?"

"That's one of the great things about Sally. I never have to ask." Cape bent to give Linda a kiss. "Sure you don't want a ride?"

"I prefer to walk."

Cape smiled. "I know you do."

Chapter Eighty-eight

Sally served the tea to her parents' cups before serving Cape. When her own cup was full they drank. Sally sat perfectly still. Cape occasionally unfolded and refolded his legs.

The tea was green jasmine and tasted like memory—sometimes bitter, sometimes sweet. Cape thought about the past week. After a while, Sally asked him how Rebecca was doing.

"About as well as can be expected. She lost a family she never really had."

Sally didn't say anything for a long time, lost in her own memories.

"Will you see her again?"

Cape met her gaze and smiled. "Not in the way you mean."

"You're learning."

"Don't count on it."

"I take nothing for granted where you're concerned."

"Did I ever say thank you?"

Sally shook her head. "No."

"Just checking."

Sally smiled at their private joke.

Cape drank some tea. "I might surprise you one day."

"Anything can happen."

"Yeah," said Cape. "I know that now."

To receive a free catalog of Poisoned Pen Press titles, please contact us in one of the following ways:

Phone: 1-800-421-3976
Facsimile: 1-480-949-1707
Email: info@poisonedpenpress.com
Website: www.poisonedpenpress.com

Poisoned Pen Press
6962 E. First Ave. Ste. 103
Scottsdale, AZ 85251